RAVENCRY

The Raven's Mark
BOOK TWO

ED MCDONALD

This edition first published in Great Britain in 2019 by Gollancz

First published in Great Britain in 2018 by Gollancz
an imprint of the Orion Publishing Group Ltd
Carmelite House, 50 Victoria Embankment
London EC4Y 0DZ

An Hachette UK Company

1 3 5 7 9 10 8 6 4 2

A CIP catalogue record for this book
is available from the British Library.

ISBN (Hardcover) 978 1 473 22205 2
ISBN (Export Trade Paperback) 978 1 473 22206 9
ISBN (eBook) 978 1 473 22207 6

Typeset by Deltatype Ltd, Birkenhead, Merseyside

Printed in Great Britain by CPI Group (UK) Ltd,
Croydon, CR0 4YY

MIX
Paper from
responsible sources
FSC® C104740

www.edmcdonaldwriting.com
www.gollancz.co.uk

This one is for Kit.

Acknowledgements

'Sure, the second book will be easy!' I said.

Hah!

When you write a book, you tend to get all the credit, but a novel is a team effort. Significant thanks are well deserved by:

My editors Gillian Redfearn, Jessica Wade and Craig Leyenaar for their invaluable contributions in terms of story development, bouncing ideas around, keeping me focused when imposter syndrome or complete befuddlement threatened, and teaching me that 'gotten' is not an actual word.

My agent Ian Drury, to whom I am immensely grateful for placing his trust in me and sending me tumbling down the rabbit hole.

The hard-working teams behind the scenes, including Miranda Hill, Stevie Finegan, Alexis Nixon, Jen McMenemy and everyone else who has played a role in helping this series along.

Gaia Banks and Alba Arnau at Sheil Land, for all their amazing work in getting this series into an ever-increasing number of languages.

Everyone at London Longsword Academy who has trained and sparred with me over the last four years, your heads have provided fantastic targets to test out the fight sequences.

Andy Stoter, who named his first talking +3 war hammer

'Spoon' and lived a dozen different lives with me through the worlds of our imaginations.

A special note of thanks must go to my grandparents, Mollie and Leslie, whose stories of life during the second world war provided a great deal of inspiration for this book. I doubt that I've done real justice to their stories, but in a sense, I have been able to share some of them.

In the time between *Blackwing* was released and writing these acknowledgements today for *Ravencry*, I have relied heavily on the infinite patience of two people who deserve special thanks. My long-distance friends, Taya and Meg: we may not have met in person, but you listen, and there is nothing worthier of thanks than kindness.

And finally, my ongoing thanks must go to my mum, who from my earliest memory was instilling me with a desire to create and tell stories, and my dad, who put the first wooden sword into my three-year-old hand. My obsession with goblins and dragons may have puzzled you at times, but I hold you both entirely responsible.

Blackwing: What Has Gone Before

The Nameless and the Deep Kings have been at war for longer than anyone remembers. The Deep Kings seek to enslave humanity and turn them into drudge – enslaved, deformed creatures that worship them. The Nameless, cruel and caring only for the final victory, stand in their way.

It has been eighty years since Crowfoot unleashed the Heart of the Void against the approaching enemy forces and, in doing so, created the Misery – a toxic, mystic wasteland where ghosts walk and mutated creatures scavenge the sands, and neither distance nor direction are ever quite what they seem. It can only be navigated by specialists taking readings from the three moons.

Ryhalt Galharrow is a Blackwing captain, magically bound to serve Crowfoot, one of the Nameless, and charged with rooting out dissenters, traitors and spies. On a mission to save Ezabeth Tanza – a Spinner, able to manipulate light energy into magic, a woman he'd loved and lost twenty years before – from drudge attack, they made a terrible discovery. That Nall's Engine, the weapon that protects the Misery's border, was unpowered, allowing the Deep Kings to bring their vast armies to bear in their war against the Nameless.

Together Galharrow and Ezabeth, along with a swordswoman, Nenn, a navigator, Tnota, and Ezabeth's brother Count Dantry, uncovered a web of conspiracy that led to the very top. Prince Herono was being manipulated by Shavada, one of the Deep Kings, and though Galharrow defeated the prince it was too late. Nall's Engine had failed, and the drudge were on the march.

In a desperate fight, they found the secret that allowed the Nameless to defeat King Shavada and save the city, but not without cost. In saving the city, Ezabeth was destroyed.

Now rumours abound of a ghost that lingers in the light network, a spirit seldom seen ...

1

Levan Ost's note insisted I come alone.

The clocks were poised to strike four as I approached the meeting point. The night carried a purplish cast, Rioque and Clada both waxing, unobscured by cloud. I stepped briskly through the winter cold. Hooded. Armed. Alert. The last time I'd met Levan Ost, he'd tried to shank me with a broken bottle. But that had been a long time ago and, truth be told, I'd probably deserved it.

The smell of the canal met me three streets before it came into view. The waterway was blacker than oil, the streets around it mostly deserted. Nobody wanted to live near that stench. Valengrad's canals had never been fit for swimming in, but after the Siege, we'd tossed all the dead drudge into the canals to rot. Bad magic isn't so easily washed away though, and the pollutants had stained even the water. Four years later, it still bore the memory.

Ost wanted to meet on a barge docked along Canal Six. It was an old waterway on the western edge of Valengrad, out past the stacked rows of soldiers' tenements. I passed barges loaded with cut stone, floated south for the ceaseless construction work on an immense phos mill being built in the Spills. Hundreds of tons of masonry sat low on the reeking water, waiting to become part of the Grandspire. Canal Six wasn't one of the worst, but the stench still forced itself all the way to the back of my throat.

I paused in the deep shadows at the street corner. Narrow boats and barges were moored against the banks, cargoes lashed down tight. We'd suffered two quakes in the past week, and nobody wanted to fish spilled stone out of the polluted water. I watched silently from the shadows, let the minutes tick by. No need to be impatient.

Nothing moved on the black water. The light tubes were dim, humming low. No sign of anyone on the decks and the barges were dark, empty by night, with only a single cabin window giving light. It had been a pleasure barge once, but hauled cargo through the indignity of its retirement. Forty feet long, bare deck. An odd place to lay a trap, if that's what this turned out to be. I shifted the gear beneath my coat, but if you walk into a trap, it rarely matters if you're armed. It was Ost's name, our old association, that had brought me out here alone. My recruits would scowl and gripe if they saw me abandon the caution that I drilled into them, but the rules were for them, not for me.

I placed a hand beneath my coat, cocked the hammer on a flintlock pistol.

'Ost!'

The black water took my words, flattened them.

A shadow appeared against the grime encrusted glass. A bolt grated as it was drawn back and then the cabin door opened. A gnarled and narrow figure was silhouetted against the cabin light.

'Captain Galharrow?' a gruff, smoker's voice asked. 'That's what they call you now isn't it? Wasn't sure you'd come.'

Levan Ost looked like he'd been on lean rations for a year and then tumbled down a hillside, maybe more than once. He had an untidy, clubbed-together shape to his body, muscle slowly losing the battle with age. His beard was long, the colour of ashes, but his eyes were still keen. His face had a peppering of circular scars where he'd suffered from Misery-worm.

'It's good to see you, Levan,' I said, although it wasn't.

'Come in. Letting the heat out,' he said, and by the way he swayed as he turned I figured he was drunk. I had plenty of experience with drunks.

He didn't look much like a threat. If he'd invited me here to end what his broken-glass assault had started all those years ago, he'd prepared badly. I eased the pistol lock slowly back to rest, though I didn't take my thumb from it altogether as I climbed aboard.

Unlike the cargo boats filling most of the docks, the barge had been a luxury river cruiser once, the kind the nobility spent dainty afternoons drifting about on. Then had come debts, boredom, or the blackening of the canals, and its owner had either sold it or turned it to shifting fruit up and down the waterways to cut a profit.

'Any crew aboard?' I asked.

'No.'

The cabin was a simple room, twelve by twelve with a few worn chairs and an old-fashioned oil lamp hanging from a hook in the ceiling. Ost offered me a seat. I didn't take it. He seemed unsure of himself, adjusted a few items on a simple table. A folio of papers and a bottle of wine, a vintage that spoke of neither wealth nor taste. An empty bottle stood beside it. Another lay on its side up against a wall. A basket-hilted broadsword lay scabbarded on the table. I didn't think that Ost intended to use it on me but I wasn't worried if he tried. He was old, he was out of shape and he was drunk.

'It's been a long time,' I said softly. In the deep night, some primal fear of the dark makes us favour hushed tones.

'I suppose,' Ost said. 'Haven't seen you since the day you fought Torolo Mancono.' His voice had retained its self-assured roughness. He may have never held a rank above navigator, but that had still earned him respect and a place in the command tent. He'd never liked me, because he was

3

common stock and I'd been born with cream for blood, and in fairness I'd been a cocky bastard.

'Still bitter about that?'

Ost shrugged.

'I always liked Mancono,' he said. 'He listened, even if he was born rich as a prince. You gave him a bad death, but I suppose you can't shoulder all the blame. He asked for the duel.'

I hadn't come to relive the past or settle old grievances.

'You said you had information vital to Valengrad's safety,' I said.

'Wine?' Ost asked. The cups on the table were smudged with fingerprints so I probably shouldn't have, but I took one all the same. I'm not one to turn down a smudged cup of worst-quality wine, no matter the hour or the situation.

Ost looked over my uniform. He noted the long, close-fitting black coat that fell to my knees, with its dual rows of silver buttons. He noted the raised silver wings stitched to the sides of the shoulders. Once, I'd sworn to never wear a uniform again, but time, money, and prestige make liars of us all, and this was a coat of my own colour. I let him look as I drank, and waited for him to speak.

'Looks like life's treating you better than it has the rest of us,' he said eventually.

'Depends on your point of view.'

'You got a nice operation going with Blackwing now, don't you?' A hint of resentment. Hard to describe Blackwing as nice; hunting down deserters, spies, traitors and the miserable bastards that the Cult of the Deep got their claws into hardly made me popular, and having to answer to Crowfoot was no tea-dance. 'You're on the up since the Siege, back in favour. Seems like the princes have thrown you a sack of gold to keep order around here and half the world's afraid of you.'

'Guilty consciences breed fear,' I said. 'Some people should be afraid.'

Ost nodded. He ran a hand over his balding scalp. He had to be sixty years old, maybe older. A proud man. It was taking him time to work up to whatever he needed.

'I didn't want to come to you, but you're the only one I can trust with this,' he admitted at last. The only reason you ask a man to come alone and at night is either you're planning on killing him or you need something you're too ashamed to ask for in the daylight. He hadn't tried to kill me. Not yet, anyway.

'Talk.'

'Where to start?' Ost said. He threw back his wine, bared his teeth, locked his jaw. 'I got mixed up in something. Something bad. The kinda thing you hang men for. I'll tell it all. But I want a deal.'

'You think I need to give you one?'

Ost's chin jutted proud and raw. He wasn't impressed and sure as hell wasn't scared. He'd navigated the Misery for forty years, a lot longer than I had. Up close I could see the tiny green veins beneath the skin, little slivers of corruption that had taken up residence. He'd seen dulchers and skweams, he'd fought drudge and seen men evaporate into mist. I was just an ugly man with more grey in my beard than colour.

'It's not for me. It's for my daughter and her kid. If I run my mouth, I'm done for anyway, but my family are clean in all this. I want you to make them disappear, somewhere beyond the states. Hyspia or Iscalia. Somewhere they can't be reached.'

I watched him carefully, and figured he was telling the truth. Something about kids brings out the few remaining strings of sympathy on my bow.

'What do they need protecting from?' I asked.

The canal barge began to rock, slightly at first and then harder, rattling the shutters in the window frames. The wine bottle fell from the table with a smash as the boat rose and fell

5

on sudden waves and glass streetlights cracked and shattered, dimming the banks. I gripped the table to stay upright.

'Shit!' Ost yelped as he lost his balance and fell hard. A bunch of raincoats fell from their pegs to bury him in oilcloth.

The earth rumbled and groaned. Somewhere distant something unstable, something that was probably somebody's home, collapsed with a crash. And then, with a growl, it was done, the tremor passing as quickly as it had risen. Ost ignored my hand, preferring to pick himself up.

'Third earthquake in a week,' I said. I didn't like that. Anything out of the ordinary is usually something to worry about. But, as Valiya had told me, even Blackwing couldn't do much about the earth heaving.

'Let's go out on deck,' Ost suggested. 'I could do with a smoke and the barge owner gets pissy if I light it up in here.'

'Why are you living on a barge?'

Ost shrugged. 'Cheaper than anywhere else, if you can tolerate the smell.'

Outside, the cold had left the air tight and brittle. Clada was starting to sink, giving way to Rioque, the purple light turning redder. The phos lights along the streets were set to one-third power and one of them sputtered, crackling at a bad connection. I lit up a pair of cigars and passed him one. A gesture of understanding, if not of friendship.

'Pol is innocent,' Ost said. 'She don't even care to see me, lot of bad blood there. But I owe her.'

It seemed a fair trade.

'You give me something heavy, I'll see she finds a new life in some other city.'

'Good enough,' Ost agreed. He took several heavy draws on his cigar. 'I took a job. Misery work, navigating out with freelancers. They gave me false names, but a true location. A fixed point, Tiven's Dale. You know it?'

I nodded. It was four days ride into the Misery, a place where the boulders were perfectly spherical. About as far as our regular patrols went, these days.

'They were thirty, well armed, heavy crossbows for the most part. Good armour too. Tough men. They had a pair of Spinners with them, and they were paying a lot – practically a pension. So I figure we're going relic digging. I know, I know, that's not legal. Misery contraband ain't permitted, but collectors will sell their horse for an Adrogorsk gold-mark. The money they were paying would have set Pol up real good.'

'And?'

'So. We get out there and I know there's something wrong with the soldiers. They pitch up camp the first night, and none of 'em laugh. None of 'em joke. Just sit there, silent all night. You and I know that there's little laughter to be had in the Misery, but what really got my goose? They weren't scared neither.'

'Experienced men?'

'They're the ones that should be most scared. Only an idiot ain't scared in the Misery.' Ost said the name with care, like he was holding a wobbling candle over a bowl of blasting powder. There's no power in the name, but only a fool disrespects it.

'True enough.'

'So we get to Tiven's Dale and there are drudge there. I hit the dirt, thinking we've stumbled into some crazy long patrol, only the Spinners don't unleash their magic on them, not even when I see there's a Darling down there. Had to be, for all he was as changed as the drudge, and I ain't never seen that before. Face like a fish, you know, but definitely a Darling. Had a fucking tail too, if you can believe that. Anyway, the Spinners, they go talk to him awhile. Then they come back and say we're going back. That was it. They just talked to him, then we come back.'

7

Short of the Deep Kings they serve, there is no creature more bent on the destruction of humankind than a Darling. Even the mention of one is enough to make most soldiers reach for an amulet. Darlings commanded power far beyond that of our own sorcerers, a gift from their terrible masters.

'Who were they?' I said.

'I don't know.' Ost said it slowly, as if I'd missed that detail. 'They gave false names. Blue, Pikeworth, Dusky – sometimes they forgot what they'd called each other. They didn't try and explain nothing, just kept telling me that there was more money than I'd ever need waiting for me back on the Range. They repeated it far, far too often. But after what I'd seen, I knew they wouldn't let me live once the walls were in sight. Only needed me to navigate for them, right? So I abandoned them a day from the walls. Left them there to rot. Maybe they'll die out there. But I ain't often that lucky.'

'So you can't tell me who these mystery men are?'

'No. But if they make it back, I can point them out to you. There aren't that many Spinners.' He shivered. 'Only if I spill on their boss, he'll get to me. The only time they showed any kind of emotion was when they mentioned him. Terrified of him. No doubt about that. And anyone that can terrify a Spinner sure terrifies me too. I'm a corpse on legs, Galharrow.'

'Makes me wonder why you haven't run.'

'I'm going to run, believe me,' Ost said. He sucked on his cigar, coughed a little when he took it down by mistake. 'Far as I can, long and hard. Maybe I'll get clear, who knows? I lasted this long.' He sucked on the cigar again, quick, tense puffs. Even talking about it scared him.

'So who's the boss?'

'A deal for Pol. Then I give you the name,' he said. The cigar smoke drifted between us, catching the phos light, gleaming like oil.

'I can pull strings, get your girl and her kid on a ship to one of the western colonies. They're always crying out for women. If your information is good then you got my word on it.'

I was glad that in his final moments, I was able to give him that small amount of relief. He looked grateful, for all that he still hated me for killing Torolo Mancono.

Ost's abdomen exploded outwards. Bits of offal and bone spattered the deck. It took me a moment to realise that he'd been shot. A small river of blood and pulped organs ran from his gut as he staggered across the deck. He looked up at me once before a flash from my left heralded the second shot. Not the crack-flash of matchlock fire but something else, something blue and gold, paired with the sound of a lightning strike. A second hole appeared between Ost's ribs. He stumbled to his knees, mouth agape, eyes wide.

My arm stung where the shot had grazed me. That one had been meant for me.

I saw them coming as Ost collapsed, broken. Two men on the north bank, one more from the south. They had firearms, two with matchlocks, one packing something with a long silver barrel. That one took aim at me.

The battle-rush came on hard.

I hurled myself down between stacks of fruit crates. A matchlock boomed, and then chips of wood and pulped citrus fruit rained down around me. The bastards had me surrounded. I reached into my coat and produced both pistols, flintlocks, primed and loaded.

I heard voices as the assassins came closer, risked a glance out. They wore masks, simple things made from canvas sacks cut with eyeholes. Their military buff coats were standard issue, but that silver-barrelled weapon wasn't. It was a flarelock, a handheld phos cannon, long made obsolete by matchlocks. Never expected to see one of those again. The military hadn't commissioned a flarelock in fifty years.

Who were these people? A single glance at Ost confirmed he wasn't going to do any more talking.

Me, alone and pinned. Three killers with firearms, closing for a kill.

Bad odds.

Voices. Too hard to make out with those muffling bags. I tried to make a move for the cabins and the flarelock roared again, spraying me with splinters as a crate exploded. I stayed put.

'I am Blackwing Captain Ryhalt Galharrow,' I yelled. 'Throw down your weapons and surrender yourselves to me, or by order of the state you are fucking dead.'

I heard the muffled voices again, but they seemed in no mind to give up.

'Give yourself up and you will be spared,' a man called back. His voice was flat, emotionless.

I couldn't leap for the bank. There were men on both sides and I'm a big, heavy target even when I'm not full of cheap ale and cheaper wine. No way I'd survive a dash down the street, either, if any of them were even half-competent marksmen. Nor was time on my side and as soon as one of them had a clear shot at me I was a goner. I thought it through, then took the only remaining option. Hunkered up to a spring position, counted *one, two, three. Go.*

I swung the pistols out and opened up, blasting off a shot in each direction, and then I ditched them and ran for the barge rail. The flarelock returned fire as I launched myself in what I intended as a graceful dive, but probably just meant slinging myself belly-down into the reeking canal. I punched through an inch-thick layer of rubbery shite on the surface and then I was down in the ink.

The cold hit me like a sledgehammer to the chest. Freezing, bitter as deepest winter, and utterly dark. I went in with a lungful of air but the moment I hit that icy blackness I knew that it wasn't enough. I kicked, tried to get myself turned around and suddenly had no idea which way I was facing. The water was slightly too viscous, a gravy of rotting drudge corpses and an echo of bad magic.

Which way was up? I opened my eyes and the filth-dark water burned them, so I closed them again and kicked hard and thought to myself, *spirits of fucking mercy, the fucking indignity of it if I die like this.* My head banged against something, maybe the barge, maybe a bank. It was there one moment and then as I thrashed around, gone again.

Air. You take it for granted until it's gone. Then you'd trade everything you've ever owned for just one more lungful. My chest screamed at me, and I couldn't blame it.

The cold gathered around me. The weight of the water bore me down.

Blind, flailing, certain to be shot the moment I poked up into the night air I started to see lights dance before my closed eyes. Something hard met my foot and I stopped caring if I was shot. Anything was better than choking on this toxic slime.

I pushed away only to meet a hard, flat surface. No air that direction, and it wasn't the bottom of the canal. I was trapped beneath something. Beneath the barge. My lungs convulsed as they fought to keep me conscious. My chest was collapsing in on itself, ribs aching to implode in an ignominious, silent death, out of sight of men and spirits.

My hand caught an edge. On reflex I punched up, through the filth and into clear air.

I broke the surface, gasped in a grateful, piercing breath. Not dead yet.

I was in a dark room, dim light around the frame of a door. My eyes stung, the bad magic that had leaked from the drudge corpses burning like lime. I could taste the Misery at the back of my throat, like sickness, and salt, and suffering as I bobbed in the narrow hole, confused, until I realised I'd somehow gone under the barge and by sheer luck had come

11

up through a privy in one of the cabins. The former owner had been too fine to shit over the side like a sensible man. I'd never been so grateful to be neck deep in a shithole.

Heaving myself from the water was not easy. I was a strong bastard, but I was also big and heavy and the hole was small and the water was reluctant to let me go. The black filth clung to me like a great shiny leech, reluctant to retract until I undid the buttons on my coat and let it slide away into the darkness. Some kind of fortune was still with me: my sword was still in its sheath and with a blade in my hand, I never counted my luck done altogether.

No time to waste. Ost was dead, but the bastards that shot him surely knew what the fuck he'd been talking about. They also had to assume that I'd perished in the canal after I didn't come up. I could hide out. Go unnoticed. But the raven tattooed on my arm peered up at me impatiently. Crowfoot would boil my blood in my veins if I let a plot this big go. Spinners negotiating with Darlings. It was un-thinkable. And while he may have let me be for some time you do not, under any circumstances, fail a wizard who can melt mountains. Time to get moving. Time for answers.

Past the shitter was the barge's storeroom, dried sausage hanging in coils from the rafters, stacked crates of flour, only one way out. I listened, heard nothing, then slid it open and peeked into the next room. No bag-heads. Maybe they were fishing for my body. I advanced as stealthily as my three hundred sodden pounds could, looked outside. The three bag-heads were standing around Ost on the barge's wide platform, relaxed, weapons slung over their shoulders. They weren't expecting me to come back up out of the obsidian sludge.

'Kick him into the water,' one of them said. A Range ac-cent, that amalgamation of every known language all com-ing together to make something unique. 'Get him under the boat. Long as he's in there a few hours, nobody's going to recognise him. That water will eat through anything.'

'Thought that big guy was going to give us a fight,' another said. Different accent. Hard-edged, city speak. Lennisgrad.

'Glad he didn't.'

There were three of them, and there was only one of me, and those are bad odds. I don't fight for losing causes and I don't fight outnumbered. I'd done my share of heroism and the only thing I'd earned for it was a leg that stabbed at me when the temperature dropped and a never-ending headache. But Ost had said enough to get me worried, real worried, and those men were my only link to the Darling, and the threat to the Range. Like any gambler, I know that when your luck's in, you run with it.

Surprise is a powerful thing. We fall into bubbles of calm and become sluggish. The kill in our brains gets turned off and the fight-or-flight response gets clouded. These men weren't professionals. Opportunists, maybe. They wore city-swords, the kind of spindly things that have a fancy hilt to impress at parties and a blade that wouldn't cut cheese. I doubted that they had ever been charged by a big, angry, determined man with a cutlass in hand.

Life is all about new experiences.

The first of them had just shoved Ost's body into the murk when they saw me, started yelling. One bag-head grabbed the firearm slung over his shoulder and had nearly brought it round to parry when I cut him from shoulder to hip. He was dead before the pieces joined Ost in the muck. The others bolted and I went for the closest. He threw down his spent matchlock and drew his duelling sword, the blade narrow and thrusty. He got a parry in and sparks spat across his bag-face but he couldn't drive back against my heavier blade and I whipped his sword out of the way and took his wrist with the back edge. He shrieked, stumbled back, tripped on a coil of rope and followed the first man over the edge.

The canal would finish him. Turn and kill and move and fight and don't stop for anything less essential than breathing. The last of them had leaped for the bank. Turning, I realised that he'd reloaded the flarelock while I was swimming and now, with range, he drew back the cocking lever and sighted down the silver barrel, past the phos canister and the protruding copper wires. At that range, he couldn't miss.

Shit.

He had me. He might put me down in one shot. Head, heart. Failing that I might reach him, make him pay before I succumbed. He looked at me calmly, neither anger nor panic in those eyes, and I heard the click of the firing lever.

A high-pitched whine rose from the phos canister attached to the weapon. For a fraction of a heartbeat I saw a shape behind him in the darkness: the outline of a woman, radiant in flames, a black silhouette within the fire. And then the flarelock's canister erupted in a blaze of flaming, hissing moonlight. Sparks sprayed thirty feet in all directions. I covered my face with a hand and ducked as the embers sprayed me, a thousand wasp stings sizzling as they struck.

As the fireworks faded, peace descended over the canal, disturbed only by the barking of distant dogs, still riled by the quake. I was burned, and my lungs were blazing like I'd inhaled a sack of bees, but I was still alive.

There was no sign of the man who'd fallen into the water. I guess he wasn't a swimmer.

No sign of the woman in the light either. She was burned into my vision until I blinked and then she was gone, and I was left wondering whether I'd really seen anything there at all.

No. Of course not. Wishful thinking. That was all.

The man whose weapon had misfired was making the last

sounds he'd make in this life. He probably didn't understand what had just happened. Flarelocks were unstable things, with a delicate backlash-venting system to handle the discharge of phos energy. When those systems failed, the results weren't pretty. In this case the steel phos canister had detonated, spraying him with white-hot shrapnel, his body torn and bleeding from dozens of bloody tears.

He made a few hopeless noises. Then he was dead and everything was quiet save for the wheeze of my own heavy breathing. I was getting as out of shape as dead old Levan Ost. Still. Four men had just died, and I was still standing.

I made the leap to the bank and looked down at the tangled, ruined man who'd put his faith in the light and been punished for it. I stripped the bag from his head. Odd. He looked familiar. An ordinary-looking kind of man, brown hair, a moustache, his only distinguishing feature a large mole beneath his left eye. And yet, I was sure I knew him.

I did, I realised. I'd killed him three weeks ago.

2

Devlen Maille had spent most of his life raising pigs on a farm someplace where mud was plentiful and money was not. Then had come a wife, and with her, gambling, drinking, and putting his fists to work. It was fair to say that Devlen had been a grand piece of shit long before he realised that his wife's brothers were planning to throw him down a well, and he was still a shit when he fled to the Range and got a job mopping the floors in a phos mill. Steady work, but paying little more than the pig shit he'd only just escaped. So, when a plucky profiteer suggested he settle his debts by stealing battery coils and selling them on the black market, Devlen Maille had leaped at the chance. My jackdaws had busted him red-handed, he resisted arrest, and I shot him dead.

Nobody had mourned him the first time I killed him, and I very much doubted that they would mourn him the second time either. I very clearly remembered shooting him, and just as clearly recalled my jackdaws slinging his body onto a cart, so it was surprising that he'd just tried to shoot me back.

The river water stank, congealing on my clothes as I dripped through the streets and spent a solid half hour puking my guts out in the alley behind the Blackwing offices. I'd done my part in the Siege, and after seeing Valengrad nearly destroyed, the princes had finally realised that adequately funding both the citadel and Blackwing should have been higher on their list of priorities. As a result of the money they'd thrown my way I could now at least afford a decent building to throw up behind.

'You look like the hells, boss,' Meara said, yawning at the desk. One of my best jackdaws, she was the biggest woman I'd ever met, and she filled the space behind it. 'You find your man?'

'I did. Anyone else in yet?'

'It's ain't yet six, sir,' Meara said. If she had questions about my being soaked through on a dry night, or what the terrible smell was, she had the sense not to raise them. 'Biggest quake so far, neh? The clock in the hallway fell down and broke.'

I found the strongest coffee I could get my hands on, empowered it with brandy and tried to scour away the taste of the canal. It was right up there, behind my eyes, chemical and sour and putrid. I finished my coffee, and shortly found myself back in the alley to see it emerge again.

The streets were still dark. There was no phos network in this part of the city, and nobody was paying to have the old lamps lit. I liked it dark. The lack of phos tubes was one of the reasons I'd settled on this location.

In the few minutes between my staggering outside and finishing heaving out strings of oily grime, someone had tacked a yellow paper flyer to the office door. Spiritual nonsense proclaiming that sightings of the Bright Lady heralded a new era of justice and freedom. They saw visions in the light, or at least they claimed to, and had attached the usual promises to it. There's no hour of day too ungodly for the servants of religion, and they were everywhere now. I scanned the street for the culprit, but there was no sign of them save for the same yellow papers tacked to every door in the street. I tore it down and tossed the crumpled paper ball away. I wasn't about to let that nonsense into my office, even if the toilet rags were running out.

The stink wasn't going to fade without help, so I stoked the kitchen fire and filled a metal tub. It was intended for dishes, comically small to fit me, but better than nothing. I scrubbed my head with soap, tried washing out my eyes, and the water quickly turned dark, took on an oily glimmer. Whatever bad magic the Deep Kings put into the drudge, I'd managed to soak myself in it. Couldn't tell whether the nausea inside me was because of the magic or my reaction to it, but it was best to imagine the latter. My servant, Amaira, had laid out a fresh uniform for me, assuming that I'd end up working late and sleeping in the office again. I had a big house that I seldom visited, and the office felt more like home. Amaira had guessed that I'd end up here again come dawn. Maybe there was hope for her yet.

Dawn hadn't yet worked her way into the sky but Blackwing had come a long way in the years since Shavada's doomed assault on Valengrad. I had men on my payroll around the clock, so I sent a cleanup crew to deal with the mess over at Canal Six. The team would cart the bodies over to the morgue for an examination, what was left of them anyway. Dead men don't do a lot of talking, but if they were marked by the Deep Kings, then we'd find out.

What a fuckup. I should have taken a team with me. I'd let sentimentality interfere with my better judgment and I'd very nearly died. Ost had been part of my past, and I preferred to clutch that close. Keep the shame hidden away, as nothing to do with the man I'd become. Couldn't afford that kind of mess again. I wasn't as young as I'd been and I had responsibility now, people who counted on me. I had to be smarter than that.

Clean-ish and dressed again, I sat at my desk and swept yesterday's paperwork from the table. Old rumours, half reports. It had been weeks since anything serious had come our way. Perhaps that was why the bag-heads had taken me by surprise.

I was tired, drained and had to keep spitting into a bucket but when two hours had passed and the coffee was cold I was starting to feel human again. A luxurious office with its dark wood panels, leather chairs and good traditional oil lamps helps the spirit. Or maybe it was the brandy. We surround ourselves in luxuries as though decadence and wealth will stave away the true concerns of the world for a time. Perhaps they do.

'Looks like you had a rough night,' I said when Tnota ambled in. For a man who could navigate the Misery better than nearly anyone, he had the worst discipline in the states. His shirt was untucked and he smelled like a brewery. He sagged down into his own overstuffed chair with the air of a man who was suffering from the deepest of self-inflicted misfortunes.

'Looks like yours was worse,' he said.

Explanations were made. I'd been out killing, he'd been out drinking. A regular state of affairs, though more often than not I was giving orders rather than swinging a sword myself these days. Tnota had transitioned smartly from navigator to being my right hand, which was ironic since he was lacking his own.

'You haven't slept again,' he said. 'Got that glazed look. You need a bed.'

'I'll sleep tonight,' I said.

'You say that every day, and half of those you're a liar,' Tnota said. 'Big Dog says,' he started, but he broke into a yawn himself and I was saved from any holy canine wisdom for the time being.

I shivered, though the fire was banked and blazing. If Death came for me through a chill I caught swimming, I was going to kick her in the bollocks.

Valiya arrived at the office, soaked and frozen. She was scowling as though the sky had given her some kind of personal affront, and if I'd been the sky, I'd have fled to the hills. She blew into the office as she blew through life: a force of nature, intolerant of ineptitude, fixing everything that lesser beings had buggered up. She even managed to drip with an air of refinement as she carefully hung her heavy raincoat on the stand in front of the fire. A sweep of auburn hair obscured half of her face, which was often useful, as it was a distracting face. She was making a better job of her thirties than most women did their twenties, or at least that's how I saw it. When she turned up three years back, she'd said she'd run the place better than anyone else could, and she'd proved that every day since. Now she practically ran not only the offices, which she was supposed to, but my intelligence network, which she wasn't. It wouldn't have paid to try to stop her.

Valiya wrung water from her bedraggled hair.

'This place,' she said, frowning, 'smells bloody awful.'

I told her what had happened, asked her to find out where Devlen Maille's body had been tossed to rest the first time. If I could work out how he'd managed to walk out of his grave the first time, it might help me find out how he'd ended up in one for a second.

'What a twat,' she said. 'How does someone manage to get killed twice by the same person? Leave it with me, Ryhalt.' She wrote down the details and glowered the clouds into submission as she headed back out into the faltering rain.

'First-name terms is it now?' Tnota said.

'You don't call me "Captain" either,' I said. But it was different, and we both knew it.

'Is it too early for a drink?' Tnota asked.

'Yes,' I said. It was half past eight. I was trying to push back against our worst habits. Drinking made me drowsy, and there was no time for sleep. 'Here. What do you make of this?'

I took the remains of the flarelock that the bag-head had dropped and put it on his desk. It resembled a matchlock in shape, with a stock, a barrel and a firing lever, but it was a far more complex weapon. A phos canister fed into the ball chamber, where a small discharge of light would fire off the shot. The canister was largely missing and the stock had been badly damaged in the detonation, but the long, silver barrel was clear enough. It bore a maker's mark, a stylised letter F imprinted into the steel.

'These things should be left in the museums,' Tnota said. 'Too expensive and dangerous to be worth firing when we got powder arms instead. Phos isn't cheap. Unstable, too.' He looked it over, inspected the trigger mechanism and the residue along the barrel. 'Don't recognise the maker's mark. Must be a new workshop,' he said eventually.

'Doesn't make sense. Matchlock's a better weapon all round. A lot less chance of blowing yourself to pieces.'

'He was an idiot to use this thing,' he said. 'Phos should be left to the Spinners. And look what happens to them, covered in burns of their own making.'

'I'm sure the man who blew himself apart with this would agree.' In my mind, I ran through what I remembered of the conversation I'd had with Ost. 'Ost said his employers had met with a Darling. Out at Tiven's Dale. Why meet there?'

Tnota rubbed at his morning stubble, winter-grey against the richness of his skin.

'Tiven's Dale ain't an easy nav. It's small, and the compass shifts around it like the hands of a clock. It'd be a good, private place to meet. You got to wonder what they'd be doing ranging that close, though, if they aren't up to something.'

'They don't have the army to push the Range again,' I said. 'Nall's Engine crippled their capability for that.'

Tnota did not look comforted.

'Yeah. Doesn't make you feel better though, does it?'

*

'Morning courier's been, Captain-Sir,' Amaira said brightly as she skipped in and placed a stack of brown-paper envelopes onto my desk. She'd been orphaned during the battle for the walls, like a lot of kids around Valengrad. In the months after the Siege was broken, I'd felt a duty to put at least some of them to work. One by one they'd wandered off, died or proved incapable of honesty. Amaira was the last of them still working for Blackwing.

'Anything I'm going to like?'

'You got an invite from Major Nenn. She wants you to go to the theatre with her.'

'She send anything for you this time?'

'Not today.' She sounded despondent. Nenn had taken a liking to the kid, kept bringing her something whenever she came back from the Misery. Amaira's growing collection of oddities included a long, four-jointed finger that crawled about on its own, a stone that cried if you stroked it and an indestructible grasshopper perpetually frozen mid-jump. Misery shit. I didn't see there was harm in it as long as the kid didn't eat any of it.

'Probably for the best.' I began to leaf through the letters.

'Can I come to the theatre with you, Captain-Sir?' Amaira asked.

'I don't have time for theatre,' I said. I could feel the night's exertions and lack of sleep coming together as a pounding in my head. I needed more coffee. Too much work to do to rest now.

'But it's a play about the Siege,' Amaira protested. 'I heard they have this puppet that looks like Shavada, and it's filled with men on stilts using poles to move it around.'

Tnota gave a mocking, staccato cackle. I put down the papers, gave him a level stare.

'They got some nerve dragging that shit here. Doubt any of those fucking actors had even heard the sky howl before they got sent here.'

'Fuckin' actors!' Amaira grinned.

'Watch your language,' I snapped.

'Yes, Captain-Sir.' She hesitated. 'You all right, Captain-Sir? You don't look so well. You want me to bring some eggs? Or wine?'

She was right. I didn't feel right at all and it went deeper than just tiredness. I was used to being tired. I lived on four hours' sleep most nights, and sometimes none at all.

I blinked myself alert again as I realised someone was speaking.

'Your son passed out drunk on the stairs again last night,' Amaira said primly.

My son. Of course, he wasn't my son. He was an old man in a child's body, and his name was Gleck Maldon. He'd been the second greatest Spinner of his generation before Shavada had twisted him into the form of a Darling. Then I'd shot half of his face away, so it was fair to say that I felt somewhat responsible for him. He looked like a child, and people tended not to ask me too many questions, so false parenthood was a good enough reason for him to be hanging around.

'Did someone take him to bed?'

'No. He refused to move. Then he was sick on the carpet. I don't know where he is now.'

I shrugged. He'd do what he'd do and buggered if I could make any real difference. Mollified by telling on him, Amaira strode away with the glad energy that only an uncorrupted child could have. She claimed she was fourteen, which meant she was probably twelve.

'You don't look good, boss,' Tnota said. I was getting tired of hearing that. He looked down toward his own papers, as he always did when he wanted to say something I wouldn't like. 'Maybe you should get some sleep.'

He was right, but I wouldn't. For the same reason I wouldn't allow phos lights in the office. I knew what

23

awaited me in the darkness. I knew that when I closed my eyes, I would see her in my dreams. Reaching for me, always reaching. Trapped in the light. Asking for my help. And I would reach out for her, and our fingers would slide through one another's like smoke.

3

'How much do they hurt?' Amaira asked. She sat across the table from me, looking at my forearms as I ate a hunk of bread stuffed with pork belly.

'What?'

'Tattoos,' she said. 'How much do they hurt?'

'It's someone sticking a needle in you, over and over,' I said, 'it hurts as much as you'd think that would hurt. Don't you have work to be doing?'

Amaira frowned at that.

'Hm,' she said, but made no move to get up.

'Don't even think about getting yourself inked,' I said. 'You're too young. If I find someone's inked you, I'll beat their ears until they're on the inside of their skull.'

'Why?' she asked. She was an annoying child, although in my experience that's the only variety. She had the dusky skin and lightless-black hair of the oasis kingdoms, but her blue eyes argued for at least one ancestor of more northerly descent. Valengrad was a place where you'd find every colour, every mix of man that ever walked the earth and her mixed heritage was common as sparrows. Amaira never spoke about her parents. It was a silence that I could respect.

'Because once you mark yourself up, it's permanent,' I said. 'And I've seen a lot of people regret a lot of bad tattoos.'

'I like that one,' she said, pointing to the raven on my forearm, his talons curled around a longsword.

'Trust me. That one hurts the most.'

I ate my way through half a loaf of bread, dunking it in cold gravy. The woman who cooked for me kept loading my plate until I refused more, and it turns out when you don't sleep, you're hungry all the time. Sometimes I ate six times a day. The food never takes away the blurriness, or helps your memory, which cracks and splits and lets you down. Things could get foggy.

'I think I should get one the same. So people know where I work,' Amaira said, with all the confidence of a kid who has never gone under the needle.

'No.'

'But I – '

'No,' I said firmly. She lowered her eyes.

'Yes, Captain-Sir.'

'You've got work to do. Go and get on with it,' I said. Amaira gave an overly dramatic sigh and flopped her way out of the room, ensuring that her displeasure at having to earn her keep was duly noted. I finished the last of the meat, stretched out, sank what remained of the coffee and set my minions to work.

I knocked on the door to Valiya's office and entered. The neatness of her little world was almost a reprimand to the chaos of my own, and I found that I was tucking my shirt in to comply with the sense of order she'd created. Her dress was immaculately pressed, her hair as precisely ordered as her room. She was working through the payroll of our – my – employees but she put the ledger aside when I entered.

'Levan Ost's dead. I don't know where he lived before that barge. I don't know where to find his daughter. Think you can track her down?'

'If she's here, she can be found,' Valiya said. She sipped from a delicate porcelain cup. She loved the mud-flavoured, terrible tea they brought in from the distant west.

'You mind taking this one yourself?' I asked. 'Keep it quiet?'

'Of course. Have you considered looking for the men who hired him instead?'

Valiya had a way of asking questions that felt like instructions, and she watched me over the rim of her cup. There was an admonishment in that tea. She disapproved of the rampant drinking that infested most of our operation, but then she didn't have to go out in the Misery or do any of the killing work.

'Ost said that there were thirty of them, and he figured two for Spinners. He didn't even have their names. Not much to go on.'

'You're looking at it all wrong,' Valiya said. 'Soldiers might be hard to find, but navigators aren't so common. How did they find Ost? Most navigators are on the citadel payroll. Not many go freelance. Maybe Ost wasn't the first they approached.'

She was right. Should have thought of it myself. Had to wonder maybe whether I might have done if the fog would just lift from behind my eyes. Maybe there was value in drinking mud-flavoured tea after all.

We all have our vices. I preferred to stick to the ones I knew best.

'Remind me to come to you first, next time I need to think of something,' I said. 'Thanks. I'll be out of the city until tomorrow.'

I got up and made to leave.

'Ryhalt,' Valiya called after me.

'Yes?'

'Take another bath. You still stink of canal,' she said. She didn't look up from the ledger as she spoke, but I swear she was trying to keep a smile from her face. I didn't see her smile often. That was a shame.

I didn't follow her advice, but I changed out of my

27

uniform into old, rough clothes, the kind I'd spent the worse half of my life wearing and headed out of the city's southern gate, following the supply road. I passed Station Two-Five and Station Two-Four, both of which looked well kept and manned. This close to Valengrad they were always wary of inspections and the commanders all sought to take a position as close to the city as possible. I overtook a couple of caravans as they creaked slowly down the Range, but there was a small amount of traffic in both directions. The road was in need of maintenance, but then, what road isn't in winter?

I met travellers heading in the other direction too, up-Range toward Valengrad. Provincial types, farmers, labourers, craftsmen – ordinary folks with high-piled wagons and wide-eyed children. They seemed cheerful despite their proximity to the Misery and wore their yellow hoods proudly: pilgrims of the Bright Order. I gave them a friendly nod as I passed but didn't stop for conversation.

My destination was a half day's ride. The Range Stations occupied the Misery's border, but a couple of miles from the desert's edge a small town – if it could be called such – had grown up to house the diggers and scavengers who dared brave the Misery. Teak's Alehouse had appeared there at some point, because men who've been into the Misery need liquorice and they need beer. It probably shouldn't have been there, but the alehouse had an undeserved reputation for brewing the best beer in the states. It was rumoured that even Marshal Venzer had visited it on occasion. I tried to picture him, small, old and disguised, licking his lips as he rode in along the single, dusty street. The subterfuge would probably have appealed to the Iron Goat, and that made me smile.

Teak's Town had a ragged, unsavoury air to it. Other shops and stores had grown up around the alehouse – the usual trades you'd expect in a town founded on digging shit out of the Misery and alcohol. Gambling, whores, fighting and pawnbrokers. There was no phos network out here, and the buildings were all wooden except for Teak's, which dressed in stone as if lording it over its neighbours. I didn't like Teak's Town. It attracted the wrong kinds of people, the kind that thought there had to be a way of turning a profit in the Misery. Levan Ost wasn't the only man to think he could get rich digging up Misery shit and selling it to curiosity collectors in the west. The diggers didn't usually delve far, the chance of getting turned around was way too high more than a few hours onto the sands. Gangs of them loitered in front of Teak's. Although it was winter, a wave of heat had washed in from the Misery and it could have been high summer, driving the patrons outside. The scavengers were obvious by the shaking of their hands, the desperate expressions. Only three kinds of men enter the Misery willingly: the stupid, the greedy or the desperate. These men looked to be all three.

'You looking for goods, mate? I got the rarest stuff you ever seen. You a buyer?' one of them asked me as I hitched Falcon to a post. I'd dressed down into scuffed old leathers and a soft-brimmed hat that had been with me fifteen years, but the horse gave me away for a richer kind of man than these. The digger had a twitch in his cheek, a nervousness that would never go away. He'd seen something out there that he couldn't forget. Happened, sometimes.

'Not today,' I said.

'I've got something real special,' he said. He reached into his coat, no doubt to bring out some kind of curio but I gripped him by the arm.

'Not today,' I said again.

I pushed through the swing doors into the bar, which was nothing special. Old rushes on the floor, the smell of spilled beer thick in the humidity. Eyes turned to me in the gloom and the woman working behind the bar gave me the once-over, figured me for just another desperate treasure hunter and went back to working her drop spindle. The few afternoon drinkers that had chosen to tolerate the heat in order to be closer to the bar ignored me. They had enough worries of their own.

I went to the bar. The casks of ale and bottles of what was probably meant to be whisky pleaded with me from across the counter, but I ignored their suicidal whining for now and addressed the barkeep. She had her hair in a stack of red curls up on her head to display a gold chain around her neck. At least someone here was making money.

'I know you,' she said. 'That coat ain't fooling me any. You step careful around here. There's some boys might not want to be seen.'

Deserters, most likely. You'd think that men who fled the service would head away from the Misery, but we tend to stick to the places we know.

'Point them out to me, if you see them.'

'If you're hunting trouble, do it outside.'

'I'm not after trouble. I'm looking for navigators,' I said. 'Any around?'

'Nolt's around,' she said. 'At least, he was in here yesterday. Weren't looking for work though. His nerve's gone. Mostly just sits telling his stories now.'

I thanked her, and despite my good intentions took a couple of drinks of whisky. It wasn't half as bad as I'd expected it to be. I paid more than it was worth and turned to leave, only to see three aggressive shapes blocking the doorway.

'Well,' I said. 'You look like you're wanting to talk to me.'

Perhaps 'talk' was the wrong word. They were dressed in oddments of armour, poor-fitting and speckled with rust, suits cobbled together from other men's harnesses. One of them was short with an eye swollen shut. The second, taller, was missing some of her teeth. The third was heavy in the gut, mutton-chop whiskers framing a drinker's face. They hadn't drawn steel, but they must have seen me ride in, gone and got themselves kitted up while I was busy with the whisky. Drinking would be the death of me, that's what everyone thought. These three were taking the idea too far.

'We know who you are,' the woman said. She seemed to be their leader. The only one with any brains behind her eyes. I recognised them as well – not personally, not by name, but I knew their kind. To be a soldier takes some guts, some discipline, and some hardness. To be a deserter only takes the last. They felt strong here, on familiar territory, with numbers, and their scavenged plate. They thought that I was here gunning for them, and if I'd known who they were, maybe I would have been. But I'd not been expecting a fight and I'd come lightly armed.

'I'm not here for you,' I said. 'Best for everyone if all I can see of you is dust in less than five minutes' time. I'll give you a head start. Want me to count?'

'You strung up Binny and Wilks,' the woman said. The heavy, whiskered man growled. 'They were vets. Survived the Siege. And you hanged them because they'd had too much Misery-time and couldn't wash it anymore. You shouldn't have done that.'

Binny. Wilks. A couple of runaways, at least a year ago. Men I'd almost forgotten. The alehouse patrons seemed to sense that the atmosphere had gone to the storm, and were moving quietly to the sides of the room.

'Go plead it to the law,' I said. 'My business isn't with you. Don't make it about you now and maybe you get to keep running that mouth of yours someplace that people want to hear it. Picking a fight with me isn't smart.'

It wasn't smart. But unlike on the barge, I didn't have surprise on my side here, and Luck won't favour you if you push her. If the deserters went for me, I'd be best off throwing myself through the nearest window.

The acrid, woody odour of burning slow match reached out to me. I heard the lock of a firearm getting cocked.

'You folks need to back the fuck off,' the barkeep said. She sighted down the barrel of a matchlock. 'Keep your swords in their scabbards and go get on your flea-ridden mules and get the hells away from my bar.'

The deserters glared at the barkeep, but her fingers were steady on the firing lever.

'I'm looking for a navigator,' I said, trying to move their minds to something that didn't involve laying me open. The barkeep only had one shot and even if she hit, the odds would still be against me. The deserters weren't just fronting: they feared going the same way as Binny and Wilks, and did it really matter if someone shot the fat one? They were all playing through the scenarios in their minds.

'I'm looking for a navigator. A freelancer. You know where I can find Nolt?'

'Nolty?' the woman said, narrowed her eyes. 'What's he done?'

'Nothing I know of. He's not in any kind of trouble. Not with me, anyway. Just tell me where I can find him and go on your way. Then keep on going so I don't ever see you again.'

'Find him yourself,' she said. 'Come on boys. Tide ain't waiting.'

We were a long way from the sea, but they saw which way their sails were trying to take them and the deserters backed through the alehouse doors. The barkeep breathed a sigh of relief, lowered the matchlock and killed the slow match. The drinkers ambled on back to their usual tables. Order had been restored in their hazy world. I turned back to the barkeep and ordered another drink. Now I just had to wait.

Nolt came to me. Word gets around a small town fast. He limped in on a crutch, a haggard man who'd seen better days, missing most of his left leg below the knee. He was dressed in shabby outdoor leathers and looked like everybody's father, but he had a yellow hood around his shoulders. He sat beside me at the bar, and it was clear that he was more than happy to talk as long as I was buying him some of that sweet Teak's ale. He practically thrust his face into the mug, glugging like he'd been denied water for a month.

'Good?'

'What can I say?' Nolt said. 'Times are tough and money's short.' He gestured down toward his missing foot.

'What got you?'

'Gillings,' Nolt said. 'Twelve years navigating, and then one night my buddy dozed off on sentry. Woke up because I needed a piss, found the little bastard had made his way up this far.' He shook his head at the bad luck. 'Hard to find decent jobs since then. Citadel don't want me, no matter I can still ride. You'd think they would. Bloody good navigator, I was.'

'That's what I heard,' I said, which was a lie.

'I heard you were looking for a navigator. Thought you ran with Tnota. Now, he's a man that knows his way around the Misery. So what can I do for you? You got a job for me?'

Nolt's tone, his posture, said that he was interested in work. Wanted to show that he was still as good as any other nav, even if he was down a foot. But behind his words, his tone, there was a silent plea. *Don't send me back there*, it said. *Don't send me back into the cursed wastes, to see the ghosts and the things that don't have names. Please. Please don't.* I felt sorry for him. Can't be easy to wake up and find a little red thing sucking on your bone marrow.

'No. I'm looking for someone who might have offered you a job. Navigating to Tiven's Dale.'

I'd hit the mark. He feigned sadness that I wasn't looking

to hire him, but the relief ran far stronger. I bought another round of drinks to ease his story out.

'I'd have taken the job,' he said. 'I could do it, you know. Not an easy nav, but I could do it no sweat.' He wanted me to believe him. To accept that he was still the man that he'd been. I didn't ask why he hadn't taken the job. He'd have been forced to lie.

'You did the right thing to turn him down. You remember who approached you?' I asked.

'Yeah, I remember him. Odd type for Misery work. Posh voice. Lennisgrad accent. Not cream, but not far off. Educated. Ego the size of a fucking barn.'

'He give you a name?'

He thought about it a few moments.

'Nacomo,' he said eventually. 'That was it. Nacomo. Like the town.'

It wasn't a common name, but it wasn't rare either.

'I have to track this man down. Anything else you can remember would help me.'

Nolt had reached the end of his line as far as Misery work was concerned, pretty understandable given the circumstances. He'd been given an honourable discharge. But he was still a patriot, still a fighter at heart. His desire to serve hadn't been chewed away with his foot.

'Medium height, brown hair. White. Young-looking, but old hands?' He thought for a few moments. 'There was one thing. Whenever the sky howled, and it was howling fierce the day he came looking for navs, he'd practically jump out of his seat. Made me think he was new on the Range. Really had me wondering what he was doing wanting to go as deep as Tiven's Dale. He make it there?'

'He did, I think. Thanks, Nolt.'

'Any real work comes up, you let me know,' he said, but the tremble of his jaw said the opposite. I gave him enough money to stay in beers for the rest of the week, which was a heavy payoff for a name and a handful of details. I'd pass them to Valiya and see what came of it.

It was long past dark by the time I made it back into Valengrad. Recently the streets were always busy with traffic. A lot of new arrivals, their life's possessions stowed in wagons. They were ordinary people, tradesmen and farmers, some with skills, some with nothing more than determination and mouths to feed. There were plenty of empty houses waiting to be occupied, if they wanted them. So many had died during the siege, both those who had gone down battling atop the wall or beneath it, or those who had hidden and been found, or run and been caught when Shavada's troops entered the city. There was something unremittingly bleak about moving into the dust-covered, untouched home of a person who'd died saving you. But four years on and people seemed to fill the city. They came with purpose, yellow hoods a declaration of their devotion to the cult that had taken root in every walk of life. If it had been up to me, I'd have treated them like any other Doomsayers and stamped their fledgling religion into the dirt, but there were a lot of them and the less I had to do with them the better. They called themselves the Bright Order, and I hated them.

I settled down at The Bell with a jar, dark ale, bitter enough to bite the roof of your mouth. It wasn't good but it was cheap. I could have afforded better. Hells, I could have bought the whole louse-infested joint on half my yearly pay, but old habits cling stronger than ticks. Across the room, shabby-looking men and women passed a bowl of white-leaf back and forth. Off-duty mercenaries lounged in a half circle around the fire trying to outdo each other with largely fictional stories of highly unlikely conquests. After the Siege, Tnota and I had practically taken this place over until duty and work got away from us. Some of the kids who'd looked after us were still there, working. When I gave the place over to him, I'd made Sav promise both to keep them on, and not to let any of them whore until they were full-grown.

I'd sunk three beers in quick succession by the time Tnota joined me.

'Valiya talked to the cemetery boys. They received Devlen Maille's body but that's where their records seem to end. They didn't remember him, and they didn't write down which pauper's pit they chucked him in.'

'It was a long shot,' I admitted. 'What else?'

'None of the usual whisper-men had anything,' he told me. 'Tried the mercenaries too. Looking for a thirty-strong troop recently back from the Misery with Spinners in tow. Nothing there either.'

'You try the boys at the east gate?'

'Valiya did. No leads.' Tnota signalled to the girl for wine. She grinned at him. They all loved Tnota, for some reason. He'd been a regular on top of The Bell's lads before the Siege, but he'd mellowed out since his injury. He'd not lost his grin, but he'd lost more than just his arm. Like Nolt, his nerve was fried, both for navigating the Misery and navigating around a bed. Didn't even glance up at the bare-chested lads lounging along the balcony.

'Nothing at all?'

'If your boy Ost hadn't been shot over it, I'd not believe a word.'

'Makes me wonder if he was just mixed up in something local. Looking to have me fight his battles for him. Only they went in close, after he was down. Real determined to make sure he wasn't getting back up.'

'Here's trouble,' Tnota said. He nodded over to where two middle-aged men had just walked in, shaking the rain from their long cloaks. Their hoods were yellow. Bright Order men.

'Maybe they're not the arsehole type,' I said, but I didn't hold out a great deal of hope on that front. Most people were exactly that type, whether or not they subscribed to a newborn religion. The newcomers approached a table of old mercenaries, tried to foist flyers on them and were duly told to fuck off, which sent them over to us. They had the look of provincials, with accents to match.

'You're wasting your time, son,' I said. 'There's only two things people come into The Bell for. One gets you drunk, the other gets you laid. No amount of talking about visions in the light is going to change that.'

The Bright Order man mostly ignored what I'd said. He took on an almost apologetic air.

'Don't worry, I'm not going to try to convince you to believe in anything you've not seen for yourself. Your beliefs are between you and the spirits,' he said. 'It's just an invitation, for any honest men who are fed up with paying more than their due. There's a public meeting to protest the marshal's latest tax. We'd love to hear your opinions.'

He pushed a damp flyer toward us. The rain had got into his bag and made the ink run, turning it mostly illegible. Seeing that he'd get nothing further from us, he and his companion moved on around the room.

'Awful lot of those Bright Order converts coming into the city these days,' Tnota said.

'The Grandspire,' I grunted. 'They treat it like a holy place, and it's not even finished.'

'They might be a bunch of bores, but at least the place isn't a ghost town anymore. Good for the tradesmen, at least,' Tnota said. 'Big Dog says that more bodies on the Range has to be a good thing. They can't all be witless.'

I wasn't so sure about that. Their faith seemed to be an accumulation of spirituality and revolutionary philosophy pasted onto the visions of the so called Bright Lady that had been happening all over. Word was that the High Witness

37

was coming to Valengrad to help spread the Bright Lady's message – maybe when he did he'd be able to explain their ideology more coherently than the peasants clogging up the streets.

Tnota and I drank, played a game of tiles. Tnota was a terrible opponent and I usually had to let him take back a move or two just to make sure the game didn't end before it had started, but I blinked and found he'd trapped half my pieces. Maybe it was the fug in my head, or maybe my mind was just somewhere else. I lost half my front tiles to a trap I should have seen a mile off.

'I saw her again,' I said.

My one-armed friend nodded. Like he'd guessed already what I was going to say.

'Lot of people seen her,' he said. 'That's why they're coming here, isn't it? All them yellow-hoods think they've seen her. They think she signifies a new world order's coming. That what you think, Ryhalt?'

'No,' I said. 'And it's not the same. They say they see a woman in the light. What I see – it's not the same. She's dead, and I've made my peace with that. Whatever's left in the light – it's no more her than a footprint is a man. But ... I saw her.'

'You saw a big flash of light,' Tnota said. 'You've been in battle enough to know that when your blood's hot, you won't remember everything clearly. When was the last time you even slept?' Tnota knocked ash against the table, put his hand over the top of his beer. That meant he was getting serious. Talking, not drinking. 'I know it's not easy, Ryhalt. You found Ezabeth and you lost her, and somewhere in that dented old skull of yours you can't help but blame yourself, for all that you done as much as anyone to make sure we aren't all drudge now. But you want my advice?'

'I don't know. Will I like it?'

'No. But I'll give it all the same. You need to get some

sleep. You're burning the candle at both ends and roasting the middle over a fire. You keep this up much more and you'll be doubting everything you see.'

'I see her when I sleep,' I said.

'Just dreams,' Tnota countered. 'We all have bad ones.'

'What if Dantry was right? What if she's not dead? Not completely.'

'That man had a brain the size of a city,' Tnota said, 'And no common sense at all. But even if he was right, that there's something more than an echo of her left in the light, he couldn't figure out shit about what to do about it. You ain't some mathematical genius like he was, but if you want to believe she's going to come dancing back, maybe you should go join the cult. A hood would suit you.'

'I wish he'd come back, wherever he went,' I said. I meant it, too. Dantry Tanza had stuck around with us for a couple of years. I'd let him board in my house. Then things got difficult. He wasted his fortune obtaining an ancient book, became obsessed with it. The Taran Codex. It was written in Akat, a dead language. Taran had been Nameless a thousand years ago. Nobody alive could read more than a handful of words in Akat, only those that remained on crumbled monuments and broken statues. Dantry employed researchers, linguists, the best academics in the states in his efforts to translate it. He believed that if he could decipher it, he might find a way to save Ezabeth. It was wasted energy, a fool's errand. I couldn't endure his constant talk about his sister, his certainty that she lived on, trapped in the light. I believed it too, at first, but as the days wore by, my faith wavered, then snapped. The living woman had been flesh and blood. Whatever part of Ezabeth remained, it was just phos. Just an echo. It was too painful to talk about.

Dantry had become obsessed. He worked endless calculations based on that damn book, but I couldn't see how numbers and lines on a page were ever going to make a woman flesh and blood again. I think that he saw it too, in the end. One day he took his impenetrable book, went out and never came back. Our relationship had grown so strained that I didn't even notice for two days. I regretted that.

'I should have helped him.' I sighed. 'Dantry was the only one trying to work out what the fuck she'd become. I wish he'd come back.'

'So do I,' Tnota said. He gave a wicked grin. 'He was a man I could really have got behind.'

I grunted.

'Yeah, I bet you could.'

4

My leg ached. Rain fell. The same people brought me their suspicions and somehow I found myself giving in to the most powerful force of coercion ever known: the continuous demands of a child. I dressed the part, looked at myself in the mirror. I looked fucking ridiculous.

I couldn't believe that I'd agreed to attend this farce of a play.

'It's what all the court folk wears, that's what the tailor said,' Amaira said.

'Nothing about that makes me want to wear it.'

'I think the ruffles is nice. They hide your chin a bit,' Amaira said.

'What's wrong with my chin?'

She gave me a look that said that honestly, if I didn't already know, it wasn't worth the telling. Kids have no tact. It's one of the reasons I like them. The tailor had cut the clothes to a good fit but it had been a long time since I'd tried to dress up fancy, and I could have waited a few more years. Preferably until after I was dead. Lace, frills, silver buttons, gold brocade, slippers made from some kind of material so soft it was a wonder it didn't fall to pieces on contact with the air. I'd worn this kind of garbage as a matter of course back before Adrogorsk and my disgrace, but I'd been a different kind of man back then. I had the distinct impression that these clothes were dressing up in me more than I was them, and resented me as much as I did them.

'Fuck it. I'm changing.'

Amaira made disappointed sounds.

'Go get yourself into that frock the major sent you. Get Valiya to help you with the laces. See if she can curl your hair too.'

Amaira scampered away singing. We conducted a lot of serious business at Blackwing, but having her around livened the place up. If we could all just remain kids forever I doubt that there'd have been a war, or an Engine or cannon and swords in the first place.

Sad to think that she was going to turn into an adult, and would probably become as unbearable as everybody else.

I changed out of the crap the tailor had sent me and into one of the new uniforms. Black breeches slashed to show the maroon lining, a close-fitting jacket with military buttons. Suitable, practical clothing for unsuitable, impractical work. I wore a long black tailcoat with it. Far better. I slung on a sword. The nobility wore weapons to the theatre not because they expected to use them but because a finely crafted weapon allowed them to show off their wealth and taste through gaudy, expensive decoration. Their weapons were more about the hilt than the length of steel attached to them. I'd allowed a smith to craft me a dress sword with fancy hand protection but I'd had him replace the feeble little duelling blade with one capable of hacking a cow's head in two. I didn't expect to have to defend myself against any deadly bovine assaults but you can never be too sure.

'You look boring!' Amaira pouted when we got into the carriage that Nenn had sent. She had a pretty pink-and-blue party frock that fell to the knee with long boots. It was a fashion that wasn't going away and it seemed too adult for Amaira's boyish figure, but then what did I know about children? In faraway Hyspia, they married them off at her

42

age. Of course, if they tried that in Valengrad, we cut their dicks off.

The carriage rolled through the city to the absurd and decadent theatre that served to entertain the nobles who lived out in Willows. Rows of carriages were assembled in order of the ranks of the nobility who had arrived in them, insignias proudly displayed. Drivers were constantly reorganizing as higher-ranked nobles arrived, whilst a fraught clerk tried to work out whether a viscount had greater status than a ranker colonel. There was a new class of nobility along the Range now, and they were keener to fight than the old crowd had been. The cream who had fled in our blackest hour had encountered a spree of tragic accidents after Nall's Engine threw the drudge back. It could have been coincidence, but after the bodies of the leader of the Red Flight mercenary company and Count Orvino had been found in the woods, together and engaged in acts of bestiality, I was certain that another of Crowfoot's agents had turned his retribution into a game. I didn't know which of Crowfoot's captains was putting so much energy into entertaining themselves with that bloody work. Which was probably for the best.

Entertainers were warming the crowd up with juggling and sleight of hand, which seemed an odd choice for a play about the biggest catastrophe since Crowfoot burned the Misery into existence.

The punters had gathered in small groups. It was opening night so a single ticket was enough to bankrupt most small businesses, but anyone who could afford it was there. They loitered in hierarchical groups, with each person of status gaining a little clutch of hangers-on, like a mother duck and her ducklings. Attempting to join a group that significantly outranked you was considered a laughable error in judgment. As I looked at them all now it seemed hard to believe that I'd once played these games, had spent my hours preening and writing out lists of who I needed to speak to. I'd had ambition. So many of the young dandies in the foyer could have been me. The young women could have been Ezabeth. I avoided looking at them.

'Can I get spun sugar?' Amaira asked. She was practically hopping from foot to foot. I'd know no peace until I acquiesced, so I gave her some coins and she hurtled away toward a seller as if she'd been launched by a catapult.

The cream moved aside as Range Marshal Davandein moved through their ranks. At forty-five she cut an elegant figure, but she had a sculpture's beauty, perfect lines that gave no warmth. A clever tailor had managed to cut her a dress that was both ostentatiously splendid but retained something of a military turn, and her dark hair was netted with a web of precious stones, glittering blackly. She'd not been in the post long. Marshal Wechsel had been capable, but he'd been old and the task of rebuilding our defences had taxed him. He'd passed quietly in his sleep. Davandein was related to two different princely lineages, too much cream in her blood for my liking, not enough mud. But, she was blunt and confident, and that counted for a lot when dealing with the hard-arses serving on the Range.

The main thing I liked about her was that she unquestioningly accepted the power of Nall's Engine. I was the only mortal who knew the truth about it. A few falsified documents here and there and the Order of Aetherial Engineers was running as it always had. Everyone who'd known about the phos-supply discrepancy – that the Engine ran not on phos, but on the power of an immortal's heart – was dead. After Nall's Engine had obliterated our enemies, the Nameless had sealed the heart, replaced the phos tanks, and reset everything to look just like it always had. The illusion continued and nobody was any the wiser.

I caught Davandein's eye and she beckoned me over to introduce me to someone. I cringed, being in no mood for small talk with freshly arrived cream. On her arm, a slender man pushing forty smiled at me as I approached. His hair was dark, thick, his beard short, peppered with grey that only seemed to make him more handsome. Where Davandein glowed in spectacular tailoring, his coat was plain, white wool lacking motif or embellishment, and he wore no sword on his belt, not even a dagger. I recognised him, or something about him. I'd met him before, somewhere, sometime. He gave an odd little smile, sensing my confusion.

'Captain Galharrow,' Davandein greeted me, pleasantly enough. 'Allow me to introduce you to Governor Thierro of Valaigne. The man behind the Grandspire.'

It had been nearly twenty years and boyish youth had been replaced with gentlemanly elegance, but the moment she named him I remembered. Thierro's smile widened a little further as he saw my new dawn of understanding.

'I don't imagine you ever thought to see me back here, Ryhalt,' he said. He held out a gloved hand and we shook, and then in a rare display of affection I grasped him by the shoulder as I allowed myself to match his smile. He wore a staggering amount of cologne, an overwhelming, musky scent.

'It's been half a lifetime,' I said. 'How in the hells are you doing?'

'You're already acquainted, then?' Davandein asked. She tried to mask how annoyed that made her. I'd stolen her thunder.

'We studied together at the university,' I said. 'Served on the Range together too, for a time.' I didn't go into any further details, and Thierro didn't offer any either. His time in the military had not ended well, and my own fall from favour had followed shortly after.

'Ah, but we were young then, weren't we? Fresh as spring and twice as green. It's good to see you.'

'You too,' I said, and meant it. We look for the strings that lead back into our pasts and follow them as though what lies behind us is the secret to passing through the labyrinth. Those things that sleep in our wake seem simpler, to be cherished for it, because all of the confusion of our lives has been washed from them.

'Governor Thierro is newly arrived to oversee the final stages of the Grandspire's construction,' Davandein said, trying to reclaim her status in the conversation. 'Thierro holds the commanding stake in the Westland Frontier Trading Company. Were you aware of that, Captain?'

I hadn't been, and it was a surprise. Westland was a vast trading emporium, dominating the trade routes to the colonies. Over the last ten years, they'd become rich as princes. Like me, Thierro had come from money, but we'd known luxury only as the second sons of noble houses. By contrast, Westland Trading commanded fleets of ships and bought and sold whole towns. If the Grandspire was their project, that meant that it was Thierro's project.

That certainly explained the marshal's cosying up to him. They made an unlikely pair, she as striking as lightning, he as drab as rain. The popinjays around us carried collapsible fans painted with miniature masterpieces, the hilts and guards of their swords worked in sparkling twists of gold and silver, embellished with the jewels that Westland's mines pulled from the earth. For a man of Thierro's considerable standing, he seemed to be entirely without entourage or any means to defend himself from attempts to kidnap and extort, and that was as unusual as his sober attire.

'I'd not expected to see you back on the Range,' I said. It was no doubt a sore point for him, but the griffin in the room needed to be pointed out. Thierro had been at Adrogorsk with me, leading a detachment of sharpshooters. A Darling had sent a killing spell, a toxic cloud of fog that had rolled over their emplacement. Thierro was one of the few to get out alive, but his lungs had been ruined and after he'd been carted back to the Range, he'd been discharged. I'd sometimes wondered which had hurt him more, the burning fumes, or seeing his men choking and dying. He'd always been a sensitive man. The military had not been the right choice for him, no matter our dreams of glory.

'Never thought I'd see that damn sky again,' Thierro said. 'But fate and faith blow us in strange directions. I can't say that I'm missing Valaigne, though. I went there for the good sea air, but it's a grim place of dark forests and biting insects. Quieter, though.' He glanced upward at the sky, but it remained silent.

'We'll have to catch up over a glass of the forty-nine,' I said. It had been an old favourite, cheap and dreadful wine that our classmates had once swilled with great abandon. Probably worth a small fortune twenty years on, if any of it still existed.

'Or perhaps a cup of tea,' Thierro said through a thin smile, and I wondered whether the sea air hadn't done his burned chest quite as much good as it was meant to. 'In fact, I have a matter that I wish to discuss with you soon. The Range Marshal here tells me that you're the man to speak about tracking people down. I'm told you have offices here? I'll have my people make an appointment.'

I agreed. Davandein was keen to show him off to the cream, so Thierro and I shook hands and I headed inside, hoping to escape the mountainous pungency of his cologne, but the whole place smelled of perfume with a back-of-the-nose hit of old, spilled wine. Despite it, I was buoyed by running into Thierro. We had never been close friends, just acquaintances really, but it was good to know that at least one of the old class had done something worthwhile with his life. I'd been to too many funerals along the Range for boys who'd stood up to receive their degrees with me.

Nenn had a stall up among the gods, though not as high

as the princes. Banners had been hung from the gallery boxes to proclaim their occupants' lineage. Status, status, and more games around status. What a crock.

'You made an effort, then,' Nenn said, as I entered the box.

'You're looking pretty special too,' I said.

Nenn hadn't even got changed. The leather buff coat she wore was stained and colourless at the elbows and cuffs, her boots had been up and down the Misery. No courtly small-sword for her: she wore the sword I'd had made for her, a real bastard of a blade made for splitting heads. She got up and embraced me. She'd had a new nose carved, smooth black wood, glossy enough that the light danced from it, but the one thing that surprised me was the smell. Nenn usually smelled like ale and horses, but tonight she was as perfumed as any of the ladies in their finery.

'Can't believe you dragged me here to watch this shit,' I said. 'We get to see our own life stories retold by some fuckers that never dug a ditch in their lives.'

'If I have to suffer it, you can suffer it with me,' she grinned. 'Meet this man. He's all right.' She jerked a thumb toward the only other occupant of the box who wasn't clearly a servant or bodyguard. Soldierly, a bit older than Nenn, a bit younger than me. Handsome in a way that might have interested me in my more experimental days at the university. Neat, well-groomed, but undeniably masculine.

'Captain Betch Davian,' he offered me his hand. I shook it. I looked him over feeling suddenly like a father overseeing his daughter's first dance. Stupid, but that's how it felt.

'State troop or free company?' I asked.

'City of Whitelande state,' he said, 'though I've never been there. I was born on the Range.'

'You here during the Siege?'

'No. I was down at Station Four.'

'I suppose you wish you'd been here to see it.'

Betch raised an eyebrow that made me immediately like him.

'Wouldn't wish that on anyone in the world. I know you were involved. Nenn told me how she got to rank up.'

So it was first-name terms? Good. That meant that they were fucking, and Nenn had always needed someone to fuck her good and often.

'Fastest climb from private to general in the history of the states. She tell you how quickly she managed to climb back down?'

Betch's smile said she had, and he didn't disapprove. Nenn had been de-ranked once for every time she'd managed to assault a highborn squawk. In four years, she'd dropped all the way down to major, but she was better suited to front-line work and the men didn't care. They loved her all the more for breaking the noses of colonels and boot-shiners. The idiots mocked her for her thin blood, but after she spilled a bit of theirs to prove that it was the same, none of them had the guts to challenge her to duel. Which was good, because they'd have lost, and even though they were arseholes we still needed generals and officers.

Nenn was fussing over Amaira like she was some kind of lap cat.

'Don't tell me you've brought her more Misery crap?'

Amaira held up the trinket Nenn had just given her. It was a clump of what appeared to be hair. Maybe human, maybe animal. As I watched, it twisted itself into the shape of a little figure, maybe a farmer dragging a plough. It uncurled, then returned to the farmer shape. More pointless, terrible magic from the Misery.

'Don't put that anywhere near your mouth,' I warned the kid, and then set about getting through enough of the house wine to make this ordeal bearable.

To my surprise, it wasn't as terrible as I'd expected. The playwright might even have been in Valengrad during the buildup. He'd made Marshal Venzer his protagonist, and the story focused on the dilemma of whether or not to activate Nall's Engine to defend Valengrad, or to wait to the last moment to ensure that Station Three-Six was also protected. That's how we'd spun it. In the end Venzer had chosen to hang himself when the Engine had failed, but nobody knew that except me. I suspected that toward the end of the performance we'd see him holding the last defence of the wall and going out in a blaze of glory.

'You notice that we don't seem to be in this play.' Nenn grinned. She leaned forward as a pair of young lovers were about to kiss, and yelled, 'Come on, give it some tongue!' The players bore Nenn's frequent disruptions with good grace, and some of the lesser cream even emulated her crudeness, much to the chagrin of their drinking partners and the older, more settled elite. Despite Nenn's derision, I was sure that there was a tear in her eye when one of the lovers she'd been mocking was butchered by the drudge. She covered it by adjusting the straps that held her nose in place.

'You mind if I talk shop?' I asked.

Nenn glanced at her beau. Betch was having to endure a stream of questions from Amaira, who was entirely uninterested in the play. He was weathering the barrage admirably, giving us a chance to talk.

'Hit me.'

'Remember when the Darlings animated dead bodies and sent them at us during the Siege?'

'Hard to forget.'

'Well, I got a man in the morgue that I swear I shot dead three weeks ago, but he was walking and talking two nights back. You think someone can do that without being marked by the Deep Kings? Think they can raise up dead men?'

'Like a puppet?'

'No. Like he was alive again.'

Nenn thought on it.

'Sorcerers can do all kinds of shit,' Nenn said. 'Spinners are the only common type and even among them, the tricks they pull with the light isn't regular, is it? I got me a Spinner in my battalion that can make mirrors out of sand.' She picked at her blackened teeth with a splinter of wood. 'But raising the dead? Making a body move is one thing, but actually bringing someone back to life? Can even the Nameless do that?'

I looked down at the raven on my arm. The deal that bound me hadn't quite done that. Close, but not the same. The dead didn't return. I grunted my acknowledgment. I'd come to the same conclusion, but a second opinion never hurt. The mystery wasn't growing any clearer. Devlen Maille had gone into the dirt, and that's where he should have stayed. The only thing I knew for sure about the men who'd murdered Levan Ost made less sense than the dance routine taking place down on the stage. I reached out to pick up my wine and winced as I tried to curl my fingers. They wouldn't flex. I took my left hand in my right, only to find that my fingers were ice-cold. As I watched they turned white as bone, numbness creeping up my arm.

'Shit,' I said.

'What's wrong?' Nenn asked.

'I don't know.'

I winced. I'd not been aware of the cold creeping up through my arm, but it extended from fingertip to elbow. Above that my arm was ordinary and warm. Below it, my skin had taken on an unpleasant, bluish cast and a painful ache rose from the back of my skull. And then I felt something stir within my flesh, close to the bone. Something foreign that had not been there before.

'Shit,' I said again. 'You'll have to excuse me.' I moved quickly out of the box to find the bathroom. It was manned by a theatre employee in a fine red doublet, who offered me a scented towel as I went in, and I took it and shut myself inside a stall. I sat down on the bench as something grim and cruel stirred within me, bared my arm and rolled my sleeve as far back as it would go. This was a good shirt. It was going to get ruined.

At least, I thought, the intense cold was going to numb the agony that inevitably followed.

To some extent I was right. It still hurt, only in a different way. Usually there was intense heat, softening the skin and helping the bird to tear its way through into the light. Instead my skin was cold and hard and the bird struggled. Halfway through it seemed ready to give up. My blood was spilling from my arm, sluggish and cooler than blood ought to be, and I'd felt it flow often enough to know. But as it struggled to free itself from the hole that its beak had torn in my skin, I saw that something was wrong.

Ordinarily Crowfoot's messengers took a certain angry enjoyment from tearing through and cawing their message at me. This one seemed small, feeble, unable to pull its wings through the tear it had made. I took hold of it and with a cry dragged it out with a slithery sucking sound.

'Sir? Are you all right in there, sir?' the attendant called.

'I'm fine,' I said quickly, though my mind was sparkling with pain and my chest constricted with it. 'Fuck off and let me shit in peace!'

'Very good, sir,' the attendant said, but he didn't sound convinced.

I looked down at the bird that Crowfoot had sent me. It was misshapen, one foot withered and small, lacking half its feathers and one eye was milky, blind. It sparkled as if with frost, little ice crystals locking its feathers rigid. It opened its beak to deliver its message.

A hissing, crackling noise emerged, a sound like pine needles being thrown into a fire, spitting and popping.

'Sir ...' the worried attendant tried again. I ignored him

and gave the bird a little shake as though that might improve the sound. The crackling only intensified. And then, as though from a great distance, I heard that angry, hateful voice.

'GALHARROW,' it snarled. '... KINGS TRYING TO ... OCEAN DEMON ... WILL DEAL WITH ...' A wave of crackling rushed up, and the bird's one good eye swivelled in its socket as though its brain rode a carousel. '... HAS TAKEN ... THE VAULT.' More of the message was lost to the interfering sound. And then finally, the crackling fell away and a frustrated, angry snarl said quite clearly: 'GET IT BACK. DO NOT FUCK THIS UP.'

Well. Not the most helpful message I'd ever received. I expected the bird to self-combust as they always had before, but this one just flopped, lifeless, head hanging at an uncomfortable angle. I gave it a shake, but it was unreservedly dead.

'Sir, I'm going to get help, sir,' the frightened-sounding attendant called.

'I'm fine,' I called, but he was already gone. I tossed the frost-speckled bird corpse into the shitter as I used the towel to mop up as much blood as I could. Now that the bird had gone the feeling was returning to my arm, and that was no good thing. I could feel the jagged edges of the tear in my skin, the torn muscle, the discomfort of the bones. I would heal up within an hour, but for now I needed more wine. I'd bled on the floor and all over my trousers. Once I'd turned the scented towel entirely red I tossed that down the hole as well. My head was pounding and my arm burned as the cold left it. My back was a mess of knots and tension, my eyes were dry. I was glad that the attendant wasn't there to see me stumbling out of the stall. What he'd make of the blood on the tiled floor, I had no idea.

I was shaking as I quick-marched back to the stall, a greasy sheen of sweat across my face. The message had been fragmented, but I already knew what had happened. Something had been taken from the vault. A shiver ran down my spine. It shouldn't have been possible.

'Unexpected visitor?' Nenn said as I rejoined them. Concerned. I took the wine bottle and drank most of the contents as quickly as I could. My arm was jabbing at me with pins and needles as though I'd fallen into a pit of hedgehogs. Captain Betch appeared to have been briefed by his lover not to ask me any questions, because he stared toward the absurd puppet monster on the stage as though nothing untoward were going on in his box, artfully distracting Amaira by explaining how it worked. I could see why Nenn liked him.

I was about to tell her when a man stepped briskly into our gallery box. He wore a frown over a sweat-soaked citadel uniform, cheeks flushed, half-breathless. He'd been running.

'Captain Galharrow. I need you to come with me, urgently.'

'What's wrong?' I asked. But I already knew what he was going to say.

'It's the vault, sir,' he said. 'Crowfoot's vault. It's been breached.'

5

When you're an immortal wizard whose power can level cities and tear holes in the sky, inevitably you pick up a few things worth keeping over the years. Sentimental keepsakes, souvenirs, weapons of horrifying barbarity – the usual things. Crowfoot had his own store of history's most awful mementos, squirrelled away beneath the earth a few miles from the city. Heavily warded, heavily guarded. It should have been unbreachable.

'I want to go with you, Captain-Sir,' Amaira protested with a frown. 'I'm Blackwing too. I should go with you.'

'You're not Blackwing, you're a maid at Blackwing,' I said. 'There's a difference, and you should be grateful for it. Stay with the captain, he'll see you home when the play's done.'

'But you'll miss the end,' she protested.

'Don't worry. I know how it ends.'

Captain Betch nodded to me. Then Nenn whispered something to him, and he laughed and she flashed him a wicked grin as we followed the citadel man.

A carriage waited for us outside. The sweating young officer didn't offer us any further information. He'd obviously been told to keep his mouth shut and we rolled out of the city at a breakneck pace. Between the wine, the blood loss and a road ill suited to a city carriage, I was swaying in my seat with dizziness whenever the potholes weren't trying to bounce me out of it.

We were going to Narheim. I hated it there.

During the fourscore years that Nall's Engine had protected the border of the Misery, Crowfoot had been an infrequent visitor. He came and went, but for a span of three years, long before I was born, he'd been a semipermanent feature. He'd lived in a palatial mansion a short way from the city, a grand house whose design spoke of a staggering lack of taste. He never officially vacated it, but he stopped coming back to it and nobody knew why. For obvious reasons, nobody was interested in taking up residence in it after he had gone and not even the most desperate thieves dared steal inside to loot the candelabras and finely carved chairs.

We rolled up and disgorged on the weed-choked gravel driveway. Other horses and carriages were gathered there and it looked like a whole cavalry regiment was standing to attention nearby. They looked nervous. Naked sabres rested on shoulders.

'How's the arm holding up?' Nenn asked.

'Hurts. Crowfoot was trying to tell me about the vault, but his messenger didn't make it.'

'What does that mean?' she asked. Men saluted us as we passed by. Nenn knocked salutes back to them. I just gave nods.

'I don't know. Nothing good.' Nenn snorted.

'You should have cut that damn thing out of your arm years ago,' she said. 'Get me a knife, I'll do it now.'

'Trust me, you wouldn't come away from that well,' I said. Nenn raised an eyebrow but I didn't want to say more. I'd tried it once, in the very worst days. Only, Crowfoot had measures in place to deter that, and Crowfoot's preferred deterrent was usually destruction. In this case, of me.

Guards had been posted at the entrance. The officer led Nenn and me past them and through the great double doors. Everything was just as it had been left, covered with thick

layers of dust and cobweb, a grey shroud for a splendour-
ous cadaver. The guard detail stationed here didn't touch
anything that they didn't have to and it all smelled cold,
stale. Dead. Footprints led through the dirt on the carpet
alongside animal tracks. People might be too fearful to pry
into an absent wizard's affairs, but rats and foxes felt no
such trepidation.

'This place makes me want to shit,' Nenn said.

'You spend all your time in the Misery finding crap to
give to Amaira, and an old palace gets your toes hairy?'

'The Misery is simple. Shit's weird. You stick it with
sharp things and it dies. Narheim feels like it dropped right
out of time. And there's always the chance that he might
come home and find us tramping about in his place. They
say that when he left, all his servants died within a year.
Fifty of them, housekeepers, gardeners, even the kennel
boy. Just wasted away into bone and nothing.'

'People talk a lot of shit,' I said. 'I heard a story about how
you were the Iron Goat's lover. Or his bastard daughter.
Heard that you were some Iscalian princess too.'

'They say that you're funny as well. People really do talk
shit.'

We were talking exactly that because we were nervous.
It wasn't just the dust, or the darkness. The place felt dead,
like we were stepping into the hells. I half expected my
mother's ghost to rise from the dust to curse me. Maybe see
my wife throwing my children from a balcony, or maybe
Levan Ost rising to ask why I'd not done a better job of
protecting him.

The young officer led us down a flight of stairs, cork-
screwing into the ground.

Range Marshal Davandein met us. Her blue-and-gold-
brocade dress was much better suited to the theatre than
this dead place; here, it was an affront to the stillness.

'Captain Galharrow, good.' She raised a well-styled

eyebrow in Nenn's direction. 'I didn't send for you, Major. Any reason you've brought her, Commander?'

'The play was boring,' Nenn said.

'You ever tried stopping Nenn doing what she wants?' I said, which wasn't much of an apology. Plus it was an academic point since Nenn was already there, and Davandein decided it wasn't worth arguing over.

'Follow me.'

She led us through the cellars. The tunnel was built for a person of mean stature so Nenn had to stoop, and I was nearly on all fours. The discomfort in my gut was taking on a hard, certain quality. I'd hidden something away down here, after the Siege.

Shavada's Eye. The one that had been living inside Prince Herono's skull all that time.

'Shit on a stick,' Nenn said.

The corridor opened onto a cellar with a vaulted ceiling and a huge door at the far end of the room. Getting to it would mean getting our feet wet, as the guards who had been stationed here were involuntarily creating a puddle. Or to be more accurate, the pieces of them were. It took a minute to let that sink in. There was an empty, chemical tang to the air. Something familiar about that.

'How many men did we have here?'

'Twelve,' Davandein said. Her voice was raw, cold. Angry.

'They all here?' I asked. Davandein's eyes roved across the butchered pieces that had been somebody's father, somebody's brother, uncle or son. The sight of congealing blood argued that the wine I'd drunk ought to see light again. There was an odd precision to the way that the bodies had been dismembered. Neat, orderly, cut into pieces like a side of beef being diced for a stew. I'd gracked enough unfortunates to know that this dismemberment hadn't happened as part of the killing. Killing a man isn't so hard. You stick him through or carve him up a bit and that'll do for most.

Separating an arm into three or four separate sections takes work. Whatever had done it, it had gone to some trouble to make this mess.

'Hard to say.'

'You count the heads?'

'There are only nine heads. But there are twenty-three feet.'

Nenn did the math on her fingers. Counting had never been her strong point and I let her catch up. She frowned.

'What killed them?' she said.

'We don't know,' Davandein said. 'But look here.'

She indicated one of the brutalised heads. The eyes were rolled well back, blood had run in streams from eyes, nose, ears.

'Reminds me of mind-worms,' I said. She nodded, her angular face set hard.

'A Darling, here?' Nenn growled.

'Maybe,' Davandein said. 'Whoever did this was in and out of the vault before we could respond to the alarm.'

In and out. Beyond the bloody ground lay the vault. That left me even colder than the remains of the soldiers and the prospect of heads gone missing. The citadel maintained a squad of guards stationed at the vault, if only for posterity. Old boys mostly. It was easy retirement work to supplement a pension, if you could stomach Crowfoot's old place, and I doubt they bothered to put on armour more than once per year. Probably should have, judging by how things had gone. Whatever had happened here had been fast, and brutal.

'They got off a message?'

'No. They managed to hit an alarm switch,' Davandein said, pointing toward a lever on the wall. 'Sends an alert direct to the citadel. That alarm hasn't been touched in more than fifty years and at first, nobody was sure what the siren meant. Took the engineers twenty minutes to figure it out and when they did, the fourth cavalry charged over here, but whoever did this was already long gone.'

'You keep sayin' "who",' Nenn said. She stuffed blacksap into her mouth, chewed twice. Annoying fucking habit. 'You sure you don't mean "what"? I seen things in the Misery that could do this to a bunch of tough guys. Dulchers. That thing with all the heads. Sand-weepers.'

'Those things don't break into vaults,' Davandein said. She was in a foul mood. Taking it personal. Maybe she'd sent some old friends down here to see out the last few years of their career, rewards for good service. Best not to ask.

It would have taken more guts than I had to try to break into Crowfoot's vault. Not many things this side of the hells had that kind of nerve. Hard to imagine even a Darling would. I made sure my sword was loose in its scabbard, for all the good that would do me if one of the little monstrosities was lurking around somewhere.

'What did they take from the vault?'

'That's what you're here to tell us. You have a special relationship with the Nameless. I figured you were the least likely to get eviscerated stepping in.'

Deadpan. Not a hint of a smile. Perhaps it wasn't meant to be funny. She flicked a finger that we should follow and we squelched across the puddle.

The vault had a great thick door of brass and iron, not wholly dissimilar to the one that protected the heart of Nall's Engine. There was no discernible way to open it, no handle, no wheel to turn. Just a big plain disc. It stood slightly ajar.

I stopped there.

'These men were just tokens meant to keep the curious away,' I said. I sniffed at that dry, acrid flavour in the air. 'The real defences were the wards that Crowfoot left behind. I'll need help if I'm going in there.'

'You want a Spinner?'

'I've my own resources to call on. Most of that new crop of Spinners are as likely to burn their own dicks off as disarm a trap set by the Nameless. I got someone else in mind. I want you lot to clear out of here. Get rid of the horsemen. They'll draw attention where it doesn't need drawing.'

'You want to take charge of this?' Davandein was a hard woman with the weight of the Range on her shoulders. She was used to giving orders to thousands. She still sounded relieved.

'Want' was a strong word, but I nodded anyway. Better in my hands than anyone else's.

Maldon was drunk when Tnota brought him out of the carriage. The soldiers had gone some hours before, and I was glad that they didn't get to see the state of the little shit. I'm often half on a buzz, but I function on it, whilst he was long gone to that place where all things grow obnoxious.

'It took me an hour to steal this bottle,' the kid said. His voice rolled drunkenly up and down the words. 'It's harder when you don't have any eyes.'

He looked about ten years old, although with the scarf wrapped fully around the hole where his eyes should have been he could have been older or younger. His skinny form was clothed in garments I'd procured for him, simple stuff, the shirt hanging open at the front to show his scrawny, hairless chest. As an adult he'd possessed an awful lot of body hair.

'You know you can just take it straight from my cellar, Gleck,' I said. 'The key's under the clock in the hall. Anything but the southern white.'

'Where'd be the fun in that? A man's got to have some fun,' he said. He gave a dry, mirthless smile. The expression belied the age that lay beneath that youthful skin.

'Then stop complaining. I'll owe you a bellyful of my best

61

whisky by the end of the night. Nenn give you the score?'

'Dead guards, broken vault, Crowfoot's treasures at risk, blah blah blah,' Maldon said. He tripped on a flagstone and wheeled around for a few moments.

'You sure he's in any state to help us?' Nenn said.

'I'm in the only state in which I can help anyone,' the blind child crowed. 'Which is to say it's the state I plan on being in for the rest of my eternally long life.' He took a long chug from the bottle, which seemed too large for his childish fists. I'd seen Gleck Maldon drunk more times than I'd seen him sober, but his boozing irked me. He'd had a great mind, once.

'Come on. Just you and me.'

'I can feel it from out here, you know,' Maldon said, drawing a deep breath. Shivered. 'Crowfoot's essence. It lingers, like factory smog in the winter.' He shuddered, and I wondered not for the first time just how different the essence of the Nameless might be to Shavada's essence. The Deep King's power had festered inside Maldon's tortured form for months, before I'd cut a deal and set him free. What I was asking of him was not easy. Some might have said it was cruel. But then, I had a cruel master.

'Now that's familiar.' Maldon sniffed and grimaced as we got to the remnants of people.

'I'll keep you from stepping in anything that will squelch,' I said. 'But I guess you never get used to the blood.'

'Blood? No, not that. When you've smelled your own blood boiling inside your skull, blood doesn't bother you. No, that other tang. Old magic, ancient power. It's bitter in the air. Thick as mist. You can't smell it?'

I thought for a moment. Frowned.

'Darling magic?'

'Like that, but different. A Darling's magic is like a river in flood, freezing but bursting with violence. This is like a glacier. Timeless. Colder. Steady.'

Maldon knocked back the last of his own backwash and tossed the bottle away. It rolled through the red-liquid carpet. Gleck Maldon had been the strongest Spinner on the Range before Herono had betrayed him to Shavada, only when I'd severed him from Shavada's influence and stripped the Darling magic away, his light-spinning abilities had gone with it. He'd once told me the loss of that power was worse than losing the eyes I'd shot out of his face.

Spirits alone knew how he'd survived that. Darlings had always been hard to kill. In the days after the Siege, I'd contemplated running a knife over his throat a dozen times. Maybe I was overly sentimental, or maybe I was just sick of all the killing. Whatever had kept my blade in its sheath, he'd proved useful since. It was hard to tell whether his ordeal had driven him crazy, or just nasty. Tnota and Nenn both thought I should have ended him, but trapped in that remoulded child body, he wasn't a threat to anyone.

I showed Maldon the open vault. He stopped in front of it and even drunk as he was, I could tell he sensed something in the air. He breathed slower, shivered.

'This was heavily warded. Strong. Whatever Crowfoot put on it, just the residue is making my balls shrivel back into my body. Such as they are. If someone had tried to force this without disabling the wards, they'd still be here. They'd be painted across the walls, but they'd be here.'

'How the fuck could someone break Crowfoot's wards?' Nenn frowned.

Gleck chuckled.

'You're asking me if I understand the Nameless's magic, which I don't. "Who" is a better question than "how". Not many in the world that could unravel his magic. There's the other Nameless, of course. I doubt that a few static wards would provide much impediment to one of the Deep Kings, but if they were here, we'd have bigger problems to worry about.'

'But someone unpicked them,' I said.

'What about an ordinary sorcerer? A Spinner or a Mute?' Nenn asked.

'Doesn't seem likely. Maybe a cabal – six or seven sorcerers working together, strong ones. Even then I don't know where they'd begin. Their power isn't the same as Crowfoot's.'

'Could a Darling get through them?'

'Maybe. Depends how good he is. There were a few who might have been capable, but the Engine got most of them. Maybe they've made new ones since then, but who'd want to risk tackling Crowfoot's wards just to get in here? There's nothing of value in here anyway.'

'There was.' I'd put it there. 'You think we can pass through without getting torn apart?'

Maldon shrugged. Then he just walked through. The courage of a drunk, or a hope it would end his miserable existence. He almost seemed disappointed that he hadn't been turned inside out. I'd brought Maldon in so he could tell me whether it was safe. Hadn't planned on using him as a dummy.

I stepped through the circular door. A backwash of something unclean passed through me, but it was brief and then it was gone. Even Crowfoot's defunct magic left a calling card.

The vault lit automatically. The phos tubes crackled and cast a flat blue light across rows of pedestals holding the things Crowfoot didn't want the world to see.

'What's that?' Nenn snapped, sensing movement in the shadows at the far end of the room. Something living. Struggling, pinned in place.

'Ignore it,' I said. 'It's not important. Don't touch anything. The entry spells were broken but I expect there's something nasty on each pedestal as well. Look and don't touch. No matter how shiny it is.' I said the last as pointedly as possible. Nenn scowled at me and spat blacksap onto the floor. Didn't matter to her that we were standing in the Nameless's own sanctum. I'd sooner have been able to teach poetry to a horse than manners to Nenn.

It all looked much as it had the last time I'd been here. I'd paid a visit to deposit Shavada's eye, and I knew, despite the strange oddities on their podiums, that was the deposit which had gone.

The first pedestal held an old porcelain doll, one eye open, slowly swivelling to watch us. The second, a six-stringed musical instrument inscribed with foreign letters. Third, an old bronze sword, brittle and green, balanced miraculously on its point. Four and five held clocks, their hands both in sequence and impossible to read. Six, nothing but a pile of grey dust. The pedestals stretched back, twelve rows of twelve, and I knew that everything upon them was dangerous, mystical and not for our hands. Nenn couldn't keep her eyes from the back of the room where the moving thing was.

'What is that?' Nenn asked.

'Don't know,' I said. 'Probably hasn't stopped struggling like that since the last time I was here.'

It was shaped like a man, swaddled with bandages from head to toe. Arms wrapped tightly across its chest, the figure wrestled against its straitjacket, seeking to free itself with a frantic energy.

'Who is it?'

'Best not to think about it too much. Maybe something from the Misery. Maybe someone that really pissed the boss off. No idea. I don't need to know.'

'Is it a person?'

'Best not to think about that either.'

I walked between plants, held in vases both ornate and mundane, a bowl of blinking fish eyes and a dusty, tan-leather book that seemed to whisper my name as I passed.

I stopped before an empty pedestal. It had not been empty before. I'd filled it myself.

'It was there, wasn't it?' Maldon asked. He cringed away from the empty pedestal, teeth bared. 'I can feel it. Like an echo of its passing. The same essence that he poured into me. Shavada.' The taste of the canal rose stronger at the back of my throat. I nodded.

'Shavada's eye.'

'Shit,' Nenn said. 'The one that crawled out of Herono's face?'

'The same. This is where we stored it. It was the only thing in here that really mattered. And now it's gone.'

6

I tore Valengrad apart. I employed a dozen tough men and women, jackdaws as they'd come to be known. Casso was the most senior, a quiet, dangerous man who spoke seldom and scowled continuously. Beneath him were my lead thugs, Meara and Traust, employed more for their intimidating size than because they were really good at anything. I gave them all free rein to lean on anyone they could, and buried the complaints. They turned up nothing more than mud and attempts at appeasement.

Marshal Davandein loaned me more manpower, but for all the marshal's horses and all of her men, I couldn't find the Eye or the thieves that had taken it. She stationed fifty good soldiers and two Battle Spinners at Crowfoot's former home, because that open door was a problem. I suggested bringing the building down on top of it with gunpowder but the marshal wasn't prepared to risk infuriating the Nameless, no matter how long he'd been absent. I consoled myself that Crowfoot's remaining treasures would probably burn the skin from anyone that laid a finger on them, or that the would-be thief would find himself flopping around without any bones. The door was only a formality: it was the wards that held the thieves at bay.

Only, one thief had managed to untangle some of my master's deadliest spells. They'd known what they were doing, and disentangled magic on a level well beyond Maldon's understanding. That was a deeply troubling thought.

The degrading truth was that reaching Crowfoot for more information wasn't within my power. He was off doing whatever it was he did in his war. He'd stuck around briefly after the Siege, whilst Nall was getting the Engine back into shape, but not only had Shavada's Eye now escaped him, his attempt to inform me – which I was confident the frozen bird had been meant to do – had failed. I didn't know what to make of that. There was some small comfort in knowing that, for the moment, I couldn't inform him that the Eye had been taken.

'Good morning, Ryhalt,' Valiya said as she entered my office. Four hours past dawn, a slow grey rain draped the city. Eala's crescent was the only colour interrupting the morning's gloom, but the cloud banks kept the Misery quiet and the golden moon dim.

'I've yet to find anything good about it,' I grumbled. I had half a headache, and a need to eat something that dripped grease.

'Cheer yourself up,' Valiya said. She passed me a parcel of wax paper containing a couple of warm pastries, squashed flat in her coat but stuffed with butter and smoked bacon.

'Thanks,' I said. 'What's this for?'

'You're better when you aren't hungry. And you're always hungry. You just don't realise it.' I couldn't argue with that as I chewed my way through the pastries. The bacon was on the tough side, but I wasn't complaining.

'Did you sleep last night?' she asked.

'Closed my eyes for a couple of hours.' Valiya gave me an admonishing look. She had a pastry of her own, but she picked at it without interest.

'Did you go home?' she asked.

'Too much work to do.'

Valiya showed me an arched eyebrow, but she didn't disagree. She got it. One of the rare people that understood.

The struggle on the Range was too important to rest. Valiya's battle was fought with words and papers. I'd never see her with a sword in her hand, but if she'd chosen to run a factory instead of fighting the Deep Kings, she'd have doubled its production within a week.

'Well, there's more work now. I have news.'

When Tnota had news it usually meant that he'd found a sock he thought he'd lost, and when Maldon had news it meant he'd cleaned out my liquor cabinet or wanted to murder someone, but when Valiya had news, she had news.

'The flarelock was made in Lennisgrad. I checked and the maker's mark matches up to Besh Flindt's workshop. He has a big operation, a whole team of apprentices putting them out.'

I frowned.

'Flindt's a good gunsmith, but I thought he was out of business. Last I heard, he was in the debtor's jail. Why the hell is Besh Flindt making flarelocks?'

Valiya held her hands out toward the stove. Her sleeves had rolled up, displaying the flowers tattooed across her forearms. They were works of art, beautifully and brightly coloured, nothing like the mess of cheap soldier-inks I'd collected over the years.

'Seems he managed to settle his debts, and now he's doing well enough. My contacts in the capital tell me that he's doing a roaring trade. Has been for the last year.'

I studied the black pool of coffee at the bottom of my cup. People wanted flarelocks all of a sudden, though they'd been out of fashion – with good reason – since before I was born. Perhaps there was prestige to them now? City folk are nothing if not slaves to fashion. But then, Devlen Maille had been on the Range a good while. Not a city boy at all.

I looked up to see Valiya smiling at me.

'What?'

'You stick your tongue out when you're thinking,' she said. 'Don't think too hard. That's what I'm here for.'

I returned her smile despite myself. She understood how I worked. That was another thing I liked about her. I liked quite a lot of things about her.

'Thank you.'

'I know it's hard to think of, sometimes,' she said. 'But you need to take some time. Just for you. Let someone else take some of the weight for a while. There are plenty of us here. You're not Nameless, you know. There's more to life than the struggle.' She took a pen and wrote down an address. 'Go here. Tell them I sent you.'

Valiya left me, the tails of her longcoat sweeping behind her. I placed my fingers against my eyes and pushed them into my skull. Spirits, but I was tired. The morning may have been grey, but there was a heavier bank of cloud across my mind that fogged my thoughts. Two hours of cracked and restless sleep. I'd tried. I'd tried to drift off and instead my brain had churned and whirred, throwing up those same damn images. A woman imprisoned in a field of light. For a few moments, I let the nothingness of permanent exhaustion wash over me. Moments. Minutes. I don't know.

'You want her.'

Maldon leaned against the doorframe wearing a cruel little smile. I could tell from the black stains on his lips he'd been on the bottle since first light.

'You're a real piece of shit sometimes.' I sighed.

'She's a looker. And you like her. You always did have a thing for work-obsessed, damaged women,' Maldon said. He was a nasty drunk, which meant he was nasty all the time. At times I thought that I should have put a lead ball through the right part of his skull back when I had the chance. This was one of them.

'Show her some respect,' I said before I realised that

70

saying that would only make him smirk more. 'What's made you crawl out of the cellar?'

'Hit a nerve, did I?' Maldon sat down in front of the fire and chugged wine until it made him cough and sputter.

'If you got nothing for me, fuck off back to your self-pity and let me work,' I growled. I picked up a report from the desk and tried to focus. Reading was getting harder those days. Maybe I needed eyeglasses. Maybe I was just exhausted. I blinked at the bill on my desk. I'd read it already, twice or more, but it hadn't been going in. I had to laugh at it now.

'They're taxing me because of you,' I said. I held it up for him to see. 'The marshal has created a child tax. Because of the public services you use up. A tax on children. It's like Davandein is doing her abject best to make herself unpopular.' I balled the paper and threw it at the fire. They could go stoke their own arses if they thought I was giving up money for that. I'd have to ask Valiya to draw up a bill of exemption for Blackwing personnel, only she didn't like Maldon and I didn't want her to have anything to do with him. Maera and Traust were no good for that kind of work and Tnota's penmanship was worse than his swordplay.

'I'm worth every grinny,' Maldon said from by the fire. 'I'm a blessing. That's what they say about children, isn't it? That we're blessings sent from the Spirit of Joy. So be joyful.'

'It wasn't the Spirit of Joy that made you,' I said, which was cruel, but he wanted a fight. 'Write me a bill of exemption and I'll give you the money instead,' I said. Maldon was missing his eyes, but that didn't mean he couldn't write, or see. Magic. It makes no sense.

'Tempting,' he said. 'But I can't. I'm busy.'

'You look real busy to me,' I said, nodding toward the bottle he cradled. 'I've been that kind of busy as much as you have, remember.'

'I want to make you something,' he said, and his nasty little expression became a still-nasty grin. 'I need that.' Maldon rose and walked to Tnota's desk where the flarelock still lay. 'And I need some other things too.'

'What are you making?'

'It's a surprise,' he said. 'But you'll like it.'

I wasn't sure that I liked the idea of a drunk ten-year-old playing around with unstable phos technology in my office basement, but I also knew that if I denied him, then he'd just find a way to steal them anyway. Moreover, I always tried to remind myself that Gleck wasn't really a child. He was over fifty years old, and had the mind and experience to handle himself.

'Write me a list of what you want,' I said. Another wave of tiredness had just washed over me, as had the smell of Maldon's wine. It was too early, I told myself, though I thought that often, and the thought seldom won. 'But be sober later. I want us to continue with my lessons.'

'You've no talent for languages,' Maldon said.

'And you've none for teaching. But you're the one that knows the drudge language, and I'm the one that wants to learn, and as long as I'm risking my neck by letting you live in my house, you'll make yourself useful.'

'Teaching you is very frustrating. And boring.'

I called him a shit-sucker in drudge, which was one of the first things he'd taught me. He laughed and swayed away.

Maldon had learned the drudge language when Shavada had taken his mind. He'd learned other things, too, awful things. Some of them I'd glimpsed when I stole into his mind, and I had no desire to know more. There was a darkness within Gleck Maldon that would never leave him. Why had I spared him? I'd felt sorry for him. He'd been a friend, and now he was ... this. The broken bones in his face couldn't heal, as they would if he were still a Darling, and the matchlock shot had taken his eyes. It took souls, he'd told me. That was how the Darlings regenerated, stripping the life and vitality slowly from their victims to replenish any damage that they sustained. But Maldon had lost that power now, the damage was permanent. The one magic that seemed to have remained was the one that kept him perpetually young. His body had not aged in four years. That would be a problem, when Valiya or Amaira noticed.

There was a larger problem, though, something that we both knew and neither had spoken about. Maldon had no eyes, but he could see. He could write, he could draw, he never walked into doorframes and always knew who had just entered the room. So there was magic in him. But of what kind, I could not be sure.

7

I am bad at taking advice, but it's easier to stomach when you get all complex over the person that gave it. Maybe want to impress her, stupid as that thought was. I was Valiya's boss. She wanted me functional because she was as committed to the Range as I was. That was all.

I found the address she'd given me, a big, unobtrusive building on a quiet, unobtrusive street. It was a leisure house, the kind known for its closed curtains and quiet discretion. I felt like an idiot walking in there. It was the kind of place Dantry Tanza might have enjoyed. What would people think if they heard that Ryhalt Galharrow was getting himself sorted out in a leisure house? There is humiliation in letting other people see you at your most vulnerable, and I had built my sense of self around the fear I struck in others. I stacked enough money on the counter to ensure that the staff would keep to silence.

A quiet, dignified young man led me to a private chamber with a tiled bath set into the floor. He started up a quiet little phos-driven water heater, which murmured ocean-wave sighs as it brought the water to steam. He lit candles, kept the light down low. I stripped off and got in, and the attendant seemed poised to add scented oils, flower petals and salts, but the water had darkened to grey after only a few moments. I felt ashamed. I didn't look at the man as he quietly drained the water and refilled the bath without a word. He spoke only when he had to, letting me sink into this quiet little world of relaxation. Gentle music was being played in an adjoining room, mellow pipes and a slow, subtle drum. I smelled apricot and orange, soft and gentle aromas. Steam rose around me. I closed my eyes. There was nothing there.

I dozed, or maybe I slept. Time passed.

I got out when the water started draining, unsure how long I'd spent in the bath. It had been long enough that my fingers had wrinkled. The water had been hot, and my skin felt raw and scalded. I figured that I was done, but the attendant brought me over to a table and made me lie facedown. Lying prone and naked was an odd sensation, but I'd trusted him this far. He massaged my legs, working slowly from my feet and all the way up, calf, thigh, buttocks, back, neck. He knew his business, fingers pushing firmly, kneading, hard and focused until the knots relented. He murmured little comments about tension, always letting me know what he was going to do so that the cracks and pops from my joints didn't come as a surprise. At one point it felt like he was going to tear my head off, and then my neck gave a huge *crack* and something hard loosened up. By the time he was done I felt hazy, distant from my own body. I didn't want to speak and the attendant seemed to understand. He gave me towels to wipe the oils away before bringing out my clothes which, somehow, had been freshly laundered while I was bathing. I put them on, almost reluctant to return to life outside this quiet, gentle bubble of peace.

I went to a second room where I was given a cold bottle of water, and was asked to sit while a cheerful woman took scissors and razor to my face and hair and another equally cheerful woman used a little file to shape my fingernails. I almost didn't recognise the man who stared back at me in the mirror, less because of the haircut and more because it was a long time since I'd bothered with mirrors. My hair had gone to grey across the flanks, which wasn't such a bad thing. If you fear getting older, then you're losing every second of your life, and I was always determined to win the battles that I chose to fight.

A bath, a massage and a shave. Nothing complicated about those things. Nothing that should make such a difference. But when I came to leave, something inside me had relented. I couldn't have said what.

The city had a brittle feel to it, and not just from the constant rain. Against the lavender bath-scent that lingered about me, I could smell the drudge-stink in the air, rising from the canals like mould and sickrooms. Preachers gabbled on the streets, but nobody seemed to be listening.

'I had a thought,' Valiya said, as soon as I stepped in through the door. She had a shadowy excitement to her, as she always did when she dug up new information. She'd come up with something good, and it was hot on her tongue. She looked me over, noting that I was clean and presentable, trying to keep a smile from her face and only managing to purse her lips. I frowned, abashed, and carried on past her. 'I thought about what the navigator told you. This recruiter, Nacomo, was educated, unused to the Misery sky. Lots of ego. So, who's going to be well educated, full of themselves and a recent arrival from Lennisgrad?'

'Go on,' I said. She started ticking items off on her fingers.

'Probably not soldiers. Not labourers. Engineers? Possibly. But then I thought, who can you really count on to be halfway up their own arse?' Valiya said. 'Actors. I checked around. There's an old stage performer called Marollo Nacomo, played a short run of *The Tower of Leyonar*, before it got cancelled. He was a big name in Lennisgrad, but fell on his face here. Only came to Valengrad a couple of months back. He's your man.'

'You're sure?'

'Oh, please, Ryhalt,' she said. Her eyebrows rose halfway up her face. 'Have I ever brought you something that wasn't worthwhile?'

Valiya had a hard energy about her, knowing that she'd started the hunt for me.

'I ever tell you how smart you are?'

'Not often enough,' she said.

I rustled up my jackdaws and we swooped. Casso and Meara went in the back, I led four through the front, weapons bared and ready. The house was old, one of the many properties abandoned during the Siege, claimed by new tenants as the city repopulated. The front door stubbornly resisted the axe. When we finally got inside, we found Nacomo in a nightgown, shaking in bed. He was a handsome man, brown hair askew from sleep, surprisingly youthful for the age Valiya had put to him.

'How dare you lay hands upon me!' he declared. 'Do you even know who I am? I demand a lawyer! How dare you!'

'Are we sure that's him?' I asked Casso. 'I thought he'd be older.' My lead jackdaw shrugged, and then took a firm grip on the captive's hair to get a better look at his face.

'You have the wrong man!' the prisoner declared. 'My name is Nacomo and I'm fifty-three! You must want someone else!'

That settled the matter, though not in the way Nacomo had intended. Casso shut him up by stuffing a rag into his mouth. Nacomo would be put to the question, but we'd do it back at the offices.

'My wife saw him in that play,' Casso said. I didn't know he was married. He didn't talk much, except to complain. 'Stupid bollocks about a king, and a tower that fell down. She said the monologues went on for bloody hours.'

'Didn't take you for a cultured man,' I said.

77

'Me? Can't stand that shit. Why do you think I didn't go with her?'

I set two of my men to tearing the place apart. They turned up a good stash of money under his floorboards, but there was a feeling in the air, down in the cellar, that left me unnerved, and a foul, lingering odour that I thought that I recognised. Excitement growing within me, I sent someone to fetch Maldon. He arrived looking pissed, his nightly coma having been interrupted. The scowl left his face when I took him down to the cellar. He wouldn't go in, arching away like a cat being thrust toward a bath.

'It was here,' he said. 'Definitely.'

'How long ago?'

'Recently,' Maldon said. 'Shavada's Eye was here.'

There was no chance of Nacomo being the vault-breaker. Anyone capable of breaking through Crowfoot's wards wouldn't have been taken so easily. He was a middleman, perhaps, passing it along? Or just a man in possession of a big house to hide it in for a while. Had I thought that the Eye might have been here, I'd have brought in Spinners and Nenn's boys. Instead I had my men dig up the cellar floor, just in case, but there was nothing to find. It had been here, and now it was gone.

I smashed a set of expensively painted dinner plates in frustration. Had we missed it by minutes? Hours?

Nacomo didn't say anything during his interrogation. He seemed confused and couldn't account for his recent whereabouts. He'd not been working: laid off by the theatre after the news sheets delivered scathing reviews, leaving him with a hefty debt on the house and no prospect of work. He knew that he was in it up to his eyeballs, and speaking would only lessen his chances of surviving the week. Questions about the Eye made him snap his mouth shut, refusing to look at me, or at anyone in the dark little room. He endured two hours of questioning. Traust screamed in his face, cuffed him around the head some. Repeated the same questions over and over. *Who were you working for? Who did you lead into the Misery? How are they planning to betray the Range? Where is the Eye?* He just stared ahead blankly. A change seemed to have come over him, like he wasn't even there at all.

'You want me to bring out the hammer?' Traust asked. His ugly grin was a little uglier than usual out of frustration that his intimidation had yielded no results. Nacomo might as well have been a statue, staring into space, unfocused. Blank as a fresh canvas.

I glanced over at Valiya. There was no judgment on her face. She knew that we'd do what had to be done.

'No,' I said. 'Throw him in the white cells.'

Traust manhandled him away.

There is more than one way to break a man. The white cells were a hard place to endure for even a day: so narrow that a man could only stand. No food, nothing to drink, and the guards beat a cymbal every twenty minutes to make sure the prisoners didn't sleep on their feet. Threw salt water over them if they managed to. Powerful phos lamps maintained a continuous, intense, brightness from all angles. The cells worked differently from a hammer. They broke the mind down, got it confused, muddled. Pliable. I'd never known a man able to resist questioning after a few days in the cells, but I was too eager to get at the information in Nacomo's head. Every hour that I had to wait saw me pacing, drumming my fingers, snapping at the servants with impatience, but I had to leave Nacomo in there until he broke down. Weaker men lasted only hours. I hoped that a single day would see Nacomo's tongue running loose. Letting him out too early would merely give him a reprieve. A week would have shattered him for certain, but I couldn't afford that long.

I was about to fetch him when Amaira announced a visitor. Governor Thierro, the old acquaintance that Davandein had reintroduced me to at the theatre, was dressed again in his long white coat, white gloves, tan belt, tan boots. Amaira admitted him, that obnoxiously strong cloud of cologne trailing in his wake.

'I apologise for arriving without an appointment,' he said. 'But business never waits. Might we talk?'

'I have to attend to something urgent,' I said.

'I'm looking for a noblewoman,' Thierro said. 'Lady Ezabeth Tanza.'

I was already reaching for my coat, slung over the back of a chair, but Ezabeth's name stayed my hand.

'Amaira. Ask Valiya to go and pick up our friend from the cells. Bring him over here.'

I mostly had Amaira make me coffee and clean my clothes so she was excited to be asked to convey an instruction relating to actual Blackwing work. As she reached adolescence, suddenly things that had never mattered before had become important to her. She scampered away with the message as I took Thierro through to a sparsely furnished reception room. It didn't see a lot of use. The office's visitors weren't often exposed to comfort.

'Hard to believe we were ever that young, isn't it?' Thierro mused. Bringing up our shared history. Drawing me closer, emotionally. Building a bridge between what he wanted, and what I had.

'Feels a lifetime ago,' I agreed. 'You want something? Brandy? Wine?'

'Herbal tea, if you have some,' he said. I didn't, so we didn't have anything. I was going to light a cigar but remembered in time that Thierro's chest wasn't strong. It seemed needlessly cruel to expose him to the rough tobacco of the Range. I put the cigar case back in my coat.

'What do you want with Ezabeth Tanza?'

'I need her help,' he said. 'She disappeared four years ago and it's widely assumed that she was killed during the

Siege. That was where she was last seen. Or at least, that's what people believe.'

'Ezabeth Tanza is dead,' I said.

'Perhaps,' Thierro said. 'I'm sorry if this is painful for you to talk about. In the course of seeking information about her, I came across a rumor.'

'Rumours are dangerous things.'

'It's idle gossip, most likely. Rude speculation. But there was a suggestion that you and she were – you know. More than friends.' We had been, briefly. But not many people knew that. Thierro's diggers must have gone deep to unearth that, this long on. But then, he had the money to pay for the best.

'Best not to insult the dead, Thierro.'

Thierro nodded, solemn. 'I apologise. I had to ask. Lady Tanza was an exceptional mathematician, physicist, lunarist and scholar. The Iron Sun is based upon designs she wrote about in her thesis on phos manipulation.'

'What's the Iron Sun?'

'You'll have seen the sphere of black iron at the pinnacle of the Grandspire,' he said. 'It's a venting device, which can be turned into a weapon to defend the city if necessary. An astounding piece of engineering, based on Lady Tanza's schematics.'

He wanted to dredge the past out of me, tangled weeds dragged from a lightless riverbed.

'Ezabeth Tanza died in the Siege,' I said tightly. 'I'm sorry I can't help you.'

'That's what people say,' Thierro agreed. 'But there was no body. No grave.'

'A lot of people were crushed when the wall came down. She was likely buried under ten thousand tons of rubble. You'll need someone else to help with your phos mill,' I said. I'd never spoken of Ezabeth's death to anyone except Dantry, Nenn and Tnota. She was our greatest hero, but just hearing her name was painful. To have it broadcast across the city-states would have been unbearable, so I'd kept her sacrifice silent. Selfish of me, perhaps.

'The Grandspire is so much more than just a phos mill, Captain,' Thierro said. And for a moment there I thought that there was a spark of something more energised in him. Something he actually cared about. To men like him, a million marks was pigeon feed, the creation of wealth nothing but a game in which to rank himself against other merchant overlords. But this had engaged his passion. 'The Grandspire is a symbol of hope to the people. They've had their share of terror. The Grandspire tells them, *"Here is the work of man, far greater than anything the enemy can ever dream of. See us reach into the sky."*'

'Not so far from the Bright Order's teachings,' I said. 'Is that it? You're a believer?'

Thierro ignored my question.

'Westland has invested more money in the Grandspire than most towns could scrape together in twenty years. It has risen over the city in just four years. No great work like this has ever been undertaken before, not in such a short space of time. Do you know why I ordered the project started, Captain?'

'Phos makes a lot of money,' I said. 'You're all about the profits, I'll wager.'

'Profits matter, I won't deny it,' Thierro said. 'But no. Not in this instance. You remember how it was, back when we all joined up? You, me, the Eiderstein brothers, Pep, Salia, all the rest. Half of our class signed up to fight. And we believed in those days, didn't we? Really wanted to make a difference.'

'We're none of us born smart.'

'Serving your country isn't foolishness. And I know you don't believe it is, or you'd not be here, fighting the long fight. I always dreamed of making a name for myself here. Being remembered as a great soldier. Maybe even making marshal.

We all dreamed that, didn't we? But after Adrogorsk ...'
Thierro's cool visage faltered just for a moment. It's never
easy to relive the worst day of your life. His gunners had
peppered a Darling with matchlock fire, blown its head clean
off, but even that hadn't stopped it casting sorcery at them.
I'd have bet the memory of that low-hanging, brown-stained
haze drifting toward him would haunt him all his life. The
head had been laughing at them the whole time. 'I was sent
back before the real heavy fighting started. I never wanted to
leave, but I couldn't stay on the Range. I could barely breathe
while the Darling's magic lingered, and the Misery's poison
only made it worse. They sent me away, out to Valaigne,
where the "clean air" did nothing for my health, but it did
let me prosper. I bought coal mines, and they turned out
to be diamond mines. I turned money into more money,
and that into more. I am good at breeding coins. But I never
wanted that life. I always wanted to be here. A fighter. I
would have been, if not for that Darling's magic.'

'You don't have to convince me that you wanted to serve.
You were given that bastion to hold because you had the
guts to do it,' I said. 'So now you've built the Grandspire.
Paying your debt of service another way?'

'If only life were so simple,' Thierro said. 'A significant
astrological event approaches. A solar flare. Two years ago,
I learned that the Grandspire must be completed before it
passes.'

I could have become a businessman like Thierro. My life
would have been very different, if I had. I'd probably still
have my old name, a family, and no damn raven tattoo on
my arm. But I had always hated the wheedling money-play,
the spinning of coins and promises. I'd always rather have
enemies who'd come at me with a spear in hand rather than
the kind who'd buy my boots out from under me.

'If you need Ezabeth Tanza to finish it for you, you're
long out of luck.'

'You know of the Bright Order and the teachings of the High Witness. Do you believe?'

'I'm yet to be persuaded.'

Thierro seemed to think that over. Then he leaned forward.

'A cigar, if I may?' I frowned. Didn't think that was a good idea, but it would have been rude to refuse. He took a pair from the tin, lit both and then offered me one.

'I saw her,' he said. 'The Bright Lady. Not just a glimpse, either. A true vision.'

'Lots of people make that claim. It's not going to end the war.'

Thierro considered the cigar carefully. He placed it between his lips, drew, then blew smoothly.

'I didn't believe it would either. But then I saw her. She cured me, with her fire.'

I said nothing. Hearing people talking about Ezabeth here, in my sanctuary, was like having a long needle driven into my spine. A feeling of terror for her, lost, alone and trapped. Pain for me, for what I'd lost. And envy. Deepest, deepest envy that these true visions had never been for me. I dreamed that I saw her sometimes, in my half-awake state, reaching for me with one hand, imploring. But Tnota was right. I saw what I wanted to see. And then she appeared to the likes of Thierro. The lucky few. Witnesses.

It hurt.

When the ghost in the light first appeared, Dantry had gone searching for her. People around Valengrad were experiencing visions, glimpses of a woman in the phos network. The visions had seemed random: a woman appearing to startle a baker; glimpsed by a guard on the wall; appearing to a clerk in the citadel. She was an aftershock, an echo. Then we'd heard more. Stories from other, farther-away places, and not just the cities but anywhere they had a phos network. Down a mine, even aboard a ship. All across the

Dortmark city-states, people saw her: the Bright Lady. The spirit in the light.

Smoke curled between us, only my cigar tasted flat, dead.

'I understand your reluctance to accept it,' Thierro said. 'But when she came to me, she healed me. She burned the dark poison out of me, and I feel her still, deep in my heart.' He placed a hand over his chest. 'And she told me the Grandspire must be ready for her coming. She needs it, if she is to be reborn.'

I'd wanted to believe, too. In something that went beyond just a simple flicker in the night. That Ezabeth still lived on, somehow. I had chased the visions, and chased down those that experienced them. But she was nothing. Just an echo. A shadow lingering in the phos network, frozen in time at the moment of her death. Because if she'd been anything else, she would have appeared to me. And not just in my dreams.

Thierro looked so earnest that I didn't know what to say. It was one thing to believe that Ezabeth had appeared to him. Reports of the Bright Lady were plentiful enough that one more made no difference, and the preachers were proclaiming their visions in the streets, day after day. But nobody had claimed to have *heard* her before. I was a born cynic, and years of tracking down spies, deserters and seditionists had only toughened me to lies.

'If we weren't old friends, I might be hustling you over to the Maud about now,' I said. 'You got better, and I'm glad of that. But if you're hearing voices, then maybe you should be laying off the leaf-pipe.'

Thierro sucked on his cigar, released a cloud of smoke into the still air. It hung there, blue and white, glazing the distance between us.

'Scepticism is understandable,' he said. 'But she didn't just heal me. She gave me a gift.'

He held out his free hand, palm up. After a moment, a small ball of light grew there, cold and blue-white, mirroring the colour of the smoke. It crackled a little, but gently. Perfectly controlled.

'You can spin,' I breathed. The light rotated slowly over his hand as I stared.

It was impossible. Spinners' ability always came through in adolescence. Thierro had been twenty-one when I fought beside him at Adrogorsk, and he'd never had the power. I stared at the impossible ball of light. It twisted, took on a faint golden hue, and for a moment it bobbed a little circle. He was still calm, still presenting that pleasant, businesslike pressure.

'Ezabeth Tanza was the greatest Spinner in generations. A mind like few others. Stories of her prowess during the Siege still linger. And she disappeared the night that Nall's Engine activated. The night the drudge inside the city were annihilated by a light-storm that nobody has ever been able to explain.' He looked me dead in the eye. 'Tell me the truth, Ryhalt. It's her, isn't it? She's the spirit in the light. Ezabeth Tanza is the Bright Lady.'

My jaw had locked rigid and I couldn't speak. Thierro's businesslike visage shifted. He smiled. My silence had told him all that he wanted to know.

'Don't fear,' he said gently. 'The secret is safe with me. I just needed – '

The door banged open and Valiya staggered in the doorway, sweat slicking her face, hand clutched to her collarbone. Blood stained the front of her dress.

'Nacomo got loose,' she said.

8

Marollo Nacomo's escape had not been a masterstroke of planning. Valiya and two jackdaws had been escorting him through the city when he'd grabbed a dagger from a belt and gone slash-wild. None of them were badly injured, but he'd shed enough blood to stop them from getting their hands on him. One of the jackdaws looked likely to lose a couple of fingers and the other wasn't going to be winning any beauty contests in the near future, but in fairness, he probably wouldn't have won them anyway.

I had Amaira show Thierro out.

'Thank you, Ryhalt,' he said. 'Things will get better. Trust me.' We shook hands.

We got Valiya patched up. Amaira brought bandages while we waited for a surgeon to come and suture the wound. It wasn't deep, just messy.

'I should have been more careful,' she said. Her anger at her own mistake hurt her more than the shallow wound. She was right, so I didn't patronise her with contradiction. I'd become so used to her competence with papers and numbers that I'd tasked her with thug work. The failure was more mine than hers.

'If you live through your mistakes, there's always something to take from them,' I said. 'We'll get him back.'

'I'm sorry. I fucked up, Ryhalt. It won't happen again.'

'Just take it easy,' I said. 'I need you fixed up. Rest. We've got the gate sergeants on the lookout for him. He won't escape the city.'

I pulled in all my manpower and set them to searching. We questioned Marollo's acquaintances and colleagues from the theatre, but they'd not seen him in weeks. He'd become a recluse after he fell from the spotlight. Nenn's Ducks were enjoying their Misery leave but they were more than happy to kick a few doors in and scare a few snooty actors if they were getting paid for it. I had a pair of eyes watching Nacomo's house too.

I'd had him by the throat and my carelessness had let him slip from my fist. My employees could sense the violence of my mood and kept a safe distance.

I received a request from the marshal to attend her in the late afternoon. Davandein liked to send her orders like they were invites to a summer garden party, elaborate calligraphy sealed in scented envelopes, but there was a sense of urgency about it, and it read more like an order than a polite invitation. She knew I hated being bossed around, which meant either she was angry, or she was in a lather about something. I was already sporting half a brandy buzz and I wasn't in the mood to talk to her, but her tone set me on edge. Nenn had been summoned as well, and we waited together in a sitting room whilst Davandein entertained whoever had gone in before us. Nenn wasn't her usual foul-mouthed self.

'Gut's playing up,' she admitted. 'Has been for a while.'

'Probably all those chillies you get through. Can't be doing your insides any good,' I said. Nenn's urge to eat raw red chillies had not diminished in the years since I got her fixed. She frowned, massaging her belly where the drudge blade had pierced her, years ago.

'Can't,' she said. 'The flesh remembers what it wants. Can't say no.'

'What does Davandein want?'

88

'Damned if I know,' Nenn said with a shrug. Something was eating at her. I asked annoying questions until she broke.

'I worry about it. When it hurts,' Nenn said grudgingly.

'About what?'

'About what's inside me,' she said. 'About what Saravor took out and about what he put back in. Sometimes I wonder if I'm all messed up in there.' She tried to make her voice light, careless, but she had no skill at acting. 'Like, if I could get pregnant. Shit like that.'

We rarely spoke of the deal I'd had to strike with the Fixer after Nenn took a drudge blade to the gut at Station Twelve. Saravor had been the only sorcerer with the skills to save her. I'd never regretted making that deal – monstrous though he was, Saravor had saved my best friend's life. But he wasn't a healer, and he hadn't repaired the parts of her that had been damaged. He'd replaced them.

I was no good at talking to people about the things that matter to them. Never had been. Nenn's comment hung between us, dirtying the air until I couldn't bear the awkwardness anymore.

'That what you want? Little shits under your feet?'

'I don't know. I'm getting old for it anyway.'

'You never seemed like the maternal type before,' I said. It was hard to think of a woman less well suited to motherhood than Nenn, but then, being a parent wasn't achieved through merit. I asked her, 'This your idea, or someone else's?' And by someone else, I meant Betch.

'Just something I was thinking on. Sometimes I feel that there's a window and it's slowly closing on me, shutting off the light.'

Misery soldiers weren't overly given to worrying over family and future. You get used to the danger. Gain an expectation that you probably aren't going to see thirty. Then you hit thirty and forty seems an impossible goal. Those few who made it to fifty were known all through Valengrad. But Nenn had hit thirty running, and I guess everyone mellows with time. Even someone as full of kill as Nenn. I'd had my chance at fatherhood, and I'd failed. Some men aren't made to be fathers, and some don't deserve to be.

We were led out onto the citadel's roof by a servant. I was glad to be saved from having to discuss it any further. I didn't have anything useful to say.

The wind blew high and hard, the salt-and-chemical stink of the Misery sweeping into the city where the factory runoff couldn't disguise it. It helped to wake me up, the usual layer of fug pushed back from my thoughts and eyes. The jester's-hat projectors of Nall's Engine loomed vast and black above us. Silent, inert. For now.

The marshal looked immaculate in a high-necked white blouse, braces and black, three-quarter-length trousers that were probably a fashion that had yet to reach the Range. The wind whipped away the smoke of a cigarillo that she inhaled through a long-stemmed holder and lips painted strawberry red. She stood alone, but her cabal of Battle Spinners weren't far away. They were young, peacocks and daffodils every one. A group from the Order of Aetherial Engineers conversed separately.

'The thing that was stolen,' Davandein said sharply. 'Talk to me.'

'There's not much to report,' I said. 'And it pains me to admit that. I've had my men dropping bribes in every quarter, but the property that got taken isn't the kind of thing that's going to get fenced in some back-alley pawnshop. Whoever took it wanted it for something specific.'

'How much danger are we in from it?'

'We're on the Range,' Nenn said. 'How much does a shit stink?'

It wasn't the answer that Davandein wanted but she glowered at the broken sky rather than at Nenn.

'Do you need more resources?' she asked. 'Would my Spinners help?'

'No,' I said. 'Leave it with me. I'll get it back.'

I wasn't making the promise just because I felt responsible. I *was* responsible, and the frozen raven that had torn itself free from my arm had been sent to alert me. It had not arrived in time, though, and its half-ruined message had not been coherent. I expected to get another message from Crowfoot at any time, but why his bird had failed to get through worried at me. It wasn't like his power to be misspent, or like his workings to go awry. That in itself was troubling.

'Didn't need to come all this way just to tell you that,' Nenn said. She'd been winning at tiles and hadn't enjoyed being interrupted.

'No,' she said. 'I want you to keep an eye on the Bright Order. Both of you. If they step out of line, or overstep their mark, I need to put them beneath my heel. Their presence here troubles me.'

Davandein flicked the cigarillo from the end of the holder, loaded up another. I glanced at Nenn. She didn't like the marshal much.

'They're just crazies,' Nenn said. I hated to admit it, but talking with Thierro had bothered me. He was a smart man. Brilliant in commerce, even. As a student he'd been fond of drinking, fond of shooting, and fond of taking a girl around a dance floor and the dance that followed. We hadn't been close, but I'd have called him a friend. I'd been a shit to him once, at one of those very dance halls. He'd beaten me at cards earlier that night, so when a girl to whom he'd written a hundred love sonnets had gone with me and I'd seen him scowling at me, I'd tipped him a mocking little salute as I led her out the door. But even when I'd made him angry, Thierro hadn't done the rash thing and challenged me to a duel – as Torolo Mancono would do two years later. It would have been a foregone conclusion; even then I'd been big, and I'd been much better than him with a blade. Instead of throwing his dignity onto the fire, Thierro had been calm, composed. He'd taken the loss, ignored the barb and moved on to the next girl. He'd got her too, as I remembered.

For a man who exhibited that level of self-control even when drunk to be convinced of the Bright Lady's coming worried me much more than the preachers on the street. An uneducated man can be led to believe anything that suits his mood, but the Thierros of the world were a rarer breed. Only he knew something that the other believers didn't. Maybe that counted for something.

'I need to know if the Bright Order are telling the truth,' Davandein said. She ejected the words as though they'd rotted beneath her tongue. 'The High Witness is coming here, to Valengrad. He claims that a new world order will begin here. That justice will be restored. I need to know what he plans.'

She was worried about her own power, I thought. Her position.

'Valiya has a dossier on them,' I said. 'There are four Witnesses in total. They've travelled the states, preaching the message. Hard to pin them down. Hard to get any information on any of them. We know two names: Valentia, and Glaun. But they travel secretly. I know next to nothing about them, other than that they're expected to arrive in Valengrad in the next two weeks.'

'The Bright Order edge perilously close to outright dissent,' Davandein said. 'The High Witness has garnered considerable support, even here. They take wild, crowd-pleasing steps to win the mob and trumpet revolutionary diatribe alongside their dogma. I want them squashed.'

'But you don't want to question their religion, because if they're telling the truth, then you'll be wrong and look stupid,' Nenn said. Davandein's glower turned on her this time. I let them clash antlers as unwelcome memories re-surfaced, bubbles of gas rising through the fetid swamp.

'Fuck.' No amount of cream and powder would keep that much anger from Davandein's face. 'Fuck it all. The High Witness will make trouble for us. I need to counter them. Somehow.'

'I've ignored the Bright Order for too long,' I said. 'I should have got a leash around them before they got this big. There are thousands of them now.' I'd let my personal feelings about their beliefs dissuade me from looking into their activities, and that had been foolish. Maybe Thierro believed the preaching of the Witnesses, but he was wrong. I was sure he was wrong. Wasn't I?

'Find me information that will bring them down,' Davandein said. 'And find whatever was stolen from that vault.'

We left the roof. I was glad to get out of the biting wind.

9

We rode quickly through the streets, pallid rain fizzing against the phos tubes. My armour was going to need oiling as soon as I got it back home. It's all very impressive to look at, but if you have to take care of your own gear, it rapidly becomes a pain in the arse.

'There's a public commotion,' Tnota told me. 'Condition Blue.'

'You're the only one who uses those categories,' I said. 'I don't even know what "Condition Blue" means.'

'It means that there's a public commotion,' Tnota said. He gave me his most infuriating grin.

We clattered through the Spills, toward the Grandspire. It thrust high toward the sky as if seeking to pry open the white-bronze cracks. Nine hundred feet tall, taller than any tower had a right to be. Thierro's engineers had done something with phos-welded pillars of twisted steel and despite its vast size it had survived all of the recent tremors. The ground had been shaking only that morning, a mild quake, but it put everyone on edge.

Thierro had been right. The Grandspire was an astonishing monument to man's ability to create. It wasn't beautiful, too blocky, too practical, but it was easy to imagine the Bright Order pilgrims' awe as they approached the city and saw it towering into the broken heavens. When the Witnesses arrived they were probably going to do a jig.

The tower was nearly two hundred feet wide at the base. They'd had to demolish a good bit of the Spills to make room for it and nobody missed the slums that had been levelled, nobody whose complaints mattered, anyway. When it was finished, it would be the greatest phos mill the republic had ever seen, the moonlight filtering down through a hundred lenses, floor after floor, to the Spinners at the base of the tower. The Westland Frontier Traders were doing their part to see that Nall's Engine was adequately supplied. Or at least, they believed that they were. I knew better, of course.

A crowd had gathered in the spacious plaza that led to the big double doors leading into the Grandspire. Gawkers tended to get in the way or get hurt when things got out of hand, today fear steamed the air between the scattered masons, carpenters and engineers. They held tight to their hammers and saws, stood in disordered clusters. The workers came in every colour and shape imaginable, brought in from across the breadth of the known world to raise the Grandspire in just a handful of years. The next shift would be arriving soon, and the plaza would become even more crowded.

A troop of men with shouldered firearms were marching in poor step toward the Grandspire's open doors. At their head, I was surprised to see Governor Thierro. I shouldn't have been. It was his Grandspire after all. I gave Falcon my heels and intercepted them.

'What's the deal here, Governor?' I said.

'Something from the Misery entered the Grandspire nearly an hour ago,' he said. His face was serious, his eyes as intense as always. 'I'm going to bring it out.' He wore polished, heavily engraved armour as befitted his status, and this time he was armed. Not with anything so clumsy or mundane as weapons: a Battle Spinner's harness formed an X across his shoulders, two phos canisters strapped to his belt.

I'd been shaking down whisper-men for any signs of Nacomo when I'd received a message saying something similar. In all my time on the Range I'd never known a Misery creature to get into the city.

'Wait for the citadel soldiers,' I said. 'If it is from the Misery, then they've the experience to deal with it. Whatever it is.' I looked over the men that Thierro was leading. They were company men employed by the Westland Frontier Traders as security, but some of them wore the yellow hoods of the Bright Order: religious zealots. Not the best men to have at your back.

'Should bring up Davandein's Battle Spinners as well,' Tnota said. I'd filled in everyone who mattered about Thierro's spinning abilities.

Thierro didn't like to be told what to do by a man of no rank. His eyes said everything about his disdain for Tnota, who admittedly was dressed like he'd fallen out of bed and into a random assortment of clothes.

'We're going in now,' Thierro said firmly. 'Every minute that the workmen are stood idle, Westland loses thousands of marks.'

'You don't know what you're dealing with,' I said. 'It's been a long while since you've had to deal with the things that crawl around in the Misery.'

'Trust me, Ryhalt, I've met my share of monsters. Those that saw it describe it as a man without a face,' Thierro said. 'The workmen all got out and I'm burning money just standing here talking to you. If we used to handle bottles of that forty-nine back in the day, I'm pretty sure that you and I can handle someone else who's off their face. Besides, these are good men. Solid.'

I gave them another look. Mostly in their twenties or thirties, their gear middle-of-the-range, some of it old, some new. Nobody looked incapable, but they lacked the toughness you see with professionals. About half of them were packing firepower, and that's when I saw the gleaming silver barrels of flarelocks among them. Tnota had spotted them as well. There were six of them, tubes and wires connecting the phos tanks that provided the weapons with ignition. As I glanced across them I saw that of those carrying them, every one was wearing a yellow hood. I said nothing about it, tried to give nothing away, but Tnota glanced my way. He'd seen it too.

'They look sound,' I said. 'Good enough.'

The security force bristled with pride, shifted the piece-of-shit flarelocks on their shoulders. Thierro was calm; we could have been discussing the price of wheat. Men like him don't fear the night; when you're lord of the dance, you think yourself indestructible.

'I'm coming with you,' I said. Thierro tipped his head toward me in acknowledgment. To Tnota I said, 'I take it you don't want to come?'

'Someone should stay down here and deal with the Condition Blue,' he said.

'What's a Condition Blue?' Thierro asked.

'A public commotion,' I grunted.

I checked my pistols over, tested the action and loaded. They had barrels the length of my forearm, and my forearm was longer than most. Flintlock mechanisms, expensive, heavy things with walnut stocks and engraved metalwork. For a man who didn't like fancy things I seemed to own more than my share of them.

The Grandspire was surrounded by a broad plaza, mostly choked up with stacks of stone and timber needed for the frantic construction. Crowds of men in heavy leather aprons, oil stained, hair lifted by static charge, watched us approach the doors. I was at the fore, clicking metallically in my half armour, black-steel lobster plates covering most of my squishy bits and my poleaxe on my shoulder, a blade at my side and pistols holstered across a bandolier. Standard kit for gracking monsters. As we neared the Grandspire we ascended the broad tiers of steps leading toward the doors.

'I don't suppose it's on the ground floor?' I said. I didn't have much hope.

'It was heading upward when the labourers fled,' Thierro said. He twisted a dial on one of his phos canisters and a light began winking. Primed. 'Ready weapons, lads,' he said. He'd been out of the military for a long time, but he'd retained his sense of command well enough. Given his success overseas, he probably could have made Range Marshal if not for Adrogorsk.

'Keep those things away from me,' I said. 'If I'm going to get gracked today, I'd rather it was by the faceless monster than by one of your weapons exploding.'

'The Bright Lady's faithful have no fear of the light, Captain,' one of the soldiers said to approving murmurs from the militia. 'These weapons are holy. They draw their power from her.'

Guns driven by light. It made sense, to them at least. Levan Ost's killers came into mind. I didn't think that any of these security men had any relationship to those men just because they carried the same kind of hardware, but perhaps Develen Maille had been Bright Order. He'd been desperate, and desperate men are bent to religion all too easily.

Worth thinking about when there weren't monsters to hand.

'Just don't throw them around,' I said. I kept a cautious distance.

The doors were open. I let the militia go in first. Never know what might be waiting beyond a door.

The Grandspire was not finished or running yet. The brickwork was raw, no panelling, no plaster, the skeleton of a behemoth only. Gaps in the ceiling sat ready for vast lenses, some as broad as fifteen feet across. It was an old design, the dream of a great scholar two hundred years dead, finally coming to fruition now that the princes had opened their purses. I wondered whether this new mill would be better for the Talents, the poor bastards who worked the light. Ezabeth had pitied them, and I had never forgotten her tale about her friend, worked to death in a mill.

What was most incredible about the Grandspire was that it hadn't simply collapsed during the recent earthquakes. There was a rigid solidity to it that told me that it would take more than a few tremors to shake the dust out of this tower.

The ground floor was broad, high-ceilinged and empty of near everything except building supplies.

'Scour the place floor by floor,' Thierro said. 'Quick now. Time's wasting.'

The bones of the Grandspire were in place, but it was still very much a work in progress. So much bare, undressed stone made every footstep echo. A winding stairway led up and up. There was supposed to be a phos-powered platform within an enclosed shaft to transport people and machinery up to the higher floors, but Thierro said that it wasn't connected yet, which meant that I was going to have to climb all the way in armour. If the creature had gone all the way to the top, my bad leg was going to be screaming agony by nightfall.

'This is going to take all day,' I said, as we reached the fifth floor. I was sweat-drenched inside my steel already, wished that I hadn't worn it. I wasn't as young as I used to be. Thierro seemed to be holding up just fine.

'Good show. We'll split up. If we're in groups of four, we can take three floors at a time.'

I didn't think Thierro's troopers were as keen on the idea as he was. The safest option was to go back down and let a thousand grenadiers in here with Battle Spinners, but it was too late now. Whatever the faceless creature was, it didn't seem to have killed any of the workers. Not that we knew of yet. Thierro sensed the apprehension too, and addressed his men. 'Every minute we spend here is a minute that work has ceased,' he said. He raised his voice. 'The Bright Lady needs the Grandspire to be completed.'

'For the Bright Lady!' the hooded militia chorused, which was the stupidest thing I'd heard all day. Those without yellow hoods either looked away or joined in anyway, if without much enthusiasm.

'Bastian, Elta, Hemley. Go with the Blackwing captain. You three with me on the seventh floor. The rest of you on the eighth. We'll meet on the stairwell after each sweep. The Lady comes.'

'The Lady comes,' the soldiers intoned, bowing their heads. I huffed with irritation and headed off up the stairs. Two men and a woman followed me. Two of them were packing flarelocks, carried reverently, which may have been religious sentiment on their part, but I was glad to see the weapons weren't being banged against the floor or jogged about. Falling through one of the lens holes in the floor was a better way to go than getting melted into your own weapon.

'Got any experience with monsters?' I asked, as we began to move through the corridors of the sixth floor. Fine stone dust lingered in the air, and we were soon speckled with white powder.

'No, sir.' Bastian was in his twenties, but his face hadn't quite left his teens. 'I was a clockmaker's apprentice before my vision.'

Elta could have been a musician, and Hemley should have been off tending cows somewhere the wheat grew long and thick. Maybe they carried their weapons so reverently because they were unused to holding them, rather than from a sense of spirituality. They were greener than cut summer grass and probably less use. The only thing I could have said in their favour was that they knew which end the shot came out.

'You aren't soldiers,' I said. Not a good time to knock their confidence, but heading into action with untried troops at your back is a recipe for getting a blade through it.

'We're the people's militia,' Elta said.

'You could be acrobats or goose tamers for all I care,' I said, 'you aren't soldiers. You got any idea how to use those swords you're wearing?'

'I do,' Bastian said eagerly. He had a short, scratchy beard and an energy that said he always thought himself right.

I shook my head. I didn't know what we were facing up here, but I hoped that Thierro had taken his best with him. He'd not given me anything worth spit.

I went first down the hall with my poleaxe on my shoulder and a pistol in my left hand. I hissed at my spring buds to be quiet as I went ahead, glancing through empty doorways into empty, unfinished rooms. First time I'd been in the Grandspire. I had to say, I was impressed.

The floor was empty of anything other than cigar butts, piecrusts and piss stains left by the labourers. Most of the chambers housed spaces for giant lenses in both the floor and ceiling. I jumped half out of my skin when I looked up to see one of Thierro's men peering down from the floor above.

'So how'd you wind up carrying arms for Westland?' I asked. 'You got a Whitelande accent. You aren't local.'

'I carry arms for the Bright Lady, and the Witnesses,' Bastian said.

'Sure. Imagine that's what I asked.'

'I saw her. In my own home,' Bastian said, sombrely. 'She looked so sad. I knew at once that she was the Bright Lady I'd heard about, and she chose me over my brothers, all six of them.'

'I saw her too,' Elta agreed. 'Clear as day, she was.'

We picked around a clutter of tools and workbenches, abandoned by the labourers. This place should have been ringing with the sounds of chisels, trowels and buzzing, phos-powered saws. The emptiness made it feel curiously lonely. I turned a corner and scanned for signs of inhuman things. Clear.

'What about you? You see the Lady too?' I asked Hemley. He was the most reserved, the only one I thought might actually be worth something in a scrap. He also had a smoking matchlock rather than a flarelock, which made me like him more.

'No,' he said, but his voice was no less assured. 'Not yet, anyway. The Witnesses say that in time, we all will.'

His accent placed him as from some country village, someplace where milking a cow was the highlight of the day and a tree falling would be talked about for years in fable.

'So what are you doing here?' I said. I nosed around a corner, pistol leading the way. Clear.

'The Order came recruiting,' he said. 'And they spoke a lot of sense. About how the wealth's all the wrong way around. One man in a thousand has more wealth than all the rest put together, and even if some fellow tries to raise himself, he can't earn a title. All this on the Range – the Grandspire, the wall, the soldiers – it's all important, I suppose, but out in the states the people are taxed to their limit, while the princes sip sparkling wine from diamond cups. It can't go on.'

'You think there's revolution on the table? That's why you came?'

'I think the Bright Lady is a sign that something better is coming,' Hemley said, and as much as I didn't want to, I felt a treacherous twinge of hope that he was right.

'But you don't believe?'

'Of course he does,' Bastian said fiercely.

'Sure, of course,' Hemley said, though I didn't find him terribly convincing. 'People have seen her in visions, haven't they? Enough people that I don't doubt their sincerity.' He shrugged. It didn't seem terribly important to him.

As we neared the end of our sweep there came a deep, earthy boom from far above us. A fine drift of dust sifted down.

We backed up and regrouped with Thierro and the others on the stairs. His men, who had previously worn expressions of pious solemnity, looked like they'd woken up to the situation. Sweat on their brows. Fingers getting twitchy near firing levers.

'Higher,' Thierro said.

'Higher,' I agreed.

Seventy-five fucking floors. I ditched my axe. Wished that I wasn't wearing armour. My leg protested, the old wound stabbing at the bone. This was a young man's game. By the time I saw daylight ahead of me I was wet through with sweat and blowing steam.

I was the last to reach the roof.

The top of the Grandspire was a vast, flat platform of perfectly clear, phos-hardened glass with a low curtain wall. Through the three feet of glass I could see the floor below, and the lens holes leading down. I felt nervous about stepping onto it, like I stepped onto the perfectly still surface of a pool of water. The glass platform's only feature sat in the centre, the Iron Sun, a twenty-foot-wide globe of black metal on a pedestal, its outer surface armoured in a series of overlapping metal shells. Smoke rose around it and the glass floor was cracked and splintered into chips of fused glass, the smell of blasting powder lingering despite the fierce wind. The soldiers were mostly clustered on the other side of the Iron Sun, some upright and some kneeling, but all of their weapons trained on a lone figure beside the curtain wall.

A familiar figure stood beside a hole that had been

blown in the wall, looking out across Valengrad. He wore a long white nightshirt, which fluttered around his legs in the high wind. The same nightshirt we'd arrested him in. His shoulders worked up and down in time with laboured breaths. Even only able to see his back I recognised him well enough. Marollo Nacomo, star of the stage and traitor to the Range.

Thierro and his troops had formed a ring around the figure but they kept their distance. I panted up to stand among them. In fairness, I wasn't the only one short of breath or soaked in sweat. It was a hell of a climb.

'What now, sir?' one of them asked. A man with a flare-lock. His weapon was cranked and ready to fire and I thought for a moment that he was speaking to me, but then I saw that their eyes were all on Thierro. The governor took a step out, ahead of his men. He seemed composed. Unafraid, but tense as a stalking cat.

'You there. Do you hear me?' he called. 'Can you speak?'

'Easy,' I growled quietly. 'I need that man alive.'

Fate is a capricious comedian. She'd given me back the only lead I had to both Levan Ost's killers and Shavada's Eye, and then perched him on the edge of a thousand foot drop. A man in his position might be inclined to take the less painful way out rather than face the white cells and interrogation again, but if Nacomo had noticed our presence, then he didn't show it. His shoulders trembled slightly. His toes brushed the edge of the platform. A strong enough wind would send him hurtling down to the plaza below.

'He do anything since you arrived?' I asked. I was all too aware of the perspiration dripping from my jaw. Thierro by contrast had only broken a mild sweat. Bastard.

'No,' Thierro said. 'He's just standing there.'

'What caused the damage?'

'I don't know,' he said, eyes narrowing. 'Whatever it is, it's slowing us down. Men, present arms.'

The security men awkwardly arrayed their weapons to point toward the man's back.

'He took my face,' Nacomo said. He kept his back to us. 'He took my face. I didn't want him to. I didn't want to give him my face.'

'Nacomo,' I called. 'Nacomo, listen to me.' Thierro glanced my way, surprised, but refixed his attention on the man on his rooftop.

'You know him?' he asked.

'Leave him to me,' I said. There was blood streaked down Nacomo's white gown. Probably some of it belonged to Valiya and my jackdaws. I found my teeth were clenched hard together.

'I never meant to do wrong,' Nacomo said. His words were faint, the wind tearing at them. 'Didn't want to get mixed up in anything untoward. I'm not a bad man.'

'Step away from the edge,' I called, 'step away, and lay down any weapons you're carrying. You're still under arrest.' He didn't respond. 'You know who I am, don't you, Nacomo? Turn around. Slowly.'

'I know you, Captain Galharrow. You're the footsteps of death to men like me. They said I was too old to play Leyonar. Too old! How the stage betrays us all, in the end. I wanted a fresh start. To go back to Lennisgrad having taught my critics a lesson. Vanity. What a thing to die for. A face. My useless face.'

'What is he wittering on about?' Thierro muttered, but he made no move forward. I shrugged. Nacomo sounded like he was on the verge of doing something stupid, and he was standing on the edge of a drop that would definitely allow him to do it. He knew that I'd hang him, once I broke the information out of him. I just wondered why he'd choose this instead of the rope. Someone was going to have to go over there and retrieve him, and I didn't trust any of the men around me to do it. I drew a pistol, cocked the hammer and took a step forward. Needed to keep him talking. Keep his mind from jumping. If I lost him to the drop, I'd never learn who he'd been working for, or where the Eye had gone after it left his house.

'What was wrong with your face?'

'Nothing,' Nacomo said. 'I realise that now. It was just my face. But they mocked me. They called me an old hack in the news sheets. I had to do something! ... there was a young man. I said I'd like to look like him. I didn't realise what that ... creature would do to him and when I learned what happened I didn't want to wear that face anymore. But what could I do? And when I failed him ... he took it back.'

He'd looked wrong when we arrested him. Too young to be the man we were after. I should have seen it. I should have realised. 'Who took it back? Who did this to you?'

But I already knew. There was only one damn sorcerer that shifted flesh from man to man.

No. It couldn't be. I had to be wrong. I told myself, I had to be wrong.

Nacomo began to laugh, a maddened, pain-filled choke that shuddered his shoulders.

'But I'll have the last laugh,' he said. 'None of you shall have me. Not him, not you, none of you bastards get to hurt me any more. I'll exit the stage like Leyonar, bringing the tower down around me.'

For all that he was babbling, the hairs on my neck leaped to attention. He'd lost it, but we were standing on a huge piece of glass and that early boom above us echoed in my thoughts. Nacomo began to laugh again, and behind his cackling, a fizzing sound began, a sustained cat's hiss. It crackled and splintered, an unnatural noise, but it suddenly clicked in my head. I suddenly understood the detonations we'd heard below.

I raised both pistols, squinted hard and fired. One of them misfired, the flint failing to spark but the second roared. I hit Nacomo in the shoulder, not where I'd aimed but you get what you get with a pistol at range. My guns were custom-made, bigger and heavier than most, more powder and bigger ammunition. Monster killers. The impact spun Nacomo on his heel, and as his damaged arm flailed, he let go of something, something wet and ragged, landing wetly on the platform. A mask. No. *A face.*

They'd been right to call him a monster. Flesh as red as rare steak gleamed wetly around staring eyes. Black, putrid rot had liquefied what should have been his cheeks, while thick dark scabs crusted across his brows and jaw. Deep cuts framed the damage done as it had been cut away, a mane of crusting, congealed black wetness. His eyes had no lids, his teeth were stark white behind skinless lips. His eyes, bloodshot, pained, boggled madly as he laughed. Maybe the pain had broken his mind. Bloody fluid spat from the raw muscle as his jaw worked in mad laugher.

The ruin of his face was a distraction and it took me a moment to see the grenadoe in his hand, a long stretch of fuse blazing as it ate toward a grapefruit-sized ball of dark iron. It held blasting powder, high explosive. As I took it in I saw the second and third bombs hanging from his belt. When one went off, those others would follow.

Nacomo laughed through blackened lips as the sparks raced along the fuse, raised one hand to the sky in contemplation, a final theatrical gesture.

'I'm no traitor, I never was. But look what he did to me!' He held up the grenadoe like a royal orb of office. 'That monster thinks to rule me. Me, the great Marollo Nacomo! But I've undone what he did to me and I'll exit the stage my own man. I am no puppet – I am an *artist*. Those talentless critics wanted to see a true Leyonar? Well here I stand. Observe me now! I'll bring this tower down; one final encore for the greatest actor of the age!'

'Fire! Fire!' Thierro roared. Matchlocks and flarelocks

discharged, a couple hitting him but most of the shots flying wide. Nacomo rocked, but he didn't fall. Thierro made a strangled noise. He had a ball of burning light around his hand but was unwilling to throw it; any light spinning he threw at Nacomo could detonate the grenadoe and damage the glass platform, and if that collapsed, then we all went with it. Nacomo raised the iron ball over his head.

I threw myself flat. I am not a natural hero. But Bastian, adherent of the Bright Lady, former clockmaker's apprentice, decided to take the single bravest action of his life. He dropped his weapon and ran at the faceless figure. He collided bodily with his target, both men hurtling over the low wall and out into the sky where they hung together in midair for the briefest of moments. And then they were gone.

Seconds passed, and when it came the blast seemed farther away than I'd expected. Still loud, but a hollow thump rather than a deafening crack.

'Bright Lady! He saved us!' Elta gasped.

'Lady's breath,' another muttered.

Governor Thierro had done as I had and got the hell out of the way. His fine white coat was smeared with grey cement dust, and it was in his eyebrows, his hair.

'Bastian saved us,' Elta said. She wiped tears from her eyes. 'A true hero! He travelled all this way, just to ... Spirits. Lady!'

Brave young Bastian had knocked our quarry right out into the open air. They'd detonated together a few storeys above ground. Peering down, there didn't seem to be much left of either of them, but for a liberal red circle on the pale grey slabs, a thousand feet below.

Thierro went to Elta and bound her close with one dusty arm.

'He *was* a hero,' he said softly. 'The High Witness will know his name. He will be remembered.'

The morons around him nodded and muttered their agreement. Belief in the Bright Lady was comforting to them. In fairness, it was a time for comfort.

I limped over to the scrap of skin that Nacomo had discarded. Must have taken a hell of a lot to make a man cut away his own face.

Marollo Nacomo had escaped me, for a much worse fate.

10

'What a fuckup,' I said as I rejoined Tnota outside. The rain had slowed to a fine mist and the air was heavy with moisture. My hands were shaking. The realization I'd made on the rooftop hummed within me. I tried to tell myself that I was wrong. I didn't want to be right. I wore the bravest face that I could.

'Big Dog says men shouldn't fly,' he said. 'What made him go pop?'

'Grenadoes,' I said. 'Wanted to go out in a blaze of theatrical glory. Fucking actors.' I shivered. 'Tell you one thing though. We can stop looking for Marollo Nacomo.'

'Couldn't see much of him before,' Tnota said. He rubbed at his forehead. 'Guess I can see quite a lot of him now.'

No arguing there. A fine red spray had decorated a broad swathe of the street. Spectators were slimy with it.

Thierro's foremen were already herding the workers back inside or scurrying up the scaffolding like apes. Not a moment, or a grinny, to lose. I watched Thierro as he oversaw it all. The faceless man had shaken him and he looked pale, but wore his discomfort stoically.

My mind was racing from possibility to possibility. Denying what was right in front of me. There had to be another explanation.

My gaze drifted to the silver-barrelled flarelocks carried by the yellow-hooded security men. Devlen Maille had been carrying one the night he murdered Levan Ost. Holy weapons, these men told me. Could Maille have been Bright Order? Could be, but I was grasping for leads. It didn't mean much even if he had been: there were thousands of them in the city, pilgrims from all across the city-states. The exploded hero, Bastian, had willingly given his life for the Grandspire. His belief had been ferocious, and I didn't think he had the wit to deceive me, whereas Devlen Maille hadn't seemed the type to believe in justice and a new world order. He'd struck me as a piece of shit who'd worked for himself and nobody else. It's why I'd shot him the first time.

I tried to imagine Thierro ordering his men to take out Levan Ost. Tried to imagine him consorting with Darlings, exerting pressure on Marollo Nacomo to destroy the very spire he was building. It didn't add up. Thierro was a real believer – nobody invested so much without a degree of fanaticism, and his loyalties were laid at the Bright Lady's feet. Nacomo had been sent to locate a navigator, to consort with traitors, then to hide Shavada's Eye. And then, after his escape, someone had cut the skin from his rotting face. Sure as the hells he hadn't done it to himself. What had he said? *I didn't want to wear that face anymore ... when I failed him, ... then he took it back.*

The inescapable conclusion clanged hollow bell-tolls inside my skull. My mind insisted that I was wrong, that it couldn't be him. But I knew what kind of bargain Nacomo had struck.

And I knew how Devlen Maille had come back from the dead.

The acceptance hammered home with a surge of fear strong enough that a bit of piss came out.

I got hold of myself. Shook my head to clear the fear and push those dark feelings to some recess.

'You all right, boss?' Tnota asked.

'I don't know,' I said. I left him there, hurried away into

the city. Nacomo was no use to me. I had to find a corpse.

The paupers' cemetery lay on the edge of the city, even their bodies were shunned for their lack of finances. I rode there on Falcon, a good horse for getting somewhere in a hurry. He was a natural biter with hooves the size of dinner plates, and people got out of his way fast. A foul taste simmered in my mouth all the way. It had been there ever since my dip in the canal. The edges of my fingernails had retained a bruised, purplish cast too. The black water had not done me any good.

The cemetery warden admitted me through the iron railing fence without argument. What did it matter to her whether someone looked at bodies so unvalued that they ended up in communal pits? She took me down into a cold, underground chamber, a good old-fashioned oil lamp lighting the way. The smog was heavy inside; it had flowed down through the ventilation grills, as if the cold, dark house of the dead wasn't grim enough without it. It didn't bother me. The dead were nothing to me.

The warden checked her ledger, then led me along rows of arched alcoves. The morgue had probably been a cellar before it housed the dead – Valengrad was always in need of new cemeteries. The bodies of the unburied lay on rickety old tables, some dressed in the clothes they'd died in, others washed and dressed in whatever their family could afford to give over to the dirt. They'd stay there until someone paid for a plot or until they decomposed enough that they could be tipped down the drain. The warden stopped at an alcove where six bodies were piled on a table that threatened to collapse beneath their weight.

'What exactly do you want with him?' she asked.

'Got to check that he's actually dead, for one,' I said. She snorted.

'They're all dead down here.'

'You'd hope so.'

'Well, you can stay down here as long as you want. Not like it's going to bother these folks none. But don't do anything unsavoury, neh? The boss comes by sometimes and he might stop down here. So. Nothing weird.'

'Sure. Nothing weird.'

The six corpses were stacked in a pyramid. It had been almost two weeks since I killed Devlen Maille for the second time and these cadavers smelled appropriately vile, death transforming them to unpleasant colours. Their skin was slippery and loose and detached from the muscles beneath as I shoved the bodies around, pushing them onto the floor to get to Maille at the bottom. Teeth dropped free from open mouths, clattering across the floor like dried peas. One of them released a great wet fart sound, but that wasn't abnormal with bodies this old. Even so, I was glad I'd not eaten anything.

My heart was pounding like a drum. This would prove it. I had to be sure.

Maille's body was in better shape than the others. For a two-week-old stiff, he looked a lot better than I'd expected. The lamplight was poor, and I couldn't tell whether his colouring was really as yellow as it seemed. What was left of him was a mess. His jacket was tattered and burned, pieces of the exploded phos tank still jutting from his flesh.

I had only recognised Devlen Maille because of the over-sized mole on his face. I had just met a man whose face had been cut away. Why would anyone cut a man's face off?

What if they wanted to stick it onto someone else?

I turned the cadaver's head, and there it was. The match was very good, the skin tones almost an exact pairing. But the meld was not quite perfect. A face can only stretch so far and, along the faintest of lines, the natural angling of his stubble changed. I'd been right, damn it. I *had* killed Devlen Maille. The man whose flarelock had detonated had just been wearing his face.

The bell clanged in my head a final time. Certainty.

'Saravor,' I said into the fogged darkness. I'd wanted to be wrong, but the last hope of doubt that I'd clung to shattered like glass.

There were plenty of reasons a man might want to change his face. Marollo Nacomo had changed his because he craved youth. The killer who'd worn Devlen Maille's face had been a professional, whoever he'd been. Maybe he'd wanted to wipe out his own past, erase his misdeeds from history with the slash of a scalpel. Maille had just been a cheap source of body parts, rotting away in a pauper's cemetery.

There was something to be said for being able to call upon experienced killers who couldn't be identified.

It all carried the mark of Saravor's work. He was back, and doing business in my city, only now he wasn't just fixing up those that came to him. He was using them to do his dirty work in some greater scheme. He'd changed Not-Devlen-Maille's face in exchange for a hit on Levan Ost, because he was consorting with Darlings and Ost was the loose end that could link them all together. And after Maldon had sensed that Nacomo had been storing Shavada's Eye in his basement, that meant that Saravor had it.

Deep Kings aside, it could not have fallen into worse hands.

I left the bodies where they lay on the floor and went up the stairs fast. I felt bad about that, but it was going to be a messy job getting them back on the table.

Saravor terrified me. He'd always scared me, even back when I'd paid for his services. Admitting that wasn't a sign of weakness, any more than it's weak to be afraid of a tidal wave. He was powerful, he was sadistic, and he was brilliant. When he'd fought Maldon, their magic bouncing around inside my skull, I'd done the unthinkable: I'd let him take the sliver of Shavada's power from Maldon. Just the tiniest thread of essence from a Deep King, but I'd given it to him and his grey children all the same.

A lot of power in that thread.

My hands were shaking as I led Falcon from the cemetery. I needed to think, and that meant that I needed to drink. I hit a bar and slugged brandy and growled until the bar was done and spilled us all out onto the street. It was the middle of the night, and the smog hadn't lifted so I walked Falcon back through banks of heavy grey cloud until I reached a crossroads.

If I turned left down the street I'd take a couple of turns and be at my own house. A full house, these days. A big one. I hadn't been there in two weeks. I employed a house-keeper, and she basically lived as though she were a wealthy, unloved mistress. Turning right took me back to the office. It was past eleven, which was early to finish drinking, but late enough given the time I'd started. My earlier fug had started to clear and I felt tired. The big bed in the house would be cold, empty, and I doubted the housekeeper kept a bedpan warming it. The office would be warm. The decision wasn't difficult.

I made my way up the stairs with all the stealth that a drunk, three-hundred-pound man can manage. I didn't fancy the smell of the whale-oil lamps so I lit candles instead, a warmer kind of glow. Maldon had already left a list on my desk. He hadn't wasted any time making his demands: copper wiring, canisters, wood, brass pipes. Sets of workman's tools, a pair of the crystal-lensed goggles that Talents wore, the components of a small forge, and a dozen rifled barrels. None of it was especially hard to come by, but rifled barrels were damn expensive, and I wasn't thrilled at the idea of Maldon's building a forge underneath my office, not with the amount of wine he was getting through. I sighed and rubbed my aching, dry eyes. If I hadn't known better, I'd have thought he was trying to put together a new light loom or something similar, but when Shavada had been forced into his mind, his light-spinning abilities had been taken. We didn't know why. The drudge couldn't spin light any more than our sorcerers could use mind-worms. Perhaps an affinity to light cannot coexist with that much darkness. Who knew? Maldon was the only Spinner ever to have been forced into that situation.

My crazed not-a-child's shopping list was not exactly ideal. I'd get him what he wanted, if it kept him out of trouble, but decided he'd have to set it up at my house. That showed where my priorities lay, because I wasn't going to risk the office. I wrote a note to my accountant instructing him to release funds to reputable craftsmen for the required amounts. At least if Maldon had something to work on, it might keep him from trying to kill himself.

I knew about two of Maldon's failed attempts. I didn't know how many he'd made. Once, he'd hanged himself from the cellar's rafters, but the fall hadn't been long enough to snap his neck and he'd discovered that he didn't really need to breathe. He'd been livid with frustration and boredom by the time I cut him down. The second time he'd slashed his wrists and bled all over my bathroom, but I was confident that he knew he would survive that one, no matter how much blood had stained my towels. It wasn't much of a life, a never-ending childhood, eyeless and deformed, stripped of the vast powers he had once commanded. Letting him have a project was the least I could do.

I yawned. Not as young as I once was, and a day of pounding up stairs and hard drinking will sap anyone's grit. I clattered myself out of my armour, making an awful racket.

'I didn't expect you back tonight,' Valiya said from the doorway. 'Care to make any more noise?'

'Couldn't sleep,' I said. I was still half-abuzz with the drink, and now keenly aware of the dried sweat that coated me, the less-than-delicate bouquet that probably now filled the room. 'What are you doing here?'

'Working,' she said, then relented. 'Amaira wanted to

sleep in the kitchen again. She's lonely here. I read to her.'

'She has a room at my house,' I said. 'She just doesn't use it, for some reason.'

'And you don't see why she chooses to be here, instead of a cold and empty house?'

I ignored the question.

'She's too young to be running around here all night. I should send her somewhere that provides a future.'

Valiya gave me an admonishing look. No matter how high you are in life, a woman can always give you that same disapproving look and make you want to improve. It is in such looks that life is given meaning.

'You'll do nothing of the sort, Ryhalt Galharrow. I am very fond of that girl, and I will be furious with you if you dismiss her. Especially if you do it when you're all the way drunk. When did you last sleep?' she asked. 'Your eyes are redder than Rioque.'

'My eyes can rest when I'm dead,' I said. The drink was making me surly.

'That all sounds very tough, but you're no use to anyone if you collapse from exhaustion.'

It was even more annoying when people came along with facts, especially when you didn't want them to be true.

'I'm sorry,' I said. 'I shouldn't be curt. Strange day.'

'Have you eaten anything?' Valiya asked.

I felt momentarily embarrassed, but drunkenness is stronger than shame.

'It's pretty late for us to go out for dinner,' I said.

I realised Valiya looked tired too, hollow shadows beneath her eyes. But there was a light blush to her cheeks that I hadn't expected. She hid it behind a fall of auburn hair that fell across her face.

'I'm not inviting you for dinner, you arsehole,' she said primly. 'You need food. And sleep. You're no use when you're dead on your feet. Come on.'

I didn't get up. She was right. I was so damn tired. Everything felt distant, as though I were viewing it through a spy tube that made everything small and dim. She reached out a hand and helped pull me up out of my chair.

'Go and wait in the mess hall,' she said. I did as she bid.

Time passes strangely when you don't sleep. Minutes slip away without being noticed, suddenly an hour might be gone and you're standing in the same place, staring into nothingness. At those times I wonder if I was sleeping or if I'd simply lost my capacity for thought. Where do you go when that happens? We accept that when we sleep we retreat from the world, but what happens when we're neither? I could have been sitting in the dining-room chair for a few minutes or it could have been an hour. I had no way to judge.

Valiya appeared. She brought a tray loaded with the kind of comfort food you make for a dying relative. And tea, awful green tea. I didn't complain about any of it. It wasn't Valiya's job to feed me. Shouldn't have been, anyway.

I ate and I talked. I told her about Devlen Maille and Marollo Nacomo, and about Saravor. I told her things that I'd never told anybody before, about confronting a Darling before the doorway to the heart of Nall's Engine, about the hold that Saravor had had on me, and how I'd bought him off.

'Saravor is the one that fixed Major Nenn, when she was wounded at Station Twelve, isn't he?' Valiya asked gently. I nodded. 'She's not in any danger from him. If he's fixing men in exchange for their service – or making deals with him – then he has no hold over her.'

I hoped that was true. I buried the fear for now. I'd been afraid enough for one day.

'I know,' I said. 'But there's more. Maldon said Shavada's Eye had passed through Nacomo's house. That means that Saravor is the one who took it. It makes sense. He's more powerful than any regular sorcerer, because I gave him that power. And he's used it to take possession of another part of Shavada.'

Valiya ran her fingers over the flowers tattooed along her forearms. Thoughtful.

'What can he do with it? Barter it back to the Darlings in the Misery?'

'No, I don't think so,' I said. 'Saravor was always mad for power. It's the only thing he truly wanted. If he has it, then the question is, what does he plan to do with it?'

11

After the Siege of Valengrad, there had been a rumour that Saravor was dead. It had seemed reasonable. He'd undergone a terrible battle with Maldon, the Darling as he then was, before vanishing with a sliver of Shavada's power. Mortal creatures aren't supposed to hold that kind of magic. When Shavada was destroyed, I'd hoped his magic would die with him. I'd tried to take steps to ensure Saravor could never use it, but he'd slipped away before I could get to him.

I'd hoped that he had died during the Siege. Failing that, that he'd fled, never to return. Both hopes now seemed to be worth about as much as a paper helmet.

I felt a powerful urge to check on Nenn. Her boys were all on post-Misery rest, which they always got after a long spell on the sand, so I rode across to her place, tied Falcon up in the rose garden and rang the bell. Nenn answered it herself wearing a towel, her nose, and nothing else. An early-rising neighbour appeared to be scoffing at the outrageous lack of decorum, but in truth he was probably taking in her largely unconcealed and well-muscled legs.

'Get a good look, you perverted old fart!' she called. She held the door open for me, then flashed him her arse. She was laughing as we adjourned to the parlour.

'You're in a good mood,' I said.

'It's a good day,' she said. She stretched, raising the rim of the towel well past decency. Nenn had given very few fucks for propriety before her elevation in status. Now she had abandoned any pretence at giving any, but this was a particularly blatant display, even for her. 'You want some breakfast? I've a bottle of twelve-year-old whisky around here somewhere.'

It was tempting, but not what was on my mind. I was about to say something when I heard a noise from an adjacent room.

'Servants?' I asked. Tense.

'Probably some around here somewhere. But that's just Betch getting cleaned up. Poor guy's scratched to shit.' She looked at her nails and grinned. She was not a gentle lover, and she revelled in the power that Betch's desire for her gave her. Nenn hadn't always had it easy. Now she'd found a man who made her feel beautiful. An important thing, that. In typical Nenn style, she wanted to show it off to the world. Or show the rest of the world what it was missing out on, anyway.

'There's food too,' she said.

'No. I need your help with something. But first, how's your stomach these days?'

Nenn frowned at me.

'I haven't eaten anything bad, if that's what you mean.'

'No. Your gut. The one I paid Saravor top marks for. How is it?'

She shrugged.

'It never felt totally right. Not like what I had there before. And I never stop wanting to eat chillies, though I have to when Betch is around or I get the juice on my fingers, and then it gets, well, you know.'

I really didn't want to know.

'It's not still hurting? Hasn't made you feel like, I don't know, going shooting people? Nothing like that?'

'I always want to shoot people,' Nenn said. She uncorked

the bottle of what I guessed was the twelve-year-old whisky, poured herself a dash of amber.

'Fuck it,' I said. 'Just one. But then we have work to do. I have this feeling that Saravor might be back in town, and if he is, it's time that he left again. In a casket. Preferably in pieces.'

Nenn gave me one of her old, slice-'em-open grins. She knew I only asked her to help out with the kind of work she enjoyed.

'Fine. But I need ten minutes.'

'I'll wait here.'

She shrugged.

'Suit yourself. But I bet you end up waiting outside.'

She slipped back into the bedroom, and after the first few energetic noises I did indeed prefer to wait outside.

We rode into the Spills at the head of two dozen men. I can't deny it felt good.

By day the Spills looked worse than it did at night. Darkness is an amicable companion to ugliness, and the Spills was as ugly as the city got. Public services still weren't what they'd been, and they'd not been up to much in the Spills to begin with. Garbage and sewage coexisted peacefully in potholes and gutters, the rats were trying to outgrow the dogs, and there were people everywhere. New arrivals, looking for work and finding it, and a lot of yellow-hoods about. Everyone scattered away from the snarls of black-uniformed soldiers.

The Grandspire cast a long shadow across the Spills. High above, through open windows and unfinished walls I could make out tiny figures at work, laying bricks, planks, or bearing loads of steel cabling or delicate glass tubes for lighting. Nacomo had been a temporary bump in the production and nothing more.

We turned a corner, and there it was. It was four years

since I'd been back here. Hadn't had a reason to, and I didn't know what I expected to find here now. Nothing, probably.

I had tried to kill Saravor, following the Siege. The only time in my life that I've tried to murder a man. Saravor deserved it, nobody would argue against it, but I wasn't a murderer. I'd sent men – twenty grenadiers, big men with nasty grins – with orders to shoot first and keep shooting until there was nothing left of him. The sliver of Shavada's power he'd taken was a bite too much for any man to possess. But my killers had found nothing but an empty house. Saravor had not stuck it out in Valengrad when the Siege came.

Now, we were back with twenty of Nenn's Ducks, and I'd even managed to borrow two Battle Spinners from Marshal Davandein. The Ducks – a name that Nenn had given her men in mockery of Davandein's Drakes, who thought themselves a cut above – were about as hard-nosed as they came while the Spinners seemed young and arrogant. I didn't like them.

The big old town house was much the same as ever. The shutters hung loose on their hinges and the whole place sagged inwards like some kind of dark, withered old grandmother, slumped and defeated in a chair. We reined in outside.

'You notice anything strange about this street?' I asked.

'There's less shit in the road than I'd expect in the Spills,' Nenn said. She was eyeing the big old house with some trepidation. Maybe I'd been wrong to bring her. This place couldn't harbour many pleasant memories.

'Yes. It's too quiet.'

I tried the door. Gave it a few solid thumps. Waited. I half expected one of those grey-skinned children to open it, but my knocking went unanswered.

'You really think he came back?' Nenn asked.

'It all fits,' I said, and gave the door another good thump. Nothing. 'Break it down,' I said.

One of the grenadiers took an axe to the door and it fell into planks without much effort. The soldiers flowed in quickly, pistols cocked and smoking. Nenn and I came last.

The house had a grim, deserted feel to it. Mould had blackened the walls, puddles had gathered in the corners and a quick tour of the place showed that the old shelves, once filled with jars of fingers, noses, feet and eyeballs in preserving fluids, were gone. It even smelled empty. The Eye had not been brought here.

'I nearly died in this room,' Nenn said. It was a small, cramped little box room, much like many of the others. The bed she'd lain in was gone, and the air was chill.

'There were a bunch of rooms you nearly died in,' I said.

'Do you ever regret dealing with him?'

'Stupid question,' I said. 'Not for a moment.'

'Do you think they can ever be good people? Fixers, I mean.'

'I don't know. Are there even any others like Saravor?'

Nenn shivered, and I don't think it was the cool air that caused it.

'I wonder, sometimes. Wonder whose guts I have inside me. He pulled the damaged ones out, the ones the drudge blade cut. Put in new ones, then sealed me up like he was patching a coat. You know what the worst thing was?'

'It all sounds pretty bad.'

'I was awake the whole time,' she said. 'I could feel it all. He immobilised me, but I felt the cuts. Felt him slicing pieces of me out.'

'You're alive. That's what matters.'

'I guess.'

The grenadiers finished their sweep.

'Nothing, Major Nenn,' the sergeant reported. 'Nobody's been here for a while. Maybe years.' She dismissed her Ducks, let them fall out.

The place gave me the shivers. We left through the

remains of the front door, mounted up and rode to the nearest place that would serve us a stiff drink. It was an open-fronted shop calling itself a wine seller, which took some nerve given the watered-down crap they were serving. Still. A drink's a drink.

'Waste of a morning,' Nenn said. She stretched her bare arms and clicked her neck. 'Plenty I could have been getting done instead. The citadel want me to take on some lads from the south country, green as grass and not even as tall.'

'Good Fixers,' I said, harking back to our earlier conversation. 'Why did you ask that?' Nenn hesitated, her eyes turning to a smoulder all of a sudden. She turned them on a couple of Spills locals who'd stopped to gawk at the two well-dressed folks sitting in this shit heap. We were probably scaring away other customers, but besides a table of Bright Order, the place hadn't exactly been heaving when we arrived.

'I think about it sometimes, all right?'

'About what?'

'What do you fucking think?' she snapped. 'People call me "Noseless," Ryhalt. You think I like that? You think that's what I want?'

'You don't give a shit what anyone else thinks,' I said. 'And your man Betch likes you well enough.'

'Well. Maybe. Sometimes I wonder if it's me he likes, or if I'm a way for him to climb the ladder. I appreciate the fucking, don't get me wrong, but it seems strange that he'd choose me, missing half a face. Lots of prettier girls out there. Not hard to be prettier if you've got a nose.'

'He doesn't care. Likes you fine as you are.'

'Nobody likes me as I am,' Nenn snapped, voice cracking like a whip. 'Not even me. I look at scarred men and it doesn't get me tingly. It makes me turn away. I hide it under this wooden thing, but whenever I'm with Betch, the fear is there. The fear that really, he's repulsed. That he doesn't want to have to look at me.'

'Sounds to me like you're fighting your own demons, not his,' I said. I thought of Ezabeth, scarred and burned, and how it hadn't mattered a shit to me. I could have said as much to Nenn, but Ezabeth had kept her true face from the world and only revealed it to me. It would have been a betrayal to speak of it, even if she was dead and gone. Even if it would help Nenn. 'Love's not an easy thing to bear. Makes us doubt ourselves in ways that don't make sense. Don't fuck things up for yourself because you're afraid to be happy.'

'I'm not happy,' she said. 'I have a horrible fucking hole in my face.' She shook her head, annoyed at herself. 'So yeah. Sometimes I think maybe I should find a decent Fixer, get him to stick some poor dead girl's nose on my face.'

There wasn't much that I could say to that. I never was very good at comforting people. I signalled for another bottle of wine instead. That was about the best that I could manage.

'How are you holding up, Ryhalt?' Nenn asked. Shifting focus to me. 'All these Bright Order people coming into the city. It can't be easy on you.'

'No,' I said. 'I guess it isn't.'

'Still dreaming of Ezabeth?'

'If I sleep,' I said. 'The worst part, though? I want to believe the Bright Order. I want to believe she's going to appear in a flash of light and thunder. Governor Thierro believes it. Sometimes, I wonder if he's right. And then I remember that she funnelled an Engine's worth of phos through her body and wrote herself out of existence. She's gone.'

'I know,' Nenn said. 'But you're not.'

'Not yet.'

12

Day slipped to dusk, dusk turned to night.

A beautiful song rose over the city. It began at the far edges of hearing and grew, drawing closer. Louder and louder, high and nasal, rising and falling with wordless melody until it demanded all attention. It ended abruptly, with an explosion louder than any cannon that I'd ever heard fired.

I fell from the chair I'd been dozing in, landing in a flurry of reports and spilled ink as I knocked the bottle from the desk.

'Shitting fuck!' I exploded, half because I'd been woken by an immense boom and half because I was covered in ink.

As my brain reengaged, for one terrible moment I thought someone had activated the Engine. I panted in my ink puddle, listening for the new apocalypse, but nothing followed the detonation save the frightened barking of a hundred dogs. The last lamp had burned down. I must have drifted off, but that ephemeral song had cut into my dreams, if it had been real at all. I went to the window, rubbing at the stiffness in my neck and shoulders. Sleep must have crept up on me, and I felt worse for it.

The night was deep as Eala sat fat and golden over the city. Valengrad never truly went dark, but a mile distant, over rooftops and chimney stacks, I saw a trail of strange light, green and purple and yellow, rising alongside smoke and the red glow of flame. Over in Mews, a civilian district.

People had died.

The city was awake now, babies, children, dogs, a chorus of voices joining a discordant orchestra of fear and panic. The door flew open and Amaira burst in, wide-eyed and red-faced from running up the stairs. It was touching that she'd looked for me before the doorman.

'What the fuckin' hell was that, Captain-Sir?' she shouted.

'Language,' I snapped, taking out my anxiety on her. Were we under attack? The noise, the lights, neither boded well. My head began to take up a slow throb as my body remembered how I'd driven it over the last week, protesting at the interruption of its much-needed rest.

'Was it the drudge?' Amaira asked. I put an arm over her shoulders, which felt strange to do because I don't do hugging, but she was trembling and scared and that's what you do with kids when they're afraid. Her fear drove me to nonchalance.

'I don't know what it was. Maybe just an accident. Not the drudge.'

She looked at me with big, terrified eyes. It had only been four years since the drudge shattered the wall and orphaned her. I gave her a smile and that unfamiliar expression seemed to help somehow. We looked out at the swirls of bright colour that spiralled up into the sky. 'I should probably go find out what's happened,' I said. Amaira didn't need instructing – she went and found my sword belt, glad to be useful. I put on my long black uniform coat and belted it over the top.

'You know what I did with my boots?' I asked.

'Took 'em down to be polished,' she said.

'When did you do that?'

'After you fell asleep.'

I almost said she should have been sleeping too, but coming from me I doubted it would carry much weight, and besides, she'd been doing me a favour. Never mind how she knew I was still at the office or how she knew when I'd fallen asleep. Fight the battles you can win, run from the ones you can't. Best lesson I ever learned.

I found cold coffee in a pan in the kitchen and forced it down, as though it might help with the throbbing that was growing behind my eyes. My doorman looked shaken. He'd placed a broadsword on the counter, as if expecting an attack at any moment and eyed the longsword that I was carrying in addition to my standard-issue cutlass. I didn't expect to find action out there, but it never hurts to go prepared.

I called at my own house to pick up my pretend son. My housekeeper seemed glad to see me, even more glad that I was taking Maldon out of the house.

'There's a demon in that boy,' she told me. 'He's too clever by half and too nasty by far.'

'You'll not hear me disagree,' I said, and she didn't know the half of it. Technically, the demon had been removed, but he was doing a good job of being just as unpleasant. I asked her to wake him, and loitered in the hallway.

The house was more than I'd ever expected to possess again. Carpets, a broad staircase, enough rooms to house a small battalion. In the dining room there was a table that could have seated sixteen, but I'd never used it. In the hall-way, a ceremonial suit of parade armour stood on a stand, where it had been since I was given it as a thank-you for the part I'd played during the Siege. It would have been ideal for the battlefield two hundred years ago, but like all things of beauty, its time had passed. There was a lesson there, I suppose. One drunken evening Tnota and I had taken it out into the courtyard and shot pistols at it, but despite its lavish ornamentation, the smith who'd made it had taken pride in his work. The engraving was elaborate, but the steel was the best in the states and our shots had pinged off it. There was a lesson there, as well.

Maldon was not in the room that I had allocated for him, and the housekeeper found him sleeping down in the cellar, in the clutter of what was going to be his workshop. He wasn't happy to be woken, and of all the people in Valengrad, he'd managed to sleep through the strange song that even now was calling in my ears. He had a sour-vomit smell about him and a smear of some kind of oil across his brow. I began to wonder whether allowing him to work on his potentially dangerous project whilst keeping up his drinking had been the best of ideas, but then, I'd always combined alcohol and fighting and I was still around.

'I was having a lovely dream,' Maldon said, evidently wishing he was still having it. 'Remember those girls we met over Enhaust's shop?'

'Not now,' I said. My housekeeper looked very disapproving.

We rode double across to Mews. Falcon was a belligerent animal, but he wasn't spooked by the people who had ambled out to make a lot of noise in the street in their nightclothes and overcoats, muttering fearfully about the song. It seemed of more interest to most of them than the following explosion and more than one was trying to replicate it.

The damage site was busy with people and fire and a number of buildings in a row of tenement houses had been demolished. I'd seen buildings hit by heavy ordnance before, the cannon balls chewing holes in the walls, but that was nothing compared to this. The buildings were not just damaged; they were gone. Reduced to piles of rubble and broken timber, debris spread liberally across the road. Even the windows of the houses opposite had been blown in and the guts of an adjoining building were laid bare, displaying the former occupant's bad taste in armoires and decor. The rubble seemed to glitter slightly, twinkling as if the stars had descended to take residence amidst the destruction.

Somewhere, a woman was wailing her grief.

Anybody who had been in the levelled houses would have been killed instantly. A fine dust permeated the air and fire had spread to the surrounding buildings. Teams of aldermen, soldiers and locals battled the flames, forming bucket chains that ran down the street to the water pumps. They worked efficiently: the fires were small and would be brought under control quickly, so I rode past them to get a better look at what had happened.

'What a bleeding mess,' Maldon said. For once, his usual coldness had thawed.

Now that we were up close, I could see no sign of the swirls of colour that had been visible at a distance and began to wonder if it had been some kind of colossal accident. If I hadn't heard that singing sound, I'd have guessed that a store of blasting powder had gone up, destroying four homes in the blast. The bodies of their residents were still buried beneath the rubble. It would have taken a lot of powder to cause that kind of damage, though, and this was a residential street not a military store. But stranger things had happened. Maldon was sniffing the air like a hound.

'Something familiar about the smell,' he said.

'I don't smell any explosives,' I said. Blasting powder has its own special flavour, a scent I've always enjoyed, partly because the drudge don't use powder weapons. Their technology is a way behind ours. But it wasn't present here. Maldon was picking up something else. I'd brought him because I needed his unique understanding of things dark and unexplained.

'It wasn't a powder weapon,' he said. 'Sorcery did this.'

'A Spinner?'

'No. Even a well-trained Battle Spinner couldn't do this – certainly not easily.'

I felt the pressure behind my eyes intensify, tried to squint it away.

131

'Ezabeth could have done it,' I said. Maldon snorted.

'I suppose. But she was rarer than wings on a pig. At my strongest, with ten canisters, I'd have struggled to do this.'

I tried to smell whatever he was getting, but all I could get was stone, and night, and grief.

'These were just civilian homes,' I said. 'Nothing special or important. I don't know who lived here, but a glance up and down the street tells me that all of them together were poorer than this was worth. One thing's for sure, doing this didn't come cheap, whether it was done with powder, phos or some other power.'

We stood and watched the scurrying firefighters. They went about their work efficiently. Some were weeping for neighbours as they passed buckets down the line, or maybe their tears were despair at the pointlessness. I saw black-uniformed citadel soldiers, the troops of private units in mismatched livery and yellow-hooded Bright Order militia all working side by side. Valengrad knew how to pull together in a crisis, at least when it meant stopping houses from going up in flame.

I dismounted and crossed to the rubble, coughing in the dust-laden air. It sparkled, glittering like a sequined party gown and though someone shouted that I should keep away from it, I didn't sense any danger from a pile of broken house. The light caught on a small fragment of something, winking at me in the dark. I knelt and picked it out, turned it over. It was hot to the touch, not hot enough to burn but warm enough that I didn't want to hold it for long. A piece of dull, cloudy rock crystal with a vaguely yellow hue. I looked for the light to catch on something else within the debris of roof tiles, shattered beams and broken bricks. Sure enough, I quickly picked out another chunk of crystal, jagged and as long as my finger.

'What the fuck are these?' I grumbled aloud. Maldon had joined me and I passed him one.

'Looks like common rock crystal to me,' he said. He held it up in front of his face, as if he could see through his scarf to examine it. A reflex, or something else? It was definitely rock crystal. Had to wonder what the hell it was doing here, in among the rubble. The blast site was littered with it. It wasn't worth much, the kind of thing kids find entertaining. Certainly nothing explosive about it.

The crystal confirmed Maldon's conclusion. This was not some powder-store accident. Somebody bore the responsibility for what had happened here today. Someone had to pay for it.

I lingered at the site as the fires were put out and grim-faced labourers began digging. Some of the beams were heavy and had to be dragged clear by horses, but most had been splintered to the point that a few workmen could heave them aside. The first body they found was a boy in his teenage years. The blanket he'd died under was black and red. He was unrecognisable, his skull flattened, and though a nearby grandmother wailed and tore at her hair, there was some kind of mercy in that. He wasn't recognisable as a person and at least it had been quick. I forced myself to watch as the workmen placed the bloody blanket back over him.

They didn't understand, nobody did. Valiya got it, the need to observe, to fuel the anger that stokes the need to fight. I watched, and I saw the dreadful grief on that grandmother's face. I made myself listen to it. Fuck sleeping. Fuck people's fearful stares, fuck the lack of respect from the squawks and the cream. This was what we fought: this cruel and indiscriminate waste of life. How the hell could I sleep when there was this much darkness in the world? Ezabeth had fought it. She'd stood against it, shown the way. But she was gone, destroyed, nothing of her left but a whisper in the light. It fell to me, now. I didn't trust anyone else enough to pass on the responsibility.

Three hours after that first blast, a second song rose over the city.

I heard it sooner this time. Faint at first, but growing rapidly in strength. I looked up to see the source of the unearthly song, somewhere above and away, out across the Misery. There was a raw, alien beauty to it, and this time I detected more than one voice amidst the soar and the lull before I saw it in the sky. It began as a faint, distant light. Those same pastel hues, purple and green and yellow, shimmered together in a sphere of light, tiny as a star at first but growing larger. It shot past the cracks in the sky, seeming to gain speed as it did. And then the descent. No longer a phenomenon of the sky, it arched down, down, down toward the city. For one terrible moment I thought, *this is for me, this one comes for me*, but then it slammed down somewhere else. The thunder came, a roar of detonation as it met the ground, and sparks and coloured lights leaped up into the sky.

'Spirit of fucking mercy,' I said. Maldon had his hands over his ears to block out the echo of that song as it passed through the streets.

'Agh! My head!' Maldon exclaimed. 'My fucking ears! That sound, it burns.'

He staggered and went down to his knees. I placed a hand on his shoulder but he shrugged it off. Whatever mess Shavada had made of his body and brain, he was overly sensitive to magic. Whatever we'd just seen, it was fucking magic all right, and it was being thrown clear across the damn Misery.

A terrible chill ran through me. I had to grit my teeth against the sudden swell of uncertainty and fear that rose within me. No lone sorcerer had that kind of power. But a Deep King might. The possibility did not bear thinking about.

The great red letters on the citadel's walls flared bright

in the night. COURAGE disappeared, and instead they read: COMMAND COUNCIL SUMMONS. I hadn't seen those words displayed so brazenly since Shavada had laid siege to the walls, and I remembered how poorly that had turned out for the council.

But then the song came again. And again. And before the night was over, there was panic in the streets.

The morning's death toll was 178 souls. The drudge's missiles killed indiscriminately. A granary suffered a direct hit, the flour inside igniting and magnifying the power of the blast fivefold, reducing Tenth Street to rubble. Homes, shops, animal pens, the blazing missiles came down in and around the city seemingly at random. The terror struck home like a knife.

The drudge sent twenty-seven missiles in all, each preceded by that voiceless song. Sixteen either fell short or soared past the city altogether, exploding out in the recently ploughed fields or churning up great clouds of stinking Misery dust. But eleven hit, and each one of them caused chaos. Soldiers tried to keep order, but there was nothing they could do to protect anyone from those descending orbs of death.

A single orb arced down toward the citadel. Before it could come down upon the projectors of Nall's Engine, the light-sphere detonated in midair as if it had slammed up against a wall of hard air. Most of the Engine was below-ground but Nall had also left his device some protection. I watched the fires from a balcony on the fourth floor of the citadel, wondering if the whole building was protected, or just the Engine itself.

'Monstrous,' Nenn said, looking out at a dozen blazes across the city. It took a lot to throw her off her stride. 'It's barbaric,' she said through her teeth. 'This isn't war. It shouldn't be war.'

'It's not as though the Deep Kings spared a thought for civilians during the Siege,' I said. 'They're not going to now. They've been quiet for four years, but we knew that it wouldn't last. They'll never be satisfied until they've destroyed us all. Our respite is over.'

I thought of Crowfoot and his Heart of the Void, and what he'd done to the people of Clear, Adrogorsk and all the towns and villages that lay around them. What he'd done to the world, even to the sky.

'There's no defence against this,' Nenn said. 'What can we do?'

It was a good question.

'We'll persevere,' Betch said. The handsome captain put a consoling arm around Nenn's shoulders, but she shrugged it away. She didn't want comfort. She was too raw, too angry, and when you get the kill inside you, comfort's like vinegar to a wound. She leaned against the railing and smoked, glowering at the sky. It was quiet now, and a red dawn was making her way across the Misery's distant horizon. The cracks in the sky had been quiet all night, as they listened to this new symphony of terror.

'Lot of questions need answering,' I said. But, in my heart, I knew that whatever this was, it was out of my hands. This was for the citadel to deal with, not Blackwing.

'The marshal will devise a plan,' Betch said.

'Maybe. For now, we're lucky to have survived it. Not everyone can say that.'

One hundred and seventy-eight people. Wasted lives, wasted ambitions, wasted dreams. The poor bastards probably never even knew it was coming. The orbs came down with a little warning, but nobody could say where they would fall until it was too late.

Davandein worked with her commanders all night, but finally saw me as the sky turned from blush to blue. At least, as blue as it ever gets by the Misery. She looked none the worse for having been up all night dealing with an attack that we'd never seen coming. She wore a long, pleated skirt that fell to her heeled ankle boots, beneath a military coat with gold and silver skulls and cogs around the epaulets. Black opals glittered at her ears. High fashion and military pragmatism combined.

'Keep it brief, Commander,' she said. 'I don't have to tell you how much I have to do, and this isn't one of your monster hunts.'

'It isn't, but it might become one,' I said. She'd redecorated Venzer's old office in a sparse, elegant fashion, but when I looked at the beam from which he'd taken his last jump I could still almost see his crumpled old body hanging there. I looked away.

'How so?' Davandein asked.

'There are two things that spread the seeds of cultism among the population,' I said. 'The first is hope. The dream that there's something better, that the Deep Kings are actually beautiful gods. The second is fear. When they don't think that they can win, they'll side with the worst devils from the darkest hells if they think it will give them a chance. That's what this bombardment is designed to do.'

'It's doing a lot more damage than that,' Davandein said.

'The damage is negligible,' I said. 'Two hundred dead, maybe? And that's when we weren't prepared. Maybe they'll try this again, but if they do, we'll have precautions. If two hundred is the best they can manage, then they're trying to bring down an oak by sending a mouse to nibble at it.'

'Two hundred a night will fell us sure as a chisel will take down an oak, given enough time,' Davandein said curtly. She was a passionate woman at heart. She took the losses personally.

'They took us by surprise,' I said. 'It's bad. I understand that. But if they try this again tonight? We'll have your cabal of Battle Spinners up on the citadel, where they're protected, trying to bring the orbs down before they reach the city. We can warn people to hide in their basements.'

'If this wasn't just a test,' Davandein said. Her face was grim. 'This might just be the beginning. Tomorrow perhaps we face a hundred of these attacks. Perhaps we'll see a thousand. Maybe this was just them drawing range on us, have you considered that?'

'It's not my job to consider that, Marshal,' I said. 'It's my job to ensure that this doesn't stir people toward the Cult of the Deep. If people fear that you can't protect them, they'll turn to those that can, even if their promises are founded on sand. I put down one traitor today. Either we give the people hope, or before long it won't take a Bride to turn them.'

Davandein mulled it over.

'I need the people to hear the right message. I need all of the major news sheets on our side, putting out a good-news offensive.' She nodded to herself. 'Yes. We tell the people that our Spinners have stopped more than half of the orbs. Lift them with stories of children saved from the rubble by brave volunteers. Make them grateful. Show them that they need us.'

She was a strong woman, but proud, and the deaths had wounded her. That could be dangerous, but I had to admire her pragmatism.

'I'll see to it,' I said. 'Give me a citadel seal and I'll see to it that the news sheets are telling the stories that we want told.'

'A citadel seal? You want a licence to do whatever you want?'

Suddenly I didn't like her tone.

'Don't I have that already?' I said. She met my eyes and I didn't look away. Davandein knew what Blackwing really was, and my connection to Crowfoot, a secret entrusted to each Range Marshal when they took the office. She knew better than to suggest asking my master for help. It didn't work that way, and she knew it.

'Do it,' she said. She opened a drawer in Venzer's vast old desk and threw me a brass lump with the citadel's insignia on one side. 'But once the printers are singing our song, I want that back.'

'We need to know where those sky-fires are coming from, and how,' I said.

'Every squad I can muster is heading out into the Misery,' Davandein snapped. 'But it's like looking for a lost hair in a herd of sheep.'

'You have Gurling Stracht here?' I asked. Stracht was our best scout. He was seldom in the city, but I'd run into him in a bar not long ago. Davandein nodded. 'Tell him to go the crystal forest. Some of the fragments that came down looked like rock crystal. Not many places to find it in the Misery. It's a fixed point, but it's deep. It's where I'd look first.'

'I'll get it done, thank you, Galharrow,' Davandein said shortly. But she'd noted it, however little she wanted my help. She saw accepting assistance as showing weakness, even when it was a long shot like the crystal forest. But it was the best I had, and the only help she was being offered.

'Have you had any reply from the Lady of Waves?' I asked, changing the subject. The Lady was the only one of the Nameless to have a permanent residence, and so the only one we could try to contact when we needed help. I had to assume that Davandein had sent her a message.

'It was the usual response,' she said. 'Her priests say that she's currently dormant, whatever the hells that means. The prince of Pyre wouldn't attempt to rouse her from her slumber just for a couple of hundred dead citizens.' She shook her head. 'We're on our own, as usual.'

'Of course we are,' I said. 'We always are. Even when they're here.'

13

The day was cold, but the rain held off. It was the smallest of mercies for those digging bodies from the rubble.

Somehow I'd known that safety would come with the dawn. The night brought forth the terrors and the coming of the sun showed that our ordinary lives were still there, no different than they had been before. At least, not for those whose homes were still intact. Bread needed baking, drains needed unblocking, cutpurses cut purses and bankers counted other people's money.

The parasites emerged, traders and con men feeding on people's fears. I gave Casso and the jackdaws a clear directive: tolerate no sedition. Accept no arguments. I made a morning call around the four major print-works and checked over what they were planning to put out. I changed the headline 'TERROR FROM THE SKY' to 'DRUDGE SCORE FIFTY-TWO MISSES.' It wasn't true, but it was the news sheets so it didn't have to be. The editor complained when I told him to burn the first thousand copies he'd printed, the ink still wet, but when I explained the term 'seditious profiteer' in terms of the white cells and confiscation of assets, he found himself persuaded.

My investigation had stalled. Nobody had anything to talk about other than the death that had borne down on us from the sky, but I still had a Deep King's missing Eye to locate. Knowing who'd taken it hadn't made my task any easier and though Casso was out trying to catch any scent of Saravor, so far he'd found fewer leads than it takes to walk a dog.

By the time night fell again, a blood-pounding headache had set in. The headache was nothing unusual, but I must have let it show, which was.

'You look like you've been dragged through hells,' Valiya said. 'Can I get you something to help you sleep?'

'No potions, no tonics,' I said. I looked at the purpling around my fingernails, which had not faded as I'd hoped. Not good.

'How about something stronger?' Valiya put down a bottle of vodka and two glasses. 'They make this in my hometown and I don't expect many more bottles will come this way with the sky-fires falling. I thought you'd appreciate it.'

She sat opposite me, poured and drank. The vodka was smooth, mildly lemony, and we drank and talked through a number of dead-end leads on the Eye, discarding each in turn, and I realised partway through that I considered her an equal.

'You know, Ryhalt,' Valiya said after a while, 'this bombardment we're under makes you think, doesn't it?'

'Makes me not want to think, in some ways,' I said. 'Anything particular on your mind?'

'Some things.'

She hesitated then. Her resolve faltered, maybe, or she was gearing herself up to say something important. I was too blind to understand what it was.

She reached out and placed her hand over the back of mine.

Her hands weren't small by a woman's standards, but they were half the size of mine. Her skin was much paler and the tattoos that snaked across it were artful while the skulls grinning up from the back of my hand were faded and crude. Her hand was warm.

I hadn't been touched so deliberately by a woman since the day we burned the world. Not since Ezabeth and I lay together in the deep cold of the Engine's heart. I thought of her then, remembered her face. Not the pretty, seventeen-year-old face that had melted me. I saw her scarred, the skin tight and raw on one side of her face, crow's-feet around the other eye. She was the only thing that I'd ever really loved, besides the bottle. I found that my tongue had fallen immobile and my throat had clenched up tight.

'It will be dark soon,' she said.

'It will.'

'Do you think that the song will come again? The sky-fires? That's what people are calling them.'

'I don't know. I hope not,' I said, my mind still elsewhere. Had it been only one, or three, maybe even a handful then I would guess not – but they'd hurled twenty-seven, and struck with an alarming regularity, over and over, which spoke of method and process.

'Makes you think, doesn't it?' she said.

'About what?'

'How we could die, at any moment. Gone, in a heartbeat, in a flash. Puts things into perspective, don't you think?'

She looked up at me, and her eyes were bright, and alive, and nothing about them was burning or dead. I turned my hand over so that I could take her fingers in mine. Her hand felt like it fit there.

'None of us can get out of this life alive,' I said. It was lame. It was all I could think of to say.

'It makes me think about choices we make. How we choose to spend time. How we waste the time we have.'

I didn't say anything. I knew that I should, but I didn't. Four years had done nothing to wear away the pain I'd felt when Ezabeth died. Four years of knowing she was still out there, still entombed in the light. I'd failed her and let her destroy herself, and there was nothing I could do to save her. I'd tried to keep that door closed, tried to smother the memory with work, and drink. Tnota always told me to let go. But I couldn't let go.

I flinched away from her.

'You should go.'

A moment of silence, then Valiya rose and left. She looked back from the door as if she wanted to say something more, but I turned my back on her and after a moment the door closed. Maybe forever.

14

I feared the coming of the night.

'I want you to go down into the basement and stay there,' I told Amaira.

She looked cross. It is a foolish man that angers an adolescent girl. We are not made to withstand their fury.

'I don't like it down there. It smells funny, and it's cold.'

I could have suggested that she go and sleep at my unloved house, but I might at least pick a battle that I had a chance of winning.

'I'll get you some blankets,' I said. 'It's safer down there. I can't protect you from things that come out of the sky, but the building can.'

'What if the building falls down on me?' she asked.

'Then I'll dig you out.'

'Do you promise?' Amaira said.

It is a bad idea to promise things to children. Adults, having seen dozens of them shattered, understand that circumstances change and that a promise is, at best, confirmation of what you intend in the moment. A child remembers a promise through all seven hells and will hold you to it, strong as chains.

'I promise,' I said. 'I'll keep you safe. I promise.'

I believed it, too, as I took Amaira down into the cellars. She normally slept alone in the servants' quarters at the back of the offices, but while a direct impact from one of the sky-fires might well collapse the building into the cellars and kill everyone anyway, being down there was safer in the event of flying debris or a partial impact.

I'd got hold of a few things for her on a table. A plate of raisin biscuits and a jug of small beer, a phos lantern in case she was afraid in the night. A book with pictures of wild animals and exotic creatures from beyond the sea.

'Stay down here until morning, no matter what you hear,' I said. 'And if you hear the song, get underneath the table. Meara is at the front desk and she knows you're here. She'll come and get you if necessary.'

Amaira didn't say anything, and I left her there in the dimness. Don't make them promises, don't get attached to them either. They either die or grow up into people that you wish you'd not met in the first place.

'Captain-Sir,' she said. 'I'm scared.'

I hesitated for a moment. I almost turned back to her.

'Stay down here,' I said. Then I left her alone, with only a lamp for company.

There were only thirteen projectiles that night. Two went down in the Misery, three overshot and two detonated harmlessly against whatever shields protected the Engine, but enough of them caused damage. The Spinners that Davandein had placed on the citadel's roof tried a number of volleys, but the sky-fires were moving too fast and if they hit any of them, they didn't have any effect.

The morning death toll was somewhere between fifty and seventy. Not so bad as the first night, but still a lot of dead people. A lot of fear.

The tension was thicker than smog as I rode back through the city the following day. Businesses were closed and people stood out in the street, gazing upward as though they had to be sure that it was over. Doomsayers had appeared on street corners proclaiming that the final battle was upon us.

I would have them rounded up later, but I was too run-down even to make a note of their faces.

A single voice of positivity stood out among the pessimism and defeat. A middle-aged man in a bright lemon coat stood atop a crate, a pair of attractive young farmer's daughters standing beneath him with armfuls of pamphlets.

'My friends, do not fear the night,' he called out to the crowd who were gathering to hear him speak. He had a Whitelande accent, a city man. 'The dark of the past will be burned away. Yes, we have suffered this night, but what good was ever achieved without suffering? The Bright Lady is coming, reaching out to us, and when she appears she will defy the Deep Kings and send them back to the darkest of the hells, whence they came. Her faithful will know victory, and she will reward her followers. Who here has seen her?'

He looked out at the people expectantly. Nobody said anything. For one insane moment I thought about raising my hand. Someone else did.

'I've seen Her,' he said. 'She appeared to me from the light. A beautiful woman, young but powerful. Her hand was outstretched, reaching: for justice! She told me that Her Witnesses were coming.' Well rehearsed, clearly orated. He was a plant in the crowd, working his lines. They'd probably go district to district doing this show throughout the day.

'Praise be, a true vision!' the orator proclaimed. 'No sooner did these troubles begin than the Witnesses sought to come to the Range, to protect you all from the terrors of the broken sky. The broken sky spits thunder down upon us, but the Witnesses shall be your shield. The High Witness has sworn to protect you.'

'What are they going to do? Wall off the sky?' a less co-operative observer shouted back.

'The Witnesses command the power of the Bright Lady,' the speaker declared. He thrust a finger skywards as if that made his point. 'Not the weak, barely trained incompetents

146

employed by the citadel. Each of the Witnesses is blessed, chosen, powerful in their art. What do the princes do to protect you? To guard you? Do they offer you shelter in their fine marble halls? What good do your taxes serve now? Taxes that have burned your hands, wearied your legs, crooked your back?'

An interesting shift in tone, one that struck a chord with a number of the onlookers. I saw a lot of nodding.

'All right, that's enough of this crap,' I said finally, pushing through the crowd. People didn't like being bumped, but there wasn't much that they could do about it.

'And who might you be?'

'Captain Galharrow of Blackwing.' He hadn't recognised the uniform, but he understood what that meant. My reputation had travelled over the last few years. The orator straightened up, but he didn't cower.

'A pleasure to meet you, sir, a fine and noble ally in our struggle against the enemy.' He extended his hand to me. As he did so, the ground shifted ever so slightly beneath my feet and the low rumbling sound that announced another earth tremor began. People grabbed onto anything nearby for stability. I hunkered down low and waited for it to pass. It wasn't a big one, but the smashing of falling crockery sounded from nearby houses. The Bright Order preacher lost his balance and his attendants had to catch him.

'Now stay off that box and piss off,' I said when the earth's rumbling subsided. I raised my voice. 'Everyone needs to go back to work, not to have their heads filled with this Bright Lady nonsense. Go on, all of you, go do something productive. If you don't have anything better to do than stand around listening to promises spun on the wind, then I know some canals that need dredging.'

The small crowd had started dissipating as soon as they heard the word 'Blackwing' but now they scuttled faster.

'We're doing no harm here, Commander,' the city man

said unhappily. He shrugged up the collar of his lemony jacket. 'I'm giving the people hope. You should be applauding me.'

'Yeah, well, the only clapping I do is with irons. Get out of here before I decide I don't like the way you're looking at me.'

The attacks continued for another two nights. The war with the Deep Kings was usually fought out in the Misery, minor skirmishes between long-range patrols, a hundred miles from civilization. The Deep Kings hadn't managed to strike a blow against the Range since Shavada assaulted Valengrad directly. The theatre where we'd watched the absurd play lost its roof. The Grandspire took a hit, but its phos-welded core had deep foundations and of all the structures in Valengrad, it took the blast on the chin. A bar was blown to pieces, and a grocer's shop, and houses. Endless houses.

We didn't know how they were doing it. Didn't know which of the Deep Kings had dreamed this nightmare up to torment us with. Didn't know what they hoped to achieve by it. But the missiles fell, and things burned, and people died. Our ignorance was no shield.

On the fifth night, I went to the wall to meet Nenn and watch the fireworks, but nothing came. The siren never sounded and no death came hurtling out of the Misery. The next night was the same and we began to believe that whatever it was, it was over.

The seventh night saw that same piercing song rise again, its return accompanied by the grinding wail of the siren. Casualties for that night reached 212. The death toll rose above a thousand. Another earthquake shook the city, collapsing a tavern where people had been sheltering from the missiles. Some of them got out, but not all.

People began to flee the city.

It started with boarded up windows on shops, and then the better streets fell quiet. Employees failed to appear for work, ovens went unlit. Some of the greener recruits deserted in the night and those that had the means to pack all their belongings onto a cart began to leave. Better to sit out the nightmare with their families in some quiet rural neighbourhood.

Marshal Davandein took steps to ensure that the city did not falter. An official dictate was passed: nobody employed by the military was free to leave, which was half the population, and neither were public servants or anybody who supplied the military, which was basically everybody else. The only people allowed to leave the city were those too poor to do so.

Her child tax, and the protests against it, had laid the kindling, and now the containment orders tipped the perception of the Range Marshal from an antagonistic overlord to a dictatorial enemy. Angry protests swelled, and then bloomed into full-blown riots.

A mob is like a living beast, an animal that moves in accordance with its base desire. When they reached the citadel, chanting 'Save us from the skies,' and 'Give us back our taxes,' the mob had grown from its humble origins of a few hundred to thousands. I watched from a high window in the citadel as Davandein sent her cavalry out. They rode big black horses, curved sabres held to the shoulder, but Davandein hesitated to order them to attack. Slashing heavy cavalry through Valengrad's population would be a disaster for her political standing. After a tense standoff, the mob was dissuaded, but by that time it had grown even larger and lost all sense of why it had begun or what it wanted. As it dispersed it swept back into the commercial districts, destroyed the barge market on the canals and struck through the tailor's quarter. A fire started. Bodies were left in the seething wake of man's communal stupidity, where they lay untouched in gutters. Who they were, why they were killed, was lost in the press.

Riots, in Valengrad. It defied belief.

When the first song rose that night, I went to check that Amaira was where I'd told her to be. The barrel cellar was cold, but she'd turned one corner into a den, hanging sheets over a big table, forming drapes around her bed to keep the warmth in.

'Amaira?'

'I'm here, Captain-Sir,' she said, but her usual vivacity was diminished. It hurt a little to see her flagging. She pulled back one of the sheet-drapes. She had a good pile of blankets beneath the table, some for lying on, some to pull over her. I thought that, dismal as the cellar was, it wasn't so very bad. I'd slept in worse places, both in the Misery and out, and at least it was dry.

'How are you holding up?' I asked.

'I'm doing my job just fine, Captain-Sir,' she said. She gave me a little salute, and I didn't stop her. It didn't seem very important. I knelt beside the table-bed.

'Are you scared?'

She paused for a moment, then put her arms around her knees.

'I try not to be.'

'It's all right to be scared,' I said. 'We're all scared. It's normal to be frightened when things are bad.'

She nodded, but her eyes were downcast, her energy sapped. Fear will do that to you. It takes a bright and vibrant person and reduces them to a shadow of what they were. I crawled in under the table, where Amaira had a candle burning inside a glass jar. Not a lot of room for me under there.

'It's going to be all right,' I said, though I was probably wrong. 'We're safe down here. You're safe.'

'That's what my parents told me,' she said. 'They said we

were safe. That we had the Engine. Then they were gone.'

I didn't know what to say to that. You can't spin a few words and suture wounds that have scored so deep through a person's core. So I lay down beside her, because sometimes being nearby is the best you can do. She'd pinned a number of sheets of paper to the underside of the table. I recognised some of them from books that had been in my office. Books that would have a substantially lower value now their pages had been torn out.

'I'm only borrowing them,' Amaira said.

'It's fine,' I said, glancing at them.

Poems. Valiya had been teaching Amaira to read. She'd struggled with it, having started too late in life, but she was managing and Valiya was insistent. She was determined that Amaira was going to have every skill a girl needed.

'Do they help?' I asked.

'Well,' Amaira said quietly. 'I thought that if I keep reading them in the night, then even if I died, I'd be looking at something beautiful. And then maybe I wouldn't be scared.'

Several moments of silence followed, and then she put her head on my shoulder. I put my arms around her, and I don't know whether I clung to her to give her comfort, or whether she was giving it to me. I shouldn't have. She was a servant and I was her employer. I was not her father, not her uncle, or brother. But she was a frightened child, and I was supposed to have the answers. I was supposed to be able to make it all safe, and calm, and all right. I wished that I had the power to end the terror, to stop the destruction. But I didn't. Nothing makes you feel more powerless than failing a child.

'It will be fine,' I lied. 'Now, try to sleep. It's hard, I know.'

'Do you have to go?' she asked.

'I have to work,' I said. I always did.

As the missiles faded with the night, the mob rose with

151

the dawn, unleashed like some pent-up beast. It emerged somewhere different each day, then grew and spread, casting waves of chaos through the streets. The rioters kept their distance from the citadel and its soldiers, but shops were looted, homes invaded, old grudges settled in the anonymity of the herd. Only the fourth day of madness brought a reprieve, as the skies opened and a colossal downpour kept all but the most die-hard looters from venturing out onto the streets. The mob realised that whilst it was very, very angry about a lot of things, it wasn't so angry that it wanted to get wet.

Valiya brought me paperwork, as subdued as Amaira. She didn't meet my eye as she stood there, spine straight. I'd hurt her. She'd loosened her armour and I'd given her a bruise to show for it. 'I found something,' she said. 'If you aren't busy.'

Formal. Distant. I guess I was bruised too. I nodded, unsure what to say or how to act around her. Nothing had passed between us. Nothing, but something as well.

She rolled out a map of the city. The cartographer had done a good job, some of the distances might even have been relatively accurate. The citadel, the wall, Mews, Spills, Gathers, Wicks, Willows and all the other districts were clearly labelled. It had probably been worth a fair bit before someone had drawn all over it.

'You bought this?'

'No. It was yours,' she said. I grunted. She'd ruined my map. I should probably have been annoyed that she'd done that without my permission, but I wasn't.

It was simple enough to see, laid out on the desk. Valiya had marked all of the impact sites, then numbered them according to the night they had struck. The first night was the most widely distributed, the second slightly more clustered. As the nights passed, the clusters drew together with fewer and fewer outliers.

'They're targeting the Spills,' I said. 'Or at least, more of their projectiles are coming down there.'

'Yes.'

'But why? It's the poorest, shittiest district in the city. There's some argument to be made that destroying it might be a blessing in disguise.'

'It not the Spills that's being targeted,' Valiya said, tapping the map. 'It's the Grandspire.'

'Maybe,' I said. There was more to the Spills than the Grandspire, although nothing else quite as valuable. 'But the Grandspire is just a big phos mill. Even if the drudge managed to destroy it, there are other mills.'

'But it's not just a phos mill, is it?' Valiya said. She could snap her voice like a whip when she wanted to. 'It's a symbol, isn't that what Governor Thierro told you? It's drawing all these Bright Order fanatics to the city. And if he's to be believed, it can generate enough power through that Iron Sun at the top to bring their beliefs to life.'

'I don't believe that.'

'But maybe the drudge do,' Valiya said, harshly. 'And maybe you should consider it.'

I wanted to. What I wouldn't have given to believe it. Every time I closed my eyes and saw her reaching out to me my chest lurched and my breath grew still. Every time I heard another preacher telling me that she was coming back, I tried to block it from my mind while gnawing hope scratched away at the edges. But now, if the drudge were trying to bring down the Bright Order's symbol of her return, couldn't I allow myself to at least acknowledge that I could be wrong?

'No.' I said it firmly.

'I know all about her, Ryhalt,' Valiya said tiredly. 'I know about Ezabeth Tanza. It's not exactly a secret among your friends. So stop ignoring what everyone is saying. Maybe the Bright Lady will appear. Maybe they're right.'

'I listened to what the Bright Order said about the Bright Lady. I listened to what Dantry Tanza had to say about the Bright Lady. And I listened to what Governor Thierro said about the Bright Lady. You know what they all had in common?'

'No.'

'It's wishes and dreams, and nothing more solid than that. I've seen what that obsession can do to someone. The people? They listen to preachers whose aims are as political as they are religious. Thierro? He blossomed late as a Spinner, and suddenly he thinks he's a prophet. He's about as rich as a man can be, and still he's looking for more. People will believe what they want to believe. That doesn't make it real.'

Valiya chewed it over. She wanted me to be wrong, but she knew no more on the subject than any of the rest of them.

'It doesn't matter whether it's true or not,' Valiya said eventually. 'The drudge think that it is. That has to be why they're focusing their attacks on the Grandspire.'

I looked over the map, the coloured inks. It hadn't even occurred to me that there might be a pattern. If people could be evacuated from the Spills by night, we might save a lot of lives. A lot of people to move, though, and Davandein's orders hadn't been popular lately.

'I'm lucky to have you,' I said. Didn't mean to. Beneath the fog of sleeplessness and unhappiness it just got out.

'Blackwing is lucky to have me,' she said. Her face was empty, the spark that had lit it in these past weeks extinguished and buried beneath rubble. 'You don't have me. You're the commander, but you're not Blackwing. One day, you'll be gone, and I'll still be here.'

'I'm not going anywhere,' I said.

'That's what my first husband said,' Valiya said. She looked me dead in the eye for the first time. 'So did the second. And they were liars both.'

15

'Spirits damn us to the hells, Ryhalt, the city's going to shit,' Nenn said. She was angry and she was sober, and whilst one was more common that the other, neither was improving her mood. Another week of sky-fires and bloody unrest had us all rubbed raw. Captain Betch rode alongside her, passing no comment on her outbursts. He seemed unfazed. Solid.

One of Davandein's men had tipped Nenn off that Davandein was planning to move against the leaders of the Bright Order, probably in the next few days. I felt a certain sense of obligation to tell Thierro because we'd been friends, but mostly because the city was too highly strung for that kind of conflict. People were already rioting. Acting now was like tossing embers into a powder store. The Witnesses had proved hard to track down, until tonight: now they'd called a public rally at the foot of the Grandspire, which had already inflamed the situation. I saw my city trembling on the fire, ready to overboil and spew scalding water over those unfortunate enough to be caught.

The road leading into the Spills was packed with people, a slow, shuffling herd of yellow scarves and hoods. Night had fallen and while they waited for the song to rise again, the Bright Order faithful gathered to hear their High Witness speak. The first public appearance. Nenn and I were mounted and people struggled out of our way to avoid getting stepped on.

'Davandein won't listen to me,' I said. 'You need to make her see reason.'

'She isn't listening to anyone, damn her,' Nenn said. She spat a wad at a man who stubbornly held his ground in front of her horse. He turned with eyes blazing but couldn't match her stare.

Rioque and Clada were high and looked close enough to touch, only Eala was absent from the sky tonight. Purple and blue daubed the world in shades of bruise. The cracks in the sky glowed fierce and bright, pulsing slowly.

'All these people gathered together make a nasty target,' Nenn said. Davandein's attempts to get people out of the Spills had only caused them to dig their heels in, and Thierro had refused to stop his building operation even for a day. The Bright Order's obstinacy had forced her to move her plans forward. She could be proud and headstrong, but ultimately, she felt responsible for the citizens in her care. Nenn shook her head. 'If one of the sky-fires comes down in the crowd, we'll be sweeping up body parts for days.'

Weeks was more likely, if anyone was left alive to pick up a broom. We ought to have been seeking shelter, but if Davandein moved against the Witnesses, the city could go up in flames. I hadn't expected this call-to-service to go out, clogging the roads.

We reached the plaza that surrounded the Grandspire, which was already packed with people, tradesmen, soldiers, children, even a smattering of the cream with their entourages. Yellow hats, yellow hoods, yellow everywhere. On the broad flights of steps that led up toward the Grandspire's double doors, four figures, robed in gold, stood before the crowd. Our horses forced passage through the people until we had a good view.

The four Witnesses faced each other. No doubting who they were, eyes down, hands linked. A heavily scarred, hairless Spinner had his back to me. To his right was a woman whose face was astonishingly beautiful. She flowed with vitality, and was strangely familiar, as if I'd dreamed of her once and then forgotten her. Her small hand was enveloped in the paw of a huge old woman, not just wide but tall, almost scaled up. Her back was hunched, oversized hands jagged with bone and mottled with spots of age, a stark reminder to the vision by her side that youth never lasts. One was a grown man's fantasy, soft coils of golden hair and the promise of soft curves, the other, a child's nightmare.

The fourth was Governor Thierro.

I was only surprised for a moment. He was a full-on believer in the Bright Lady, and if his story could be believed, then she was the one directing the show, through him. It made sense for a man with such a desire for control to have taken it. But he hadn't told me he was a Witness, and that made my eyes narrow and my fingers twitch.

Each of the Spinners's wrists were wrapped in copper wires that ran away into the Grandspire. The atmosphere was charged, and not just from the expectation hovering over the nervous crowd. I could feel the energy in the air, could smell the hot, metallic odour of the phos. The Witnesses were loaded with it.

'Do not be afraid,' Thierro said, his voice enhanced to roll out over the crowd, over the rooftops, over the city. 'The Bright Lady sees the purity in your hearts. She sees that you desire justice above all things. She will guard you in the dark night when those who should have failed you.'

Nenn and I shared a look, Nenn's brows arching in hostility. That was dangerously close to seditionist talk, inciting public discord against the ruling elite. I glanced at the clusters of nobility and saw that they nodded along. I noted, with even greater concern, how many of those small clusters were attended by high-ranking officers. Old, small Colonel Koska stood alongside a countess, enraptured by these advocates of his new god. Lieutenants, a few majors and plenty of lords and ladies stood shoulder to shoulder with newly arrived farmers, coffeehouse workers, thatchers, teachers. My father would have spat his port across the plaza to see it.

But maybe, just maybe, there was a hunger for something slightly less corrupt. The people grew quiet, watching. They'd heard the calls to abandon the Spills, broadcast by citadel officials throughout the day, but faith was proving stronger than their fear. It must have been comforting to trust in something so strongly that they were willing to risk their lives for it. I'd never had that kind of faith in anything, except maybe Ezabeth. The irony of that was not lost on me.

Neither Thierro nor any of the Witnesses spoke, concentrating instead on whatever they were planning.

The song of the falling sky began, a distant, beautiful cadence rising far across the Misery. A ripple of fear shot through the crowd, children crying out. They knew what followed. Hands were linked, children clutched to breasts. But the Witnesses had their attention.

'Do not be afraid!' Thierro proclaimed, though he sounded breathless. His message was stark in contrast to the blood-neon letters on the citadel that flickered and changed to read TAKE COVER.

As the song grew in volume, the Spinners began to glow, phos smoking from their skin in incandescent wisps. Sparks and crackles of blue-gold lightning spat around the phos drums as they grew brighter still. I needed to see this for myself, but I couldn't look directly at them as they grew hotter, brighter, filling the whole plaza with flat white light. And then the phos surged along the wires and into the Grandspire, a stream of brilliant white-gold rushing upward, blazing out through the windows and rising floor by floor.

Atop the Grandspire, the Iron Sun began a harsh, mechanical roar of its own, a dry-mouthed answer to the beautiful death song that brought fire down upon us. A glittering sky of stars erupted from the Iron Sun, rushing out over the city. They were joined, bright golden points of light, by blue-white threads of power, high above us. A net of energy.

Every eye stared skywards. I saw the missile coming in, and felt the fear rise around us, an enveloping death shroud across the assembled believers. Faith suddenly seemed a misplaced defence: the sky-fire was aimed right for the fucking Grandspire, just as Valiya had said. It drew in fast, trilling its nightmare song –

– and exploded, shattering into a cloud of twinkling sparks, high above our heads. The shield projecting out from the Grandspire held strong and that first missile disintegrated into nothing.

'Holy shit,' Nenn said, barely audible over gasps from the crowd. 'They're protecting us.'

The net of sparkling light, conjured in the name of the Bright Lady, glowed over the city.

The Spinners had to force their hands apart and attendants came forward to unwrap the wires from their wrists. As the crowd began to chant their praise for the Bright Lady, I watched the Spinners move. There was nothing holy about what they had just done. They'd focused their energy into a web and then sent it through the Grandspire, using the Iron Sun to magnify their power. I had to wonder, if the Grandspire could let them do that when it wasn't even operating as a phos mill, what power would it command when it did? Could Thierro really try to break Ezabeth's shadow from the light that bound it? I suddenly understood why the drudge were so determined to bring it down, even from such colossal range. If the Witnesses could do this, what else could they do?

I should have listened to Valiya. Always, I should have listened to her.

There was joy in the air, all around us. Real, palpable joy. The people had been losing hope, terrorised for days, and as death had hung over them, Davandein had sealed them up like kittens in a bag. They had placed their dwindling faith in the Witnesses, and they had appeared right before them, their saviours, glowing and steaming with power as a bright net of stars held back the night's terrors. It wasn't long before a second missile came arcing in, heading off target toward Wicks this time, but it also met the star-net and detonated harmlessly.

People were actually laughing.

I was not laughing.

I was looking at Thierro.

He'd spotted me, standing out from the crowd on the back of a massive black horse. He gave me a self-satisfied smile and tipped two fingers to me, a little salute. The same I'd given him when I stole that girl from him at a dance so many years before. A salute that said, *'I'm winning.'* I stared back. Winning at what? Our methods might have differed, but we fought for the same side.

Didn't we?

'People of Valengrad, loyal citizens,' Thierro said. 'The Bright Lady has loaned us her gift. We are merely witnesses to her power. It is she, not we humble servants, that protects you.'

A bugle called from the back of the crowd, high and insistent. People were crammed in. They shuffled around, trying to see. I turned in my saddle to see a column of heavy cavalry on dark horses forcing their way down the Rain Boulevard. Their helmets bore rampant-dragon crests, Davandein's Drakes. She rode at their head, decked out in her fancy armour, her dark hair bound up tight. One of her own Spinners rode alongside her with a hand against the small of her back, unobtrusive but putting his power through her. When Davandein spoke, her voice boomed across the crowded plaza, echoed from the Grandspire.

'People of Valengrad. I am Range Marshal Davandein, first daughter of House Davandein. You are all under my authority. Make way.'

Nenn and I exchanged fearful glances. Davandein had moved a lot faster than Nenn's tip-off had suggested. Nobody made way. They glowered and gritted their teeth.

Her timing could not have been worse.

'Shit,' I said. 'She's going to do something stupid.'

Davandein had misjudged the situation, badly, and I had to stop her before this turned volatile. I began to wheel Falcon around in the press. It wasn't going to be easy to get through to her, but Falcon was a biter and his hooves were the size of a child's head, and even the most faithful observers didn't want to get their feet crushed.

People shouted, started yelling abuse as part of a general rush of noise declaring their dissatisfaction, disgust, frustration. They weren't afraid of men on horses tonight. They'd just seen their worst fears shattered harmlessly overhead.

'Range Marshal, you are welcome here,' Thierro said. His voice was even louder than hers, augmented by his own power. I kicked at Falcon's flanks, urging him to knock people out of the way if he had to. Davandein was blind to the public anger, and the resentment all around her, assured of her invulnerability as Range Marshal. Secure atop her fine horse.

Range Marshal Davandein did not see herself as a politician. She had been raised to understand that the spirits had ordained her right to rule by virtue of her blood. She could trace her mother's family back for nine generations. They had been coastal lords, taxing fisher fleets to the north of Ostermark. Her father's family could count back seven patriarchs, and they were sea captains and men of the

Range. Soldiers. Her bloodline counted counts and more than one unsuccessful bid for a princedom. She'd lost an uncle to assassination as he strove for control of Ostermark, and a famous feud had caused her grandparents to wipe out a would-be royal household in a pitched battle.

There was no way in seven hells that she was going to take being welcomed by Thierro well. This was her city, and she was its absolute master. But she kept her composure, the straightening of her back the only sign of her anger.

'Witnesses. Good people of Valengrad. I am your Range Marshal.' She looked up toward the sky. 'We thank you for helping the city in its time of need.'

'What have you done to help us?' an angry voice came from the crowd. Davandein's self-control was tight as she kept her focus only on the Witnesses. I kicked urgently at Falcon's flanks.

'You are my people. I am ordained by the spirits of Justice and Mercy as your protector,' Davandein said. The words were meant to soothe, but to the crowd they were salt in a wound. 'Witnesses. You have done great work tonight, all can see that. Undoubtedly, you have saved many lives. But, good people, you must disperse. The Spills is not safe. The Grandspire draws the fury of the drudge. I cannot keep you safe here.'

'You can't keep anyone safe anywhere!' a heckler shouted.

'Our working tonight has indeed saved many lives,' Thierro said, his voice echoing from the stonework. The other Witnesses, the scarred man, the beauty, the crone, stood alongside him. A formidable group, even drained as they were. Enough Spinners to make anyone back down. 'The people need no longer fear the night. They are safe beneath the Bright Lady's shield. The Grandspire will not fall. *We* will not fall. But we welcome you among us, if you seek her protection.'

Something snapped inside Davandein. I heard it in my

soul. Born too high, the air too thin, for years she had been surrounded by yes-men who told her that she deserved power, that she was born to command, that others had to obey. Her growing failure to control the city had challenged that belief. She sought to reassert it now in a moment of blood-deep fury. Davandein thrust her finger forward like a lance.

'While I command the Range, my orders will not be questioned. I am the Range Marshal, and this is my city. This gathering *will* disperse!'

She urged her horse forward, her Drakes moving with her, just as Falcon persuaded the last of them to get out of her way.

'Back down!' I shouted, uncaring of the disrespect, forgetting her title in the sense of black panic that had welled within me. 'Back down and get your men out of here. There will be blood.'

Davandein looked at me, her fury contorting her face to match a gargoyle's glower.

'I will not cede control of my city to these zealots,' she snarled. One of her Drakes moved forward to block me, a man half my age, just as tough.

'Don't do this,' I said, but she was already pushing on into the crowd as it struggled to part, her Drakes forming a wedge around her.

'The city belongs to the people, Range Marshal,' Thierro said. 'It always has.'

'Marshal,' I hissed. 'Please. You can't win here.'

Davandein teetered on the edge. Her pride was battered, her control fraying into the wind. She glanced in my direction, and in her eyes I read the years of sycophancy falling away, the dawning realization that she was just one more body among the crowd. The circumstance of birth and capability had built her a tower on which she'd gazed out over the world and had begun to believe the legend that had grown in her mind.

The crowd trembled. Emotions were high, balanced for a week on a blade's edge. People had been burning and dying, and here was the woman who had done nothing about it, the woman who had trapped them, suddenly threatening the only people to have offered hope. Individual people can be highly intelligent, but put them into a mob and they change. They become something else. Something really, really fucking stupid.

Everything went to the hells.

A flarelock went off in the crowd, and one of the Drakes clutched at his neck and went down. Thierro tried to bring order, shouting for calm, but it was no use. Soldiers respond to threats as they have been trained and, under fire, their instincts flared. Their captain rose in his stirrups and yelled the charge. Angry, afraid, Davandein and her men spurred forward against the crowd in sudden panic as though they faced an enemy battalion instead of one idiot. Sabres rose, bright and gleaming beneath the web of stars, then sabres fell. Screaming, loud and shrill. Men, women, children. The Drakes got fifty yards into the crowd, ploughing toward the Witnesses, before they met resistance. The Bright Order's militia flocked to the steps, formed up around their leaders.

'Enough. Withdraw! Don't fire!' Thierro cried. But the militia's blood was boiling and half of them only heeded the last word of his command and unleashed a volley of flarelock fire into the Drakes. Men and horses screamed, and the soldiers spurred harder. The threat they had to reach was clustered around the Witnesses and they drove a path toward them, Davandein borne along in their midst.

'Spirit of Mercy,' Nenn breathed. The Drakes had left a trampled mess of wounded and dead civilians in their wake. They were taking casualties, but they were heavily armed and armoured, rode heavy chargers, and body by body they cut a path toward the Witnesses. They didn't seem to care whether those bodies were men, women or children. Only that they were in the way. The Drakes were as protective of their commander as the Bright Order were of their prophets.

'Stand down!' Thierro screamed, but it was no longer clear to whom he was giving orders.

The Drakes' captain reached the steps, his warhorse bloody, his sabre rising high.

The scarred Witness had had enough. He raised his hands and let fly. The lead Drake was torn from his horse, and then the other Witnesses joined him. A series of blinding, silent flashes detonated among the soldiers. Horses screamed as they were torn in two. Men were silenced as they became pieces of men and a warm rain fell across the scattering crowd. The Drakes' advance was hurled back and Thierro stepped forward. His eyes were ablaze with white light, his body smoked with a Spinner's power. His robe had burned away from his torso, revealing the massive, swirled burn scars that covered his chest, oversmooth skin framed by a circle of chest hair. 'You gave me no choice, Range Marshal,' he boomed, looking down on her and the men that remained to her. Her horse was dead, and there was blood in her hair, across her face. Davandein was not the only one to have been pushed past breaking point. Phos steamed from Thierro's fingers, judgment blazed on his face. Had he wanted to, he could have obliterated them all there and then. 'This is no longer your city, Davandein.'

The Range Marshal saw that the game was up. Her best men were dead, her Spinner had been killed. She rose slowly, standing small and fragile amidst the wreckage. Unable to believe. Unable to accept the breaking of her power. A man pulled her up to share his saddle, and she gathered together what remained of her personal troops and fled the city, beating a trail west toward Lennisgrad.

By dawn, a second banner had joined the Range's emblem

above the citadel. A woman's silhouette against a field of gold. The Bright Order.

I should have been able to do something. Anything. But I was just a man with a sword and a handful of thugs in my control, and so I sat and drank and watched as the remaining officers welcomed High Witness Thierro into the citadel and declared the Witnesses the protectors of Valengrad.

16

I brought my people together and told them what had gone down. How things stood in the city now. After their light show and shield, the Bright Order were the Guardians of the Range.

The generals had remained loyal to Davandein and beat a retreat with her. They'd not seen it prudent to risk long-standing positions for a change in the wind, or to remain in a city under siege. Colonel Koska, who I'd seen among the crowd in the plaza, was the highest ranker left. He met with High Witness Thierro, and they agreed to share power temporarily while an envoy was sent to the grand prince requesting that he install a new marshal. The Order didn't go as far as to declare themselves lords of the Range. Thierro was running his show with a diplomat's touch.

Outside, celebrations rang through the streets. People were dead, their bodies cooling in makeshift morgues, but somehow the populace felt liberated. They waited for the shield to rise over the city again that night, as though the Bright Order's defiance of the drudge's missiles were some kind of victory. Maybe it was.

My own little group was more realistic about the situation we now found ourselves in. Tnota, Casso, Maldon and I sat together over a few bottles of Whitelande firewater and tried to plan a new move. Valiya sipped her tea.

'Our situation is unchanged,' I said, having thought about it long and hard. 'The Eye is still our priority, and until it's back in that vault we'll keep hunting for it. What happens to the city next depends on how the grand prince reacts and at a guess, he will appoint a new marshal. Probably Marshal Herrich, from Three-Six. If not, then Marshal Ngoya, down at Station Four. Either way, our duty is to retrieve the Eye.'

'At least people are being allowed out of the city now,' Casso said. He had a sweaty look about him, eyes a little fried.

'That what you want? You want to get out of here?'

'The bombardment isn't over,' he said. 'I been thinking about it.'

'You're free to go if you want to,' I said. 'I won't hold you here against your will. You aren't sworn to serve.'

He thought about it a few moments, looking increasingly uncomfortable.

'Reckon I'll stay for now,' he said. I nodded, poured him another drink and whizzed it across the table to him. It's the small gestures that we remember the most. Loyalty is more easily bought with a few cups of spirit than salary or duty.

'I need to go,' Casso said, embarrassed, shortly before dark. He'd wanted to see the gathering in the Grandspire's plaza for himself. A yellow scarf protruded from his pocket – didn't want to put it on in front of us. I made no comment, but my own people were starting to believe as well.

The siren began right alongside the song and the night's terrors had begun. We watched through the window as the shield appeared over the city again, a glowing web of stars across the night.

The others had drifted away to huddle with their families in their cellars, not ready to place all their trust in the Witnesses' protection even though they'd saved most of the city the night before. But not all of it – three of the sky-fires had made it through. Valiya, Tnota and I took a look at the vast weaving in the sky, thousands of glittering points of light, then retired beside the fire. Why didn't we seek shelter? Sheer bloody-mindedness, maybe. Then Tnota fell asleep in his chair, snoring and it was just Valiya and I.

'What's the order of business tomorrow?' she asked. 'Where do we even begin?'

'Maybe we should take a holiday,' I said. I allowed myself a smile. It felt the first in a long time. 'Get away from the city whilst all this boils itself dry. Where should we go?'

'I heard that the sky gardens on Pyre are worth a look,' Valiya said. It was still awkward between us. She reached up and pulled free two of the pins that stacked her hair up on her head and shook it loose, fingers combing out the snarls and flattened patches. I didn't mean to get caught up watching her, but she noticed. 'What?'

It wasn't just the shape of her face or lazy sweep of her hair, it was the set of her shoulders, the way she controlled the space around her. Her intelligence, her determination. Her dignity.

'Not worth the journey,' I said, bringing myself back. 'The crossing to Pyre will leave you sick for a week. Something in the gardens runs off into the water, makes the whole place stink. They're beautiful, but only if you put a peg over your nose.'

'I didn't take you for a traveller,' Valiya said.

'My parents wanted me to see the world. Visited all of the city-states at one time or another. Crossed over to Hyspia, the Iscalian cities. Even stopped in Angol once.'

'I liked Angol. Once you get past all the cannibalism, anyway,' Valiya said. She smiled, and I thought to myself, *yes*. In a different life, a life where the damage had never been done to us, I could have loved her. I'd met Valiya after I gave up sleeping and it felt as though she'd always been slightly out of focus, hidden behind a wash of winter grey. In the dim candlelight, I saw her clearly now.

'Why did you really come all this way?' I said. 'Oster-mark's a long way off. You must have left family behind. Friends. Why come here, to the broken sky and the never-ending war?'

Valiya swirled the wine in her glass, her legs tucked beneath her on the divan. She'd removed her shoes and the tips of stockinged toes protruded from the hem of her dress. It felt like something intimate, to see them. An element of trust. A sign that the bruise I'd given her might be fading.

'You ask as if there was a choice,' she said, not meeting my eye, her voice tinged with pain. 'There's a war. It needs winning and I don't trust anyone else to fight it better than I do. I'm smarter than most people. A *lot* smarter. How could I entrust the fate of the world to people less capable?'

The fire cracked and popped in sympathy. She wasn't saying this to impress me. She knew that it wouldn't. But maybe she guessed it was the same feeling that kept me awake all the long night.

'My first husband didn't like how hard I worked,' Valiya said. 'He didn't understand. He made a lot of money on fishing fleets, while I was organizing an intelligence net-work to monitor the counts around Ostermark. Do you know what he said, when I told him that I'd outearned his fishing boats?'

I didn't say anything. Wasn't my place.

'He said that I'd made us abnormal. That if word got out, his social circle would snicker at him. He told me to give it up. Sell the business. That I should run the shop he'd given me and forget about spies and whisper-men.'

'And did you?'

Valiya's smile barely reached her face.

'I did. I wanted it to work. I wanted it to work so much, I'd have done anything for him. But, if you want to know the truth? When his ship went down, I wasn't heartbroken. I was relieved.'

I had lost a spouse as well, and felt no relief. I'd not loved her, not as I was supposed to. Not as I'd intended to, even. But her passing had still hollowed me out. I looked down at the flowers on my arm, the ones tattooed there to remind me of those that she'd taken with her that day. The ones for whom I'd sold myself to the crow.

'And your second man?' I asked. Just words to fill the silence.

'A good man,' Valiya said. 'The best man. Killed by the drudge.'

She didn't offer anything more, and though I knew it had been six years, clearly that wound was still bleeding. We were both walking casualties, the sutures never quite holding us together.

'And what of you? Your Ezabeth.'

There are wounds that won't heal, and then there are wounds that are still being inflicted. I had loved Ezabeth with a ferocity that could have driven the drudge back to their side of the Misery on its own. In a way, it had. I couldn't speak of her. Even thinking of her made me feel that I was betraying her with Valiya. She'd given her life for me, for us, for everyone, for the world. And now, while whatever remained of her was imprisoned within the light, I was getting shy around someone else.

'We should sleep,' I said. 'There's a lot to be doing tomorrow.'

My words were harder, flatter than I had intended. They settled down between us, alien. Vinegar. No way back from them.

'Yes, Captain. Of course. A lot to do.'

Valiya put her shoes on, and then she was gone and I sat in the dim light of the lamps and rubbed my tired eyes, only then realizing that Tnota's snoring had stopped sometime ago.

'Big Dog says you could do a lot worse than that very

good woman,' he said without opening his eyes.

'She's an employee,' I said. As though that mattered.

'Ain't nothing to do with it,' he said. He nestled deeper into the side of the chair. A single eye opened to look at me. 'You want my advice, you go find her, apologise and let nature take its course.'

'I didn't ask for your advice,' I said. 'What do you know about women anyway?'

'Men. Women,' he said, 'we're all the same where it matters. Can't live your life alone, Ryhalt. Shouldn't, anyway, not when there's good people that want to hold us. Here we are sitting getting shit-faced in a city that's being pelted with heaven-fire and we might die at any moment, and you're going to turn down a good thing because you're still hurting over a woman that's been dead four years.'

His words punched arrow holes into my chest. It's one thing to know it yourself, it's another to hear someone else say it. I should have snapped something back but my jaw had decided to wire itself shut.

'We both know that that shield's not Ezabeth's doing,' Tnota said. 'She's gone and there's some kind of impression left in the light. We both know that ain't her either.'

'It is her,' I said. 'The ghost in the light. It's her.'

'It ain't,' Tnota said. 'She was flesh and blood, and that thing in the light don't have neither. But there's a woman you just drove away got both, and each of them hot for you. You want to be lonely forever?'

'I want Ezabeth back,' I said, like I was tearing the arrow free. It must have been barbed because it hurt even worse coming out the other way.

'Let me be honest with you, Ryhalt,' Tnota said. 'When you imagine that somehow she makes it back, imagine her getting out of the light, what do you think that would be like? I mean, when we ran into her all that time ago back at Station Twelve she was rich. Cream. Used to the fine things. And us? We were practically in the gutter. You got yourselves thrown together when things got all hot and chaotic, but if she'd survived, what then? You think she'd be here, watching you drink yourself sick? Nah. She was better than that. She was fine-as-you-like cream, and clever with it. You really think she'd stay here on the Range?'

'It doesn't matter,' I said. 'We'll never know, will we?'

'We won't,' Tnota said. 'That's all the more reason to find some kind of happiness with a good woman who brings you pastries and tries to look after you, even though you don't really deserve it.'

Somewhere else in the city one of the singing projectiles came crashing down through the Witnesses' shield. It could have been here, could have fallen on us. But it didn't, and our survival had been assured once more by luck. As it ever is.

17

I woke Maldon from his usual drunken stupor with a kick.

'Get up. I have work for you.'

'But I'm dreamin',' Maldon said. He tried to fend the toe of my boot off with a softly flailed arm. It was unsuccessful and earned him another kick. 'Fine,' he grumbled. 'But it delays your new toys.'

'They don't look to be getting made right now anyway,' I said. 'How much did you have? It's past ten and you're still wrecked.'

Maldon was in a state. His hands and forearms were shiny with gun oil and he smelled of phos residue and ground iron. I didn't want to ask.

We rode double through the dark city over toward the Spills. The faithful had left a lot of litter in their wake, discarded, indestructible piecrusts, empty bottles, horse and human manure, scraps of greased paper, and all the other detritus that people on the move leave behind. Amazing to say it, but the Spills seemed even dirtier than usual.

The previous night's activity didn't mean that the workmen had stopped. They were going hard, shifting vast timbers that would form runners for the looms. Some poor bastards would end up more or less chained to those beams, spinning light through dozens of focusing lenses. The nasal drone of phos-powered saws came from high overhead.

'Ugh,' Maldon said. 'The smell of the phos residue is

incredible. It's like the Engine just fired.'

'That will be the shield, I guess,' I said. I could taste it too, a metallic flatness to the air. Maldon was far more attuned to it though, and I needed that attunement to invisible things today.

We rode in a wide circle around the Grandspire, then closed in and rode a tighter one. Workmen didn't even glance up at our passing, but they weren't the only ones there now. Men with silver-barrelled flarelocks had taken up position on the stairs, at the entrance, in pairs walking a perimeter. They eyed us, but a man with a child doesn't inspire a great deal of interest. The Grandspire was our defence against the drudge and it was only right that it be guarded, but if they were citadel men, they were wearing Bright Order colours and carrying the Bright Order's holy weapon. Back when the man who wasn't Devlen Maille's flarelock had exploded, they'd been rare. Now they were everywhere.

'Getting anything?' I asked.

'The phos residue is powerful,' he said. 'What am I meant to be getting?'

I reined Falcon in and he was happy to stop. He might have been built like a charger but he was a lazy old cob at heart. We dismounted, stretched our legs out. The saddle had been thumping me in the balls something awful.

'I was hoping for traces of the Eye,' I said. 'Nothing?'

'You think that I'd keep it quiet if I picked that up?' Maldon said. He was tense as a violin string and just the mention of something connected to Shavada caused him to flinch. Poor bastard. 'Why do you think it was here?'

I looked at the vastness of the Grandspire, a tower that nearly reached the clouds.

'It seems too strong,' I said. 'The shield. The Witnesses are clearly powerful Spinners, and they wire up and make the shield together. But even so I wondered if Saravor was involved. The Eye is a fragment of a Deep King. I don't know what kind of magic can be wrought with it, but he wanted it, for something. Wondered if it was this.'

'If it was here, then I can't smell it,' Maldon said. 'So it wasn't here for long, if it was at all.'

'It was a long shot,' I said.

'You dragged me out here just for this?'

'No,' I said. This part was harder to ask. 'The phos you can smell. Tell me about it. Is it ... normal?'

Maldon thought about it, then said, 'It smells old. Like it's been stored for a long time in a battery coil. Years, maybe. Why? What else were you thinking?'

Maldon's assessment confirmed what I'd suspected. The shield was the work of four talented Spinners running their power through the Iron Sun at the top of the Grandspire, and whatever that Iron Sun was, it was more than just a vent for excess power, as I'd been told. But whatever it was, however clever the technology behind it – the light-shield had required astonishing power. Thierro had told me to believe. Valiya had struck at my doubts. Even my own people were wearing yellow. Since I saw the Witnesses raise the shield, a doubting little voice had been hammering away at the back of my mind. Insistent. Relentless. I had to know.

'I have to be sure. Does the Bright Lady make the shield?' I asked.

Maldon's face lit up in a leering grin, and he almost spoke, but the words faded away, the leer dying as quietly as it had come. He didn't have eyes, so I was spared seeing pity in them. I hated to be pitied. But it was written there on his unnaturally childish face all the same.

'No, Ryhalt,' he said after a while. 'It's not her. It's a phos working, channelled through some kind of system inside the Grandspire. If you're asking if there's something more at work than that? No. It's colossal, and it's impressive as the hells, but it's just phos spinning. Whatever they say, it's not her.'

Was I relieved by that? Disappointed? I didn't know. I felt empty, mostly. Lost.

'Fine. Let's get back. I'm sure there's a bottle in my cellar you've not opened yet.'

We'd ridden back a few streets, Maldon seated behind me, when he dug his fingers into my ribs to get my attention.

'I think we're being followed,' he said. 'Don't turn around.'

'How do you know?' I asked.

'How do I know anything? You want me to explain how all this works now? Really?'

'Fine,' I snapped. 'Who?'

'Two people,' he said. 'Hustling along after us on foot. But one of them is big. Really big. Bigger than you. The other is just big.'

Reassuring.

'How long have they been following us?'

'The Grandspire,' he said. 'I clocked them back there. But they've kept up with us even when we turned down Clatton Street, and stayed with us when we went back onto Barrello, and that's an odd route to take.'

It was. I took Clatton Street, a little used side road, because a year back I'd raided a tea shop on Barrello Street. It hadn't gone well and people had been hurt – not abnormal when dragging a couple of Cult of the Deep practitioners out into the night – and had left sore memories behind. No need to grate the feelings of the innocents left behind. So I avoided Barrello Street when I could, and we'd cut through Clatton. A longer ride home. A strange route to take.

'They armed?' I was.

'Not sure.'

'Let's find out.'

I turned Falcon down Nowhere Row, then immediately

off the road and into a narrow alley. The big horse didn't like it in there, a thin strip of nothing between badly made warehouses, the kind of alley the sun never reached and the rats grew bigger than badgers. I handed Falcon's reins to Maldon, who had never liked horses, and had never been liked by horses, and got ready. At a guess they were probably Bright Order men posted to investigate anyone acting odd around the Grandspire. They'd not done anything but follow us, yet, so I left my cutlass in its hanger.

The two men passed the end of the alley. Maldon had been right. They were both big men, unusually so. One of them must have been pushing six-ten, but the few men that I'd met who were that tall were lanky, mostly bone and skin. This man was mostly beef, tremendously broad and wide. I felt an irrational surge of hatred toward him for being that much bigger than me. I shouldn't have been proud of being born to be tall, but I guess that I was. His companion was about my height, which made him a lot bigger than most men in the world, similarly slathered in brawn. They wore civilian clothes, not a trace of yellow about them, and they were armed with proper swords, cutters, thick in the blade and nothing too fancy about them. Their steel was at their hips, for now, and they were unremarkable aside from their size. I took them in quickly as they went past the alley and down Nowhere Row. They'd turn right, as the road bent, and find themselves at a complete dead end. The road was named Nowhere for a reason.

Which meant that I had them in a trap, of sorts. Of course, they were big and armed, but I had a pistol in my coat, which gave me all of the advantages.

I left Falcon with Maldon and followed them, pistol cocked and held at my shoulder. When they stopped, visibly puzzled that I'd disappeared into thin air, I cleared my throat to get their attention.

'Let's not do anything that might make the cemetery

wardens have to work harder than they already do,' I said.

The two men didn't react as I'd expected. I don't know what exactly I'd expected, surprising them in this dead-end street, but I'd expected something. Unease, fear, maybe anger that I'd got the drop on them. But there was nothing. They stood there for a moment, nothing seeming to go on at all behind their faces. Thick necks, heavy shoulders. Not an inconspicuous pair at all. Bad spies. Good killers, maybe.

'How about you toss down those swords down, your knives too, and we'll practise the lost art of conversation,' I said. I kept the pistol to my shoulder. Didn't want to spook them by pointing it unnecessarily. You can really ruin a man's composure when you aim a firearm at his face, and that gives people bad ideas.

You get used to the way that men act under pressure. There's denial, a natural human response to crisis. Talk your way out of it. But before that, in a group situation, a panicked man will look to his companions. It's instinctive. We can't help it. And these men should have glanced at each other, a split second to gauge their response. But these men didn't care and the weapon at my shoulder didn't faze them. Maldon's instinct was right, they had been following us for a reason.

Simultaneously, the big men's eyes rippled, as though a stone had been dropped into a calm pool of water. Thin trickles of blood began to leak from the corners of their eyes, red tears tracking lightly down their faces. I resisted the urge to step back. I'd seen this before. It happened when a Darling got its mind-worms into you. Just like the soldiers who'd been killed back at Crowfoot's vault. But a Darling had to be present to work its dark magic, and there were just the three of us. But whether a Darling was in my city or not, I'd not led the men into a trap. They'd led me into one.

They were reaching for their swords when I aimed at the

bigger man and fired. The flint snapped home, the heartbeat pause as the powder ignited, then the pistol roared and I hit him high in the left arm. Not my best shot. Not enough to put him down. Not even enough that he seemed to notice.

There were three naked swords in the alley, just like that. I didn't trust my bad leg enough to turn and run, and more to the point, they were already on me.

The small-big man swung his blade at me overhead, a cut that would have sheared through my arm. I parried, wound his sword aside and thrust at his face. I drew blood, but now the bigger man was swinging. No finesse, no skill with the blade, blood in his eyes, I swayed back out of his arc and his sword sliced into the smaller man's shoulder. Neither acknowledged the damage, and the blood pulsed from their eyes in steady, rhythmic drops. No pain, no care. Not even a will of their own.

I backed away, trying to circle, to keep them blocking each other. The smaller man was bleeding from the deep slice his pal had put in his shoulder, but a fight rarely takes more than seconds, and I couldn't wait for him to bleed out.

The bigger man came in again, driving a swing from the shoulder. I parried it, no time for a riposte as the second man followed suit. Artless, clumsy strokes, with all the finesse of a buffalo's charge, each of them aimed at taking my sword hand. I got out of the way and there was the opening I needed, one that could be taken quick and clean and still keep me moving. I took it, the cut savage, and the smaller man staggered back minus an arm. It nearly cost me: the bigger man was an inch from carving a chunk out of my head.

There was no point in trying to talk to him. He wasn't in his own mind. Moreover, my breath was screaming through me. Too many cigars, too many brandies. Too slow by far.

My remaining assailant came at me with the same skill-less, disabling blows. I cut his forearm half-open, I cut him through the face, I left a bloody gash through the side of his shirt. Nothing slowed him. He came in close and hard and I parried, grabbed his wrist, but before I could put my own sword through his head he reached up and caught my sword arm. A big bastard, several inches taller, several inches wider and all of it was bearing down on me. I lost my footing, sprawled, and he came down on top.

He twisted his arm, sweat-slicked fingers slipped and his elbow crashed into my face. Sight shattered as bright points of light stole the world. Something soft and wet crushed up against my face, and with it the sweet, powerful smell of a surgeon's anaesthetic. The world was shaking but I locked my throat tight even as I felt the fumes trying to work their way into me. Chest screaming, half-blind, I tried to twist and lever him off me, but he was heavier and stronger than I was. I snapped my head to the side, freeing it from the stinking rag and tried to get a deep breath, my lungs snarling, but his weight was pressing down on me and I couldn't get shit. The chemical odour reached into my nose, its poison reaching to take me down.

The big man went limp, suddenly three hundred pounds of deadweight. There was a cutlass halfway through the back of his head. I heaved with whatever I had left and rolled him off me, gasping for breath, spitting and scrubbing the pungent wetness from my face with my sleeve. Maldon, blood-sprayed and grinning, let go of the cleaver, wedged deep into the dead man's skull. The man whose arm I'd taken had fled, broken through the door of a nearby house.

'You looked like you needed help,' Maldon said.

'Good time to get involved,' I panted.

'Time was that I could have turned him to ash in a flicker,' Maldon said. He snapped his fingers as though expecting a result, but nothing happened.

I looked down at the dead man.

'He's dead enough.' The stench of the anaesthetic had

faded, the light-headedness drifting away with it. My temple throbbed where the elbow had broken the skin. No time to gather myself fully. Low on his gut, the dead man's shirt was stained black and a foul odour rolled off him, stronger and fouler than the chemical he'd tried to smother me with. I knelt and tore open his shirt. Flesh had torn open in the struggle, and congealed, putrid, brownish-black fluid seeped from the seam of a mismatched patch of skin over his appendix. Like Marollo Nacomo he'd turned to the Fixer for help, only it seemed to me that when I'd given him that drip of Shavada's power, Saravor had learned a few other things too. The dead man's eyes were filled with blood.

My heart hammered harder as I thought of Nenn. What lay inside her? What had I done to her when I bargained for her life?

'Ryhalt, he smells like it. Like the Eye,' Maldon said. His nose was working like a terrier's, sucking at the air.

'Think he's been near it?'

'Definitely. Or maybe it was used to do ... this ... to him.'

I pushed myself upright. The battle-rush was fading, its heady spin draining out of me, only I had more work to do. I looked down at the severed arm: three of the fingers were at a slight angle. Slightly too small. Badly fixed together, maybe. When I'd cut it from him, the owner had bolted. Had that broken Saravor's hold over him? I needed to find him if I wanted to find out. A trail of blood led from the abandoned limb and through a tenement doorway. I retrieved my sword, wiped it off and cursed that I didn't have any more ammunition for the pistol. I'd carried it out of habit, hadn't expected to need it. Certainly not more than once.

'You're going after the other one?' Maldon asked.

'Of course I am.'

'I'll come with you,' he said.

'No. Take Falcon. Get Casso to come and clean this mess up. Make sure his body gets back to our offices. Don't let the citadel claim it.'

I set off in pursuit.

The blood made an easy trail to follow. He'd gone through the tenement, buildings too cheap and full of too little to bother with exterior locks, out the other side and then down a series of streets. Civlians pointed me in the right direction when the spatters grew sparse – it's not often you see a man with a freshly severed arm. My old leg wound was making me limp but I kept after him, even after it started stabbing at me like a stitch. I'd worry about it after I got hold of the bleeding son of a bitch, dragged him back home and drank a couple of brandies. Nothing that wouldn't heal.

Keep telling yourself that, Ryhalt.

As I jogged from street to street, the spatter slowed from regular to infrequent, and then maybe he'd managed to wrap it because I emerged onto a broad street and there was nothing. Asked an old man sitting smoking a pipe on his doorstep whether he'd seen anyone run by, but he hadn't. Nobody unusual? Nobody. He looked bored enough to note every neighbour that went by, let alone a stranger with a missing arm, so I retraced my steps down the last narrow street. Had I missed a doorway? His good hand had to be properly bloody, but there was no sign of him forcing any doors and those I tried seemed well sealed. It was only chance that I noticed a dark sheen on a sewer grill which came away red when I wiped at it. I heaved the grill aside, and made my own descent down the shaft into the dark.

There is nothing good that can be said about a sewer, but I was glad of three things. Firstly, that there was a walkway on either side of the stagnant slurry so I didn't have to walk through the waste. Second, that I had a small cigar-sparker in my pocket, and the phos light it gave was enough to see by. Lastly, that the cartilage in my nose had long been crunched into oblivion, leaving my sense of smell about as impressive as Tnota's piano playing.

Saravor's man had been here. He'd supported himself against the wall, his handprints smeared against the brick and his trail led me to a door. A new door, not rotting, not stained with age, but good hard wood, intended to keep people out. With a lock. A big, black-iron lock. Who locks something up in a sewer? Light seeped out around the frame and I killed the sparker.

It was unlocked, ajar, a final red handprint across the edge. As though a panicked man had forgotten to close it. I went through.

18

It takes a lot to disturb me. An awful fucking lot.

I've seen things most people wouldn't believe. I've seen the ghosts of a carnival skip through the Misery, burned and skeletal. I saw gods unmake one of their own in the Engine's heart, and I saw a woman unleash enough power to vanquish an entire army. But sometimes, it's not about how fantastic or strange or fucking magical something is. It's the humanity. Or the lack of it. When I went through that door I felt my world tilt.

This shouldn't have been happening in my city.

I guess that it had been a temple of some kind, back before Valengrad was raised along the Range to protect the Engine. The columns were old, some of them carved from single pillars of stone, some of them built in stacks. There was phos light, a globe at each corner of the room rigged up to the network with crude cable-splicing. Whatever forgotten god had once been worshipped here, the space had been put to a more mundane use since. It was an abattoir. It just wasn't hogs or cattle they were butchering here.

Bodies. They were suspended on hooks and chains in ordered rows. Dozens of them, the phos light running between them in cold shafts, the badly sabotaged wires emitting a hissing crackle.

Men. Women. Occasionally children. They hung from lengths of black-iron chain, meat hooks thrust through the shoulder. The taller ones had their feet on the floor, the shorter dangled. I'd seen dead in greater numbers. Had probably made dead in greater numbers than this. But the neat, ordered way in which they had been displayed, the way they all faced toward me, heads bowed, silent, pale or dark or golden – it was methodical. Precise. This wasn't a cannon blast, spraying bodies around in the name of war. It was a practice. A choice. A decision.

They were maimed. All of them, or near enough. They were missing limbs, or skin, or guts, or a face. All of them, from the white-haired old man near the door to the teenage boy three rows behind. Something had been cut away. Not ragged, hacked or bitten, but sliced. Surgically. Precisely. Old stains covered the floor beneath them, black and dry. Unwanted bones lay in piles against the walls. Saravor had been plying his trade down here in the dark for months. Maybe years. How many people walking the streets bore his handiwork on their bodies?

I felt suddenly out of my depth. I'd never expected this, and if Saravor was here, then I'd made a grievous error. The Fixer had decided he wanted me gracked – or taken alive, given the attempt to disable and anaesthetise me – and had sent his biggest goons to do it. I'd survived them, but to survive this I should come back with a hundred men and ten Battle Spinners and lay waste to it all.

Along the side of the old temple there were other doors, and there were workbenches at the back. The tables on which these brutal human tragedies took place. Hooks on the wall carried a variety of appendages, hands mostly, but there were scalps, a few feet, faces, and what I guessed was a heart. This nightmare was here, in my city, under my nose and my anger was hot, black and thumping in my head.

I passed through the forest of bodies and found my quarry lying against one of the bloodstained workbenches. He was pale, his stump cradled up against his chest and he focused on me uncertainly.

'Fix me,' he wheezed. Didn't understand who I was. He was delirious with blood loss. 'Fix me again,' he whispered, desperate to be made whole. That's what this place was. A meat locker for Saravor's vile work. There was little chance of his getting fixed, though. Not enough blood left in his system. I should go. Instead I grabbed him by the throat.

'Where is Saravor?' I demanded. 'Where is the Eye?' Shook him. Slapped him. Tried to keep some kind of light in those eyes.

He couldn't even see me. He could barely breathe. He died.

I stood and turned, and knew I should have gone when I had the chance.

A man and a woman, each carrying a smouldering matchlock, had crept between the rows of corpses and had their weapons trained on me. I froze. They'd approached from different directions and if either fired they'd put a hole the size of my fist through me.

She was dressed in work overalls, like she'd ditched her job as a pipelayer and come to take up arms against me, but he was naked to the waist. Poor stitching formed a border between the tanned flesh of his chest and a cream-yellow patch beneath his armpit. Fixed, just as Nenn had been. More of Saravor's creations. Beads of blood had gathered at the corners of their eyes, confirming my suspicion that Saravor no longer simply put men back together. He changed them. Owned them. The Darlings could take a man's mind with their mind-worms. I'd given him that magic and he'd made it his own, woven it into his own power.

'Drop the sword,' the woman said. She was at the worst possible range. No chance I could get to her before she could fire. No real chance of her missing. Her hands were steady on the stock and I had no choice but to do as she asked. The blade rang against the temple's stone floor like a funeral bell. The man came closer, never taking his gun from me.

'Turn around,' he said. 'Face her.' Their voices sounded flat and dead. I did as he asked.

I guess he smashed me in the side of the head with the butt of his matchlock. I felt a massive impact. Confusion. Pain. Nothing really made sense. I wasn't totally out – I knew they were moving me – but my brain had rocked around enough in my skull that it made little difference. I couldn't move.

My captors had laid me out on a table and tied me down. My hands were bound together, the rope fastened to a hook above my head. My feet had earned themselves a rope each. I was still dizzy and there was a milky nausea in my guts that made me want to spit.

'The master wants him Bound,' the man said. My head was swimming and I couldn't get my thoughts to come out straight, but I got the impression that being Bound was not the same as being tied up.

'Whatever deal you have with him, trust me, it's not going to work out well for you,' I said. 'You think he'll keep to his terms, now that he's in your heads?' Neither the man nor the woman responded – didn't seem to notice me at all, in fact.

'I never back down on a deal,' said a dry, breathy, whisper from between the bodies. I closed my eyes, not yet ready to see the new speaker. My head thumped away as if a child were bringing a mallet down on it. I took a deep, steadying breath, and looked.

Two grey children had arrived, blank and expressionless as desert sand. One of them held a severed head of the kind that Saravor had once delivered to me. Dry old leather for skin, the neck neatly stitched, the eyes rolled up into its grey face. This one had been an elderly woman, her hair as fine and white as silk. The grey child held it in the crook of an elbow, and the voice that ushered from the unmoving lips was dry as the rustle of fallen leaves.

'Galharrow.'

'Saravor,' I said. The pain pulsed in my head in nauseating waves. 'It's been a while.'

'So calm, Galharrow. Good,' the head breathed. 'You cost me two very loyal servants today. Had I known you would come here of your own accord, I would but have asked. Perhaps we could have struck a new deal.' The children came closer.

'We did our last deal a long time ago, Saravor,' I said. The head's eyes slowly rotated down to look at me.

'All deals come to an end sooner or later,' the dusky voice hissed. 'Our old association is, as you say, done, but new deal or no, I require your servitude. Blackwing will assist me, in these last days.'

I thrashed hard against my bonds in a sudden panic, understanding what he meant to do, and the man flinched, hand moving to a sword at his belt but the knots only tightened and dug deeper into my wrists. I was terrified. Really, deeply terrified. Saravor wasn't here in person, but there were few living creatures that inspired as much fear in me as he did. The Deep Kings, the Nameless, the jellyfish thing under the northern Misery sands, and maybe my mother. But he was up there. Him and his creatures.

He wanted to bind me to his will, like the poor fucker who'd just bled out on the floor. Like Marollo Nacomo, and whoever had worn Devlen Maille's face. His power had grown, and if he changed me, I would become one of his creatures. A slave.

'We need a part to attach,' the male said. 'Which one?'

Silence followed for several moments.

'Bring the prisoner,' the head hissed eventually. 'If I'm to keep Galharrow in his post, it must be a fresh part. The prisoner's colouration will match well, and I have no further use for him anyway.'

The grey child placed the head down, sideways, on the table at my feet, then knelt. When it stood again it was holding a saw. Rust speckled the jagged, blunt-looking teeth. No, not rust. Just something that dried the same colour. I went tense and cold all over and strained harder against my bonds but even if I was stronger than most, that didn't mean that I could snap rope. My breath came fast. Hot, staccato pants. The saw did not gleam wickedly; it was the dull, practical grime across it that really sent dread through me.

The prisoner could have been mistaken for the most unfortunate of beggars. His hair was long and tangled, at least half of its mass composed of grease and grime. His face was gaunt, the bones stark beneath the skin. If he'd seen a bowl of water in the last year, he hadn't chosen to wash with it. But his clothes had once been fine. They were a uniform dirt colour now but the quality of the lace and silk had not been destroyed by whatever horror they'd put him through.

The grey children watched as the prisoner came meekly. No fight in him, whoever he'd been before Saravor took him. He was pushed into a corner, and cringed away from the hand that forced him.

'It needs to be a limb to bind him strongly. Galharrow has shown me his capacity for resistance before,' the head breathed. 'A right hand can cause problems with signatures. A foot always affects gait and draws attention. Take his left arm. The match won't be perfect, but he can wear sleeves.'

The grey child passed the saw to the goon.

'What do you want, Saravor? Tell me. Maybe we can make a deal,' I said. Desperate. Weak. Throwing two dice and hoping for three sixes. 'There's something you want. Tell me. Let's trade. I'm good for it, you know that.'

I sounded pathetic. I was pathetic. But then, everyone is when they're about to lose a limb.

'What does any man want?' the head said. 'I want to be great. To be stronger, bolder. To control, to ascend.' The talk of power made the grey children smile. 'You can offer me nothing that I cannot claim myself,' the corpse-lips breathed. 'What would you give me? Money? Sex? No, Galharrow. There is only one thing I truly want from you.'

'Too much to hope that it's my good opinion?' I growled.

'Your teeth,' the head said. I swear that dead old woman's head almost smiled at me. 'What a prize they would be. I would wear them myself. The teeth that tore out Torolo Mancono's throat!'

'You're fucking mad,' I said.

'If you lie still, I'll get through the bone quicker,' the man with the saw said. 'If the angle is clean, the fixing won't go on a wonk. Less pain. Be your old self faster.' He smiled and pointed toward the stitching around his armpit. As though his enslavement was some glorious gift.

'Galharrow ...' the filth-encrusted prisoner's voice was weak, from the corner. He was staring at me like I was the Spirit of Judgment sent down to burn him. Horrified. His mouth hung loosely open and as I stared at him for a moment, I knew him.

Dantry spirits-damned Tanza.

I thrashed again against my bonds again, the ropes biting deeper into my flesh, straining with all I had, the flax cutting and drawing blood, and I screamed and jerked and did what I could, and all of it was nothing. I fought until I was bloody and raw, panting. They let me exhaust myself. They had plenty of time.

'Hold him,' the man with the saw said to the woman. She came forward and applied her weight to my elbows, tried to flatten them against the table. She hadn't the weight to keep me down, but the ropes weren't letting go. Saw-Man gave me a look. 'It really will be easier if you don't struggle,' he said. For a treacherous moment my fear won through and I considered not battling with all my fight, but it was only a moment. I growled and spat, but she crushed me down and I was tired and still half-concussed. The jagged saw teeth rested against the skin of my inner left elbow.

And drew back.

I jerked my arm away as the teeth bit into flesh. The saw slipped, and instead of digging into my elbow, the jagged teeth tore across the raven tattooed across my forearm.

I'd told Nenn that I'd tried to dig the raven from my flesh once. I knew the consequences.

There was a crack, as though a hundred-year-old oak had been felled. A smell, of hot tar and burned hair. The raven fought back against the saw's teeth and my arm burned as a splurge of liquid darkness flared out into the room, hurling Saw-Man and the woman against the wall. A nightmare spilled from my arm, a living blackness: Crowfoot's fail-safe in case his servants tried to cut him from their own bodies. The corruption that spilled out was formless, a cloud of boiling, hate-filled ink in the air which lashed back and forth, mindless and volatile. An oily, stinking purple light filled the room.

I saw Saravor's grey children as I never had before. All pretence was flayed away, their true natures revealed. There were no children here. I have no name for what they were, but they were old, old as the mountains, wrinkled and impure. Rows of blunt horns rose from scaly brows, and their bony thinness came not from a lack of appetite but from never being sated. They hissed and shrieked, orange eyes wide as foreign magic flared out to burn them.

Wild and uncontrolled, the corruption spilled from my arm. The wood beneath me sizzled and turned moist, and the ropes binding my arms dried and disintegrated. As I came free, the grey children gave a shrill shriek and fled.

The woman was dead, the burst of magic having rotted her flesh from her bones, but the man had only been thrown back by its blast. He picked himself up as the poisoned magic sputtered out, the flesh on the side of his face sizzling and running in streams. Half-blind, he brandished the saw as a weapon, but I was free now. My vision wasn't all there, but I got my hands on his saw and after we crashed down on the ground his neck got opened, and I got sprayed with whatever had been inside him.

I grabbed Dantry and I didn't give two shits about the pain shooting through my leg as I lifted him. When it comes to those you love, there is no pain that cannot be endured. I forgot the pain in my head and focused on getting him out of there, getting him to safety. I heard the grey children's shrieks receding into the dark tunnels as I fled. They would be back with more men, and more saws.

19

I wouldn't have fed what was left of Dantry Tanza to a starving dog. Or more accurately, I doubt that even a lean dog would have been terribly interested in trying to gnaw the gristle from his bones.

When I had first met him, out in the Misery, he'd been thirty years old, but with a certain boyishness in both look and character. Soft skin, hands more used to pen than plough, and a lightness of heart that only came from having a bank account whose bottom he'd never had to acknowledge. Then there had been his willingness to believe, a refusal to accept that – despite his situation, despite the murder of his manservant Glost – anybody might have an agenda against him.

Standing over his bedside, it gave me little joy to see he could not doubt it now.

Dantry had always been slender, but now he was skeletal. The most wretched beggars in the Spills would have pitied him. His skin was milky-white as a maggot, his hair and beard grown into a damp, matted clump. He was filthy, and he must have been wearing the same tattered rags since he was taken. A single pearl button had clung to the front of his shirt, a last stubborn memory of its former finery.

I had sent Maldon to bring Casso and Valiya. While I had washed the blood from my wrists and head, they'd stripped him down in the yard and dealt with the worst of the lice, cutting his hair and burning his rags. Dantry was in too much shock to acknowledge the indignity. I added it to the stack of grudges I held against Saravor on his behalf.

He lay in my bed, in my house, a fever bringing perspiration to his brow, alternating between shaking and lying entirely still, silent as a corpse. I hadn't seen him in over two years. All the resentment I'd felt that he'd gone sat like a traitor in my chest.

Valiya and Amaira came in with a bowl of hot water, scissors, a razor.

'Do you want to, or shall I?' Valiya asked gently. My hand had a shake about it, so I nodded that she should go ahead. My skull was still pounding, and my leg would be biting me for days.

'Why's he so sick?' Amaira asked. She was reluctant to go near to him.

'Some bad people have treated him very poorly,' I said. 'This is why we do what we do, Amaira. Because good people like this boy are hurt and in pain.'

'He's a man, not a boy' Amaira said. She was right, but Dantry would always seem a boy to me.

Valiya worked quietly. She'd cut away the tangled beard in the yard, and worked quietly now with a razor to remove the remaining stubble. Dantry flinched and mumbled. He'd been fevered by the time I'd dragged him out of the sewer, as though he'd been holding it back with all his strength before. He'd let go now, and it had him under siege.

'Who held him this way?' Valiya asked.

'Saravor,' I said. 'He had Dantry. He has the Eye. And he's going to pay for taking them both.'

'Do you know where to find him?'

I shook my head, a mistake. The motion made my head swim, dizziness and nausea striking me. Determined, strong fingers pulled me down into a chair and Amaira stepped away as I thumped into it, flushing a cloud of dust from the cushion. The whole room had a neglected air. Of course it did – I was hardly ever here, and my housekeeper looked to have abandoned her duties after the sky-fires began falling. I was exhausted, frayed at every edge, worn through and out of reserves. The fight against Saravor's puppets had taken what little I had left. I needed brandy. Or something, anything, to take the edge off. Let me get a little energy back.

'Can I get you something, Captain-Sir?' Amaira asked.

'Why's she here?' I asked Valiya over her head. 'She shouldn't be seeing this stuff.'

'You sent everyone else to the sewer, and I needed another pair of hands. Amaira, more water please.'

The kid looked downcast. Hurt. She didn't understand that I wanted to save her from this for her own good. The life of a Blackwing captain was nothing to strive for, no route to wealth, or family, or happiness. I was barely even an umbrella against life's steady stream of piss. She was a good kid. She deserved a better life.

I woke from the usual dream. Ezabeth, cold and lost in the light, reaching out to me. I reached for her but could never touch her maimed hand. Safely awake again, I shivered in the quiet, cosy room. Valiya had settled a blanket over me. Candles gave a soft light, and the fire had been stoked. Across the room, Dantry's quiet breathing whistled in and out of his chest, but the smell of his sickness was masked by a scent in the candles. My head pulsed, and I wondered what had woken me.

A jug of tea, many hours cold, sat on a side table beside some beef, winter greens and, best of all, a bottle of Whitelande brandy. I ignored the glass, settled back into the chair and drank hard. Whitelande brandy alone was worth defending the republic for. I wondered whether Valiya or Amaira had set it there, and finally decided that I loved them both in their way, and that it didn't matter. I got through half of the brandy without rising from the chair, and then heard the thunderous crash far overhead as Thierro's shield deflected a missile. The sky-fires were hammering down again. That was probably what had woken me.

I winced each time I bent my wrists. The red weals the ropes had left were scabbed and sore, but there was nothing to show from where the saw had bitten into the raven mark on my forearm. Not for the first time I wondered where Crowfoot and Nall were, what schemes they were plotting, and why they hadn't come to our aid. I thought of the frozen bird that had torn itself from my arm, deformed and failing in its ability to deliver a message. None of it was good.

I was bone weary, my legs jittery and throbbing with exhaustion, but sleep had retreated back to its swamp. My mind swarmed with things I knew, things that I thought I knew, and inevitably, my worries over what I didn't know at all. Saravor's plans were more advanced than I had dared to imagine. Sending men into the Misery, stealing the Eye from Crowfoot's vault – those had felt like the beginning, but I saw now that he'd been plotting against us much longer. Probably from the moment I bestowed Shavada's power upon him. Alone with my regrets, time passed slowly. I heard the impacts of four sky-fires that made it past the Witnesses' shields. After what I'd witnessed beneath the city, they didn't even make me flinch.

Dawn came and with it Valiya brought me hot tea and porridge.

'Nenn's back from the sewers. You'll want to talk it through with her.'

'Send her in.'

Nenn looked like she'd had a rough night, which for her was impressive. I'd sent her in with her Ducks and every other kill-hungry bastard I had once we'd got clear.

'How's the city?'

'In pieces. Four of the sky-fires made it through the

shield. One of them hit a slaughterhouse, and there're pork chops all over the neighbouring roofs. How's Dantry?'

'About the same.' I rubbed at my eyes, pried the sleep from them. 'What did you find?'

'I thought I'd seen the worst the world had to throw at us in the Misery,' Nenn said. 'That was worse.'

Nenn and the boys had stormed down there, but the grey children had disappeared and Saravor was nowhere to be seen. Maldon had gone down with them to be sure, but the Eye hadn't been stored there. Saravor had more than one hideout, as I knew he would. He might well have more charnel houses set up beneath the city, dead bodies hung like slaughtered cattle ready to be harvested for parts. Their number made it clear. Saravor wasn't just fixing people anymore. He wasn't just taking the occasional client who wanted to make a deal. He was building a force of servants he could control directly.

Maybe Nenn knew it too. She reached for the half-drunk brandy and I didn't stop her. After a few swallows she planted herself beside me.

'I was hoping you'd at least get those children of his,' I said. 'I don't know what they are, but we'd be better off if they were dead.'

'It's Saravor I want,' Nenn said. Her eyes focused on some imagined scene which, knowing her, meant hacking him to pieces. We'd left the worst fear unspoken, hoping that Saravor's newfound abilities didn't backdate to those he'd fixed up before I gave Shavada's power to the grey children.

'The book,' a hoarse wheeze came from across the room.

I got up, unsteady on my feet despite having slept for longer than I usually did in a week. I flexed my shoulders, a trio of knots in my spine cracking like crushed beetles. I was getting too old to be swinging swords at people and the fierce, abrupt action had pulled something in my shoulder and something else in my hip. I winced as I walked over to Dantry's bedside.

'How are you doing?' I asked him. His shrunken, skull-face peered back at me. He'd taken on a reddish colouring, and the sheets around him had a damp-sweat odour.

'Were my books there? Papers? Did they find them?'

'No books,' Nenn said, joining us. 'Spirit of Mercy, Dantry. You look like a pig's arse.'

'Good to see you too, General.' He managed a weak smile. It rose and fell like a ball tossed in the air. Nenn was about to explain that she was no longer a general on account of being unable to hold her fists in check, but there was time for that later.

'What book?' I asked. Dantry gestured that he wanted to sit up, so I propped him up on the numerous pillows.

'The Taran Codex. It was there.'

That damned book. Dantry had obsessed about it, before he disappeared.

'Nothing down there now but the dead,' Nenn said. She handed him a bowl. 'Eat. Get some food in your belly.'

I asked Nenn to get more brandy, wanting her out of the room. I'd sent her and her Ducks into the sewers on reflex, but after what I'd seen, it was better if she wasn't party to our conversation.

Between mouthfuls of nourishing oxtail broth, Dantry recounted what he remembered. He'd lost all track of time down there, and we both thought he'd been a prisoner for most of the two years since I'd last seen him.

'I knew who he was,' Dantry said. 'Saravor. He looked like he was made of patchwork pieces which didn't quite fit together. He knew I had a copy of the Codex. He lured me to meet him, claimed to be a linguistics expert, but there were men waiting for me. They took me belowground and into a cell. I haven't left it until now.'

'Why?'

'He made me help him with the book. To understand it.'

'But you couldn't read it?'

'I couldn't. But Saravor translated it from the Akat. He knows things, Ryhalt. He's so old. Or those children are. There are things in that book that nobody should know. Taran was Nameless, and he codified what he knew about how to breach reality a thousand years ago.' He paused. 'I wish that I could un-know what I learned, and Saravor only showed me glimpses. Only the parts that he couldn't understand. He made me work calculations for him.' The spoon trembled in his fingers. 'He used the mind-worms on me, tried to scour my mind for information. But he couldn't force me to think for him. They don't work that way. He can make puppets of men's bodies, can read their memories, but he can't force them to think something new.'

Astronomy and mathematics. They had always been Dantry's gifts, and he had laboured at them, alone and in the dark. Sometimes his lantern would burn out, and they would forget him for days. Then one of Saravor's minions would replace the oil and tell him to get back to work. If he didn't work, he didn't eat, that was the deal, and so he worked.

'What did he want?' I said. Dantry closed his eyes and laid his head back against the pillow.

'Everything,' he said. 'To learn what Taran once knew, and unlock the secrets of the Codex. He wants to become like the Nameless. Or the Deep Kings. But he was always afraid. He feared the Nameless.' He looked straight at me. 'He feared Ezabeth. For a time, anyway. He kept bringing me details of the Bright Lady sightings. They were growing more frequent. He wanted to know what she was. But the more we learned, the less he was afraid. He started to believe that she was gathering power with each appearance, and when I threatened him, said she was coming back to save me, he laughed and gave me more of the Codex to read.

Forced me to prove what he'd already deduced.' He looked at the blanket in his lap. 'I'm sorry, Ryhalt. You were right. It would take more power than the Heart of the Void ever held to reach through to her in the light. She's trapped in another world and not even Nall's Engine commands the kind of force necessary to breach that barrier. There's no way to reach her.' He looked so pained.

'The Bright Order believes she'll come back,' I said. I had refused to believe it for so long. But somewhere, deep inside me, I'd held to the faintest glimmer of hope. With his words, that hope cracked in half and disintegrated into dust.

'Her world isn't ours anymore. She can no more bring herself back than we can reach through to her. The laws laid down in the Taran Codex proved that.'

I thought of Dantry, alone and wretched, slowly doing the calculations to prove that all his hopes had been in vain. If I ever got a chance, I'd tear Saravor apart with my bare hands, piece by stitched-together piece.

'Then why would she be gathering power. If there's no way – why?'

'I don't know. Though Saravor proved that's what she was doing. He found something else in the Codex that interested him more. The things in that book – Ryhalt, I know how stars are born. I understand how to split the tiniest particles that make us all. It's staggering. I only know of a handful of academics in all of the city-states who could have worked those equations.'

'But you did.'

Dantry stirred his broth.

'What choice did I have?'

'No choice at all,' I said. 'I'd have worked them too. So what's he planning?'

'I don't know. Not exactly,' Dantry said. 'But I deduced parts of it. He plans to pit two opposing magics against one another. I don't know what, but colossal forces. He needed to know how to avoid being destroyed by them. Spirits save me, Ryhalt, I showed him. Whatever he's planning, he knows everything he needed to. He ran out of uses for me.'

Except as spare parts.

'Rest,' I said. 'When you've slept, start writing down whatever you can remember. Anything that might help us. Whatever he knows, we need to know it too.'

'I'll try,' Dantry said. 'Ryhalt – I'm sorry.'

My mood had turned too dark for comfort. I hadn't any kind words for him.

I left him to his rest. Nenn had to get going. She'd worked through the night, but with Colonel Koska in charge in the citadel and Bright Order men running the show, I needed a steadying hand up at the citadel. Her soldiers were already on the streets, in the cold, tense air.

Nenn and I bumped into Valiya at the door. 'Unless you need me, I have to get some rest,' Valiya said. She looked as worn as the rest of us. She hadn't needed to stay all night, but telling Valiya to stop working was like telling me to stop drinking. 'Major Nenn, could you put a couple of men on the door?'

'Manpower's stretched taut as rope right now, but I'll find someone,' Nenn said. Both of them hesitated, waiting for the other to leave. Nenn won the standoff, crossed her arms and watched Valiya walk toward a hired carriage. The sound she made was half grunt, half laugh.

'What?' I asked.

'Just funny. She's been trying to get inside your bedroom for a while. Probably didn't imagine it would happen like this.' She took out blacksap, put the disgusting stuff between her teeth and began to chew.

He words rankled. We'd talked this way for most of the last ten years, but I didn't think it was respectful to talk about Valiya when she wasn't around. She was proud. I couldn't imagine that she'd have appreciated it. I told Nenn as much.

'She'd forgive you soon enough if you lifted her skirts and went to town. You should do it, too. Might loosen you up a bit.'

'And here I was hoping Captain Betch would fuck some sense into you.'

Nenn niggled a bit of grit from her blacksap and spat it out into the front garden.

'I'm not embarrassed to say that I like fucking, Ryhalt. It's the way the spirits made us, and I'll be damned if I'm ashamed to say that I enjoy it. That's your problem, you know. You only want things that you can't have. Only you can have her, you've just convinced yourself you can't. I doubt you're paying that woman enough to have her making you soup through the night. Read the news sheet, as they say.'

'Piss off and stop bothering me. Go save the city or something.'

We clapped hands together, and for all our jabs and insults, we were still close as pigs in the mud. That wouldn't be the case in my next conversation.

Maldon was down in my cellar, in what he'd turned into a workshop of sorts. He'd lit the place with traditional lamps, no phos to be seen, but I could smell it in the air even against the hot ache of smelted steel. He had a big workbench, a small furnace, and all kinds of metallic wizardry that simpler men like me couldn't begin to understand.

The blind child worked, alone, humming to himself. He wasn't wearing his blindfold so I could see the hole in his skull, the wound that would never heal and never kill him. The rhyme he sang was an old one that chilled me. *The night is dark, the night is cold . . .*

'You've been busy down here,' I said. He didn't look up; what would have been the point?

'Busy is better,' he said. 'Pass me that spanner.'

I found it on his cluttered workbench among a series of rifled matchlock barrels, the deconstructed parts of at least two flarelock firearms, gears, cogs, steel winches, leather straps, and other assorted metallic junk and tools. He took the spanner, adjusted it and tightened two bits of metal.

'What are you making?' I asked.

'Weapons,' he said. 'That amateur Besh Flindt thinks these flarelocks he's making are something to be proud of, doesn't he? I'm going to show him what a real phos weapon can do.'

'Can you make something more stable than the flare-locks?' I said. I picked up a phos canister that had imploded, the iron shell crumpled inwards.

'I'm not sure. I was working on similar ideas a long time ago, but I always ran into testing issues. Now it doesn't matter if I make a mistake. I can blow myself up a number of times, can't I? So far all my calculations show that there is a substantial chance that my weapon will explode after firing. But if it doesn't, it would make one man worth an army.'

I was confident that Maldon would probably survive any malfunctions that his project experienced. I wasn't so sure about my house, but I'd allowed this, and it did seem to be keeping him out of trouble. He didn't even seem drunk, for the first time in several years. Empty bottles still cluttered the edges of the room, but not as many as I'd expected.

'What does it do?'

'I'll show you when it's finished. Did you want something, or were you just checking I'm being a good son?'

'There was something.'

I laid out what we'd discovered beneath the city. Maldon kept tinkering at first, but when Saravor's name came up he put the revolving discs he'd been screwing together down and sat back in his chair.

'I would have beaten him, if you hadn't taken my power,' he said. His voice was very quiet. I sensed a hint of resentment there, even though he knew that had I not taken his magic, he would have killed me.

'I know.'

'Saravor had some raw power. It was strange, not like anyone or anything else that I'd encountered before. Not that anyone is generally the same, where magic is concerned. But it came from somewhere dark. Someplace that shouldn't be touched.'

'I gave him the power that Shavada had put into you,' I said. 'That's how I beat you both. We made a deal and those creatures that serve him took it. How powerful could he be, now?'

Maldon shrugged his bony shoulders.

'How far is a Misery mile?'

'He took the Eye, too,' I said. 'What can he do with it?'

'The Eye wasn't worth much after it came out of Prince Herono's face,' Maldon said. 'Indestructible, like any physical part of a Deep King. Remember when we fired that cannon at it? And it just kept grubbing around on the floor.' The memory raised a smile, but it didn't last. 'But when Shavada was destroyed, any power the Eye contained was lost. It's an empty vessel.'

'An empty vessel,' I said slowly. 'Could it be filled?'

'With what?'

'Phos?'

'No,' Maldon said. 'I doubt it, anyway. When Shavada took me, I lost all of my spinning ability.' He snapped his fingers as if expecting a spark. Nothing happened. 'They're different sides of a coin. You can't put light into darkness.'

It had been a wild theory. A layman trying to guess how forces beyond his control worked. Better to leave it to the experts and focus on finding the damn thing. I lingered in the workshop as Maldon went back to his work, not quite able to bring myself to say what I needed to. Maldon put down the screwdriver again.

'Spit it out,' he said. 'Or go away.'

'Saravor has changed,' I said eventually. 'He's controlling people. I'd assumed that Nacomo was being paid, or blackmailed, but now I'm not sure. He'd changed his face and to free himself, he cut it off. He didn't want to be Saravor's puppet anymore.'

'Hard choice to make, I guess,' Maldon said. 'Keep your face or your mind. He chose right, I guess.'

'When Saravor takes them they seem clumsy, like someone else is pulling their strings. Others seem normal. Kind of. I'm not sure they even understood what he was doing to them. But Saravor fixed Nenn, four years back. You think he can get in her head?'

Maldon didn't have an answer for me. He picked up two pieces of metal, tried them together. Spun a little wheel on a greased axle.

'I don't know. That was before he took Shavada's power and his puppeteering is a new trick that he learned since. Let's hope he can't. I like Nenn. She doesn't look on me with pity.'

I nodded.

'I have to ask something of you.' Maldon lifted his hairless chin, only I couldn't bring myself to say it. Maldon understood, chewed his lip, then nodded. A slow nod. A killing nod.

'If it comes to that,' he said. 'I'll do it. The Range asks a lot of you, Ryhalt, but not even I'd ask you to do that. If she's lost to us, send her here to collect my old journals. I'll make it quick.'

I'd asked him to do it, and he'd promised the right things. But in that moment I hated him nonetheless.

We both jumped as a bird flew headlong into one of the high windows that ran close to the ceiling. It collapsed, dazed, beyond the glass. It was just a bird, and there was nothing unusual about that, only it was a raven, and I pay particular attention to ravens. It had a mantle of white feathers around its shoulders and running up the back of its head, and it struggled back to its feet. For a moment it examined us through the grimy pane, then began to peck and scrape its beak across the glass. *Tap, tap-tap, tap-scrape. Tap-tap-scrape. Scrape.*

'Crash must have addled its brain,' Maldon said. 'It thinks it's a woodpecker.'

'No,' I said. I stood and listened. 'It's communicator code.'

'Sure it is,' Maldon snorted. 'What's it saying? Give me a worm?'

'No,' I said. 'It's saying "let me in".'

20

'What is it?' Maldon asked. 'A crow?'

'No,' I said. 'I think it's a hooded raven. But you don't see them around here.'

I reached up and pushed the window open. The raven ducked inside and fluttered down to perch atop one of Maldon's brass-and-steel contraptions.

It stepped from foot to foot in a manner I'd seen before. That usually meant Crowfoot was laughing at me, and I had a bad feeling about where this was going. The noises it was making were becoming more coherent, some of them actually starting to sound like speech, though its attempts at forming words were closer to squeaks and whistles.

'I don't like it,' Maldon said. His childish timbre made him sound fearful. Maybe he was. 'We should kill it.'

'I think that would be a bad idea,' I said.

The raven flicked its head to one side, then seemed to suddenly switch from avian squeaks to a harsh, guttural language. Short, punchy syllables ran together in blocks. Definitely a language, but not one that I knew. Maldon shrugged. The bird flicked its head again and this time it made the click-and-buzz droning of the drudge. Some of it I caught, but not much, my grasp of drudge-speak being limited. The bird buzzed and hummed, but then it flicked its head sideways one final time, and said, 'How about now? Can you understand me now?'

Maldon and I would have shared a look, except that he couldn't look at anything. Mad as it sounds, a bird coming out of my arm was familiar. A talking bird didn't seem all that strange.

'I understand you,' I said.

'Good. I wasn't sure which idiotic language you speak. I will stick to this one so it doesn't wear out your brains.'

I bowed my head.

'I am at your service, Master,' I said. Gleck had started to shuffle back across the room. He'd escaped the Nameless's notice following the siege. He feared them. Everyone did, of course, but there was a little bit of Deep King in Maldon that hadn't quite been erased when Shavada's power was stripped away, the part that kept him young and indestructible, and his greatest fear was that the Nameless would decide to dissect him to learn more about their enemy. The raven didn't seem to have any interest in him, however.

'Master?' the bird croaked. It had a high, nasal, irritating voice. 'I'm not your master, Galharrow, you worm-piss. I assume you're Galharrow anyway, not the child? Hard to tell at this proximity.'

I didn't know what the raven meant, but it was a raven, so it wasn't going to make sense.

'I'm Galharrow,' I said. 'What are you, then?'

'I'm a part of his power, obviously,' the raven said. 'He shaved me off and sent me here.'

'And you didn't come through my arm because ...?'

'Too much magical interference from the wards the Nameless have placed around themselves. Too much cold. His last message didn't come through properly, did it? He was furious about the Eye's being taken from Narheim. Not going to be happy that you've failed to get it back, either. He wants to commune with you in person.'

That struck me cold. Crowfoot was bad enough through an avatar. The few times I'd been forced into his physical

209

company had been worse. There was an evil gleam to the raven's eyes. More of Crowfoot in it than it cared to admit, maybe.

'Where is Crowfoot?' I said. 'We have death raining on us from the sky and chaos in the streets. What in the hells is he doing that's so important?'

'The hells, the hells,' the bird croaked back at me. Its eyes were as black as the feathers across its head, but they gleamed like pools of oil. 'Do you think that what's happening here is the only thing of importance in the world? Do you? You humans think everything's about you and your own lives. This war is waged on more than one front, you should know that.'

'Valengrad is the heart of the Range's defence,' I growled. 'Without the Engine we lose the war.'

'The Engine? Everything of consequence is protected,' the bird scoffed. 'You're talking about a few civilians. It's a war, Galharrow. Wars are about killing. Your hands are stained enough to know that.'

The bird looked around as if hungry. There was no food in the room. Birds can't make expressions, they haven't the faces for it, but this one managed to look annoyed. I took a deep breath. I wanted to get this over with. If Crowfoot wanted to speak to me, then he was likely furious at my failure, and I'd seen the price men paid for agitating the Nameless.

'He can speak to me through you?' I asked.

'No,' the raven said. 'He wants to talk to you himself. Ready?'

'I suppose.'

'You should sit down for this,' the raven said. He cocked his head toward Maldon. 'And you should fuck off.' Maldon didn't need to be told twice. He was up the stairs faster than I'd seen him move in years. I didn't like the sound of this, but I sat anyway. The raven cawed, maybe a laugh, maybe just a bird sound. But when I'd sat cross-legged on the floor it launched into the air, flew a tight circle around the room and then flew right at me. I raised my hands to stop him but it passed right through them and then everything changed.

A cosmic rush. Light-headedness, a flurry of stars bending time and substance as I raced through the voids that lie between all things. A roaring, a gale between mountains.

I was somewhere else. In darkness, alone with a silvery thread of insubstantial thought-essence. I groped along the link until I felt something, a huge and terrible presence at the other end. Big as a star, dark as a mountain's heart. It was Crowfoot, I realised. I was seeing him, and seeing *into* him, and I never thought that there could be so much space in all the universe.

I was myself, but not myself. No emotion. No feeling. Those things had been left behind in the body that I no longer inhabited. I became aware of more, not just Crowfoot but of the Nameless. A place, far away, so far it could have been another world entirely.

He was beyond the reach of cold. Three of them, standing as points of a small triangle. Frost coated them, snow had banked against their hunched forms. There was nothing around them but grey snow and blue ice, and a screeching wind that carried more of the same out of the north. The pale blue ice stretched on and on into forever. Flat, featureless, a place of bright paleness, and yet everything there was dead. Through the thread that led me to Crowfoot I understood that I had been brought to a place of power. I had always imagined such places to be surrounded by standing stones, a forest glade, a holy mountain shrine. Something to mark the spot as unique. But there was nothing but ice and wind and echoing loneliness.

Three watchers, three workers of power. My master had not moved in days. Maybe weeks, months, years. He didn't need to. His eyes, mouth and ears were frozen over. His body was blue and cold, solid as the glacier on which it sat. A part of it. Across the cold air sat Nall, or one of him, looking as dead as carrion. His eyes were slightly open. Perhaps he could see me, frozen stiff though he was. Shallowgrave completed the triangle, but I couldn't focus on him. He was a blur, a distortion against the eye; even while he was immobile my mind rejected him. Here were the Nameless. Our defenders, frozen, alone and locked in a silent war, immobile as they worked unseen, invisible violence. I was not the only one that made sacrifices for the war. We hated them, feared them, but we would be lost without them.

I looked down at the clouded blue permafrost. The ice plain was featureless, but there was something down there. A long way down, deep beneath the hardpack glacial ice. Shadows of something that has been buried for all the slow years in which the frozen river had claimed it, inch by grinding inch. Nothing lived down there. But there was a presence all the same.

'Galharrow.' Crowfoot's voice was slow and low, as if the words were crushed between thoughts of immense significance. 'You are failing me, Galharrow.'

I could have answered, but there was nothing I could say to appease him.

'Where is Shavada's Eye?' he grated. He wanted to display more fury, more of his rage at my failure, but to do so would have cost him. I was the barest speck of acknowledgment on the edge of his conscience.

'The Eye is in Valengrad,' I told him. 'Saravor has it. I *will* find it, Lord.'

'The children's keeper seeks to become Nameless,' Crowfoot said. 'The Earth Serpents feel it in their turning, in the very magic that drives the world. If the keeper unmakes the Eye while we are locked against the Deep Kings, we will not have the strength to oppose him. He will master us all.'

'How do I stop him, Lord?' I asked. The depth of Crowfoot's will surrounded me, crushing down like the fathoms of ice below, but even as I was crushed I felt it fading, returning to another purpose.

'GALHARROW,' the whispered roar struck at me, 'DO NOT FALL TO THE SPIRIT IN THE LIGHT. IT WILL SEEK TO UNMAKE YOU. DO NOT FUCK THIS UP.'

I became conscious as the first wave of nausea rolled through me. I rolled onto my side and threw up everything that Valiya had made for me, and the brandy besides. I was cold, terribly cold, my fingers turned white. I crawled over to Maldon's little forge where the heat sent a knifing pain through my cold flesh. The hooded raven peered down from the workbench, head cocked to one side.

'Where is Crowfoot?' I said.

'There's no word for it in your language. Your people have never been there,' the raven said.

'Why is he there when we need him here?'

'This is a war on many fronts, you self-obsessed nit. The Deep Kings have struck back. They're attempting to sink your whole country beneath the ocean.'

The bird said it simply and plainly, as though it was nothing more serious than poor weather.

'They what?'

'It's an ancient working. The kind that bound the Deep Kings beneath the ocean in the first place. There's something that sleeps in the depths of the eastern ocean, far beyond the Dhojaran Empire. Something vaster and more powerful than Kings or the Nameless, a creature that grew old before there were words to describe it. The Nameless call it The Sleeper. The Deep Kings seek to awaken it.'

That sounded like the kind of bad that went beyond the daily howling of the sky.

213

'Can they do it?' I said. The bird bobbed up and down, spread its wings wide.

'The ritual that the Deep Kings are attempting requires great power. They will sacrifice a million of their followers to generate enough soul magic to contact The Sleeper and drive it to summon waves that will swamp the land. The Sleeper's influence would tear away the Lady of Waves' control of the ocean, allowing the drudge to build ships, move freely across the sea. The Nameless cannot allow this. It is a battle of wills. You will have felt the earth shaking beneath you; when The Sleeper stirs. Such is its vastness, you feel it here.'

'They're causing the earth tremors?'

'Essentially.'

'And all those people that the Deep Kings are going to sacrifice. They're all going to die?'

'They're drudge,' the raven said. 'A million fewer enemies to deal with is an excellent prospect. Although it won't be their fighting drudge they eviscerate. But, it's all part of their war machine. Soul magic has always been part of the Deep Kings' arsenal, but they have seldom attempted anything on this scale. Shavada's destruction has left them angry, oh, so angry! They must be spitting blood.' The bird seemed to find this a positive thing and made laughing sounds. Whatever snip of power Crowfoot had created it from, it seemed his sense of humour had been absorbed with it.

'Crowfoot wants me to stop Saravor unmaking the eye, but didn't tell me how it can be done, or how I can stop him. What does he want me to do?' Crowfoot's messages were seldom hot on detail. I looked at my frozen fingers and re-membered his words. The spirit in the light would unmake me, if I let it. I had no idea what that meant. Something to keep to myself, maybe.

'Sort this fucking shit out,' the bird snarled, and in

that I heard Crowfoot's tone: anger at my incompetence. 'Crowfoot, Shallowgrave and Nall are freezing their arses to the rock to keep you safe and whilst they're gone you've managed to lose Shavada's Eye. Get it the fuck back.'

The raven cocked its head a little, then flapped into the air, up to the window.

It was clearly too much to expect that Crowfoot's little helper would have some information that was actually useful to the task at hand, rather than just an admonishment for not having done what he wanted yet, but at least the raven wasn't as unpleasant as my master's usual messengers. It made a change not to be covered in my own blood.

'I'll be watching you,' the raven said. 'And if you can't do what he wants, I'll find someone else who can. I'm going to go see if I can locate the Eye where you've failed.' With that, it nudged its way outside and flew away.

'Crowfoot is a fucking arsehole,' Maldon said, peeking in through the door.

'You won't hear any arguments from me there,' I said. 'What do you make of all that?'

'It sounds very fucking bad,' Maldon said. 'But then, you have to wonder just how much of this has been going on for the last thousand years, don't you? How often does one side or the other come up with something like the Heart of the Void?'

'Once was too often,' I said. 'The sky should never have been sundered.' I wondered how many of our people Crowfoot had destroyed when he unleashed his weapon and burned the Misery into being. Too many. Sometimes I wondered if he'd known how badly he would tear reality when he unleashed that power, but I always came to the same conclusion. It was better not to know.

'That came from far, far away,' Maldon said. He had shrunk back against the wall. Almost as though he were afraid. 'For a moment, when it flew into you, I felt

Crowfoot's presence. It was so similar to Shavada's. The power. It's colossal.'

'Best not to be on the wrong side of it.'

'One of these days you'll have to tell me how you got that tattoo, and what you owe him,' Maldon said.

'One day, maybe,' I said. I didn't mean it. Some things should not be shared.

21

I wrote a letter to Grand Prince Vercanti, giving my recommendations for the new marshal. He was away on the west coast, raising mercenaries to take back holdings we'd lost in Angol, and it would take time to reach him. The Range was going to have to endure for a while. Davandein was his blood kin, and her defeat was going to cost Vercanti face. He probably wouldn't give my suggestion much time, but I put my weight behind Marshal Ngoya anyway. Colonel Koska had done a good enough job getting the city in order, but he was no great tactician and certainly not the man to lead the Range. Especially not when he was taking his direction from a spirit in the light. One that Crowfoot had warned me against.

I didn't know what to think about that.

'Leave the politicking to the cream,' the raven cawed at me. It had shown up at the office and was currently nesting atop a pile of old warrants.

'We need leads to follow,' I snapped. 'Can't just search the whole city house by house. I'm working on it.' The raven flared its feathers out, a hostile reaction, but despite spending several days flying around the city it hadn't turned up anything, so it had no argument to make.

I was sealing the letter with wax when Amaira came in.

'I love it,' Amaira proclaimed upon seeing the bird.

'Keep away from it,' I said. 'It might have diseases.'

Amaira evidently didn't believe me and went as far as to disobey me, stroking the crow's feathers. I was lacing up my boots, in a rush.

'Why don't you put it outside?' she asked.

'Just leave it alone,' I snapped, and Amaira recoiled a little.

'Now, now,' the raven said in a voice altogether too friendly for Crowfoot. 'No need to snap!'

'It talks!' Amaira declared with delight. You'd think that she might have been more unnerved by a talking bird, but Nenn had been passing her Misery shit for over a year now, and when you grow up alongside a cracked and screaming sky, it takes a lot to faze you.

'What use is a bird that can't talk? Clever things, birds,' the raven said pleasantly. I immensely disliked its talking to her.

'Message from Tnota, Captain-Sir!' she said, and snapped me a salute.

'Don't do that,' I said as I took the scrap of paper from her. She looked like she'd not been getting much sleep lately. I knew the cellar was cold and uncomfortable, but I wouldn't allow her to be anywhere else when the barrage came in.

'Why not, Captain-Sir?' she said.

'Because you're not a soldier. You're a servant. Servants don't salute.'

'I will be a Blackwing one day,' Amaira said.

I paused with the envelope in my hands. I set it down.

'No. You won't.'

Amaira stared at me as though I'd just said I was marrying a Bride.

'Why not? I'm smart enough,' she said. 'And I can fight. You can teach me.'

I was in no mood to have this conversation now.

'When you're older I'm going to get you a job as a servant for some nice lady who lives a long, long way from the

Range. And then you'll go and live in her palace and do for her what you do for me. Maybe one day you'll run her household, if you stick at it long enough. Safe, and calm, and away from this damned broken sky.'

Amaira's brows drew in with challenge, her lip caught between her teeth. Anger didn't suit her, but I gestured for her to speak her mind. Better to have things out in the open.

'I don't want to go away. I want to stay here. It's my home. Everything I got is here.'

'Just because you've picked up a turd, doesn't mean you have to treasure it,' I said. 'You'll see that I'm right, in time. There're better ways to spend a life than running down scumbags on the Range. People don't like us, Amaira. They fear us. I don't want to hear of this again.'

She pouted, hesitated for a moment and then snapped me a salute and stalked away. I heard her banging her fist in anger against the wall panels as she went down the corridor. I grumbled in the back of my throat. Every child wants to be a soldier when they grow up, but only because they've never understood that when the game ends, everything's over permanently. Amaira was too young to understand she was dreaming of a short life of blood and danger.

'Can't turn everyone away,' the raven cawed from the corner of the room. 'Crowfoot will have to take a new captain sometime. You won't live forever, and it would make sense to choose someone who knows the ropes.'

'You'll take my people over my dead body,' I said. The bird seemed to find that amusing, stepping from foot to foot as it nodded in agreement.

I opened the note. Hastily written. I read it through once and was out the door.

I raced across to the citadel. Many of the soldiers were wearing yellow hoods over their uniforms, showing their support, or thanks for the shield that protected them, and the red-neon message across the citadel read BRIGHT LADY

WATCH OVER YOU. I scowled, and turned my collar up against the blustering wind.

I flashed my black iron seal and it cleared me a path to the muster yard. A whole lot of men were getting prepped, burnished-steel cuirasses, boots polished black. When Tnota saw me he began waving and yammering as a couple of men with yellow hoods held him back. Anger cleared men from my path.

'If you want to keep your hands, you'll get them off my man right now,' I said. The soldiers let him go.

'He's not to be allowed to go running off,' one of them said uncertainly.

'The bastards are trying to send me into the Misery!' Tnota said. He was heavy with sweat, stank of it. He'd not been back into the Misery since we'd fetched Dantry Tanza from Cold's Crater.

'You don't have to go into the Misery,' I said, scowling. 'What the fuck is going on here?'

I took a good look at the soldiers around me as they strapped packs of dry rations and ammunition onto horses. None of them looked like slouches.

'It'll just be like old times,' Nenn said, joining us and throwing an arm around each of our necks. 'You along too, Ryhalt?'

'They want to send me in up to my pits,' Tnota said. There was real fear in his voice at the prospect. He'd always had the healthy respect for the Misery that a navigator ought, but he'd taken missions without complaint. Losing a limb had changed him, as if the surgeon's knife had taken more than just his arm. I flexed my fingers; I could appreciate that.

I noticed a familiar face among the mustering soldiers. Captain Gurling Stracht had been a soldier on the Range before I began serving there. Pushing through his fifties like a log washing down a river, he'd ignored his baldness and wore what was left of his white hair long, in a tail. His face was pitted and dried, lined with cracks that mirrored those in the sky. He'd spent more time out in the Misery than anyone else living, and the bad magic had bled into him over the years, turned his skin a sallow yellow. Could spot him a mile away.

'Good to see you, Gurling,' I said.

Stracht looked at me, grunted and chewed his liquorice root. There was something deeply alien about him now. He should have retired years ago, the moment he saw that the Misery was taking a toll on him, but he was, without doubt, our best scout. It wasn't possible to really know the Misery, given the constant shifting, but he knew the place better than anyone else.

'Galharrow,' he said. 'Should have known you'd still be alive.'

'I usually am,' I said.

Stracht grunted something that could have been laughter, but it was a feeble, dusty thing, as if his lungs had given up on him. He was worn ragged, cheeks sunk, nails black with dirt. The cup of wine in his hand didn't look to have been the first.

'What's the chew?'

'Found them, didn't I? The bastards throwing the sky-fires.'

A surge of something hot and angry rushed through me.

'Where?' I could practically feel the swing of the steel, the thunder of the guns. Nenn was right. There was vengeance to be dealt.

'Crystal forest,' Stracht said. 'Nine days east. Or that's where it was, last. You know it?'

I punched the air. I'd told Davandein to send Stracht there. The crystal forest wasn't really a forest, but a broad, flat depression where thick spears of rock crystal, or clouded glass, rose from the red sand. There were thousands of them

221

in disordered ranks, covering a few square miles. When the wind blew between them they resonated, creating an unpleasant moaning. It was an unsettling, fixed point in the Misery, like Cold's Crater.

'By day, the drudge are smashing the pillars and making piles of crystal,' Stracht said. 'We snuck in by night. Killed some sentries. They have a choir of what I guess are sorcerers, eight of them. Didn't look like any drudge I seen before. Huge, they are, size of a bear. Maybe fatter. Lungs bigger than a horse's arse. It's their singing that does it. They make one hell of a racket, and then the forest all starts to glow. Then one of those piles of crystal they been smashing in the day will shoot off into the sky like a firework.'

It was a long way to throw something.

'So it's simple enough,' Nenn said. 'We're heading out there to shut the singers up.'

'Something tells me it won't be that simple,' I said.

'Nothing ever is,' Stracht said. He finished his wine, looked around for more. An obliging serving girl handed it to him whilst trying to avoid touching his hand. She probably thought that the poison that had coloured him copper could be caught. Maybe she was right.

'Steel is simple,' Nenn said. 'Bring it and swing it. Nothing I haven't done before.'

'Getting to them is the hard part. They have soldiers. I reckoned three thousand.'

'That's a lot of drudge,' I said. 'And a lot of our soldiers followed Davandein when she ran. Valengrad doesn't have the manpower to match them, not nine days deep in the Misery.'

Stracht nodded.

'You're not wrong. But all the soldiers leave at night. Don't want them to interfere with the sound, I think. There's a window where the singers are vulnerable.'

'So why didn't you grack them already?'

'They got two Darlings standing watch over them, and one of them was something special. Maybe something new. Looked like a Darling, 'cept his face was all fished-up, like a drudge and it had a tail. I weren't going to go suicide against them.'

Darlings. Of course there were. But fish-faced and tailed? That sounded like the one Levan Ost had seen, the one Saravor had sent men to meet, shortly before he'd cracked the vault at Narheim. It was the first good lead I'd had to Ost's Misery expedition since Nacomo blew himself to pieces.

Not a lot to go on. No real chance of taking a Darling alive to question it. But if their assault was linked to what Saravor was trying to pull in Valengrad? Could it be one of his two colossal forces? I needed to see it for myself.

That, and there were a whole lot of innocent lives to avenge.

'I'm in,' I said. 'What's the plan?'

'We are,' Thierro said. He had a saddle over the shoulder of his starched white coat. There were insignia crescents on his sleeve now, equivalent to the rank of general. A man on the rise, for sure. He gestured at the troops preparing around us. 'Fifty of my best marksmen, fifty of the citadel's best cavalry. Colonel Koska's two remaining Battle Spinners, Witness Glaun, Witness Valentia, and myself to counter the Darlings. We go in, grack their sorcerers and get out again.'

'*Range Officer's Manual* recommends three Spinners to neutralise each Darling,' I said reflexively.

'Six would be grand,' Thierro said. 'But we've only got five, so five it is.'

'You running the whole show now, Thierro?'

'Davandein's desertion has left the citadel badly under-strength,' Thierro said easily. 'Most of the Spinners went with her, and without Spinners, there's no mission.'

I had to hand it to him, he had balls volunteering to lead the mission himself. Only three kinds of people willingly enter the Misery. I didn't pick Thierro for greedy, stupid or desperate. Unless overconfidence is a kind of stupid.

'What do you need Tnota for? Stracht has his own navigator.'

'Had,' Stracht said. He looked weary, half-dead on his feet. I wondered whether he'd slept since he got back to the city. 'He took a bolt in the side as we were trying to get out. He's down in the infirmary now, dying. He's made his last trip.'

Tears glistened in his tainted, amber eyes. Stracht had been with his navigator a long time. You make a deep bond with a man when you ride together in the Misery. You trust each other, understand how little chance you got on your own. We're none of us an island.

'That doesn't mean I can be forced,' Tnota said angrily. 'Tell them!'

Stracht cut in before I could reply.

'Far as I know there's only two navigators alive that have been as far as the crystal forest,' he said. 'This one-armed git is one. The other has an infected gut wound, and I'm planning to offer him a loaded pistol before I go so he can spare himself the agony.'

'I'll be fucked if I'm going,' Tnota said. He spat on the floor. 'One hundred men against three thousand? Fucking madness. I'm not even military.'

I wanted to support Tnota, to say he didn't have to go. Tell him that it was OK. But I couldn't. I stood thinking it through in the clatter and bustle of the yard. A small force would move quickly, strike hard and fast and get out. I had no doubt that Nenn had volunteered her Ducks the moment she'd heard about it.

I placed a hand on Tnota's good shoulder.

'Sorry, old friend,' I said. 'We have to go.'

'You can't be serious!' Tnota said, shaking me off.

I recalled what Valiya had said to me.

'The drudge have to be stopped,' I said. 'We're bleeding out here, and I don't trust anyone else enough to do it right.'

'Glad to have you on board,' Thierro said. He shook my hand and I was caught for a moment by the potency of that damn cologne that he seemed to bathe in. I pulled him in closer.

'And with three Witnesses out of the city, what about the shield?' I said quietly.

'We're nearly out of phos batteries anyway,' he whispered back. A confidential acknowledgment between old friends. 'We can't maintain the shield for much longer. We have to end these attacks before the flare.'

'So much for the Bright Lady.'

'Not at all,' he said. 'This is her will.'

I was highly sceptical about that, but I wasn't going to get into a theological debate in the middle of the muster yard.

'You're really serious about this?' Tnota asked, sounding dismal and looking betrayed. I placed a consoling hand on his shoulder.

'You really expect any less of me?'

'I knew I'd get you lads back out there again someday,' Nenn said. She grinned like a dealer that just heard you're back on the pollen. 'It'll be just like the old days.'

Only in the old days, I knew she'd always have my back. Now, I had to watch hers, in case she turned on us.

22

'The Eye is still in Valengrad,' the raven said. It was trying to get into my carefully wrapped and stowed rations, without success. Falcon lashed at it with his tail. 'Your duty is to stay here.'

'I have to go out there because of the Eye,' I said. 'We've no other leads.'

'What do you think you'll find?'

'I don't know,' I said. 'But I'd rather be out there killing drudge and ending this rain of fire than whistling to myself and waiting for some new piece of information to fall into my lap. Whatever he's planning, Saravor needed to meet with that Darling. Finding it, and seeing that magic, is our best shot right now.'

The raven squawked, either frustrated by me, or frustrated by how well I'd wrapped the dried meat in my pack. It flapped away in a rustle of black wings.

I hadn't packed light. I was taking Falcon plus a packhorse to carry all my other crap. Falcon was a biter, the kind of horse that would sometimes throw himself out of his stall to get at passersby, and I liked that kind of spirit in an animal that you take into battle. I seemed to have readied enough weaponry to arm a small brigade, including matchlocks, a brace of pistols and a long cavalry sabre with a nasty curve. Then there was a poleaxe, a great double-handed war sword and a few others that had different functions for different situations. I was armoured in new steel, feeling excessively shiny compared to the scratched and Misery-worn armour that Nenn's boys were packing. Fifty of her best, her meanest, and I had every confidence in them. Men and women with broken teeth and the right kind of evil gleaming in their eyes.

Thierro's marksmen were a different sort, but their presentation gave me confidence. They marched up in decent order, flarelocks shouldered. I didn't like seeing those, but I'd had the argument and I'd not dented Thierro's faith in them. The troopers wore brightly coloured buff coats of lemony yellow, a simple female figure depicted in black both front and back. They were an odd bunch, took themselves very seriously and didn't speak to any of Nenn's devils. They weren't the usual Bright Order pilgrim types – Thierro had handpicked men who had served as soldiers before. They were tough, but they were also volunteering to be heroes. Didn't know what they were letting themselves in for.

I decided to give the first-timers a briefing on what to expect. Got them all gathered together. They listened attentively, solemn-faced. These men and women were the deepest of the fanatics. Thierro had assured me that each and every one of them had seen the Bright Lady appear in a vision, as though that was supposed to give me confidence that they could put out three rounds a minute.

'You're going to see things you've never seen before,' I said. 'Some of them are going to try to eat you. Some of them will want to kill you for the sake of it. Some of them will try to drive you mad. There are no people out there, unless they're our soldiers on patrol. You think you see your wife, your lover, someone who's been dead awhile? They're ghosts. Don't look at them, don't listen to them. They got nothing to say that's worth hearing. And definitely don't try to fuck them.'

It was a speech I'd given to my new guys a dozen times

down the years, and I usually got a laugh. None of them were laughing today. Bad audience.

'At night we sleep with three bodies back-to-back, and a fourth watching over you. Most likely way you die in the Misery is for a gilling to chew your foot off. If that happens, and you can't ride, we leave you behind. We'll only have supplies for twenty days so we can't afford to be longer. If you get left behind, you won't make it out.'

The Bright Order soldiers said nothing. It was like talking to a bunch of badly dressed statues.

'Above all, you listen to me, and to Stracht, and the navigator. And listen to Major Nenn. If we tell you not to put your foot down, you fucking freeze in place. If we say don't go beyond the rocks when you need to piss, you don't go beyond the fucking rocks. It's not just the things that live in the Misery you need to watch for, it's the land itself. It hates you, and it wants you dead. You forget that, even for a moment? You're gracked.'

Still no reaction, save the one who coughed politely into his hand. I gave up, shook my head and stepped back down.

'Twenty marks says we don't get two miles before one of them cracks and cries,' Stracht grunted at me.

'You think they know how to cry?' I asked. Nenn and Tnota decided to get in on the wager. I'd gone for three miles. Nenn optimistically thought that they would make it all the way to our first campsite before a mass panic set in. She frowned at them, though. Worried. I saw Thierro. He'd worn a cuirass of well-polished steel rigged with phos canisters, but even he had a flarelock mounted on his saddle.

'These are your best?' I asked.

'They're the best,' Thierro said. 'Don't mistake their discipline for a lack of passion. They're devoted to the cause.'

Dawn was a rising purple blush out across the Misery. The sky was welcoming it with a dirge for its latest victims. It hadn't been long since the sky-songs had faded. The

Witnesses' shield had been smaller and weaker than before, confirmation that Thierro's phos supply was dwindling. One of the sky-fires had come down on a temple, and nobody knew whether the priests and holy sisters within were still alive in their cellar or whether it had collapsed onto them. I'd visited the site, gathered a few of those tiny crystal shards, let them fall through my fingers. Watching the workers dragging away rubble and broken beams only firmed my resolve. Not only would we end this madness, I'd get a chance to put my sword through the heads of those that had brought it.

Tnota had shown up drunk. He hadn't slept all night, had instead gone out and got himself washed through, as though this were his last night alive. I guess it might have been. He was busy throwing up in a horse's trough.

'You'll come back safe, won't you Captain-Sir?' Amaira said. She shouldn't have come to see us off, but she was there all the same.

'I'll do my best. Look after everyone while we're gone. Do what Valiya tells you. And make sure you're down in the cellar at night.'

She snapped me a salute and tried to find a brave smile as she fought back tears.

I reached down and hugged her. It wasn't right that I did that. She wasn't my kid, but she held on to me like she was, and she wasn't the only one fighting to keep the mask from cracking.

Never get close if you can help it. When I got back, I'd send her away. Servant work wasn't hard to come by.

'Be good, and stay bright,' I said to her, then went to shout at people until I felt better.

Nobody won the bet. The Bright Order were far tougher than I'd given them credit for. They didn't complain about the baking heat when the warmth came up from the ground, nor the bitter cold that blew in on a dry wind, as sudden as a change of mind. They sat in their saddles and stared ahead, intent on the job at hand. Maybe I'd misjudged their mettle. Belief can be a powerful spur to courage.

I hated being back in the Misery. Hadn't had to chase anyone into the wastelands in some time. For a while I'd thought maybe my time here was over and done.

Within fifty miles of the Range the Misery was still scarred by the terrible power the Engine had brought to bear four years ago. In some places the craters were vast, half a mile wide, in others they were just ten paces across. The Engine was not systematic in the fury it had unleashed. The projectors had sent out annihilation, blackening and char-ring the sands into grains so small they couldn't be seen in-dividually. There were marshes where the blood had soaked in and never dried, up near Three-Six, where hundreds of thousands of drudge had been ripped to pieces. The legacy of the Engine was written up and down the length of the Range. If the drudge ever got close enough to see what we had done, they would think twice about advancing farther.

And yet, even as we rode through the depressions left in the earth, I could see that the land was reclaiming itself, erasing our touch. The craters had begun to fill with sand, their edges growing softer. There were no plants here, but there was a certain naturalness to the gradual erasing of man's influence. Close to its edges, the Misery's tendency to move around was much reduced. If we rode back the way we'd come, we might even ride through the same craters.

The Misery stank of twisted corruption. I breathed it in and it was grimmer than sewage. Stracht, by contrast, seemed more comfortable once we'd got into it, the bad magic creeping in beneath the fingernails, soaking into the skin. Perhaps it was like the white-leaf that the addicts smoked, a thing simultaneously hated and craved. Misery addiction. It was a terrifying thought.

Tnota took the readings, plotted us a course as straight and true as anything ever was in the Misery. He'd had a thick book, bound up in black leather as long as I'd known him and it was as tattered and worn as he was. The man who'd taught him to navigate had had it from the man who'd taught him. They taught Misery navigation at the military academy these days, but it was all bollocks. Some men just have the affinity for it. They look from moon to moon, measure them off and somehow they know where things are going to be in the Misery. Nothing of that can be taught in a classroom.

A few hours into our journey and the hooded raven found us. It had followed me from Valengrad and I held out my arm for it to alight on.

Nenn's men wanted to shoot it. Normally, they'd have been right to. Shoot first is the best strategy in the Misery.

'I never took you for a man who kept pets,' Thierro said. He was not coping well with the Misery's influence. His face was sheened with sweat, despite the cold, and he'd tied a handkerchief over his face. He'd remember that you can't keep out the smell or the poison that way soon enough.

'This one is hard to shake off,' I said. 'After a while they get under your skin.'

The raven was smart enough to realise that speaking in front of these people was a bad idea, but it opened its beak and cawed. I guess it found my joke amusing.

'At least we can eat it when the food runs out,' Nenn said, and then raising her voice, 'which it will if our navigator isn't paying attention.'

Tnota looked up from his hangover and waved her away. His charcoal complexion was tinged with green. So too were the Bright Order men. Nenn's veterans were faring better. Wasn't their first time out in the Misery.

One hundred men is enough to keep a lot of the Misery's things at bay. Some of them, like dulchers, are too fearless or brainless to understand that they'll lose the fight, but the skweams won't come out of the sand if they think they'll lose legs. This close to Valengrad those things were both rare, though. I was keeping my eyes peeled for nugs and gritterlarks all the same.

'No gillings,' I said. 'Something we should be thankful for.'

'They're getting rarer,' Stracht said. 'Haven't seen so many lately. We blocked up a burrow a month back, but they used to be common as mouse droppings.'

'Maybe the Misery is cleaning itself up.'

'Maybe. Or maybe there's something new in the food chain taking a liking to all those fat little red bodies.'

Stracht wasn't an optimist. That's probably why he'd managed to stay alive so long out here.

We made a camp. Some of the drag-sleds had tents on them. They weren't much, more like canvas coffins that you could sit in, but they kept the wind off. I slept alongside Nenn and Tnota, like we used to back when it was the three of us doing this for shitty court-paid bounties. Tnota had just about recovered from his night of excess, but his farts were still worse than the Misery's stench.

During the night, one of the Bright Order men disappeared. There was no sign of a struggle, no blood, no damage to his tent. He was just gone. His weapons were beside his tent, with his provisions and his canteen. Thierro wandered around shouting his name for a while, a confused look on his face, while the heavily scarred Witness Glaun scowled and muttered.

Dawn brought a pall of cloud. The cracks in the sky could still be seen beyond them, too bright and bronze to be obscured so easily, but the moons hid from our view. Tnota cursed and I held the astrolabe up for him as he moved dials and clicked wheels into place. He could still navigate, but it would be based on his estimates of the moons' likely positions, and that meant that there was a limited degree of accuracy.

The second day saw the rising of the ghosts. Nenn's boys were used to them, and they ignored them as best they could. Not always possible. A woman died in childbirth, over and over, reappearing every mile or two that passed. Eventually one of the Ducks let his friends blindfold him and stuff wax in his ears, led him along blind. That didn't stop the ghost, but it spared him the brutality of it.

She wasn't the only one, and they were all distracting. They pulled at the mind and cost us our focus. We nearly rode into a nest of deformed, crab-like things the size of dogs, because we'd been watching two aged spectres tearing at one another. Stracht managed to pull us up in time. The crab creatures were slow and couldn't cause much trouble, but we took our poleaxes and smashed their shells in and skewered them anyway. There was lots of white flesh inside their shells, and if I'd not known better I'd have thought they'd make a decent stew.

We suffered no losses on the second night. I guess that was something.

23

By night we saw them pass overhead like shooting stars, crystal missiles hurtling through the sky. Their song was more distant, softer, and since there was no chance of their coming down upon us with a boom and a roar, it was possible to see beauty in their flickering lights.

Nenn and I lay looking up at the cracks in the sky, counting the sky-fires that went by. The camp was quiet. They always are in the Misery. I've heard that in other places soldiers will sing songs, or someone has a fiddle, or there'll be laughter and stories. But almost all of my soldiering was done in the Misery, and there was never enough levity to bring out a song or a joke.

'Do you ever wonder why the cracks don't move?' Nenn asked.

'No,' I said. 'I guess they're just some kind of imprint. A reminder of what happened here.'

'These things the drudge are throwing at us seem pitiful in comparison, don't they?'

I grunted.

'Depends if you get hit by one or not.'

Nenn went silent. The cracks were a fierce bronze-white, pulsing softly, soundless. They webbed through the sky, jagged, cruel. We lay on a bed of rock, our heads close together. The stars were out, bright between the cracks. They were one of the few glimmers of beauty that could be seen in the Misery. No light from the city to push them back, and we didn't light a fire out here. Fire attracted things better left unattracted.

Nenn glanced around, checked where her man was.

'Betch wants me to stop taking linny tea,' she said quietly. The change of subject was abrupt. Must have been on her mind a while, as she slowly worked up toward telling me. I've never claimed to know much about women, but I knew enough to know that I needed to step as cautiously here as though I were creeping about in a nest of skweams.

'How do you feel about that?' I asked.

'I don't know,' she said. 'Scared, I guess.'

'It's a scary thing,' I said. 'How long have you been drinking it?'

It wasn't like Nenn and I talked much about this before, but I assumed that any sensible fighting girl was brewing linny seeds a couple of times a month. They were easy to get hold of, let a woman control her own life. But there was a price.

'Since I was sixteen,' she said. 'And I know, it might mean that I can't bring them to term anyway. It's a long time to be on seed. I never thought I'd want children, though.'

'And now you're feeling happy with your man, and you aren't sure?'

'I'm not sure,' she agreed. 'But I'm not getting any younger. I just don't know what it would mean for me if I had one. Most career soldiers choose not to.'

I didn't have any good advice to give, so I kept my big jaw shut. I'd not been a good father, as the Misery so often chose to remind me. I would never rid myself of that regret. I didn't want to. In some ways I thought that if I didn't hang that burden around my neck, I'd be making myself less human. We are defined by our guilt as much as our pride.

'And Betch – he wants children?'

235

'Yes,' Nenn said, and though she was the hardest, most foul-mouthed officer in Dortmark's army, her voice was hesitant. 'What if I ... What if I can't? What if we try and find I'm barren?'

'I don't know,' I said. 'You're worried he'd leave?'

Nenn didn't say anything. We looked up at the stars, those tiny dots of light, whatever they were. Problems come and go, and we solve them or we don't, and then new ones come along and take their place, but the stars don't change. I wondered if they had problems of their own.

'Do you want them?' I asked.

'I don't know,' Nenn said. 'My life never had much purpose, before I met you. It had been first-grade shit, in fact. I had an unhappy childhood. My family weren't worthy of the name. Life got worse once my tits came in. So I did a bad thing, and they'd have hanged me for it, so I ran away. Then I ran into you, and you gave me a chance, and I thought, "this isn't much of a life, but at least I'm free." Feels like I spent my whole life fighting someone or other. Never saw a place for children in that.'

Hard questions. For most folk it's easy enough. They see their dull futures spreading ahead of them and think that having someone else to look after will liven things up on the farm, or else it happens by mistake, or they want someone to train up to run their business when they're grey. Some just want something to love. Lots of reasons, and I had no easy answers. Nenn wasn't done though.

'And then I got rank, and I got power that nobody in my line ever dreamed of. Would I want to give this up? This Misery walking, the fighting, the drink?'

'Only you can know that,' I said. I was determined not to get involved in whatever Nenn had going with Betch. She'd make her decisions one way or the other, and there were fuck-all ways that I could help.

A ghost was walking the Misery, approaching us. It was

one of mine. I sat up and watched him walking in toward us.

'Shit,' I said. 'Never thought I'd see that face again.'

'Handsome guy,' Nenn said. She didn't pay much attention to the ghosts. She only ever got one, a heavy man with an axe in his head, whose eyes looked too much like hers for it to be coincidence. I had lots. I once wondered whether each ghost was just a different shade of our own guilt. My grandmother had died years before my disgrace, and she'd scolded me for my dirty shoes more than once in the Misery. I should have cleaned them before I saw her. A small guilt, but small failures matter when someone's gone.

'He was handsome,' I said. 'He was a good man, really. A friend, before it all went to shit.'

'Torolo Mancono,' Thierro said. He didn't look at me. He'd known the man, before he had to leave the Range.

The ghost was tall, if a good few inches shorter than me. He was limber, athletic. His eyes were bright, his hair slicked back from his face. He wore the shirt and fencing breeches he'd worn on the day that I killed him, bells on his shoes tinkling gently as he approached. Thierro stood with Witness Valentia a way off, watching the ghost approach. Valentia looked queasy, staring at the ghost as it staggered aimlessly about. One hand was pressed up against its neck.

'They say he beat you,' Witness Valentia said. 'That he was the finest swordsman in Dortmark. He challenged you to single combat because of the rout from Adrogorsk.'

I prickled.

'Adrogorsk was no summer fair. Thierro will tell you that. Mancono challenged me out of pride,' I said. 'And I accepted for the same.'

'He challenged you because you sent men to their deaths to secure your own retreat. That's the way I heard it.'

'It wasn't like that,' Thierro defended me. He rubbed at his chest as if it pained him. Maybe seeing Torolo reminded him of that hazy brown cloud of Darling poison, drifting into his lungs. He was a brave man to come out here to face Darlings again. 'I never believed the rumours.'

The Misery was getting to him. The businessman's mask slipping, by the slightest of degrees, but enough for me to see the resentment there. Thierro hadn't been there when I killed Mancono, but that didn't mean he lacked an opinion. He just wouldn't let it get in the way of his goals.

A grim smell had been following us all day, the stench of rotting meat. It seemed appropriate now.

The ghost walked past me, ghost blood running from his hanging mouth, ghost blood soaking the ruffles of his shirt. He ignored me entirely and staggered to a halt before Thierro. He mouthed silent words, and toppled over. A few moments later he was gone.

'He saved me, you know,' Thierro said sadly. He couldn't look at the ghost. 'At Adrogorsk. He pulled me out of the poison.' He scratched at the burn across his chest again.

'No, Thierro,' I said gently. 'Mancono wasn't at Adrogorsk. Pep got you out. It's just the Misery playing tricks on your mind.'

Thierro blinked hard. Looked confused. Shook his head to clear the Misery's fuddle. He said, 'Was he not there? I would have sworn that ... no. You're right.'

Witness Valentia shook her head in disgust.

'You tore his throat out,' she said.

'This place,' Thierro said, staring at the spot where the ghost-corpse had been. 'This awful place.'

He was not wrong.

'How are you keeping, Thierro?' I asked.

'Surviving,' he said. He took out a bottle of cologne and daubed it liberally on his chest and neck. He smiled a flat, joyless smile. For once I was glad for its potency as it over-came the stink of rot. 'If I'm going to get eaten, at least I'll make a pleasant meal.'

'It can't get worse than this,' Witness Valentia said. Nenn and I chuckled at that together, though it wasn't funny.

'Lady, we've barely started.'

'Give fire!'

Another volley screeched out. Spits of light roared from the flarelocks and the skweam reared backward as pieces of its carapace rained outward like wet confetti. It bellowed, a dry insect screech as it reared up, confused by the new and sudden pain.

'Give fire!' Nenn yelled, and the matchlocks boomed. The skweam staggered back as lead balls smashed into it at a thousand miles per hour. The eight back legs dug deep into the sand as it whirled its forelegs through the air as if it were beset by stinging insects. Finding nothing in the air before it, its eight eyes locked on the twin lines of humans before it.

Bluish ichor pumped from two dozen wounds. It opened its mouth and howled a demonic riddle of pain.

'Now!' I yelled and we charged it on foot. I was roaring as I swung my poleaxe, hard as I'd ever swung anything, and chitin cracked and scythe-like limbs drew sparks from my armour.

We lost three men.

I'd never seen a skweam that big before.

'He says you started it,' I said.

'I left my rum ration right there, and now it's gone. He fuckin' drank it,' one of Nenn's men growled. He was looking toward one of the Bright Order, who stood nearby with a bloody nose and a spreading red fist imprint across his face.

'Major! I need you over here.'

Nenn limped over. She was wiping blood from her hands after tending one of her wounded. Her leg had taken a swipe from something that had looked like a tree, but wasn't. The langets on her armour had stopped it from drawing blood, but she had a terrific bruise there.

'Durk, calm it right down,' she snapped, and her angry soldier strove to rein it in.

'Witness Thierro, you too. I want you and Major Nenn to get this shit sorted, right now. We got enough to worry about without the men fighting one another.'

I left them to it and planted myself down next to Stracht. It wasn't my job to keep order and they'd respond better to their own officers. Mostly the Bright Order soldiers had kept well out of the way of Nenn's Ducks, holding themselves aloof like some kind of monks. They seldom spoke, never laughed, ate separately, pissed out of sight. They'd been reliable though, even brave. They hadn't flinched, not one of them, when they had to hold the line. They'd just cocked their flarelocks and given it hell.

Stracht was the only one out here who looked content. With his yellow eyes and copper-veined skin he almost looked like he fit in. He stared off into the distance, murmuring to himself, as though he were party to some conversation that nobody else could hear.

The hooded raven perched atop my shoulder. Its head swivelled, looking to see who was near. I was riding out front, an unpleasant job that made me the bait for anything that was lurking camouflaged within the sand or behind a rock.

'When you reach the crystal forest, do you have even the beginnings of a plan?' the raven croaked.

'Don't see how I can have a plan until I've checked out the lay of the land,' I said.

'You need to be careful.'

'I didn't know you cared,' I said.

'I don't,' the raven said. 'I'm incapable of feeling anything. I was created to make sure that you don't let things go too badly while the master is off saving the world from the Deep Kings.'

'How am I doing so far?'

The raven cast itself into the air, flew up high, did a circuit around me, then returned to its perch on my shoulder.

'How do you think? Fucking terribly. You've let religious fanatics take over the city in preparation for some kind of cosmic-power ritual. You've let a lot of Valengrad's defenders get run out of the city, or killed by things coming out of the sky, you haven't recovered the Eye, and there's a dark sorcerer poised to subjugate the Nameless. On a scale of one to ten, I'd say you're in deep shit.'

'When are we not in deep shit?' I said. For all it claimed not to feel anything, I was sure that the raven was laughing.

'There's a sea of faces coming up,' the raven said.

As we went forward, a sound grew louder on the wind. Whispering, dry and steady as the rustling of autumn leaves, and then I crested a rise and saw that the bird was not wrong.

It takes a lot to turn my stomach. I always think that I've seen just about everything that there is to see in the Misery, and then one day you go a little farther and run into something that's even worse.

The grit and gravel gave way to a plain of faces in the dirt. Old faces framed with strings of grey hair, young faces with pimples. Men with beards, women with ritual scars on their cheeks and jaw, as they had practised in the city of Clear. Yellow teeth, clean white teeth, broken teeth. Blue eyes, brown, grey. Faces baked brown by the sun, faces pale from a life indoors with books and ledgers, here and there a dash of red hair, now and again the glint of gold from a false tooth.

I bent over emptied my breakfast out onto the sand. A waste of good brandy.

It wasn't just the sight of them, blending together in a

big, fleshy expanse. It was the sounds they were making. What had seemed like a general murmuring on the wind was a blur of individual words. I nudged Falcon forward, and he snorted and pawed the earth, disturbed by the sound.

'I need more milk,' a woman whispered, over and over.

'I'll be glad when this is all over,' an old man said, his voice so matter-of-fact that I knew that these were words from another time, another place.

'What's that in the sky?' a child said. 'What's that in the sky? What's that in the sky?'

He was so insistent that I looked upward, but there was nothing there save the tears in the fabric of reality.

'Ah. This place,' Stracht said, grimacing as he rode up alongside me. 'Don't worry. They're not alive. The faces are only a couple of inches deep. There's just rock underneath.'

'You tried digging?'

'Came across this place a few years back. It was farther south, then,' he said. 'There's a theme to what they say. Like that little boy there, asking what's in the sky. Lots of them ask that. I reckon that this was a town, back before Crowfoot used the Heart of the Void. I reckon these folks gathered out in their market to look up at something, and then, zap. Heart of the Void happened. This is what it left behind. Some kind of echo.'

'I thought that the Endless Devoid was the epicentre.'

'It was,' Stracht agreed. 'There ain't nothing in the Devoid. I mean nothing, in a way you can't understand without seeing it. I never got far in. This, whatever it is, was on the periphery.'

'When you see this, you wonder whether we're really the heroes in all this.'

'Heroes? Hah.' Stracht spat. '"Heroes" are the excuse we made to explain why we don't hate all men who carry swords. Pretend there's some grand and noble reason that *his* head was the one that needed splitting, not yours. But it's all piss and shit in the end. It's one of the reasons I'd rather be out here. Less hypocrisy.'

'But a lot more shit,' I said.

'Aye,' Stracht agreed as he signalled the rest of the party to halt. 'But you can get used to anything if you walk with it for long enough.'

24

Ten days in the Misery feels like ten months.

The crystal forest finally appeared as a glimmering, sparkling miasma on the horizon. Stracht led us around to the east, costing us half a day, but ensuring that our angle of approach would put the crystal spires between us and the drudge encampment.

'Can you hide us?' I asked the Spinners. They conferred, but it was beyond them. Ezabeth could have done it, I thought, but she had been the rarest of the rare. I didn't think any of our Spinners particularly able. They weren't weak, but they did lack finesse.

A dust cloud rolled in, not as fierce as some of the storms that gathered this deep in the Misery, but it turned the air hazy just when we needed it. Stracht and three of the Ducks went on ahead, picked out a path.

We wouldn't see what we were up against until we were going in, but we would have the element of surprise. The men set about fixing dust masks over their faces, cut loose any unnecessary gear. As I waited for them, my thoughts wandered. Out here, the night was calm. There was no phos light to be afraid of. No flinching at sparks, no fear of seeing a ghost trapped in the light. There was no auburn-haired woman slowly unpicking the damage that had been done to my heart, and no child to force her way into it. I found that I missed all of them tremendously.

There was a truth that I had avoided admitting to myself. Another reason that I'd chosen to come all this way into the Misery. When you're poised on the edge of doing something stupidly dangerous, the lies we tell ourselves melt like ice in the thaw.

I needed to save the Grandspire. If the drudge were successful and one of their missiles toppled it, then Thierro's dream of seeing the Bright Lady reborn died too. And no matter what Dantry had told me, no matter what Crowfoot had warned me about, no matter how far-fetched it seemed, there was one thing I desired over any other. I didn't believe that it could happen. But I have always been a gambler, and I was willing to take the smallest odds where Ezabeth was concerned.

To save her.

To be her hero.

I almost laughed at my own idiocy. It was time. The song had begun.

We descended into the crystal forest. The glassy spears thrust up from the dry, powdery sand like stalagmites, some no taller than my waist but most jutting ten or fifteen feet toward the night sky. The horses were the biggest concern as we led them between the spires. There was enough space for them to pass between the crystals, but the glow made them skittish. They were used to phos light, but they had eight days of Misery jitters behind them and the slightly translucent, light-holding pillars did nothing to calm them. Horses are built for running and their instinct when spooked is to run, run and don't worry about what's ahead. We couldn't afford that now. Soft words reached their ears to calm them. They didn't understand the words – horses are stupid – but they understood the tone. The men wore their travelling cloaks over their armour, the better to muffle the sound of our approach, but we didn't need them. The singing resonated so loud here, magnified as it bounced from pillar to pillar. If it hadn't been a form of power that sent death arcing through the sky, I might have found it beautiful.

'We have three minutes to the end of the song,' Thierro whispered. Seemed dumb to be whispering with that sound echoing from every pillar, filling the air, ruling the night. We'd counted the verses and choruses as they launched the previous missile.

'Get your men ready,' I said. 'Double line. Volley fire, one-two. Then Witness Glaun gives the signal and we go. Concentrate everything you have on the Darlings. Only a direct blast to the brain will stop them. Ready?'

Thierro cocked his flarelock. It was a finer weapon than those his soldiers were packing, a master-crafted weapon with a complex lens-sight mounted on the top. He was a good enough shot to justify it. His backup, for when his phos canisters were depleted.

'We are. Take care of yourself out here, Captain. I'd hate to see you get hurt.'

'I'm not planning on dying today,' I said. I checked my kit over. My heavy sabre was ready to be drawn, the pistols were loaded, wadded and ready on my gun belt. I had a double-handed war sword across the saddle, just in case. Then there were daggers. Knowing your weapons helps put you at ease before the storm hits. Lets you feel that you've done everything in your power to see yourself through. Of course, the smartest thing to do is turn around and ride back the way you came as fast as you can. But we run when we can run, and we fight when we have to, and sometimes the dawn comes and there's no choice but to grit your teeth, draw steel and scream against the night.

'One other thing, Thierro,' I said. 'If this goes wrong – if it looks like we'll be taken – don't let them take us alive. None of us. You think we're going to be captured, you aim for my head real slow, and you blow it clean off. If they take us, death will be a blessing.'

'I'd never let them take you, Ryhalt. But it won't come to that,' Thierro said. I offered him my hand to shake but he'd already turned away, telling his men to prime their flarelock hand cannons. I wasn't a praying man, but I asked the Spirit of Mercy to make sure none of them exploded before we even got started. I was still looking foolish with my hand outstretched and Nenn gave it a slap instead.

'Third chorus,' she said. 'Two minutes. Ready?'

'I'm always ready,' I said. She chewed on her lip, spat.

'Fuck it. Let's do this, then.'

I let Falcon feel my heels, and he moved toward what would have been the tree line in any sane part of the world. The drudge had mined away a broad swathe of the crystal pillars, leaving a clearing of stumps a good two hundred yards across. It was toward the centre of this glade that the Singers harmonized their song. Maybe this was it. Maybe this was the power that Saravor sought to drive against the Eye. Could he ascend to godhood if the drudge's missile came down right on top of the Eye? I'd thought it through, over and over, but it didn't feel right. Too physical. Too ordinary. The Singers sat in a circle, facing one another, their faces so bloated and deformed that I couldn't tell whether their eyes were open or closed. It wouldn't have mattered either way. They were engrossed in their song, and if this worked then it was too late for them now. If we'd misjudged our hand, then it was all about to go sour anyway.

Darlings. Two of them. They sat near to the Singers, the only other living things within a bow's reach. One looked like a young girl, scars on her face, hair patchy and falling out. The second had been male, but he'd not only been made into a Darling, he'd been marked and had begun his drudge changes. His face was greyish and too flat, the nose smoothly spreading into his cheeks. And there it was, behind him: a short, flexing tail. The Darling I was after. This *was* part of Saravor's plan. Getting hold of that Darling and somehow surviving long enough to force it to talk wasn't part of the plan, but if opportunity reared her head, I'd take it. I'd played on worse odds before.

Had either of the Darlings been paying attention, they might have seen us, shadows moving between the spires, but if Darlings do have a weakness, then it's their confidence. They looked bored. Of course, confidence isn't much of a weakness when you're practically indestructible and command a dark and terrible power.

'One minute,' Nenn said. I drew my sabre. Good curved steel, she sat my hand like her hilt had been sculpted for it. Through the thin leather of my glove I could feel the silver wire of the hilt. I'd had her a long time.

'Witness Thierro. Give fire!'

I gave the order. It had been a while since I'd given that kind of order. It felt good.

'First rank, ready arms!' Thierro called. The marksmen ran forward, out of the cover of the spires. They held their flarelocks out in front of them. The Singers' voices rose, soaring, vast and inhuman.

'Take aim!' Thierro called. The weapons nestled in against the men's shoulders. One of the Darlings looked up from whatever book it had been leafing through, shouted and scrambled to its feet.

'Give fire!'

The flarelocks cackled and whined, and bolts of bright light spat across the cleared plain. Two of the guns misfired, jettisoning sparks but not blowing themselves apart. Some of the men had aimed for the Darlings. Some of them had aimed for the Singers, and the song faltered and wobbled. The iron basin of crystal shards was shimmering with power, gold and purple, greens and deep, bloody oranges, but the moment the song faltered it began to sputter. Wild vents of energy spat out and one of the Singers was sprayed by what looked like hot coals. It struggled to brush them away, its limbs too large for the task.

'Second rank, give fire!'

Thierro's second rank sent out another volley, flarelocks screeching. At least one of the Darlings was hit – not an easy target at that range. I saw blood fly from her shoulder and hip. The male had flattened himself behind the stump of one of the crystals.

'Ride!' Nenn shouted. 'Ride, ride, ride!' She whirled her sabre around her head. Dangerous thing to do, that. Somebody could lose a nose that way.

I gave Falcon my spurs, let him know it was time. He responded eagerly, and as the first horse surged out the others gladly followed suit. I hunched low over Falcon's neck, reins in my left hand, gripping with my calves and spurring him on. Falcon's long legs ate the ground, but we were charging toward something straight out of my nightmares.

The girl Darling picked herself up. She wouldn't be stopped by a couple of flarelock blasts. Her mouth stretched wide as she screeched something which wasn't clear over the faltering song, as the Singers struggled to bring the magic in the iron basin under control. The Darling interposed herself between us and the monstrous creatures, shrieking as she unleashed something against us. The blast ripped up pebbles and a spray of sand as it sliced forward – and then disintegrated in a shower of sparks. Glaun and the Spinners were doing their work.

The tailed Darling tried another ploy, an old one. Faced with a charging line of cavalry he sent out the mind-worms and caught one of our riders who jerked his horse to the right, trying to crash it into the others. At a gallop, a fall onto those crystal stumps would have brought broken bones or worse, a sharp edge might split a man open.

There is an old adage that a good offence is the best defence, and in this case it was true. The Spinners saw that the

Darling had opted for subtlety and they took the opposite course. The Darling was immersed in a series of blazing bursts of phos light, gold and blue, traces of flame left in their wake.

Nenn was shrieking to match the Darlings. She didn't have a battle cry, she just liked to shriek. She raised her sword and we left the Darlings to the Spinners. They were too hard to kill and too dangerous to get close to. But the huge bodies of the Singers? They were a different matter.

Up close the Singers were grotesque, worse than I had thought. Their skin had the same clammy greyness common to many of the drudge, but they were patterned with huge stretch marks as though their thin-stretched hides struggled to contain their mass. They were vast, swollen five times larger than a man or woman should have been. Huge jowls hung from their faces, dragging the skin down beneath bloodshot eyes. They wore soft robes, their elongated ears studded with gold ornaments and their oversized bodies, altered to accommodate their great lungs, were too deformed to allow a natural range of movement. They seemed confused as they looked at the rush of cavalry about to hit them, their ponderous heads unable to swivel and eyes unable to focus. I wasn't at all sure that they understood what was happening as I rose in my stirrups and brought my sabre down on a Singer's head with all my strength.

I am a big man, and I put myself through a good deal of training and exertion to make sure that I'm as strong as my body can be. But even with a ton of horse beneath me, my sabre only slashed through scalp and the shreds of clinging hair, didn't cut through the Singer's overthick skull. It groaned like a drunk and tried waving its hands around, struggled to rise, but it was defeated by its own bulk. I wheeled around, hacked at it again, drawing plenty of blood and wails but the beast wasn't going to die that easily. It was like attacking a bull with a kitchen knife.

Pistols and carbines were cracking. Several of our horsemen had chosen to close on the female Darling, firing down into her body, unloading their pistols in blasts of dragon-smoke, drawing another and firing them off too. There was a lot of dust, a lot of smoke, and I could make out nothing of the Darling. Maybe they'd got her. Perhaps we'd got lucky.

A blast of Darling magic ripped through the air close by and cut a horse and man in two. The drudge-marked Darling had broken free of the Spinners' bindings and was blasting around indiscriminately. Armour offered no protection against that force, and another two men were cut from their saddles. Sparks crackled in the air around it as the Spinners tried to weave something new, but the Darling's rage gave it power. His half-human face was filled with that pure, wild hate that I've only ever seen on a Darling as he cast lashes of razored air left and right. I drew my pistols, took as careful aim as two seconds and a frightened horse would allow and missed my first shot. I tried a second and missed with that too. The Darling turned as the shot whipped by its face, saw me, and might have ended me right then if a riderless horse had not accidentally trampled him. The sorcerer went down in a spray of crystal dust as the horse's hooves crushed him into the dirt.

I looked at the Singers. They were bloody and wailing in deep, frightened moans. Too large, too grotesque to even flee, they bellowed feebly for help as our men slashed at them. It was horrible butchery, and a lesser man might have felt pity for these wretched, deformed things. I may not have been a Darling, but I knew how to hate. These things had killed thousands with their damned sorcery. I would kill them all, personally, piece by piece if I had to.

The drudge soldiers were coming at pace. Some came on foot with pikes and swords, others rode at us on heavy, shaggy-looking creatures. The job should have been done by now, the retreat sounded, but the Singers wouldn't fucking die. Broken bodies of Nenn's good men lay in pieces everywhere, victims of the Darlings' furious sorcery. A trio of them stood over what I guessed was the female Darling, hacking down at it over and over, struggling to make it stay dead.

I saw Nenn. She had dismounted, and like me she had a two-handed sword. She drove it all the way into one of the Singers from behind as the warbling monster tried futilely to get up. Their legs were not up to the task. The blade came out of its chest, but that didn't seem to stop it. Nenn drew the blade out again, jerking savagely to get it out of the ribs, but the Singer gave no indication that it was going to die.

'We've done all we can,' Stracht shouted. He was bleeding from the mouth where a Singer had managed to bat at him with a swollen, oversized hand. 'We can't fight all those drudge.'

He was right. Hundreds of them began to stream from their encampment, galvanised and swarming to save their sorcerers. A series of muffled thumps sounded nearby as the Spinners managed to pin the boy Darling down against the earth. His body was smoking, but still the damn thing kept twitching. The chances of getting anything out of it had been negligible anyway but I saw my best lead burn up with it.

A volley of flarelock fire spat out toward the drudge, but fifty hand cannons against that horde wasn't going to make much more of an impact than we were making on the Singers.

'Grenadoes!' I ordered. 'Light them up.'

Nenn gave me a vicious grin. I hadn't realised just how immobile the Singers were until now. The smallest of them had almost managed to drag itself a few feet. We carried grenadoes as a last resort against the bigger, stupider things the Misery can throw at you.

I rode up to the first Singer. Its big eyes sought me out, bloody veins running through flat yellow orbs.

'Kill … me …' it croaked, slow enough that I understood its drudge language. There was so much pain in its voice. The Deep Kings had ten hells of damnation to answer for when they were finally ripped out of existence, but I still couldn't bring myself to sympathise with this creature. It could have refused. It had chosen this tortured existence over preventing the murder of innocent women, men and children. I lit the grenadoe's long fuse and stuffed it inside the creature's robes. Its arms were too heavily deformed to bend enough at the elbow to do anything about it.

I began to whistle as I lit others and went around the group. Between Nenn, Stracht and I, we got them all sizzling and then ran for the horses. Stracht's horse had fled the fighting and he and I both ran for Falcon, who was snorting and prancing, flicking his hooves at the ground, but his training kept him near me. I jumped up. The drudge were closing so fast, but their mounts – ponies? Yaks?—weren't swift. They were hardy things, bred for Misery work, not for cavalry charges, and we'd be ahead of them.

'Let's move, let's move,' Stracht said. Nenn waited with us, readying a pistol.

'Get down!' she shouted, but too late. The Darling was on fire, flames raged along its leg and tail, half of its face burned away completely by the Spinners, but it was barely twenty feet away and I could see its ire burning hotter than the magic charring it. It summoned what little magic it had left to strike us down.

A lick of power came out at us, scything the air. It struck Stracht first, and I was just behind him and should have been next – but death didn't come. The energy exploded around Stracht, almost as though it bounced off him, fragments of deadly magic spraying back. The Darling took a hit from its own power, cutting itself near in half, rag-dolling over and over in the dust.

Falcon pranced, snorting and blowing as I grabbed his reins. Stracht seemed miraculously alive given that he'd just taken a full-on blast from a Darling but there was no time to ask him, as the drudge were about to arrive. Our men had retreated, only Nenn, Stracht and the dead were left. I gripped Stracht's forearm, hauled him up. He struggled, too old to be out here doing this and no stirrup to get a foot in.

'Stracht, come on,' I said. I tried hauling again, but my strength was spent and I couldn't pull him up alone. Nenn cocked her pistol. Her grin was gone.

Twin tracks of blood wept from her eyes.

'No,' I breathed.

'Thank you, Galharrow,' she said, and the voice that issued from her lips was dry and dusty as a tomb. 'I thought you were going to cause problems. But look, you've stopped the drudge barrage for me.'

'Let her go,' I said. My teeth locked rigid at seeing my worst fear come to life. Nenn pointed the pistol at me.

'How about a deal?' Saravor said through her lips. A twisted smile. Nenn could never have looked at another person with that malice. She hadn't the cruelty. 'You tell me now how to take the Bright Lady's power, and I'll let this one continue to serve me.'

The mounted drudge were nearly upon us.

'She'll destroy you,' I spat. 'Just try her.'

'An empty threat. How disappointing. I thought you would die with greater dignity. Good-bye, Captain Galharrow.'

I flinched as Nenn's fingers squeezed on the firing trigger – but not quite hard enough. Her body trembled, and in her eyes, there was still a flicker of Nenn's consciousness. Her shoulders shook, her hand wavered as she battled for control.

'I'll kill you,' Saravor whispered, but it was with an effort, and then, pained, 'Go, Ryhalt. Ride.'

The pistol dipped with a boom and an eruption of smoke, and Falcon went down beneath me. He tipped sideways, crashing down atop Stracht and spilling me onto the broken ground. A piece of crystal gouged into my face, shredding skin. I was dazed for a moment, and when I looked up again, Nenn was galloping away from the drudge, for the cover of the crystal spires.

The first grenadoe thumped, blowing the Singer wide open even as the drudge drew down upon us. A few seconds later another, then another. The drudge slowed, caring less about us now as they saw their sorcerers detonating. Milky flesh erupted violently into the air as each of the Singers died. It was a new kind of music, filled with thunder and percussion.

A hollow victory.

'Well,' I said. 'At least we stopped them.'

'That's something,' Stracht said. He swiped thick blood from the blade of his cutlass. The drudge cavalry were far too close for us to hope to outrun them now. He stared after Nenn as she rode away, too confused and too lost in the certainty of death to even ask what had just happened.

'How did you stop that Darling's magic?' I said.

'Damned if I know,' he said grimly. 'Shit, Ryhalt. We're dead, aren't we?'

I looked at the approaching ranks of drudge. They had slowed, stopped to stare at their sorcerous leaders, perhaps wondering if there was some way that they could save them, but in truth the whole area looked like the floor of a butcher's yard. Red and white, bone and meat, carpeted the ground.

I looked back toward the edge of the crystal forest. I saw Thierro there, a flarelock in his hands, and it was almost a relief. Nenn and the last of the horsemen were just reaching them. Thierro was staring at me.

'Yes,' I said. 'I think we're dead.'

Funny, how it didn't seem to mean that much to me.

I gave Thierro a nod. It was better to die than to be captured. The drudge would take us to their masters, and the Deep Kings would twist us, make us into weapons against our own people. But first, they would hurt us. They would hurt us for a long, long time. Life doesn't flash before your eyes when you see the end coming as they claim. Instead, you're hit by things left unfinished. Ezabeth, lost to the light. Nenn, lost to Saravor. Nothing that I'd done had made any difference. Distantly, Thierro aimed the flarelock at me. I took a deep breath, looked up toward the moons. Couldn't see any tonight, but the cracks in the sky were there, glowing faintly white and bronze, and in their own way, despite what they represented, there was a degree of beauty in them. For a last look, a man could do worse. I knew that Thierro was a good enough shot to put the ball through my head.

I waited. The sky rumbled. I fancied that it mourned our passing, though of course, it was just the fucking sky.

A shot cracked out from our lines and Stracht staggered, his eyes rolled up in his head, and his game was played. I waited for the shot that would take me too, looked back to Thierro. He removed his hat, and then gave me that same two-fingered salute. Then he shouldered his smoking weapon and followed the others into the forest.

'Bastard!' I snarled.

I planted my sword blade-down into the sand, drew my last pistol. The drudge were closing in on me fast. Capture was worse than death. There was only one way out.

Pressed the barrel to my forehead.

Pulled the trigger.

25

The lock snapped home.

Misfire.

The drudge swarmed around me, spitting at me and jabbing with their spears. I threw the buggered pistol at one's head, a futile gesture as it just bounced from his helmet, but then I roared at them and tried to go down fighting. I drew my sword, struck left and right. Melee is a dirty, sweat-drenched kind of hell. All that gentle swordplay they teach you in the fencing hall, the tactics and the thinking and the games, that all goes out the window and there's nothing but instinct and speed. My blade sliced the air, struck sparks from a vambrace as I snapped it out to take a wrist.

'What are you waiting for, you bastards?' I snarled at them, but they were being cautious. A dozen of them circled me even as more arrived to and cut me off from any hope of retreat. I hacked at a spear shaft, but the drudge disengaged nimbly and it struck against my breastplate. Eight inches higher and it would have struck my unprotected face, but the bastard wasn't trying to kill me.

I realised that I should put my sword through my own neck.

A spear haft cracked against my forearm, and white numbness rushed up my arm from palm to elbow. My sword fell from my senseless fingers, and the drudge swarmed me.

A fist smashed into my face, armoured and heavy with

fingers. My lip split, my cheek tore. After that I didn't get much of a count of how many blows rained down on me, but there were many, they were iron hard, and the drudge threw more than were necessary to take me down. *Bam*, I saw lights dancing before my eyes. *Bam*, the ground rose rapidly to slam into my face. *Bam*, something cracked with a snap. Half-blind, I made a grab for a big knife hanging from a belt, but the drudge knocked my hand away and went on slamming his fist into my head. Boots followed the fists, *bam*, *bam*, *bam*. The soldiers snarled and slobbered as they kicked and thumped.

It hurt. It really fucking hurt.

By the time my brain stopped bouncing around in my skull, they'd dragged me into the drudge camp, wrists and ankles bound. A persistent stabbing in the centre of my face said that my nose had been broken again. I could taste the blood that I'd swallowed. It filled my throat, my nose, gummed my beard. My face had locked up in rigid planes of swelling, one eye half-closed. I couldn't have been pretty. Or at least, I was uglier than I'd been before.

I coughed up some of the blood that I'd taken down, spat it into the dirt. This wasn't how it was supposed to go. Win or die, those had been the options. It was a struggle to think through the pain. I wished I had brandy. I wished I'd died. I wished for anything, anything than this.

And Nenn. The pain the drudge had dished out was nothing compared to seeing those red-tear tracks. I'd lost her to Saravor.

I'd lost her.

Two drudge sat nearby. They were old creatures, long since changed. Not a lot of human left in what they'd become, noseless grey faces and lidless black eyes. Looked more fish than man. One of them wore the mark of King Acradius right on his forehead. This was his operation, then, as useless as that knowledge was to me now. As the pain of the beating became bearable I took more stock of my surroundings. Not encouraging. The drudge had dragged me into their camp along with two other prisoners, a couple of our men who'd gone down wounded. One of them, a cavalry trooper, wasn't going to last much longer – an hour at best, judging by the bloody wound in his side. The second, I saw with sadness, was Betch. His foot was twisted at an impossible angle, shards of bone jutting through his boot.

Life is merciless. She doesn't care if you're old, young, man or woman, loved or reviled. The only thing you can count on is that you're going to be treated with as little fairness as everyone else.

'We're still alive,' Betch whispered, his voice shaking. He looked at the wreck the drudge had made of my face but he didn't see the blood and the blackening flesh. He looked for comfort, for some sign that this wasn't the end, that we weren't fucked beyond belief.

I had no such sign to give him. This was the end. A horror approached us.

'We aren't the only ones.'

The male Darling limped slowly across the camp toward us. It was burned, terribly burned, a stump of smoking tail dangling behind it. In places its skin was blackened and charred, in others red-raw and weeping. Its hand and forearm had been burned away entirely and I could see the bone of its leg where most of a muscle had been incinerated. It seemed to be having trouble closing its jaw and one of its eyes had melted down its face, but the one that remained was locked onto us. Nothing can hate like a Darling, and this one's fury was hotter than the flames that had engulfed it.

Even the drudge kept well back as it hobbled slowly toward us.

'Oh, fuck,' Betch said, seeing it. 'Oh fuck, oh fuck oh fuck.'

I wished that I had not come round. Being battered into unconsciousness or better yet, dead, were both preferable to this. Being at the mercy of the ire, the malice, on that half-torched face.

It stood before us. The Darling had been shot, it had been burned, and any mortal creature should have died from the punishment that it had taken. A huge gash cut right through its lower abdomen where its own power had backfired against it, but still, scarred and diminished, it was more terrifying than it had been before.

The drudge-Darling stopped a few feet away and looked us over, trembling.

'Be assured that there is nothing for you but suffering, now,' it said in Dort. Speaking made it cough and it collapsed to its red-raw knees. None of the drudge came forward to assist it.

'Do any of you have rank?' the Darling asked. The badly wounded cavalryman was shaking too much to form words and the fear had me bad, but any kind of movement sent my face into new agony, so I closed my eyes and laid my head back. The Darling coughed again, a string of bloody drool hanging from burned lips. 'Your minds will answer, even if you will not.'

'Please,' the wounded cavalryman wept, 'please, please, please.'

His mind was gone. Cracked. Hardly surprising, and probably a mercy. The man he had been was dead already, only the shell remained. That had to be better. We were surrounded by monstrosities, smelling the smoke that still rose from the Darling's burned clothing and the rich roasting of his flesh, and it seemed pretty certain that this child-sorcerer was not going to let us die quickly after the damage that we'd dealt him. "Slowly" probably didn't begin to describe it.

The drudge commander appeared, his heightened status

evident in the quality of his armour, the goldwork and precious stones studded through his ears. He spoke to the Darling, sounding angry and gesturing wildly. The Darling spat back in the drudge language. The commander pointed at us, one by one, snapping away in slower clicks and buzzes. He was not afraid of the Darling.

They had no idea that I understood their language, or maybe they thought it was irrelevant if I did. I caught the gist, either way. The commander wanted it to steal our thoughts now. The Darling said that it barely had sufficient energy to keep itself alive. It needed time to recover.

The Darling looked us over, then turned its baleful eyes on the wounded man. He was not conscious.

'I will search this one now, before it expires,' it said. 'He may know things. May have knowledge of the New King.'

'Don't fucking touch him,' I said in Dort. My swollen lips warped the sounds and the words were feeble things. They ignored me.

The mind-worms came. The wounded Duck sat bolt upright, as though a wooden rod had been speared up along his spine. His head shook violently and his eyes opened wide. Then wider, and wider, and then blood began to leak from them, to drip from his nose. He made a gurgling sound, and a river of it flowed from his mouth. His ears bled and his shoulders shook.

'Bright Lady watch over you,' Betch whispered as the man died. He was shaking from the fear, but he couldn't look away.

The wounded man's body couldn't take the pressure of the Darling's presence inside his skull. His eyes remained wide open and he continued to sit up, but he was dead nonetheless. The interrogation didn't end, though. The life was gone, but the brain was still fresh, and the Darling dug through it like a scavenging fox tearing through a pile of garbage. Minutes passed, the corpse staring, and then his body sagged, a crumpled bone heap. The Darling swayed and caught itself on its hands. Nobody moved to help it.

'He was nobody,' the Darling said to the commander. 'His commander was a maimed woman. Not one of these.'

'He was an enemy,' the commander said. 'He was still somebody.'

'Just a soldier. A common man,' the Darling said. 'I will draw more from these two tomorrow, but I must regenerate. I need lives.'

The commander glared at the Darling. Its one remaining eye was wide in its grotesquely burned face.

'The great one has already lost one of his Chosen. You would do well to ensure he does not lose another,' the Darling said. The drudge soldiers all looked away, to the ground, to the moons, to the cracks in the sky. Anywhere but at their commander or the steaming creature before it. The commander's face was old-drudge, almost featureless, grey and smooth, but I could see the reluctance there. He did not want to agree to whatever the Darling was asking.

'Take the beasts,' he said at last. 'As many as you need.'

'Beasts will not serve,' the Darling said immediately. 'Their lives carry little energy. You know what I need.'

'Then take these people,' he said, and gestured to us.

'I cannot waste them when they may be able to tell us more about Shavada's return,' the child-creature said. His words tolled dimly behind the stabbing pain in my face, a distant bell that no longer called to me. They were important, but only to the man that I had been. I wasn't anything, now. 'I need lives now. Souls to strengthen me. Your men failed to defend the Singers. This is the price that they pay.'

For several moments the drudge commander just glared at the Darling, his flat lips chewing at themselves.

'How many?' he said eventually.

'Ten. Choose whichever you wish. The sentries that failed

us, perhaps. Have them brought to my tent. After that, we shall see.' He broke into a coughing fit.

The Darling hobbled away, blood trailing across the sand. The commander watched him go, then turned and left us, his men following him. The drudge didn't bother to leave a guard. They didn't need to. Besides trying to spit at them, we had no capacity to cause them trouble, and given the state my face was in, even spitting wasn't much of an option.

Betch wept. Couldn't blame him, but the sound was just another grotesque reminder of how badly I'd failed. The Darling would return, all fuelled up, its power restored. I hadn't known that they could feed from death magic, but it didn't surprise me. Power comes in many forms, whether it's the moonlight spun by Spinners or the colossal magic that grows within a wizard's heart. It should have been no surprise that a Darling could siphon power from life.

'It will come back, and it will rip our minds open,' Betch said. 'It's going to turn us inside out.' His lips were trembling. He was right to be terrified.

'It doesn't look good,' I said. My face hurt a lot. All of me hurt, but my face worst of all.

'It's going to tear our minds apart,' he said, and then the little coherence I'd got from him devolved into meaningless gurgling.

He was right. It would learn what it could from us, and then it would soak up our life energy. Not a good way to die, out here in this shitty place. Dying might have been the intention, but as deaths went, this was a bleak one. Even as it tore through our minds we'd be helping it, teaching it, sharing what we knew.

And then it struck me like a hammer.

When the Darling set its mind-worms into me, it could riffle through my memories, and it would take my greatest secret.

It would learn the truth of Nall's Engine.

I would unwillingly spill the great secret upon which the republic depended. They would realise that the Engine would not last forever, that Shavada's heart would run dry just as Songlope's had. I was the only man in the republic who knew the awful truth about what powered the Engine, and I had placed it right into the hands of our deadliest enemies.

'We can't let them interrogate us,' I said. Betch just shook and stared into space.

I tried to get my hands free of their bonds, but the drudge who tied me had known his knots, and he'd not gone easy on them. Dawn rose, cool and blue, dominated by Clada as the other moons chose to sleep beneath the horizon. Periodically a drudge soldier came to check on us, but they weren't concerned that we might escape. A single bored old creature sat nearby, and they left our dead trooper bound to his post. Why bother digging a grave when you were breaking down your camp?

Midmorning, a battalion of five hundred drudge rode out on their hairy mounts, heading west. They were going to hunt Nenn and Thierro, try to catch up to our men. The commander wanted to have something to show when his Deep King master caught up to him. Creating those Singers must have cost Deep King Acradius significant power, and no wizard gave that up lightly. How long had they been nurturing them, growing them, training them? I wondered whether they'd been born to become those grotesque, lumpen monstrosities, or if they'd taken grown men and women and forced their bodies to adapt? Could they create more, if they had a desire to? I didn't know. I probably wasn't going to live to find out.

I didn't think that the drudge had much chance of catching Nenn. Tnota would be skipping them home using every navigation trick he knew. There weren't many navigators who could have kept up with him, and none that could catch him when he was given a head start and a damn good reason to use it. That was something.

I could smell cooking. The drudge were making breakfast. Some kind of meat, but nothing I recognised. Some animal that lived way out east, beyond the Misery. They didn't bring us any. Didn't bring us any water either. A warmth had risen out of the earth, adding thirst to my list of pains. My face was locked up pretty solid, swollen planes of flesh and drum-taut skin. The thirst was worse. They didn't take us to the latrine trench either, but I'd sweated out most of my water so when I had to let it go there wasn't much. Clada rose up, nearly made it to the top of the sky, began to fall again. The drudge ate lunch, and I worked the ropes against the post, over and over, wrists scraping against the coarse rope. They chafed away until they were raw and bloody, and then I tried again, though every twist was futile, stinging agony.

It was midafternoon when one of the drudge, slender and young, came and relieved our bored old guard. He planted himself down on a stone near to us. He was vaguely human, his changes far less pronounced than most of the creatures in the camp. He still had a bump for a nose, and nostrils, and his eyes had an equal ratio of pupil to white. He even had a straggling line of brown hair running down the centre of his scalp. He drew the sword from his belt and placed it across his knees as he watched us. It was a drudge weapon, a design entirely foreign to us, but I was a connoisseur of swords and so I paid attention. It was a mildly curved blade, a hilt that could have taken three hands and a small round guard that offered little protection. It didn't look all that practical but there was a certain aesthetic beauty to it. I wondered if he meant to use it, to take revenge for what we'd done to his Singers, because there was something in the way he was looking us over. It took me a moment to place it, but then it came to me: he didn't loathe us the way that the Darling or the commander had. He almost seemed curious.

'They put you to watch over us?' I asked. He flinched. Hadn't expected me to speak, and my voice was croaky, dry as old leaves. 'Not much point in that. Where are we going to run?'

He didn't understand me. I was speaking Dort. Weren't many drudge that understood it. I could have spoken to him in his own tongue, but if I did, he'd probably go running off to his commander and the schedule for my torture and interrogation would be significantly stepped up. The torture and interrogation was inevitable, but later had to be better than sooner.

My wrists were stinging fire against the ropes. My mouth was dry as a desert wind. Betch had cried himself to sleep, and I sat bound and helpless awaiting the coming of a furious, spite-filled Darling who would force me to reveal the Grand Alliance's greatest secret and cost us a war that had raged for more than a century.

Fuck it. Roll the fucking dice. When you're down to your last tile you play it blind and pray that the fates give you sixes.

'Your Darling consumed the lives of ten of your friends,' I said in what was probably terrible drudge. Clicks and snacks, buzz and drone. If a bee had a voice, it would sound like a drudge.

The young drudge flinched again. He had tabby stippling across his brow, and the shapes warped and moved as he frowned.

'You know talk us?' the drudge asked. In reality, he was speaking his language correctly and I was mangling it with my atrocious pronunciation, but I didn't get much practice.

'I speak your language. Yes. Lots of us do,' I said. Lying, but then I needed to get him to talk. Needed to make him angry. Needed him to take that delicately curved sword and cut my head from my shoulders. Needed him to use it to split my brain in two. I had to die before the Darling could get to me. It wasn't much of a plan, and I didn't particularly want to die, but I didn't want to be tortured and betray the Range either and maybe if I died sooner rather than later, the Darling would find it harder — maybe even impossible — to dredge out old memories of Kings, hearts, and Engines.

'You first one I meet, can speak us,' he said.

'Have you met many of us?' I asked.

The drudge smiled. It was odd to see a drudge smile. The changes that happen to their skulls and muscles tend to prevent it.

'I was one of you,' he said. 'Before glorious master, praise be to majesty, King Acradius, gave me gzzzrt.'

He didn't say 'gzzzrt,' but it was a word that Maldon hadn't taught me and I had no idea what it meant. The drudge saw me struggle with it.

'Ascension,' he said in Dort. 'Is hard me remember old speak. It mean "ascend".'

'You were a soldier from Dortmark?' I asked.

The drudge nodded.

'Before glory. Yes. Soldier like you, across Misery. Long-ago time, now.'

'How old are you?'

I don't know why I asked that. It wasn't relevant, and I needed to get him to kill me, not make him like me. It was no time to be practising race relations.

'Not measure life that way,' the drudge said. He thought for a few moments, contemplating something. 'Measure life in thoughts of master. Make sense?'

'No,' I clicked. He shrugged.

'Not can explain, then. Master think big thought. All know big thought. Not like that for unborn.'

'Unborn' was what the drudge called the rest of us.

Maldon had taught me that. They regarded us like a larval form, caterpillars or grubs. Perhaps that was why they were so indifferent to us.

'You talk like them,' Betch said. He had woken up and stared at me in horror. 'You speak like them. You're one of them!'

'I'm not one of them,' I said. Betch began to thrash against his bonds, as though this was too much for him to take, and the need to free himself became all-consuming. The guard got up and walked across to him. A solid kick to the face saw Betch's struggling die away, his head lolling. Satisfied, the drudge went back to his rock. He was almost smiling, as though he had cleared an irritating inconvenience from our attempt to converse.

'Recently, god have big thought,' the drudge said. 'Confused thought. Not understand why unborn raise Shavada from death.'

He looked at me as though that were supposed to mean something to me.

'I don't understand,' I said.

'Unborn build sky-reach tower. Sky tower for harness moon power. Very strong. Need destroy.' He cocked his head at me as if working through something very complex. 'Gods not like that. Moon power beyond gods. No work for them. Work only for unborn.'

No surprise there. Valiya had sussed their intention to bring it down. Thierro had demonstrated just what the Witnesses could do with just a few tanks of phos. When the Grandspire was complete and the solar flare hit, could he take the war to the Deep Kings?

No. It wasn't Thierro and his Witnesses that they feared. The Darling had mentioned Shavada, and Saravor had wanted the Singers stopped. I was looking at the hound without seeing the lion behind it. Unless ...

'Your god fears that the Bright Lady is going to return?'

The words escaped on a treacherous little surge of hope. I knew it was false.

'No understand,' it said. 'Sky tower bad for world. Is truth.'

'You believe everything they tell you?' I asked. 'Even when they take ten of your friends and siphon them into a Darling?'

' "Darling" is unborn word,' he buzzed. 'We say Chosen. Chosen special. Need lives. Give gladly, for Chosen and god. You unborn, no cause. Give life gladly for nothing. What point then in life? Life only have value if you give for other.'

That sounded like a lot of old horseshit to me. Easy to see why the Deep Kings wanted their subservient thralls to think like that, though. They were brainwashed to their very cores, not even their thoughts their own. At least, I thought that they were. Only this drudge had something like a spark of personality. I'd never expected that. Were his changes just not so far gone, or was it that his face could still move enough to convey his feelings? I doubted that anyone had ever conversed with a drudge for as long as I had with this one. Not without hot irons and jagged knives. Perhaps we should have.

'Your life is your own,' I said. 'Staying alive is all that matters.'

'Better to give willingly,' the drudge clicked at me. He shrugged. 'If all that matters, sad end for you. Not much time left. Chosen come, use mind-worm. You die then.'

He was right. There wasn't much that I could say to that.

26

Winter days are as short in the Misery as they are anywhere else, no matter what warmth seeped up from the poisoned earth. The guard changed, darkness fell across the world. Clada slunk away and Rioque peeked half her face across the distant horizon. A colourless night.

'You bastard traitor,' Betch hissed at me. He'd come round sometime during my conversation with the drudge. 'You're one of them.'

'If I was one of them, you'd think I'd be strapped to this post?'

'You talk like them.'

'I can speak their language,' I said. 'Can teach you, if you want. It's all about buzzing in the back of your throat and slapping your tongue against the roof of your mouth. I reckon we have at least a few hours before the Darling's done eating his own drudge and ready to mind-worm us. Want to learn?'

'Fucking bastard traitor,' Betch growled.

He'd latched onto something that he could hate. Something that he could direct his anger toward, something that could feel it. The guard had changed again, and there was no point directing his anger toward her. She was white as milk, skin almost translucent over smooth planes of bone, and had no interest in us whatsoever. I'd not tried to speak with her. She was too far gone, too deep into the change, and it hadn't done much good with the last one anyway.

'What do you remember that was good in life, Betch?' I asked. I turned my head to look at him. I'd twisted my neck something terrible during the fighting, and to look around that far hurt a lot. Sitting up against the post wasn't doing much for my back either.

'What?'

'Life. Back home. What made you happy?'

Betch's face was all sinew and fear and his eyes were wide.

'What the fuck does that matter?'

'It's worth thinking about now. Probably won't have much time later.'

Betch turned away. He didn't want to talk to a traitor, even though it was pretty clear that if I were a traitor, I wasn't getting a good deal from it. I blew out a heavy breath. I was done trying to work the ropes against the post. My wrists were swollen against the ropes, and now my bonds bit even more painfully. I looked up at the glowing cracks in the sky. If one of them could simply open and swallow me, the Misery, even the world, that would be better than what lay ahead. I was going to be the man who betrayed the Range. Not some drudge sympathiser, but a Blackwing captain. For everything I'd done, for all the bastards I'd put to the sword in defence of a country that reviled me, I was going to be the one who cast us down.

A shadow wheeled through the sky, across one of the cracks. Odd thing that. Don't see birds in the Misery, not without six heads and a scorpion tail. With any luck it was some kind of new terror readying to dive down and tear our hearts out.

'It's not fair,' Betch said then, quietly.

'No,' I said. 'Nothing ever is.'

'I always expected the Range to take me, one way or another,' he said. 'It gets us all, in the end. Breaks us. Takes us.'

'I guess we're the proof of that.'

Betch had moved through the terror, the panic. Now he was heading into melancholy. Next would come confession, then defiance, and lastly, he'd go back to pleading. A cycle that the mind went through as it tried different methods to cope with the nightmare. I'd seen it with dozens of prisoners over the years. My prisoners, usually.

'You're close with Nenn. There was a way she'd talk about you,' Betch said. 'I didn't get it at first. It made me envious. Jealous, even. I thought, here's a man she's loved all these years. That she'd rather have you than me.'

'No,' I said. 'It was never like that.'

'Realised that,' Betch said. 'But I was still jealous.'

'She got out,' I said. I wasn't going to mention that her mind had been corrupted. Warped. What was the point? I thought about her fears, that Betch only wanted her to climb the ranks. They seemed so small now. Life is like that. 'You love her, Betch?'

He gave a dry, dusty laugh, but it was streaked with the pain that his mangled foot was sending up through his leg.

'I never understood how you didn't,' he said.

A wind had picked up, and it sent the growing smell of the dead cavalryman in my direction. A bad smell, that. The corpse was only a day old, but things go nasty fast in the Misery.

'I would have married her. Maybe. I don't know,' Betch said. He looked up at me, his face as bruised and dreadful as mine. 'She's safe, now, though. We did it, didn't we? We stopped them throwing the sky-fires. They can't hurt anyone else. That's what we set out to do, and we did it.'

'We did,' I said, and though it was no consolation to me whatsoever, it seemed to offer Betch some. He didn't know that I would let the republic's most vital secrets fall into the Deep Kings' hands. Not even death was certain to take me beyond the Darlings' reach. I'd doomed us all, with one misfiring pistol.

'What about you?' Betch interrupted my thoughts. His voice was shaking. Maybe it was the undiluted pain from the broken bones protruding through the leather of his boot, or maybe he was trying to hold on to his sanity. He'd have been better off letting it go. 'What was good in your life?'

Not an easy question. 'Brandy' wasn't much of an answer, but there hadn't been as many good times as I'd have liked, not ones that I remembered anyway. A few victories here and there, but there's only so loudly you can cheer about scrubbing away mould.

'I had a woman, too,' I said eventually. 'She died. In the Siege.'

'A wife?'

'No.' I couldn't help but choke out a laugh. My throat was dry and stiff, and the laughter hurt. 'It never would have worked out. She was far too good for me. Didn't really matter, though. She made it worthwhile. So yeah. A woman.'

'That's all it really comes down to, in the end, isn't it?' Betch said. His voice drifted away.

I slept. Hadn't intended to, but exhaustion finally got the better of me. I dreamed about Valiya and Amaira. One of those dreams where nothing is happening, but you feel the closeness. I'd spoken of Ezabeth to Betch, but Valiya was there on the edge of my mind as well.

My dreams were broken by the young guard pushing a metal canteen against my mouth. I didn't want to drink it. I knew that I shouldn't drink it. I could try to die of dehydration, and only the spirits knew what was in the canteen. But my body was a treacherous piece of shit, and it drank. It was just water, stale and metallic with the taint of the moisture extractors.

It was full dark now. I wondered how long it would be before the Darling was rested and came to chew through our minds.

The camp had grown quiet. Drudge went to sleep just like anyone else. They'd loaded everything up on the wagons, would be moving out with the coming of first light, provided there were enough visible moons to take a reading.

The drudge sat down on his rock again.

'Strange sword you got there,' I said while he was screwing a cap onto his canteen. 'Not seen one like it before.'

The drudge took the scabbard from his belt, showed it to me. Good clear metal, ghosts in the steel forming a wavering pattern along the blade's edge.

'From faraway place,' he said. 'Went there, fought unborn. Now sword mine.'

He seemed pleased with himself as he stowed it away on his belt. He had a packet of some kind of dried meat, wrapped in paper.

'Want?' He offered it to me.

'No,' I said. He held it out to Betch, but he turned his head away. The drudge shrugged, chewed on another strip. His mannerisms were so familiar. He could have been any one of a hundred young soldiers, bored on guard duty, looking for a way to pass the time. I'd known thousands like him, only they'd been human beings, not some kind of monster. I wondered what the man had been like before he was twisted into this thing. Probably just an ordinary man looking to make his living from soldiering. Maybe there'd been a bad harvest and he'd found his family starving and poor, had gone to make his fortune. Maybe he'd dreamed of promotion and medals. Or maybe he'd had no other skills of worth and somebody had put a matchlock in his hand and said it made him a man. Soldiers' stories were seldom flush with hope.

A pebble dropped from the sky a few feet to the left,

kicked up a little cloud of grit. The drudge glanced up at the dark sky, but it only winked at him from its white-bronze cracks. He wandered over and picked it up. It was a little shard of the crystal that the drudge had been pulverizing to make their sorcery.

'In Misery, sky rains stone,' the drudge said. He turned the shard in his hands. 'Strange land. Kings of unborn make so. Is bad magic. Should not be rocks in sky.'

I couldn't argue with that. There definitely should not be rocks in the sky.

'Do you love?' I asked the drudge. Maybe it was a strange thing to ask.

'All things love,' he said. 'Love gods. King Acradius ascends me. Must love for that.'

'Do you love one another?' I asked. 'The other ...' and I faltered as I nearly called him drudge to his face, 'ascended. Do you love any of them?' The language failed. Perhaps Maldon had not known the word for love that didn't refer to a divine being of awesome power. The drudge word for love had connotations of obedience, servitude, worship, adulation. All the worst parts. It carried nothing of kinship, of affection, of respect.

'We know how is for unborn. Like that? No, not that,' the drudge told me. He approached and knelt close in front of me. Stared into my face as though he were looking for something. A memory, maybe, of what he'd known before.

A raven cawed overhead. It was a solitary call, a lonely bird in a place that it should not have been. The guard looked upward, frowning. And then a rock the size of my fist smacked right into his head. He crumpled in a sprawl of awkwardly angled limbs, blood running from a gash on his forehead.

The hooded raven fluttered down after it, swivelling its head left and right to see if anybody had seen.

'About fucking time you showed up,' I said.

Hope. It surged. It roared. Here, in all of this, it was the last thing I'd expected. Spirits-damned hope.

'Good to see you haven't given away all our secrets yet,' the raven squawked at me. It was a big bird, and it hopped over to the drudge. It seemed to sniff, though I don't know whether ravens can smell anything. 'Not dead. Move fast. Move fast anyway, I think.' The bird took hold of the drudge's dagger in its beak and drew it out from his belt. It was a slow and awkward process. Ravens are not designed to carry things. It managed to drag the blade through the dirt toward me.

'What the fuck is that thing?' Betch asked. Then he decided that he didn't care, as he began to whisper, 'Get us free. Get us free!'

'What took you so long?' I asked. The raven dropped the knife behind me and I began to saw awkwardly at the ropes. It was not easy to get the angle, and the skin-stripped weals around my wrists burned with every movement. My shoulders were stiff, rigid, protested at the motion. But I felt the strands of the rope beginning to fray away. Everything is weaker, more brittle, in the Misery.

The drudge on the ground made a groaning noise, his hand began to grope around on the floor and I sawed faster. The bird spoke in a staccato as it pecked away at the rope, tugging at threads to assist the process.

'Took ... a long time to find ... a rock that I ... could pick up ... that was heavy enough ... Only had one chance.'

'It was a good shot,' I said.

'Was aiming ... for you.'

I wasn't even surprised.

'Your compassion is overwhelming.'

'What do you expect? Crowfoot made me. Didn't he tell you not to fuck this up?'

'What did that bird just say?' Betch asked. I ignored him.

276

With a snap the last of the rope came free and I sawed away the rope around my ankles. That was much faster work. The drudge had enjoyed keeping his weapons sharp, and the knife was the same smoky steel as his sword.

I looked up to see that the soldier had pushed himself up onto his knees. Blood ran down his face and he clearly didn't know what was happening or where he was. The rock had left him disoriented, dazed. The way his eyes struggled to focus, the hand pressed to his brow. He could have been just another man. But he wasn't a man. He wasn't anything.

I got my hands around his throat and crushed down. He was slender, not a lot of meat on those twisted bones and his windpipe collapsed when I drove my thumbs in. He didn't make a sound. I could have used the knife, but in my anger I wanted to feel him die. In the time that I'd spoken with him, I'd found that he was more human than I'd expected, and that drove my spite. Had he been mindless, a slave to the whims of the Deep Kings, perhaps I could have forgiven him. But he had a mind. Or at least he did until I strangled the life from him.

I sat in the dust and the new quiet. We were shielded from the rest of the camp by the square tents around us, a curtain of canvas that was for now keeping us alive. But for how long? I pried my fingers free of the crumpled neck and hung my head. Everything still hurt like a kiss from the Long End, but freedom had brought with it the crashing truth of our situation. I'd solved one problem, and now a much greater one presented itself.

'Now me,' Betch said. 'Free me.' I didn't move, just sat for a moment, thinking.

If the Darling got his mind-worms into me, then the secret of Nall's Engine was done. The drudge would know, and no clever deceptions would keep them at bay. That information was too vital to fall into the Deep Kings' hands.

The hooded raven was pecking at the discarded dagger.

'You know what you have to do,' it croaked.

'Free me,' Betch said, but he was a dull little voice at the back of my mind.

The bird was right. I realised with a grim finality that it was not here to help me escape. It was here to ensure that I was dead before the Darling could get to me.

I picked up the knife, turned it in my hand. Wasn't so long ago that I'd put the barrel of a pistol against my head. Now the knife was my way out. I'd opened other men's throats often enough; how hard could it be to cut my own? Betch was still talking behind me. He didn't understand. Throat, or heart? Maybe a quick, hard insertion between the ribs. Would that work? I couldn't risk wounding myself to incapacity without making it certain.

'Get on with it,' the raven cawed.

'How's the master going to get by without me?' I said.

The raven just stared at me, and I knew the answer. He'd find some other fool willing to trade his life away for a favour. He'd grant it and that poor bastard would take my place, live my life. I positioned the point of the blade against the raven tattoo. I could drive it home, hope that Crowfoot's safeguard would be enough to rip me apart. No. It was too risky. I didn't know what would happen and the magic might just tear my arm off and leave me too weak to finish the job. I placed the cold edge up against my neck. Betch thought I'd cracked, but the steel felt very bright, very final against my skin. Bitterly, I thought that to press it home would be a relief.

It was the uncertainty that stayed my hand. Even after the Darling killed the cavalryman, it had been able to pry through his mind. If I was certain I'd take my secrets with me, maybe I'd have had the strength to drive the blade home. But to die without knowing if it would work? To end myself and fail even so? I couldn't. I couldn't give Amaira to a world in which that monster held power. Not when there was a chance.

When I lowered the blade I was panting hard, sucking in heaving gasps of poisoned Misery air. I struck my head against the pommel.

'Get on with it,' the raven croaked. 'If the Darling comes back, you know the price we all pay. All of Dortmark will pay it, not just you. End it.'

'No,' I said.

'Think, Galharrow,' the raven said. 'You're deep in the Misery, no navigator, no friends, no supplies. They haven't waited for you, they're thundering back to the city. You don't have a future. Die a hero, not the coward that cost the Grand Alliance its freedom. If the Darling gets into your mind, you end us all.'

The raven's voice annoyed me, which made me all the more certain that I should ignore it. The hooded raven was an impression of Crowfoot, but it was not my master. I did not have to obey, and I had a job to do. The fate of the republic rested on how far I could get my brain away from the drudge. The people I loved needed me to suffer this last crawl through the dust. I owed them every ounce of fight that I had. They could flay me, they could scald me, they could send a thousand scorpions to madden me with their agonies, and I'd still have fought my way through seven hells and beyond to die knowing that Amaira would grow up safe and free. No. No giving up. Not now. Not ever again.

I slowly dusted off my hands.

'Come on, free me,' Betch insisted.

I had to leave, right now, but I owed Betch some kind of explanation. He thought that we were being rescued, and he was grasping for that chance. Taking anything that he could get. He didn't understand.

'Betch,' I said gently. 'I can't take you with me. This isn't a rescue. Nenn, Thierro and the others – they're gone, and they took our navigator with them. We have no way out of the Misery. I'm not a navigator. Neither are you. Even if we had supplies, or mounts, the land will turn us around and around until we either wander into a skweam hole or die of thirst. Equal chance which. We're dead, Betch. I'm not going to escape. But I know things. Things that will destroy everything we've ever cared for if the Deep Kings learn the truth. I can't let that happen. I'm going to head out into the Misery as far as I can in the hope that they can't find me and drain my mind. Maybe if I make it far enough, something will eat me.'

He deserved better than this. He'd come all this way, he'd offered his life to his country. He loved my best friend. He was a brave man.

'Just give me the chance to run,' he said. 'Together we might ...' He looked at the twisted wreck of his leg and slumped a little. 'There has to be some chance.'

He couldn't walk. He certainly couldn't run. If I tried to bring him, he'd be in agony, he'd slow me down, and we'd be caught. If we even made it out of the camp, he might be able to endure the pain for the first mile, but when the agony was too much he'd beg me to help him. I'd carry him for a mile. Maybe then I'd drag him. And when the drudge caught us we'd both beg for death.

'You fought bravely,' I said. 'Nenn would be proud. You lived a good life.' Betch looked down at the knife in my hand, noted my proximity. Tears filled his eyes, spilled down across his cheeks. He let out a strangled moan of grief, fear, pressed his eyes tight shut. He shuddered.

'If somehow you make it,' he said. 'If you ever see her again, tell her "yes."' He stared at me very intently, pouring his will into me. Gave me what little he had left. 'What she asked me, on the veranda, on the morning we watched the dawn rise. Tell her that I said yes.'

'I will,' I said. I didn't blink from his gaze. It felt an important kind of promise. 'Close your eyes.' Betch blinked away the last of his tears, then gritted his teeth and put his head back against the post. Muscles strained in his bared throat as he forced the words.

'Do it.'

I hadn't known him well, but doing it hurt all the same. I wiped the knife against a jacket he no longer needed.

'Galharrow, if you run, they will catch you,' the raven snapped. It flapped up at my face in a flurry of wings, demanding. 'You can't navigate, you'll leave tracks, and the Darling will devour your mind. Once it is rested, you've nothing to bring against it.'

'You're right,' I said. 'Once it's rested.'

'You can't outrun it after it regenerates,' the raven cawed.

'I'm not going to run,' I said. I straightened the collar of my coat. 'And it's not going to get to regenerate.'

27

The wind had not abated, and a cloud of dust rolled in just when I needed it to. Sometimes the Misery hates you, sometimes it comes around and slackens the noose. Not by much, but a little. A storm of Misery dust wasn't something that I'd ever welcomed before, but I did then, as the stinking, blinding grit flowed into the drudge camp like noxious steam from a factory runoff, darkening the air and sending the drudge into their tents. Even the cracks in the sky were dimmed and muted.

I searched the guard, found his face mask and hooded myself against the clouding dirt. The mask not only protected me against the gusting wind and flying grit, it concealed my face from the enemy. I shrugged the drudge's cloak around my shoulders and pulled it tight. Through the storm, I might pass for one of them.

Betch was slumped forward, slack, deadweight. He was a hero. He had deserved a better death.

'Now yourself,' the raven croaked.

'I'm Blackwing,' I said. 'And I refuse to go down.'

The raven was having a bad time of it in the gusting wind, feathers getting ragged with dust.

I took the guard's sword, stuffed it through my belt, the dagger beside it. His canteen was full, and I took that too, and the dried meat. No time to make a rational inventory of what I had, and it was there so I took it. Hunching my shoulders, I set out into the camp.

Campfires had been smothered by the dust or doused so embers didn't go flying into canvas walls. The sky had grown loud as the storm picked up, growling and rumbling. We were deep-Misery here, halfway between us and them, and the heavens had more volume, more vim, than I was accustomed to. Some strange part of me felt that the Misery was on my side. If so, she was my only ally. The raven that struggled to flap alongside me certainly wasn't, reminding me over and over that the best option – the only sensible option – was to slice my own throat open. I told it to stop attracting attention, but the few drudge still braving the storm didn't even spare me a glance.

Past experience had taught me that my enemy's tent would be separate from those of the ordinary drudge. The Darlings kept themselves apart, or the drudge stayed away from them, one or the other. The Darling would have a pavilion, larger, stronger than those of its minions. I had to pick my way around the camp carefully as I looked for it, and it was a big camp. I saw bottles of what looked like wine, stopped and loaded them into a cloak that became a makeshift sack. Might not have been wine, might have been anything. Doubted that I'd have a chance to drink them, but better to take them than not.

As I passed one tent I heard grunting sounds coming from within. I wasn't sure what to make of that. Drudge voices came from another, a heated conversation. I saw the blurred shadows of figures through the thin cloth. In so many ways they were like us. In so many ways, not.

There were two Darling tents next to one another on the outskirts of the camp. Bigger, made of dark cloth bearing crudely painted glyphs of praise for King Acradius. I wondered if he'd send his creatures any thoughts tonight. Wondered if he was capable of sending a warning. I didn't think so. The Deep Kings were vast and powerful, but they were not all-knowing and all-seeing. That's what the drudge were for, to be their hands and eyes out in the world. Besides, Acradius was far away, trying to sink the world beneath the icy seas. The Darling would have no help tonight.

I needed that Darling out of action. Needed to take away its capacity to tear the thoughts from my skull. If I ran straight into the Misery, it might still catch me, and in open ground I'd stand no chance.

The Darling tents were a good hundred yards away from any others. There was no cover, and there would be guards. I had to assume that the surviving Darling, weakened as it was, wouldn't risk that a few gillings might find their way inside and take off the other arm. A worse thought struck me, one that threatened what little sense there appeared to be in this plan. If the second Darling had survived our attack and been brought here too, things could fall into the hells a lot sooner than I intended.

'What are you doing?' the raven choked through the billowing dust. 'What can you possibly hope to achieve?'

'I need that Darling,' I said.

'Then what?' the raven croaked. 'You'll run into the Misery? To what end?'

I shrugged.

'Believe it or not, this is not the worst situation I've ever found myself in. When you've faced down against a Deep King, a walk in the Misery isn't as frightening as you might think. And I have a debt to pay. Ezabeth gave everything to protect the Range. I can't ask less of myself.'

'You'd risk the security of the Range for an imagined debt to a dead woman?' it snarked.

'The debt's not imagined. And she's not dead. Not entirely,' I said.

'Did those Witnesses get into your head? You think that

the solar flare is going to bring the Bright Lady back into the world so that you can breed pink little babies?'

'I know the flare won't bring her back,' I said. 'Doesn't mean I don't owe her.'

'Tenacious bastard, aren't you?' the raven snarled. 'I should have dropped the rock on you instead.' It glared at me with nasty little raven-eyes and took up residence on a post. I'd do the next part alone.

I hunched low against the wind as it threatened to knock me down and ran for the tent. No need to worry about the sound. I was counting on the Darling still being weak enough not to pose any threat. If it had already replenished its power, then this would all be over fast.

The bodies of ten drudge soldiers lay outside the tent. They were bound hand and foot and their eyes were opened unnaturally wide, mouths hanging open, gathering sand. Their throats had been cut with the same precision that I'd offered to Betch, red crescent moons mirroring Rioque above. It was one thing to give your life for your country. It was quite another to have your throat slashed to help regenerate a monster that didn't care for you one way or another. I wondered how they'd felt as they were led here, lambs to the slaughter. Crowfoot was a callous master, hard and cruel in his punishments and ruthless when he used men in his schemes, but this was worse. I couldn't put my finger on why that was, but it was.

The Darling had taken those lives to speed its recovery. Death magic, the foulest of all the black sorceries.

The entrance flap to the tent was weighted down on the inside, but it opened easily enough when I ducked through.

The Darling had lived in some sort of luxury here. The floor was covered with carpets, and there was furniture – small, portable items, but more than I'd seen even our highest rankers bring into the Misery with them. At Adrogorsk I'd had a portable writing desk, polished walnut, legs carved like lion paws. I'd been terribly proud of it, back in the days when things like that seemed to matter. The Darling had apparently enjoyed something similar here. But it was not enjoying them now.

The room had two occupants. The Darling, maimed and burned, clean white bone showing through the charred flesh of its face, lay wheezing on a cot. Its breath was a hoarse grind, slow and dry with pain.

The second occupant was slender as a willow, a woman of middle years whose changes were subtle, lightly begun. She was reading a book as I entered. A servant or a nurse, not a warrior, dressed in a light, flowing robe. Her hair was curly, shiny and rich beneath her head scarf. She looked up at the intrusion, at the drawn sword in my hand and her presence stymied me for a moment. I had expected a couple of bruisers with big axes and meat for brains, not this rare display of femininity in the Misery. And because I'm flawed and not as hardened as I wished I was, I didn't launch in and cave her head in as I should have.

I must have looked like a drudge with the dust mask and one of their cloaks, and she had no reason to suspect otherwise.

'What do you want?' she asked.

'How fares the Chosen?' I asked in their tongue.

'He has consumed. He recovers. But much hurt.'

I walked across to look for myself. I steeled myself for what I had to do, and realised I didn't want to do it. A rare strand of weakness burned up through me. Maybe because she was a nurse and her job was to heal rather than hurt, or maybe her gentle concern reminded me of Valiya, but I felt a moment of unease. I was fully aware that if the Darling opened its eyes, then I would be in a lot of shit.

'Commander wants to know if Chosen will recover,' I said.

The drudge woman frowned at me, as though I'd said

something wrong. Probably just some inflection in a word, or I'd used an insulting synonym. Or maybe I'd made no sense at all, or maybe there was no possible way that I could have come from the commander. It was a hell of a gamble to take.

I murdered her as quickly and quietly as I could, and she did not fight. The sword slithered clear of her chest and I turned to the sleeping Darling.

It did not look like a child. It was already half-gone into its drudge changes, and the Spinners' light had taken what little humanity remained. It looked like a demon from the darkest of hells, an inhuman thing, which I guess it was, really. I did not waste time. The sword was clean and sharp and I brought it down on the Darling's neck with one wrist-jolting chop.

The Darling's half-milk eye flared open and for a moment I was sure that I was dead. Its hand reached upward, clawing at the air, and I thought that somehow I'd failed to sever the spine, but then the body jerked upright and I realised that no, I had indeed managed to part one from the other. But neither seemed to be dead.

The body rolled off the bed and began to grope about, debilitated by its missing limbs and blind to anything around it. The head posed the greater threat.

'Who are you?' it croaked. I don't know how it croaked since it had no lungs or airway to make words, but Darling anatomy never did make any sense.

The raven flapped into the tent, eyed the Darling's severed head and cackled appreciatively. The Darling began to shriek, an impossible, high sound. But impotent. It was far too weak to use any power against me, all of its focus and energy had been on repairing the damage it had sustained. I'd taken a big gamble, but I'd been confident. Self-preservation comes before everything else. I could see little threads of worming muscle were pushing down from

287

the severed neck, seeking tendrils that groped upward from the body. Trying to repair itself.

A mad idea struck me. I'd come into the Misery to learn what Saravor was planning, had come looking for this thing. I'd never expected to stand over its impotent, shrieking head. The plan was to break out of the camp and walk, and walk, and die. A solid plan. But if I could break this creature, if I could learn its secrets, then maybe there was a chance to stop him. To save Nenn. To be a spirits-damned hero.

New plan.

I needed to shut it up. I yanked its jaw open and stuffed a balled-up towel into its mouth, then stuffed it into my makeshift sack and tied the sack through my belt. The Darling's muffled protests continued, futilely.

My heart was drumming, but the only other sound was that of the wind gusting against the tent. I'd accomplished my first task; I'd killed an ally, a nurse and then a demon in its bed. It was not a story that I'd ever want to tell another living soul, and as days of my life went it had been at the shit-stinking end. Now, all I had to do was get out of the drudge camp without being seen, trek back ten days through the Misery without a navigator, without being caught, without adequate supplies, and without a mount. And if I did all that, I might reach Valengrad, where something terribly, terribly dark was manifesting.

Bad odds.

28

The dust storm was a double-edged, blood-hungry sword. It gave me the cover I needed and drove the drudge into their tents, turned their eyes down and away from the stinging grit, but the tracks that I could have followed out of the camp were swept away by the stinging wind. I needed those tracks. Scuff marks in the sand were worth marginally more than a banker's smile, but with no skill at Misery navigation and no equipment, I was willing to clutch to any driftwood that might keep me afloat. Crowfoot's simulacrum hadn't lied. I was fucked up to my eyeballs.

Odds be damned. I wasn't giving up until my last tile got flipped. The overwhelming likelihood was that my first plan – to get far enough from the drudge that they'd lose me and my secrets in the Misery – was still going to be my life's final destination, but I was angry and I'd promised Betch that I'd tell Nenn what he'd told me. I owed him that. No giving up. No surrender.

The shattered stumps in the crystal forest that had become our battlefield were the only place I knew. I headed there, hunched low and ducking my head against the swirls of dirt. The drudge had removed the larger chunks of the Singers: those bodies were imbued with magic. They'd be ground down into something to feed the next batch of sorcerers that the Deep Kings sought to breed. The enemy lacked sentimentality. Our men lay where they'd fallen, stripped of arms and armour. I didn't see any sentries, but I didn't see much of anything through the storm. The drudge had no reason to watch the crystal pillars now that the Singers had been blown to pieces, but I went cautiously all the same. I'd been hoping to find a stray horse, but they'd all been captured or had bolted to die in the Misery. Or maybe something had eaten them already.

'Faster, faster,' the raven croaked.

The cost had been high. Thirty-two of Nenn's brave Ducks were carrion, dead and staring. Some of them had been decent enough types. I came across Stracht's body. Thierro had put the shot right through his chest. He'd had to make a choice, and he'd made the wrong one, but there was no way he could have known that. Only his salute bothered me – a mocking, cold gesture to an ally certain to perish. Why had he given it?

The second Darling had not survived the point-blank volleys of pistol fire and trampling by thrashing hooves. Do enough damage to them and they will die, eventually. But it takes a hell of a lot to put a Darling down for good so when you manage it, there's not much left to look at. The head in the sack tied to my belt was testament to that.

My looting turned up just one useful item. One of the soldiers had possessed a hip flask of Whitelande brandy and I necked most of it as I limped back through the faintly glowing crystal spears. The old wound in my leg was playing up, nipping at me as though I'd been stitched up too tight. Now was not the time. I needed to be better than this, stronger than this. I wasn't going to get far if I listened to an old complaint in the muscle. Keep going. Keep moving.

The hooded raven guided me. I'd not have found our old camp at all without its caustic little comments, delivered each time it chose to swoop down and tell me which way to walk. It struggled against the gusting wind, but a pair of eyes in the sky was worth more than I'd thought.

Not much left of the camp. I could see where we'd dug the trench to shit in, and the moisture extractor had left a shimmering white residue on the earth that the dust hadn't managed to cover or displace. Discarded ammunition cases, torn powder charges, fodder bags, an apple core. My friends were long gone, and I knew that was a good thing. I still sagged down to my knees in the middle of the deserted camp and let my head hang forward. I'd got this far, but what now? This had been the easy part.

I looked across the Misery's shadowed dunes. I could walk in any direction and it would always be wrong. Even if the Misery didn't shift, it would only take one skweam, or maybe the gillings would take me in the night. Maybe the ground would just open and swallow me whole. The hardest part was over. Only the dying remained. Perhaps I should have taken some satisfaction from that. I recognised the lunacy that had driven me to bring the Darling's head with me for what it was, a battle-rush-inspired surge of hope that there was something left for me to do in this life. But staring out over the barren, empty sandscape I saw the futility. Hopeless.

No. There was always hope. When all had seemed lost and Shavada brought his forces down upon us, Ezabeth had not given up. Backed by her will, I'd not given up. We'd stood, and we'd fought and it had been enough. We hadn't known what we were doing, but we had made it work. She wouldn't have let me quit now. I spat, wiped my mouth. Get bright, Galharrow. Not dead yet.

'Over here,' the bird croaked.

A small cairn of stones had been built, a couple of dozen fist-sized rocks, carefully stacked in a pyramid. Tnota had written the word 'Ryhalt' across a flat rock that lay across the top. At least, that's probably what it said. His writing had been bad even before he lost his right arm.

'Guess they made me a grave,' I said. Some of the hope I'd

been trying to fill myself with seeped away. They'd given up on me. 'Course they had. Damn Tnota for a sentimental idiot. He'd wasted time making this when he should have been running. I felt a sudden wrench of loss that I'd not sit with the old bugger again, chewing the shit and drinking worse. There had always been a line of competitive desperation to our drinking. I looked away. No point getting all damp-eyed about it. But there was a bleak disappointment in the way Tnota inflected his letter 'Y' and the tail of the last 'T.'

'You should be in a fucking grave,' the raven snarled. 'Killed by your own stupidity. It's not a grave, you fuckwit.'

No. It wasn't.

'Course it wasn't a fucking grave. Tnota was a southerner out of Fraca. His people believed in the Grand Wolf, some kind of eternal alpha being that lived in the sky and watched over his pack. The Big Dog. Fracans didn't bury their dead. They believed life ran in cycles, mistakes repeated, glories renewed. I hadn't been listening properly when he explained it, and he'd not been that interested in explaining it in the first place, but he seldom bothered to attend funerals, and he told me once that when he died I was to stick him outside or feed him to some pigs. He'd been facetious about it, but it really was what he wanted.

This wasn't a grave. It was a marker.

I scrabbled rocks out of the way, my breath catching in my throat until I saw the glint of bronze, the dull brown hue of old leather. I pulled the items clear. His navigation book and his spare astrolabe. A navigator's tools.

Spirit of Mercy love him for throwing me the smallest shred of a chance.

'Saw that one-armed sot leave this behind for you,' the raven croaked.

'And you still tried to persuade me to kill myself.'

The dark bird preened its feathers and niggled at something with its beak.

'It's still the better option. What do you know about lunarism and Misery navigation?'

Good point. I didn't know how to navigate. I understood the basic principles. I'd seen Tnota and other navigators do it hundreds of times. But knowing how to draw a bow, and watching a champion archer ply his trade, doesn't mean you can hit the gold. Doesn't mean you can even hit the target, and you'll probably injure yourself trying.

'Any branch in a flood,' I said.

I leafed through the pages. The book had been passed down to Tnota by the men who'd gone before him, the early sections written in their easy, tidy penmanship the latter in Tnota's gambolling affront to calligraphy. He'd left it here, for me, on the crazy off chance that I might get away. It was a mad act, to abandon something so valuable out here on the possibility that he wanted me to escape. But he'd guessed where I'd go and he'd made a fucking present of it. Spirits watch over me, I'd have to buy him a whole fucking brothel for this. If I could learn to navigate before I ran out of food. Or water. Or got eaten by gillings. Or fell down a hole and broke my legs. I could go on.

'So what now?' the raven asked. 'You've got a book you can't read, a bag containing a head that keeps muttering to itself, and you're still going to die out here. Nothing has changed.'

'That's the problem with you, Crow,' I said. 'No creativity. You're just Crowfoot's spite and malice in feathered form. Now shut your fucking beak unless you got something helpful to say.'

I took a quick inventory. A sword. A knife. Good start. A small bag of rations: some kind of dried meat and hard, flat bread. Not a lot, not enough for nine days, but it was something. Going hungry wouldn't kill me. Two water canteens, one half-empty. Three bottles of what I figured was wine. I uncorked it and gave it a sniff. It wasn't wine made from anything that I knew, but fuck it, I'd drunk stuff that smelled worse.

'It's not enough,' I said. 'Not for nine days. Not unless I can work the Misery to my advantage like Tnota could.'

'Can you?'

We both knew that I couldn't.

'Maybe I don't need to get to the Range,' I said. 'What if I could get to one of our static patrols?'

The bird didn't seem impressed by the idea, but I leafed through the book all the same and found a section that listed coordinates for fixed points. The crystal forest was there. Cold's Crater. The ruins of Adrogorsk, the fallen pillars of Clear. The Endless Devoid. There were others, places and things I'd never heard of. The Spark Flats. Locust Walk. Eame's Stage. But I didn't know what they were or how I would find them. Numbers, strings of them, stretched neatly across the page. Tnota had crossed some out and added his own notes. Some of them were in Fracan, which wasn't helpful since I didn't speak it.

I went back to the beginning. The original author had indicated that he'd copied out the basics from some other navigator's book. The basics. I could start there. Learn Misery navigation as I was doing it – why not? Someone must have been the first to do it, once.

I looked up at the sky, sensing mockery from the glowing cracks. Clada was high, Eala sat fat and low. Rioque slept.

I was on a clock. I didn't have time to sit down and read my way through this. When my water ran out, I was dead, so I needed to make it somewhere – anywhere – before I died of dehydration.

'Stand with me now, Ezabeth,' I whispered. 'I need you now more than ever.' But only the wind answered.

I started walking, opened the book, and read.

29

My head hung heavy on my neck, too heavy, nodding toward the black and red sands as they passed, slow step by slow step, beneath my boots. What was left of them. Piece by slow piece they were collapsing, tattered shreds of leather and string. Something corrosive in the Misery sand was eating at them. I'd never walked so far on foot before. How long had I been walking now? Three days? Five? I didn't know. Time is rarely your ally. In the corrupted land, it never is.

My throat was a gargled clutch of razors as I tried to swallow, and liquid was too precious to waste on soothing it. I was making a hoarse, wheezing sound and tried to force my throat muscles to remember their purpose.

Dark heat, white cold. The Misery shifted between them. Everything but the pain had grown distant.

A single thought remained. I focused on it, let it envelop me, become me. Easier to function if I clung to a single determined thread of thought.

Keep going. Whatever the cost.

Every step was pain. The blisters had long since split and dried, filled with sand and grit. I hadn't removed my boots for days. Didn't want to look at my feet for fear that they'd worn away. No time, anyway. Had to walk, had to keep going. Had to press on. Back toward Valengrad. But I knew I was done. Walking without a future. Nothing to eat, not enough water. No navigator, no friends. Just a head bumping along in a sack at my side making occasional, muffled demands to be freed, and a shadow of power in the sky.

Step followed grinding step. The Misery's heat rose all around me, draining the perspiration to salt stains before it could form. No hope of making it to Valengrad, only torture and death left. I hated everyone and everything, for leaving me to die without a drink on my lips. Irrational laughter rose within me, but the laugh didn't come out right. It was an ugly, dying sound from a dying man.

So confused. My own name seemed distant. Starving to death. Alone, but for the crow. Alone would have been better.

Not alone. I took the head out of the sack, face away from me. Croaked questions at it. It said nothing. Why would it? I had nothing left to threaten it with, and even if I got my answers, I'd die out here before I could use them. I kicked sand in its face and stuffed it back into the sack.

As long as I could resist the last of my water, my will to keep going remained. My head was full of shards of glass, and every thought was like a foot stamping upon them. My energy was spent. My gut rang hollow as a bell. Never knew hunger could hurt with such intensity, or make things cloudy. Make me forget.

I thought of Ezabeth. Trapped, alone in the light. Four years of torment. If she could endure that, I could endure this. She never gave up and I couldn't let her down.

The hooded raven circled down toward me in lazy spirals.

'Land shifted!' it cawed as it alighted on my shoulder, the croaking voice too loud in my ear. I had to think about those words, to work out what the fuck it was talking about. To remember what 'land' was. I staggered and went down on my knees. The wind bit at my dry eyes.

Dunes of coarse black gravel rose in every direction. I looked back. More of the same. It had been the same all day. More than a day. Or less. The distance was lost in the shimmering haze of the heat. My arms and legs had turned to lead. So fucking weak. This was it. This was as far as my body could take me.

Blackness, for a time.

I woke to a new pain, sharp and insistent, jabbing at my eye.

'Oh. You're not dead,' the raven said, sounding disappointed as I blinked away grit.

'You trying to eat me already?'

The raven ignored the question.

'Need a new reading,' the raven cawed. Was it a little embarrassed to be caught in the act? Sleep had restored something of my mind. Enough that I could remember who I was and why I refused to lie down and die. I said Ezabeth's name, a talisman to keep me moving, and it gave me heart. I opened my last bottle of water. Took a mouthful. It hurt all the way down. I went on.

Ghosts came and went. I saw my grandmother, and I saw Marshal Venzer, his neck broken and wrung like an old dishcloth. I saw old Kimi Holst, cursing me for taking his place. And then I saw Valiya, and she was still alive, and I knew that I wasn't seeing ghosts anymore. My mind was collapsing. Whether through lack of sustenance or the creeping influence of the Misery, the core of my being had begun to deteriorate.

I staggered over something. I thought it was a rock, but it wasn't a rock. Some kind of shelled creature, black and gleaming obsidian on top, long-haired crab legs beneath. It scuttled feebly away from me, its shell too heavy for its spindly limbs. Not all of the things in the Misery were dangerous. Not to touch, anyway.

I took out the book again. Tnota's handwriting was awful. I looked up, used my fingers to track the distance between Eala and Clada, who'd only just made it over the horizon, and flipped to the pages of numerical tables at the back of the book. Cross-referenced them with the place where I thought I'd started. The bird was right. The land has moved, and though I'd been walking due east, now I was facing south. I adjusted, took another reading. I was on the right track. Maybe. I could have been completely, utterly wrong.

Did it matter? I was weeks deep in the desert. The drudge must have hunted for me, and not even they'd been able to find me. A lucky man might have made it a few days. I'd never been that lucky, and I needed more than a few.

Luck would have to step aside, and let the Spirit of Vengeance be my guide.

I pressed my hands against the Misery's dark sand. I felt her whisper to me. Felt her gently tell me the truth. I didn't know what that meant. Maybe just that exposure, dehydration and starvation were all conspiring to strip me of my mind before my bones give way, my flesh collapsed and the last rise of my chest left me out here to die alone in the dust and wind, unremembered, unknown, just another set of bones among the dead.

Every part of me hurt as I forced myself back to my feet. So weak I could barely drive my legs. I looked at the shelled creature as it slowly tracked away. There was a wetness in its wake, the hells knew where it came from. A vile odour trailed it as I stumbled after it. Everything in the Misery is poisoned. The bad magic that created the Misery lived in her creatures.

'I won't make it like this.' It was my voice, become a cracked and broken shadow. 'I've nothing left.'

I could see her before me. There was no phos network for her to come from, no power for her to steal. She wasn't some Bright Lady. She was my Ezabeth, human, fragile, born of wisps of light and tricks of luminance. I reached out for her but knew that I mustn't touch her. If I did, the

298

illusion would end. I could die now, with her, and perhaps that would not be so bad.

'Get up, Ryhalt,' the mirage said, her voice stern with command. 'Get up and be the man you always have been.'

'I'm not strong enough,' I croaked. Hardly even words.

'Do whatever you have to,' she said. 'Win. Whatever the cost. Promise me.' She reached out to me, and I reached back. If I could just touch her, just reach her, then I would drag her back to me, no matter the cost. My fingers passed through hers as if I tried to brush the wind. Lost to some other world in which I had no purchase.

'I promise.'

'I'll stand with you,' she said. 'I'll be your shield, when you need me to be, but the will to fight has to be yours. Fight for the people. You're not alone.'

I blinked with dry eyes and she was gone. If she'd been there at all. Just a trick of the Misery. Just hunger taking the last of my mind. But she'd been right. My eyes turned to the crab thing as it crawled slowly away from me.

'Don't be a fool,' the raven croaked at me, but I ignored it. I drew the stolen sword and approached the nameless creature. 'Everything here is poisoned,' the raven cawed. 'Crowfoot's magic lives in you. What will you become if you take the Misery into you? Abomination! Better to die!'

I raised the sword over the creature. I had to go on, whatever it took. The blow came down hard, split the creature's shell apart. I struck again and it went still. Its trail had smelled bad; the stench of its insides was worse. Hot oil and sulphur. I retched, even as I clawed back broken pieces of shell. My stomach was empty but it still clenched, appalled at the suggestion of consuming that.

I could feel the bad magic like smoke against my fingers as I dug at the tough, moist white flesh. I hesitated. It was sustenance, but it was filled with the Misery's poison. Soaked in it. Grown in it. Unfit for anything living. But

I had nothing else left. This was the only choice that remained.

The raven swore it would destroy me as I raised hot, dripping flesh to my lips.

Whatever the cost.

30

White fire ripped through my veins as another fit took me. My muscles locked rigid and my body shook, spasming, out of my control. My face struck the sand. Sand in eyes that wouldn't close, grit on my tongue, beneath my lip. Time lost importance and my mind drifted away, floating out of reach. I was aware of other things, things that were beyond my understanding. The drudge, the creatures of the Misery – I was easy prey for either. For an hour or more afterward I could not remember who I was, where I was, even language failed me. Then I blinked and it was all back. The acrid taste of Misery flesh lingered in my mouth, burning against my tongue.

I was not the same.

The Misery is as inconstant as the wind, but some scars lie too deep on this world for even the Misery's treachery to budge them. Dust Gorge, Adrogorsk, the Crystal Forest: they were minor waypoints, even the ruins of our cities were of little importance compared to the Endless Devoid. It was a place unlike any other on the surface of the world, because it wasn't a place. It was the absence of a place, a great and terrible nothingness. Now I could feel it, across the distance, across the miles. I knew it was there.

I stared at the remains of the creature that I had consumed. Madness had taken me in my hunger. What had I done? Better to die than to consume the Misery's essence, to let it take hold within me. But it was too late now. I'd crossed an uncrossable line, and survived.

I wiped slime from my fingers onto the gritty ground and felt the Misery creature's juices burning in my gut, its essence permeating me. I felt time differently. I could sense the Endless Devoid without seeing, though my eyes stung with grit and my body seared me with a sharp, knife-wound pain. At some point I began to walk, though any conscious decision to do so came long after I had started, and I stopped before I reached my destination. At times I collapsed to my knees in the sand, wracked with agony, my body betraying me with convulsions. Becoming something else. Knowing things I should not – could not – know. Ahead of me lay a sleeping creature that had seven names that it alone knew, and the sound of any one of them would shatter a man's sanity; I knew which way was west, and that the sun was lying to me when it rose; I knew there would be Misery water beneath a rock even before I turned it. It was black, oily, shimmering with the Misery's essence, but I knelt and put my face to it all the same. Even then I hesitated. It was liquid, but it smelled worse than corpses, even with the salt and sulphur taste in my throat.

'Enough!' the hooded raven shrieked, 'better to die than this!' It battered at me with angry beak and wings until I knocked it from the sky, and seeing it could not stop me it muttered dire threats instead as it watched me nerve myself to do the unthinkable. My throat was tight at the sight of the Misery water, constricted like two ropes twisted together and just as rough. The black water reflected my own image back at me.

No.

I turned away from it.

The bird did not seem to need sustenance. It was not a real bird, after all, and out here I felt its presence as I never had before: it was joined to me, part of me. The head in the bag at my side still mumbled curses at me, or at least I assumed that's what it was saying, muffled as it was through the fabric of the bag.

I walked for days. What I saw, what I heard, much of it was lost from my mind the moment it passed into it, whilst as I drew closer and closer to the Endless Devoid, I began to know things. Impossible things, things beyond my understanding, through the Misery. Guided by the Misery. She was a mother, or a queen, or a goddess, and I was part of her now. She ran through me, and as the magic passed into the marrow of my bones I shrieked and cried and bit down on my belt so that I wouldn't chew off my own tongue just to give myself a lesser pain to concentrate on.

But with the pain came the knowing.

The Endless Devoid called to me. It was the heart of the Misery, at the centre of the devastation the Heart of the Void had wrought. Not even the bravest of our scouts ventured there. Reality grew ever more tremulous as you approached, and I felt as if I was on a road toward it, where the light grew more and more intense until everything became white and silent, calm but racing. The Endless Devoid, the epicentre of the Misery. An error in reality, a fault line in existence.

'Turn back!' the raven cawed. 'The tear will unmake us both. Turn back, you idiot!' I ignored it and trudged on into the brightness. Perhaps I had finally learned my lesson about taking advice from carrion birds.

I approached something. Something of importance. A place that carried greater significance than the ordinary. The world grew brighter still around me, and the closer I came to it, the stronger the white glare became. Impossible to look at, too potent to ignore, a pure brightness, terrible in its purity, perfect in its corruption. White, marble white, ice white, stretching on and on into forever.

My footfalls were noted.

Along that road that was not a road I encountered other travellers. One of them looked like me, lost, desperate, his eyes aglow with yellow fire, but somehow I knew that he had died many years ago and was lost in time, his journey endless. He didn't seem to heed me, but I saw that he had a canteen, and I murdered him and drank from it. It was good, clean water with the taste of the moisture extractor that had filtered it, and it hurt all the way down. I would have felt bad, but I met him again some miles on and his water was just as good the second time. I could have become like him, but I had purpose and he had nothing. That purpose kept me grounded in time. If I let it slip even for a moment I might find myself back along the road, thinking the same thoughts, taking the same steps. I had to wonder whether I already had.

A group of the Holy Sisters who had tended a shrine in Clear sang a song for the dead, though they were neither living nor ghosts, just a reflection. I had no fear of these shadow people, but I was careful to keep my distance from the behemoths, vast creatures of jagged stone. I was beneath their notice: their footfalls could have flattened houses, and the earth shook as they took slow, ponderous steps that sometimes lasted a day or more. I passed by them, and other Misery creatures, unseen and determined, and only once did a Misery creature come against me. Insectoid, buzzing with scythes and legs, we fought a pointless, bloody struggle. The drudge sword I had stolen proved its worth with great, dismembering, slicing blows which cut through armour plating. As we fought it cursed me for staying out with the other girls, scolded that people would disapprove now that I was supposed to be engaged.

When it was over the creature's legs and heads were scattered across the ground, but my chest and arms were torn and slashed and burning with fizzing venom. For an hour or more I thought that I was done for as the wounds hissed and steamed, but either the venom wasn't lethal or the Misery creature I had consumed had given me some kind of immunity to it because having blacked out for a while I came to, and my wounds looked grim but weren't bleeding anymore. It seemed to me that it had been some time since I had eaten, and in the haze of misjudgment I tried to eat some of the dead insect. My mouth burned as though I had thrust my tongue into a patch of nettles, but the pain proved a good distraction from the burning of the Misery's essence as it moved through my spine. I threw up what little I managed to swallow and lay on the ground for some time, wishing that I was dead.

Death would have been preferable to this. At any moment since I had been captured by the drudge, a shot to the head would have been a blessing. I should have opened my throat myself. But having escaped, and after what I'd done to Betch, I couldn't give up now. I didn't press further into damnation for myself, but because a lot of people back in Valengrad were going to be destroyed. A lot of bad people, some outright pieces of shit, but there were kernels of gold among the chaff. Valiya. Amaira. Tnota. And maybe I could give them a chance.

Ezabeth would not have given in. I owed it to her not to let my pain deceive me. It was just pain. I'd felt it before. I would feel it again. I'd made her a promise.

Maybe it was days, maybe it was weeks, maybe it was a cluster of heartbeats. My sense of time grew blurred, white, racing light all around, the void howling in my ears. The greatest of the cracks in the sky lay above me, radiating out from the impact point. The Endless Devoid. A vast, empty hole in existence. The sand had turned to obsidian glass, smooth and black, and it reflected the damage that my ruptured body had sustained in perfect detail, and the mild amber glow that shone from my eyes. I approached the edge slowly, but there was no wind, nothing dragging me in or tearing at my clothes. No sound, a silence so thick and deep that my own footsteps rang bright and clear as cannon fire. Whiteness, whiteness all around me save for the black glass below; and then, where the glass ended, nothing. A sheer drop, the crystal glass ending in a razor-sharp edge.

'Well,' I said to myself, and my voice seemed to stretch out, out into the blankness. 'Here I am.'

I realised that I was talking to the bird, but it had not followed me this far. I sat down cross-legged for a moment and considered what I was seeing. Not even Stracht had made it this deep into the Misery. I sat at the heart of nightmare and it was more peaceful than I had imagined, but sad, because I knew that ultimately at the start and end of existence, this was what we would find: nonexistence. I had never been a great believer in the spirits but here lay Nihilism: Nothingness, Absence, Zero. Not even the Misery could endure it.

I sat for a time, and my thoughts were clearer than they had been for some time. I knew that the Misery had her claws in me, as she'd had them in Stracht. I had been a fool with no choices when I took her into my body. I looked at the greenish bruising beneath my fingernails, the faint, oily glimmer of copper across my skin. Stracht had soaked up enough Misery poison in forty years to take these traits. I'd eaten them into myself in days.

I dreamed without sleeping. First of home, not my Valengrad town house but my true home, the childhood home that never truly leaves you, which you call home long after you've left it behind. I hadn't been back there for close to twenty-five years, the estate with its well-ordered rows of vines and olive bushes. In my dream I saw my father, my mother, proud of me as they once had been. In my memory we were happy, and I sought their approval as strongly as they delighted in my accolades, my achievements. I dreamed of my older brother, who I had not seen since that futile duel, but who in my memory was both a child and older than me still. But they were only dreams, and they meant nothing, and they were nothing, as all dreams turn out to be.

The head in the bag was making noises again, and woke me from my reverie.

I opened the bag, but pointed the head away from me, careful not to look into its eyes, as I still didn't know what magic it might hold. It hadn't died when I cut it from its spine, and I wasn't prepared to underestimate it, no matter how drained of power it was. My own head held far too great a secret to risk that. But I held it up by the hair and took a step forward, holding it over the Endless Devoid, suspended above an infinity of nothingness.

'Darling,' I said in drudge speak. 'I am going to ask you some questions.'

'What place is this?' The Darling did not speak loudly, but its voice boomed across the gulf of nothing, vast in the silence.

'We are at the Misery's heart, the Endless Devoid,' I said. 'I do not know what you call it. The place where the Heart of the Void struck the world. There is nothing below you. An infinity of nothing.'

I tilted his head forward in case he couldn't see it. I didn't know how a Darling's physiology worked, but I wanted the point to be clear.

'Move away,' the Darling hissed.

I did not. 'I have brought you here with a purpose,' I said. 'You will tell me what I need to know. I know what you are. I know that a shred of Acradius lingers within you. But I doubt that he has great influence here. Crowfoot wrought this place, and not even his creatures can enter. Don't doubt my resolve. If I think you're lying to me, I'll drop you in.'

'You would not.'

'You will live for eternity,' I said. 'You need no sustenance. Not even air. And you will fall for the rest of time, alone with nothing but your thoughts and whatever power Acradius has poured into you, will be lost to him. Eternally far, far beyond his reach. I have nothing to lose by releasing you to this.'

'Pull me back!' the Darling growled. It had no capacity to struggle.

I did not.

'If you answer me, then I'll leave your sorry head here, on the edge. Perhaps something will eat you. Perhaps in a thousand years something will find you. Either will be better than an infinity of nothing. And if I find you've lied to me, I'll come back and kick you into the emptiness. Do you understand?'

'Yes!' the Darling shouted. 'Draw me back! Back!'

Immortality may not have been the gift it had once seemed.

'Tell me your deal with Saravor.'

'The patchwork man?' the Darling spat. 'He betrayed us.'

'How?'

'God King Acradius shared the secrets of ward-breaking with him. So that he might bring us Shavada's Eye. But he took the eye for himself.'

So much for Saravor's deals.

'What did he want in return for it?'

'To become a King,' the Darling hissed. It could not keep the contempt from its voice, even suspended above oblivion. 'He must have realised that such mortal filth as he would never be permitted to ascend. He kept the Eye for himself and found a new way. We could not act against him directly so we sought to destroy his means of ascension, but you fools killed the Singers. When the solar flare strikes, he will use the tower to ascend. The Kings will stand against him, but you have doomed yourselves.'

Darlings have a poor grip on their emotions. He couldn't keep the spite from his reedy voice.

'The Grandspire?' I said. 'It's just a huge phos mill. What does it have to do with Saravor?'

'The Eye is an empty vessel which was once part of a god. Now that power is unmade, but it still aches to be filled. Saravor is filling it with the magic of souls, as a Deep King would, and when it is filled with death he will use the power of the flare, magnified by the tower, to unmake it. He will claim Shavada's power and rise.'

I should have seen it.

Two colossal forces. Light and darkness, coming together to give Saravor the one thing he absolutely desired. Power. The butchered dead beneath Valengrad's streets – not just spare parts but fuel for his masterwork. Nacomo's desire to bring down the Grandspire after he escaped Saravor's influence. Dantry's abduction and use as slave labour. Pieces crashed into place, their implications deafening.

I had thought the Deep Kings feared the Bright Lady. Hoped that, no matter what Dantry had found in his ancient book, there was a chance Ezabeth would return to me. My feeble dream had blinded me to the truth, no matter how I'd denied it. Thierro was wrong, about all of it. Whatever whispers he'd heard in his heart . . .

. . . but of course.

The Bright Lady hadn't healed him. Ezabeth hadn't given him a Spinner's power. I'd been a fool not to see it. Saravor had seen the Grandspire, and its potential. He'd known about the Eye since he took Shavada's power, had craved it, plotted with the Deep Kings to take it. He'd taken Thierro's tormented lungs and replaced them with a Spinner's, gifted him with a beautiful lie and a burn scar to hide the work he'd done. It was Saravor's voice that Thierro heard, and the poor bastard didn't even know who was urging him on. I'd been played from the very beginning, and if I hadn't wanted to believe it so badly, maybe I could have put it all together earlier. It was all Saravor, and he had everything he needed to ascend.

I'd been so blind.

I thought of the bloody bodies beneath Valengrad.

'How many does he need to kill?'

'Tens of thousands,' the Darling said, and I felt a moment of relief. And then a greater one of dread. He didn't just have the Grandspire and the Eye: he had the city. He had an army at his disposal, zealous and eager to fight for the Bright Lady, and all the weapons and holy commands he needed to start a bloodbath. Like a key sliding into a lock, everything suddenly came together and made horrible, perfect sense. I heard the turning of that key in the silence of the Endless Devoid. My arm was growing tired. The Darling said, 'You desire this no more than we do! In this, we should be united.'

It was right. Even though we were enemies, even though his master was away trying to raise The Sleeper, and my master was trying to prevent exactly that, nobody except Saravor wanted Saravor to possess such terrible power. His capability for cruelty was spattered beneath Valengrad's streets, and I'd endured his torture on more than one occasion. He was already as inhuman as the Deep Kings, and if he claimed such power, even if they would not accept him as one of their own, they might well propose an alliance. There were few enough immortals in the game that they couldn't afford to ignore one.

I had learned what I needed. I asked the Darling's head a few more questions, and then I tossed it into the Endless Devoid.

31

I learned things there, in the Misery's heart, that no man had ever known, or would probably know again. Thought and body were not so separate there as they seemed beyond the Endless Devoid, as though the lines between what constituted something and nothing were less distinct. Existence and time became relative concepts that whirled and changed and had done so since the dawn of time. For a time, I understood the tiny instructions woven throughout our bodies that tell us how to grow, what to be. I knew how the stars had been born, and the true name of the demon that the Deep Kings sought to raise from the ocean's darkness. I understood how starlings arc their flights as they gather in their millions, and felt the pull of the force that keeps the rest of us strapped to the earth. But these were not secrets I could keep, and they blew through me as fleetingly as a spring wind. They were not true knowings and I had not earned them, and so they left as easily as they came.

I looked for the time-lost man with the good water on my way out, but I had no chance to kill him a third time, and so my thirst grew.

I left the Endless Devoid lighter by a head, but newly scarred and carrying a far heavier burden. I was the only one who knew. The only one who could try to stop him before it was too late for Valengrad. I staggered back out of the glare, beneath the dark sky and a lonely golden moon.

I knelt, pressed a hand to the dark, bitter sand. I felt her, Misery, simmering just to the other side of existence. She was the essence of change. To allow anything to remain the same would have been foreign to her.

'Hah!' the raven cawed at me as it descended. 'You look terrible.'

'Still alive, though,' I said.

'Barely.' There was no arguing with that.

'I think I have a way out of here.'

I was no longer blind. I still felt them, those fixed positions. Indistinct, but distant, and I only knew where the nearest of them lay, the way you can tell which way a sound comes from. Tnota's book told me the proximity of one point to another. I figured I might make it to Cold's Crater, if I was lucky, and if I was incredibly lucky there might be a static patrol there. As long as I could keep the fixed points in my mind, I could navigate without an astrolabe, without moons. But already the knowing, the infusion of Misery that I'd taken from the creature that I had consumed, was fading. The magic had entered me, but it was leaking out again, slowly, painfully, and I could not face taking more of it in. The clock was ticking.

'What happened to your face?' the raven asked.

'Insect thing,' I grunted.

'And your chest?'

'Same thing.'

'And your arm?'

My inner right forearm was a crust of bloody scabs.

'It was something that I had to remember,' I said. 'Something that I learned in the Endless Devoid. I knew that I wouldn't remember it later.'

'Should have written it down instead,' the crow said, as though that wouldn't have been my first choice, had I possessed the materials.

Whatever I had learned, I didn't recall it now, not a

whisper, not a glimpse of it. Only the words that I'd carved into my skin carried a shred of it. They were jagged, hastily cut, sliced deeply through the skin to make sure that they'd scar. Whatever it was I'd learned, I'd wanted to remember it.

The words in my skin read: BECOME THE ANVIL.

I wished that, whatever great and terrible knowledge I had drunk of, I'd thought to carve something I'd actually understand. But then, I'd probably not had a lot of time, and I probably hadn't been entirely sane when I'd done it either. Maybe it would help against Saravor, but I didn't think so. Problems like him were usually solved by pointing a barrel and pulling a trigger, but I didn't think that would work on him any more than it had on the Darlings in the crystal forest.

No matter. Inventing new ways to kill people was something I'd always been surprisingly good at.

As I trudged away from the Devoid, I wondered if Nenn was still alive, and if she was, what had become of her. She must have felt him inside her mind, forcing her hand, but she'd resisted just enough to dip the pistol barrel at the last moment. Saravor must have purged Thierro's mind or laid false memories to cover what he'd done to him. I hoped he wouldn't punish Nenn for her resistance. I wondered what had happened to Tnota, to the Bright Order soldiers who'd fought for us, and the remnants of Nenn's cavalry. The Misery was never friendly, and their losses had been heavy.

Tiny gleams of red and bronze sparked beneath the skin along the veins in my hands. Pollutants, moving with my blood. I wondered whether this was how Stracht had finally taken on his coppery shine. Ingested something that he shouldn't. I'd never get to ask him. Another comrade to avenge.

I had a mission, a need to get back to Valengrad. I couldn't afford to think about Nenn, or the voice that whispered through her lips. I had to focus on getting back and warning them about Saravor's plans. He needed to kill thousands to fuel his mad ambitions and he would have no qualms at all about doing it.

The sky stretched into forever.

My mouth was drier than salt, my tongue rough as old bark. The Misery alternated between intense cold and the rising heat and pain rose in me as my body fought to expel the nightmare that had entered it, a pain biting hard in my guts, piercing and cold as a spear driven through me. I dropped to my knees, retched and heaved up an oily trickle of something foul and poisonous. It was black as treacle and just as thick, but my stomach had nothing else to give.

'You're dying,' the bird said. Helpful fucking thing.

'We're all dying, from the moment we're born,' I said. 'Only thing that matters is that we do some living in the 'tween time.'

'I'm not dying,' the raven that was not a raven said.

'You're not alive,' I said. 'You aren't anything.'

'You're probably right,' the raven conceded. 'Once my purpose is fulfilled, I'll cease to exist.'

'So Crowfoot didn't just send you to annoy me, then,' I said.

'No,' the bird said, seriously. 'No, he didn't.'

I didn't ask. The bird knew its business, and since Crowfoot had made it, it was probably best not to know.

I walked the dark sand, and the sky hung angry, red, and howling overhead. Hunger haunted me, but it was nothing compared to the thirst, and I was taunted by mirages, hazy and shimmering patches of water in the distance. I pressed a hand to the ground, quested out, and the Misery acknowledged that they were lies. The sands stretched out, rising and falling in sweeping dunes, littered with charcoal-brittle rocks. I read Tnota's book several times on that walk, and before long I had much of it memorised. I was navigating in a way that had never been done before and the Misery seemed prepared to tolerate our coexistence, while her creatures preferred to avoid me.

I almost gave up. One morning, I barely had the energy to rouse myself. Hungry, thirsty, burned by sun and wind and moons, my resolve began to flag, and I wondered if I could simply lie in my shallow sandy nest and let the elements take me. But the bloody raven had changed its mind about my death, and was suddenly insistent that I continue, pecking at me until I remembered Ezabeth and her isolation within the light, and had no choice but to rise, and walk, and ignore the pain.

The raven sometimes rode on my shoulder, but mostly it flew ahead, scouting for me and keeping an eye out for anything that looked hungry. It knew we were drawing near to Cold's Crater before I did, and it saw no signs of life there. I didn't know whether that was a good or a bad thing. Any men stationed there might put a crossbow bolt in me at a hundred yards. I didn't just look like some horror dragged out of the Misery – I had become that horror. My clothing was torn, stained, hanging loose where I'd lost weight. I carried an alien sword, my boots were coming apart and the wounds that I'd taken had scarred blackly. But death did not hiss toward me. The fort was deserted.

What remained of my heart sank. I'd rationed the little water I had and there were only a couple of mouthfuls left in the final canteen, but it was another three days to Valengrad from here. No way that I could make it with what I had, even though the fort offered some shelter for a night. The last time I'd been here was on a mission to bring Dantry back to his sister, when I'd approached it from the other direction. No flags flew over the fort's walls. Abandoned. My best bet now was to be picked up by a patrol, and the chance of that was slim indeed.

Not everything can go wrong all the time, though. I entered

the fort, and saw that when the long patrol had packed their kit and left, they'd shirked the labourious task of deconstructing the moisture extractors. They were silent, no drilling whines disturbing the deadness of the fortress air, and there were no phos coils to power them, but when I pried away the storage-tank lids I could have cried. Precious, blessed, clean water. It carried the metallic tang of the extractor and it was stale, having lain stagnant in the tank for weeks, but in all my life I had never tasted anything better. Swallowing hurt, a thousand angry knives carving lines up and down my parched throat, but I drank my fill, and then sat, water-drunk and savouring the moistness on my lips. I wasn't dead yet.

While I sat there, a ghost appeared on the far side of the fort. Glost, Dantry Tanza's man. He'd died here, collateral damage in a bungled assassination. The ghost was missing its lower legs, dragging itself on its hands as it called its master's name. I watched him, resting against the iron extractor tank, until my eyes closed and I slept.

I woke to the raven shuffling from foot to foot on my shoulder.

'Don't move suddenly,' it croaked in what might pass for a crow's whisper. 'But get ready to move very suddenly.'

I opened my eyes to see them around me, hundreds of them.

Two feet tall. Red as a burn. Yellow eyes. Watching me.

'Evening master, care for a good time?' one of them squeaked.

'Seventy-three, seventy-two,' said another.

Gillings. Gillings by the score. I glanced down at my legs, checked my hands. I still had all of them. The gillings were clustered in jumbled ranks, row after row of them stretching back across the fort. I could see the gleam of the anaesthetizing venom on their jagged little fangs. Some of them looked starved, emaciated, but the closest ones were fat-bellied. Well fed.

I took hold of my sword hilt, knowing already that there were far too many for me to fight my way out. I had never heard of a swarm forming like this, and I couldn't possibly kill them all.

'The roads are a mess,' one of the gillings put in helpfully.

'Seventy-three, seventy-two,' a pair said in unison.

All eyes were on me as I stood. My sword would scythe them down six at a time if I started to swing, but I would exhaust myself before I managed to kill them all, and just one bite could take the use of a leg. They stared at me, unmoving, as if there was something holding them back.

'What should I do?' I said.

'I think this as far as we go together,' the raven croaked in my ear. 'If you can get out of this one, I'll be impressed.'

'Thanks.'

'I'll be getting along then,' the raven said, as nonchalant as if it were discussing the end of a tea party. 'I still have to find a new Blackwing captain. Especially if you're going to get eaten.'

I was backed up against the extractor's water tank, and behind that there was a high stone wall. A carpet of gillings filled the fort's yard. No way forward, no way back. I'd come a long way only to find myself in this cruel situation. The raven cawed once more in my ear and then took flight, abandoning me to my fate. It flapped away west.

The gillings' eyes followed the crow as one, their heads rotating to follow it in flight. And as they did so, their highpitched voices squealed in agonised unison.

'Father!'

It was a word filled with longing, with pain, with the torment of existing as whatever the hell they were. The word turned into a cry, then a squeal, high and shrill and dreadful in the Misery night. They clapped their hands to their heads as if in pain, shaking their fang-filled little faces left and right.

317

Then their heads swivelled back toward me. Thousands of hungry stares.

'No,' I said. I held a hand out toward them. Beady eyes latched onto it. I drew back what was left of a sleeve, displayed the crow there. They didn't understand the image. They hadn't the intellect. But I stared them down, concentrating on the essence of Misery that I'd taken into my body. It coexisted there with me. I'd been battling it, holding it back. Refusing it. Now I gave up that fight, let it be a part of me. I embraced that it had guided me through the Misery, that it had showed me her heart and revealed her secrets.

My heart thundered, and Misery wrapped me tighter.

The gillings lost focus, blinking as though I'd ceased to exist. They had not come for me to begin with, I realised. They had come for the raven. And now the gillings were as indifferent to me as though I were one of their own. The ones farthest back began to disperse, and within minutes I couldn't see a single one.

I knew what I had done to myself when I ate one of the Misery's creatures. Crowfoot had created the Misery with the Heart of the Void, but whatever ancient power had driven his weapon, part of him had infused the devastation he had inflicted. I now carried both Crowfoot's debt, and the Misery's taint. They were of a kind. The gillings' savage hunger was not brought about by a need for sustenance – after all, they seldom found prey in the toxic wasteland – but rather a need to consume the uncorrupted. And now I found myself as corrupted as they were.

Spirits. What had I done to myself?

It didn't matter. All that mattered was getting back to the Range, and revealing the black worms of treachery that had taken charge of my city. Saravor had to die, slowly and painfully, for what he'd done to Nenn. To me.

The last thing he ever felt would be my hands around his throat.

32

How long had I been out under the broken Misery sky? As I wandered into the depths of the twisted land's heart, time had turned tricks around me. It had been too long. Weeks. When I finally saw the Range ahead of me, the trees wore spring-green buds as if they'd been decorated to welcome me home. I saw blue sky, unruptured and unbroken. I could have wept.

As I stepped out of the Misery the air tasted strange. Without the poisoned tang it seemed alien to me, rare, even though it was the air I'd breathed for most of my life. Grass, and then trees appeared like beautiful statues, though by anyone's standards the trees growing so close to the Misery were shrivelled and stunted things. But the sky above was blue and pure, almost cloudless, and the natural coolness of the early year felt like a gentle caress. I was out.

I just wasn't the same as when I'd gone in.

I found a stream, deep enough that I could immerse myself completely, and the chill water was a balm against my sunburned skin and crusted wounds. The Misery filth flowed away, or at least, the filth on the outside did. I looked human again. Humanish.

My first priority was to find a Range Station. I wasn't sure exactly where I was on the Range, but I was certainly south of Valengrad. I started up the supply road, and before long I ran into a patrol, the first people I'd seen since I killed

Betch. They were wary of me at first and I couldn't blame them for that, but I spun them a tale about getting lost out in the Misery on a close patrol and dropped Nenn's name, and they agreed to escort me to Station Two-Three. There were eight men in the patrol and three of them were wearing the yellow hoods of the Bright Order.

It had taken me nearly three weeks to get back to the Range. I asked how Valengrad was faring.

'The Bright Lady has protected the city,' the sergeant told me, 'and the drudge have given up. I saw her appear, one night. Beautiful she was, reaching out toward the Misery. That's how you know she's going to end the war with the Deep Kings. It's a sight you wouldn't believe unless you was there.'

'I don't believe it,' a youngster muttered. 'I think you smoked one pipe too many.'

'There's plenty think that, and I'd be one of them if I'd not seen it with me own eyes,' the sergeant laughed. 'You'll see. The Bright Lady's message is spreading. There's a new order coming, and no mistake.'

'So long as Prince Vercanti doesn't slaughter them all,' the youngster said.

'What do you mean?' I asked, appalled at the reptilian croak in my voice. The sergeant passed me his flask of small beer and I sank it.

'You've a thirst, sure enough. You really did come out of the Misery, didn't you?'

'Why would Grand Prince Vercanti attack the Bright Order?' I asked.

'After she got kicked from her perch, that bitch Davandein went running to her kin. Colonel Koska got declared Range Marshal by High Witness Thierro, only the princes didn't take kindly to that. The grand prince, he says it's unlawful. He cancelled his expedition to Angol and he's marching his army on Valengrad to take it back for his cousin.'

Thierro controlled Valengrad. If I was right, that meant Saravor controlled Valengrad. The city, the Grandspire, all of it. But he hadn't been proclaimed king. There were good people at the citadel. The game wasn't over yet.

'The High Witness has no business interfering in military matters,' a gruff old soldier growled. A couple of others agreed, but the followers of the Bright Lady were in the majority whether they wore hoods or not.

'It was the High Witness who saved Valengrad in its hour of need, weren't it?' the sergeant reprimanded them. 'Not that butcher Davandein. Fucking cream, got no regard for the common man. The prince will see when the Bright Lady comes.'

Even among these few men, the division was evident.

We stopped at the side of the road when a violent coughing fit took me. I nearly fell from the saddle, retched and hacked and spat poisoned blackness from somewhere inside of me. The shakes were on me something fierce, and the soldiers had no liquorice to offer. I couldn't hold the cigar they gave me long enough to get it lit and one of them had to do it for me. Such long exposure to the Misery was going to take a heavy price.

Station Two-Three appeared and I'd never seen such a welcome sight. The jester's-hat fronds of the projectors sat dark and silent over the brooding fortress. I thanked my escort after they checked me in at the gate and went about getting as much food and booze into me as I was able to get hold of. I hadn't money, but the cooks saw my hands shaking and took pity on me. There was heavy dark flatbread, bowls of rice and beans, and best of all, roast lamb, pink and dripping grease as it fell from the bone. I ate more than my share, went back and took more. The gravy was pure luxury, the beer rich, dark and bitter. I found that I could only eat a little at a time, my stomach constricted, but I persevered. Never before or after would I eat a feast like that one, though it was simple fare served up and down the Range. Context is everything.

As sorry as they felt for me, the cellar man wouldn't give me brandy. I managed to steal a bottle of it anyway. There was no point trying to use my rank. I hadn't my seal to prove it, and the less attention I attracted the better. I kept to myself in a quiet corner of the barracks and drank until I could barely stumble to my borrowed bunk and crash into sweet, dreamless sleep.

When I woke it seemed that my presence had been noted, and a meeting with the station commander became inevitable, because she was sitting on the end of my bed.

'I didn't believe it when they told me, but it looks like they were telling the truth. You really did wander out of the Misery. I've seldom seen a man so affected and live.'

She was a dusky woman with a bold, hooked nose and hair like liquid obsidian. Her uniform was crisp and sharp.

'Wasn't a good time out there,' I said.

'Looks like you ran into some of the Misery's less friendly inhabitants.' Without my shirt on, the ridged black scars on my chest and face were all too prominent.

'You could say that.'

She handed me a bundle of liquorice sticks tied together with twine. I practically jerked one out and began to chew.

'You're Captain Galharrow, of Blackwing. You won't remember me, but we met briefly at one of Major Nenn's demotions. She broke my brother's nose.'

She said it matter-of-factly. I didn't remember her, but I nodded anyway.

'We heard that you'd been lost in action.'

'The others, they made it back?'

'Some of them. They lost a lot of men in the fighting. Your friend the major survived though.'

I nodded at that. I had known she would. I had done my best not to think about that betrayal. But if any of them had made it back, then Tnota must have got clear as well. They'd never have made it back across the Misery without his navigation.

'Don't let anyone know I'm back,' I said. 'I'm going back to Valengrad, but until I've put some things right, nobody can know that I'm here.'

The station commander raised an eyebrow at that, but she didn't push me. I found that I rather liked her.

'There's a shitstorm of trouble heading that way,' she said. 'The citadel is barely sending us anything these days. They're preparing for a siege. Grand Prince Vercanti and Davandein have raised twenty-five thousand men. They'd have been there sooner but they've brought up a cabal of Battle Spinners and an artillery train. They plan to take the city back by force.'

'It's madness,' I said, and coughed to clear the croak from my voice. It wouldn't shift. 'We can't fight each other for the Range. Taking the city with green, levied troops? Using guns against Valengrad? Damn it, the citadel's our stronghold. It defends Nall's Engine. They're all insane.'

'I agree,' she said.

'Where do your loyalties lie, Commander?' I asked. 'If it comes to blood, will you support the grand prince and Davandein, or will you back Koska and the Bright Order?'

'My duty is to protect the Range,' she said. 'I'll stand at my post and ensure that if the real enemy present themselves, we activate the Engine and send them to the hells again. I cannot intervene. But we've had desertions. Some of my men have gone to Valengrad to join the Order. We see others along the supply road all the time. Fervour's got deep into them.'

'The next time someone deserts, you need to catch them and hang them,' I said.

'Not a solution here. Half of the men here are believers. Count the hoods. If I start hanging their friends, next thing

323

you'll see is a yellow flag flying over the station in support for the High Witness and, more than likely, my head on a spike.'

'They're traitors. They should be punished,' I said. I could see her point, but compromise has never been in my nature. She gave me a half smile but didn't defend her position again.

We talked a while longer, about which rankers were supporting each faction. None of it boded well.

The commander was good enough to give me everything I asked for. A shirt and trousers. A waistcoat. A greatcoat, hat, belt and buckle, new boots. The foreign sword had drawn more than one eye, so I wrapped it up and requisitioned a decent, standard-issue cutlass, straight-bladed and a plain black guard. Lastly I was offered a horse from the stables. None of the horses liked being close to me – they could smell the Misery taint in my skin and they whickered and shied, but eventually I found one that would let me on her back, a docile, tired old nag only a couple of years from decorating a pie stall. She would do. I would have thanked the commander, but she had gone to oversee the shoring up of a bridge. I rode north.

Somebody had to talk some sense into somebody, and the first somebody would be me, and the second had to be everybody. Nobody had anything to gain from a clash between the citadel and the grand prince. Nobody except Saravor. Enough good people had died for that monster's ambition already.

Saravor had Thierro, dancing to the whispers of his Bright Lady fantasy, and through him, the innocent people who believed his lies. Thousands of them. Saravor craved power, but he was willing to wield it through a more-easily-swallowed figurehead. He had Koska in his pocket, and worst of all, he had Nenn. I couldn't go up against Thierro alone. He was a Spinner, and it didn't matter that the voice urging him on was Saravor's; he could ash me with a flick of his wrist.

I entered Valengrad by a little-known way that avoided the main gates, the kind of route smugglers used when hoping to avoid paying the duties. Darkness had fallen just before I arrived, at which point I'd got through all of the liquorice and had half a drunk on me from the brandy I'd enjoyed on the road. Once I emerged into Valengrad, I saw the words on the citadel, fierce and neon red, proclaiming THE LADY BLESSES YOU. No longer a message to take courage against the fears of the night, the citadel itself had gone over to the Bright Order.

I picked my way across the town, hood up and face down. There were a lot of yellow hoods in evidence, some of them a murky beige, and I guessed they'd run out of yellow dye. Doomsayers crowed on every corner, proclaiming that the Bright Lady's return was imminent, that the portents grew stronger day by day. But despite the zealotry, there was a nervousness in the way that people walked, the glances that they cast toward their neighbours.

A hard spring rain was falling, not cold but insistent. I turned my face toward it, let it run across my skin. I had never appreciated simple water the way that I did then.

The Blackwing office was dark, locked up, nobody at the desk, and I had to force the back door to get in. It was my office; I could break it if I wanted. I picked my way up the stairs, the place so familiar and welcoming after so long away. Nobody to greet me, though my orders were that the desk be manned at all times. It didn't bode well.

I lit an oil lamp in my office and sat down in the chair. My desk was empty, my cluttered papers gone, everything placed neat, unused. Tnota's was the same. The whole place was shut down, closed for business. I hadn't expected the strength of the sadness that gave me. We'd made something good here, something efficient, and I didn't like to think that it had all been for nothing. They all thought I was dead, of course. It hadn't really occurred to me that might change things here. I'd been too preoccupied with surviving.

I smelled something out of place then, the acrid smokiness of slow match. The creak of a floorboard outside the door. There was someone there, and they were armed. I was about to call out but the door flew open with a bang, and the wavering barrel of a matchlock appeared, nosing ahead of its owner. I stood as the little figure did her best to keep the heavy weapon pointed at me. She could barely keep it upright, let alone steady.

'Who's there?' she demanded, angry, scared. She saw me and the gun was aimed right at me. I looked back at her, skinny and fierce as a furious puppy.

'Hello, Amaira,' I said, and my voice was a hoarse, croaking rattle, that sounded nothing like the man who had ridden out into the Misery. She stared at me, unsure what she was seeing. My skin was baked and peeling as the sunburn healed. Fresh tracks from Misery-claws ran across my face. I'd lost weight and bulk, and my eyes had turned an unnatural amber with a faint glow in the dim light.

'A demon,' she whispered, her eyes wide. 'Are you a demon?'

It was brave of her, to converse with what she thought as a monster, although she did have the weapon and I was unarmed.

'No, Amaira. You know who I am.'

She looked at me, not sure, maybe not wanting to believe it. I wasn't the man who had left here. That man had died, and she had grieved for him, and here I was, ruining everything. I wasn't even me, I was some other version of me that didn't sit right with anything in her mind.

'How do you know my name?' she asked.

'You told me your name when you first came to work here,' I said.

'Did the Deep Kings send you?'

'No.'

I spoke soft, gentle, as I would to a skittish horse. She had a matchlock levelled at me, and after my fight through the Misery it would be an irony if I was shot dead by a child in my own office. She didn't seem to know what to do next, and the gun too heavy for her to keep straight, but she knew that if I was a demon, she'd do well to shoot me.

'How can it be you when you're fuckin' dead, Captain-Sir?' There were tears in her eyes.

My voice caught in my throat.

'Language,' I croaked. 'And don't call me Captain-Sir.'

That decided it. Amaira dropped the matchlock and flung herself at me with a sob, and I clutched her tight. I pressed my eyes shut, or else I might have cried too, and you don't let a kid see you crying when they need you to be strong. Her heart was thundering against me.

'They said you was dead! They said you was dead!' she sobbed on me. 'But I knew you wasn't! I told them you wasn't, and I'd stay here and wait for you until you come back, and I was right!' She de-clamped from me. 'You look like you got shit on, Captain-Sir!' she said. 'What happened?'

So, I gave her a version of it, and it was a brief version which missed out most of what had truly happened. Much of it I struggled to remember. My time near the Endless Devoid was the most blurred, and I had questions I wanted to ask her, about where Valiya was, the jackdaws, Tnota. But her need for answers was greater than mine. She fetched me brandy and poured for me as I recounted it all. There was pressing business to attend to, but as the rain beat down against the window and the sky gave long, aching groans, nations and princes would have to wait. Children command every room they enter. There is something built into us that insists they come before all else, and I had only come to understand that too late.

327

'Where are the others? Why isn't anybody manning the desk?' I asked, when she finally ran out of questions.

'The jackdaws is all gone,' she said. 'There's only me, Tnota and Valiya left now.'

'Where did they go?'

'They got better money from the yellow-hoods, went and joined them. There's no money, now. That's what Valiya said.' She smiled at me. 'I'm glad you're back. Things can be back like they was. I liked it that way. We both cried a lot when we thought you was dead. Valiya tried not to let me see, but her eyes was all red and puffy. I think she got the liking for you, Captain-Sir.'

'That's not an appropriate thing to say,' I said.

'It's true though. You should marry her. She's clever, and kind, and she's your age.' She said the last with a certain finality, as though that decided it. 'We could all live in a house together. I could be your servant, could do the chores while you were out doing work.'

'It's not for me,' I said. 'But you're right about her. She's good, and she's kind, and she's brilliant. But Valiya deserves better than me. She deserves love, and commitment and a man who can give her his heart.'

'What's wrong with giving her yours?' Amaira said. She pouted as she refilled my glass, as though she had a plan to get me to agree whilst I was drinking and then hold me to it.

'I can't give her all of it. I made a promise to another woman. A woman just as good and kind and brilliant as Valiya, and I have a debt to repay to her. Nothing else matters.'

Amaira looked like she was about to argue when I heard the clang of the bell down below. Someone wanted in. She rose as though she intended to answer it but I put out a hand and stopped her.

'You had anyone come knocking in the night lately?'

Amaira shook her head, frowning. The bell jangled again,

clanging with an unfriendly abruptness. A few moments later a fist was pounding on the door.

'Seems an awful coincidence that someone's come looking for Blackwing now,' I said. Only the commander at Station Two-Three knew who I was, and she might have reported it to the citadel, used a communicator to tap across a message. I got up from my chair, put on my sword belt. The heavy velvet curtains were drawn, the shutters beyond them closed. I didn't think they could have seen the weak light through them.

Bang-bang-bang, another series of blows against the door. We stood in silence, waiting. I stood by the door, listening. Someone tried it, found that it was locked. Tried it again. I motioned to Amaira.

'Kill the light.'

Amaira had a wide-eyed look, mouth pursed. I put a hand on her shoulder to try reassure her that everything was fine, but I was worried. She clutched the back of my coat, as though by being attached to me I could keep her safe.

'I need you to stay here,' I said. 'Stay here and don't do anything silly. Can you do that for me?'

She nodded.

'Yes, Captain-Sir.'

I opened my desk drawer and drew out a fighting knife, a long, flaring blade with a curve to it that could put a smile on even the dourest of faces. Then I slipped out into the darkened corridor, moved to a dark room which overlooked the street. I nudged the curtain back the smallest of fractions and looked down. There were four of them, I guessed two men and two women by their sizes and shapes. Cloaked and hooded against the rain as they were, I couldn't make out anything else. They could have been people come asking for help, or they could have been something altogether more sinister. One hammered on the door for a last time, then they turned and walked away down the road.

I returned to Amaira.

'Who was it?' she asked.

'Nobody,' I said. 'But I don't think you should stay here anymore. I'm going to take you over to Valiya's place. You can stay with her.'

'But we're the good guys,' Amaira said. She swallowed, trying to shift some of the fear from her throat. 'They're meant to be running away from us.'

'I know. And believe me – they will.'

33

I waited another three hours before we left by the servants' entrance, crossing town during a downpour. The streets were quiet, folk driven inside by the rain, which suited our purposes.

Valiya lived in a terraced house, its neat, quiet exterior entirely in keeping with what I expected. I knocked on the door a few times.

'Who is it?' she asked through the wood.

'It's me, Miss Valiya,' Amaira said, as I'd instructed her to. I didn't think Valiya would recognise my voice. I sounded like something that had died and been left to soak in the canal before it was reanimated.

She took a step back when she saw me, but she knew me at once. Her expression hurt, though I'd tried to armour myself against it, and it was nothing so strong as horror or revulsion but was shock at the least. My heart sank just a little, because whatever I'd told Amaira, in another life, if I were another man, then Valiya was better than most men deserved. She'd never have thought me handsome – she had eyes – but at least I'd looked ordinary before. No longer.

'It can't be you,' she whispered.

'Hello, Valiya.'

She ushered us in out of the rain.

There was disgusting tea to drink, and I drank it, though it was easily the worst thing I'd drunk since I'd left the

Misery. Valiya had a lot more questions for me than Amaira had and I answered them as best I could. Amaira sat with her arms around her knees in a chair near the fire, trying to understand the events that she'd been caught up in. I'd have sent her off to sleep, but she'd only have crept back to listen at the door, and having been dead for so long, I felt I owed it to her to let her stay.

'Nenn can't be trusted,' I said. 'I don't know if she realises that she's under Saravor's power, or how much of what's left is her and how much is him. Witness Thierro is his as well. I'm certain of it. How many others among the Bright Order? I don't know.'

Valiya's face spoke more of her sorrow for me than words would allow.

'The Bright Order consolidated their power quickly once you were gone,' she said. Her face was still tear-tracked. Some people are not ashamed to cry, and I think that ultimately, they're probably the stronger ones because of it. She hadn't asked about the scars I'd acquired, or how I survived the Misery. She understood that I would tell her if I could.

'After the Grandspire was completed they forced the mills to relocate all of their Talents there,' she said. 'I know you don't believe the Bright Lady's coming, Ryhalt. But every day the visions of her have grown more and more frequent – and always reaching toward the Misery. Is it connected?'

'I don't know,' I said. 'I don't think it's Saravor's doing.' I frowned. 'What does Dantry say?'

'Not much. He tried, but he's too sick to work. Mostly he just sleeps.'

'Does Colonel Koska have enough authority to surrender the city when the grand prince arrives with his army?'

'It wouldn't matter if he did. The city's packed with fanatics. They've been flooding in from the Range stations, from the inner states, and they're armed. It's not just religion

332

that the Bright Order are promising them. It's freedom from the rule of the princes, and a better world without them. They'll fight for it.'

I mulled it over, barely noticing the dismal flavour of the tea.

'They'll be slaughtered,' I said.

Valiya nodded. The fire crackled and popped in the darkness and I looked around. If things had been different, maybe this would have been my second chance. Could have been the family that I didn't deserve. All those years spent neck deep in a bottle and now, with the city going to chaos and my body turned copper and poisoned, I realised that what I'd needed hadn't been so very far away after all. This could have been our living room. A more welcoming place than my own house, a cold, dismal tomb, seldom visited.

We talked into the night. Amaira fell asleep in her chair and Valiya covered her with a blanket.

'You haven't asked,' I said eventually, because I felt it like a cold sea between us. 'About how I survived. About what I did.' I gestured toward my face.

'I am sure you did whatever you had to do,' she said. 'You always do.'

I slept in a guest bed. and in the morning, I ate eggs and bread with Valiya and Amaira as though we were that strange family I'd imagined us. Valiya gave me a cup of small beer, which was past its best and she can't ever have drunk from the barrel, but it was still beer and I didn't want to offend her. Strange, the things we do even when the world is falling all around us.

'I have to go,' I said. 'I have to try to talk some sense into Davandein. I don't want either of you to go back to the office. It might not be safe there anymore.'

'Please don't go. Not again,' Amaira said.

'How can we fight this monster if even Blackwing is forced to run?' Valiya asked.

'You can't fight him, and he probably has more people under his command than we realised. Saravor will need access to the phos that's captured by the Grandspire when the solar flare happens. He'll need to be at the epicentre of that power. But he needs to empower the Eye with the deaths of the soldiers, of the Bright Order. They don't realise it, but he's engineering a slaughter for his own benefit. If we can prevent that, his plans will fail. No new Deep King, no new Nameless. However strong he is now – however strong I made him – he's still no match for Crowfoot. Hold out until the Nameless have finished saving the world and they can crush him. End of the game.'

'Be careful,' Valiya said.

'I don't want you to go,' Amaira said. 'Please don't go.' She clung around my waist, and my chest ached. I knelt in front of her.

'I'll be back,' I said. 'I promise.'

'Yes, Captain-Sir!' she said, snapped me a salute, then turned and fled into the house so that I wouldn't see her tears.

'Look after her,' I said. 'We have to save this world for someone. Might as well be her.' Valiya nodded.

'Like she was my own,' she said. As I turned to go she reached out and her fingers brushed against my arm. I turned back to her, and her face said everything that should have been and never would be. Even now, fucked and poisoned with copper and Misery foulness. In another life, where we weren't damaged. It passed between us, the final bell-toll in a service that had served nobody well.

I turned back toward the battle that awaited me. It was easier to face. As I walked down the street I glanced back once, saw her watching me from the doorway as I walked away. Her hair was loose, stirring lightly in the breeze, half her face hidden in a sweep of red.

I got out of Valengrad as easily as I'd got in, a quick dab of palm-grease the colour of gold and no questions asked. You can always trust the men on gate duty to be the least capable, the least trustworthy. It's how they end up working a door in the first place.

As I rode out from beneath Valengrad's dark walls, I looked at the stream of people still flowing toward the city. Travellers come a long way, their wagons laden with a life's accumulations, and on every head a marigold hood. They carried their weapons openly, nervous glances cast back over their shoulders, wary of the wolf at their heels. They'd set out for some kind of land of the free, a city where the shackles of tyranny and princely oppression had been cast aside. Now they found themselves running from the harriers and outriders who had appeared at their backs, requisitioning food wagons and coaxing the better-looking pilgrims to make a few marks on their way. Their disappointment would only deepen when they found that their sanctuary was no better than any other city, and worse than most.

Davandein's army was three days march away. I reached them as dusk was falling. I seemed to be the only person travelling in that direction.

The army was not concerned about being attacked. I reached them just after they'd made camp, the cook fires struggling against the drizzle. The tents were arrayed in good order, standard military positioning, but there was no defensive earthwork around the perimeter. I rode into the camp un-challenged – they had nothing to fear from a lone, beaten-up man on a weathered horse. I knew what to look for in soldiers. The Bright Order were enthusiastic but untrained. In contrast Davandein hadn't put her faith in optimism.

Her men were mercenaries, hard-bitten companies from the west. Few men in the camp spoke my language. Iscalian swordsmen, Hyspian matchlock gunners, Angolese bowmen, even Fracan heavy infantry. Missing teeth and scarred hands, they had the look of men and women who'd spent their lives fighting someone else's battles, hard-earned marks on their bodies and nothing to show for it in their purses. Dangerous people. The High Witnesses' believers had fervour and flarelocks, but I wouldn't bet a stolen grinny on them against these hardened killers. If this came to a battle, Saravor would have his souls.

I picked my way through the camp, drawing looks despite my hood. These weren't Misery grunts, and whilst the cracks in the sky could still be seen in the distance, they didn't know the Misery and they didn't know magic. Maybe they'd seen a few carnival Spinners casting light illusions or some hedge sorcerer change the colour of his eyes, but I must have looked a strange sight to those that spared more than a glance my way.

Toward the centre of the camp I saw men in citadel uniforms; soldiers who'd fled the city with the former marshal. Some of them I recognised, but I kept my hat low, unsure where I stood with them now. There were real enemies out there that needed fighting. The optimistic pilgrims, the kids dreaming of freedom, the old sluggers only wanting to get paid – they were all puppets dancing to someone else's tune.

Finally, someone stopped me. I had my seal, got a pair of vets to send it on ahead, then waited.

'You got the shakes pretty bad,' one of the soldiers I waited with said.

'Never worse,' I agreed. I tried to clench my fists to make it less obvious, but not with a great deal of success.

'Follow me,' one of the returners said, gesturing toward the command pavilion. It was a big old thing, more suited to a summer fair than a military camp, panelled with cloth of gold and summer-sky blue.

We like to imagine that whenever we meet someone who commands a military force they will be bent over a table of old maps, game pieces arrayed to display varying forces. The reality is that maps are usually about as accurate as a piss in the dark, and the cream have better things to spend their time doing. A pair of musicians, beautiful girls, played harps while Davandein, Grand Prince Vercanti and some privileged members of the nobility reclined on uncomfortable-looking travel chairs. A pair of young men, naked to the waist, put on a sword show. They had slender rapiers in their hands, blunt blades with heavy corks pressed over what I hoped were rounded points. It wasn't clear whether the main attraction was the impressive swordsmanship that they displayed or the sight of their lean, well-muscled torsos, the kind of physique that commanded even the straightest man's attention. A pair of Battle Spinners, bodyguards, stood at the two main tent flaps, canisters at their belts.

Davandein was waiting for me, back straight as a mast, arms crossed. She was dressed in black and purple, frilled here and there with thin, elegant lines of white lace. She looked as glamorous as ever, styled in a fashion that was yet to reach Valengrad. She had lost weight, and where she had been beautiful she was now stark, bitter and hard. It somehow seemed a more fitting look for a Range Marshal, but the dark gleam of her eyes told me that she was not happy to see me.

'You've got balls of stone, showing your face here,' she said. I was glad that her arms were crossed. I didn't want them anywhere near the hilt of the elaborate sword at her side. 'You look like something that crawled out of the Misery.'

'Not inaccurate,' I said.

'Well, well, look who it is. The face has taken a weathering,

337

but it's still you behind that colour,' the grand prince of the republic added. He was a well-aged man, skin like old, well-treated wood, clean-shaven, slim, greying hair bound back in a tail like a much younger man. His garb was no less ostentatious. I'd met him long ago when I swam in such milky circles as this. He'd only been a count's son back then and his rise had been as meteoric as my fall. He said, 'The last time I saw you, you had Mancono's blood all over your face.'

'I had a wash,' I said. 'Your grace. Marshal. We need to talk.'

'Galharrow,' Davandein spat my name, 'the last time I saw you, you were defending the traitors of the Bright Order. Tell me why I shouldn't have you thrown in a pit.'

'I understand your anger, Marshal,' I said. 'But I'm as loyal to the Range as I've ever been.'

'I don't have time for you,' Davandein said, and I knew that she remembered the truth, she was just too proud to admit her mistakes. 'My rightful, elected position as Range Marshal has been usurped by the Bright Order traitors. If you sought to assist me in retaking my citadel, you're several weeks late.'

'I had pressing business in the Misery,' I said. 'Stopping the sky-fires.' I held up my hand. Blunt and halfway up her own arse Davandein might be, but she knew that kind of trembling couldn't be faked. Or the fact that I looked like forge-heated shit.

Davandein softened, just enough for me to see that her fury hadn't entirely consumed her reason. She uncrossed her arms, twisted a ring on her finger as she looked over the changes that had been wrought on me.

'Are you all right?' she asked.

I suspect that between the fresh scars on my face, the oily taint to my skin and the fact that my eyes were glowing fucking amber that I was most seriously not all right, but

I grunted something about being well enough. Never let them see you bleed.

The fencers chose that moment to engage in another intricate display of skill. I'd thought they were going at it for real before, but I saw now that they were in fact moving through well-rehearsed plays. No real fight goes that smoothly.

'A skilful exhibition, eh?' the grand prince said, evidently enjoying the entertainment himself. 'A shame to miss it. Let us wait a little until the lads have finished their display. I recall you were considered fair with a rapier.'

'What I have to say won't wait, your grace,' I said.

'Message from the High Witness, your grace,' a page announced, and a woman wearing prince's livery entered. She was carrying a heavy box in both arms.

'This was delivered by a group of the Bright Order,' she said. 'They said that it should be opened only by the grand prince himself.'

'Open it outside,' Davandein said immediately. 'Away from the tent. There's no knowing what trickery that traitor might be playing at. It may well explode.'

The messenger went a little green, but she bowed and struggled out again with the box.

'Your grace. Marshal. I have vital information I can't share in front of these court grubbers.' That earned me a few nasty stares, but I wasn't trying to make friends. The insult got the grand prince's attention.

'I've paid a great deal for this performance, Captain,' Vercanti said, indicating the fencers. One of them took that moment to disengage with a dramatic flourish and roll over the top of his opponent's weapon. His partner caught the blow, and they thumped up against one another, sweaty chest to sweaty chest, lips close enough for kissing. They stayed there while the courtiers applauded. 'Whatever you have to say, it will wait a few more rounds.'

I was about to protest, but the courier came back in with her box. She cleared away dishes of fish paste, flat bread and skewered meats with a sweep of her arm and deposited it, unclasped a couple of hinges and a side fell down to reveal a great hog's head, pink and shaggy with white hair. Dead, obviously, but I had an uneasy feeling that it was going to do more talking than the usual pig's head.

'A feeble insult,' the grand prince said. 'I would have sent its genitals.'

The pig's eyes opened, slowly, steadily, as though it were awakening from a deep and timeless sleep. No more pretence. No more slithering through dark tunnels. Saravor was ready to step into the light. I hadn't time to avoid his gaze.

Let him see. The courtiers scrambled back, but I stood my ground. There comes a time when you grit your teeth and say 'enough,' and my hatred was hot. I'd hidden, I'd run and I'd burned beneath the Misery sun because of that monster, but I was still standing. I wanted him to see me. I wanted him to know that for everything he'd done, for all his bloody scheming, he still couldn't put me down.

A courtier choked on her wine and sprayed it into a man's wig. The Battle Spinners were the only ones that took a step toward it. The fencers, sensing that their audience's attention had been stolen, ceased their well-rehearsed display.

'What demonic power is this?' the grand prince declared. 'Who is this High Witness that he can animate the head of a pig?'

'Greetings, Grand Prince Vercanti,' the pig's head hissed. Corpse odour filled the space, though the pig's head was fresh. 'And Marshal Davandein. Though marshal no longer, I think.'

'You speak for the High Witness?' Davandein demanded.

'No,' I said. 'This isn't the High Witness. It's the creature that rules him.'

'Galharrow! And I believed you lost to the Misery. Looking somewhat the worse for wear.'

'So everyone keeps saying.'

If either Vercanti or Davandein were horrified by the prospect of conversing with a pig's head, they both had the political skill to hide it, though several of their hangers-on looked ready to bolt. One of the Spinners had a web of light rotating around one of her hands, ready for trouble.

'You have refused all of our messages and demands,' Davandein said simply. 'But I see you wish to talk now. The hound comes to heel when the master draws near, after all.'

'Is that what you think?' the pig's head hissed. It sounded amused.

'The terms of your surrender have not changed, whatever porcine display you seek to divert us with,' Davandein said, trying to rally her cronies with levity. 'You will open the city gates. Your followers will lay down their arms in Muster Square and return to their homes. The Witnesses will surrender themselves, along with Colonel Koska, Major Nenn and the other traitors of rank. The guilty shall be spared execution, should they follow these directives.'

'He's not going to surrender,' I said.

'You're right there,' the hog's head hissed. 'Not when there is no threat to me from your pathetic force. But I do speak for the city. I come only to tell you to spare yourselves. Back away and surrender the city to me.'

'Your forces are untrained farmers and fools,' Davandein's voice cracked like a whip. 'We have the finest mercenary brigades from across the states. Forty thousand veterans. When the assault begins, we will retake the city in less than an hour.'

'You have the advantage in men.' Saravor's pig breathed and the nose wiggled a little. 'I have the advantage of walls. But I also command the Grandspire, a weapon of such potency that after the solar flare strikes, I will erase all trace of you from the earth.'

'He's goading you,' I said. 'Back off. He wants you to attack.' But Davandein wasn't listening to me.

'We shall have crushed you before that happens,' she snapped. But she looked concerned. She had to know the flare was a matter of days away. 'Know this, High Witness. If you do not surrender the city to us, all of our mercy shall be replaced with ire. I will put every one of your damn yellow-hooded bastards to the sword. And you? We'll see how much weight your threats hold when you're dangling from the Heckle Gate. I have no fear of your Grandspire.'

A dead pig cannot laugh, but this one did a good impression.

'You should fear it. I have arranged a demonstration at one-tenth the destructive force that it will soon be capable of.'

'Do your worst, hog,' Grand Prince Vercanti said easily. 'Whatever hand you might think that you have to play ...'

But the pig was laughing. Davandein and I shared an uneasy look which Vercanti didn't understand. He hadn't been on the Range when Nall's Engine had scoured the Misery of the drudge threat. He didn't understand the destructive use light could be put to as we did. The pig's laughter rose and rose, snorting and mocking until the snout was juddering and the hog's head twitched around on the table.

The walls of the tent, thick cloth of gold and blue, grew lighter, brighter.

'Oh, fuck,' I said.

Some idiot threw back the tent flap and looked out.

There was a new sun in the sky, an orb of blazing fire, but it was far larger than the sun and it was very clearly moving.

'Get down!' I managed, before the fireball struck.

34

Had Saravor been aiming for the command tent, my story would have ended there. It wasn't luck: he could have torched us from the earth if he'd wanted to. But that wasn't his intention. When I'd dug my way from beneath the scorching tent fabric the air was clogged with smoke, swirling embers, and the stench of a world aflame. I emerged into a scene from one of the hells.

Fire. Burning tents, burning animals, burning people. The weapon that had been built to fight the drudge had been put to new purpose, and whatever company of mercenaries had been pitched down by a stand of old oak trees were now as blackened and charred as the crackling branches. The smoke rolled in blinding clouds, and the screaming – spirits, the screaming. Fire is a terrible weapon. At Adrogorsk I dumped hot oil on the drudge and even then, in the teeth of desperate battle, part of me had regretted it.

I had no good way to estimate it, but I guessed that a thousand men, maybe two, had just burned. I could taste them on the air. Across what had formerly been their camp, a barrel of powder must have caught as a secondary explosion lashed out, casting wooden shards into the air. By comparison to what we had just witnessed, the detonation was little more than a puff of smoke and light. It was nothing. The blast was only just audible over the cries.

Saravor had just snuffed out a thousand lives, but he had

no intention to stop the army. He was trying to provoke them into an attack. He wanted slaughter in Valengrad's streets. He needed souls, death magic to empower the Eye, but first he had to draw them in closer. Faster. To ensure they attacked before the flare was done.

Davandein picked herself out from beneath the tent. Like me she was sheened in sweat and soot. Her teeth were locked together, her fury hotter than the Grandspire's blast.

'You have to pull back,' I rasped. 'You can't fight this. If you attack, you're playing right into his hands.'

'Never,' Davandein snarled. 'I'll have that bastard's head. I'll flay Thierro's skin from his face and turn it into fucking bed curtains. That fucking traitor!'

Burning embers floated around us like fireflies, lazy on the wind as the rest of the prince's command council picked themselves out of the tent. The blast had thrown down most of the tents for a good half-mile radius.

'You have to listen to me,' I said, as a dozen burning sheets of paper blew past me on the wind. 'This insanity can be stopped. But not through force. An attack on the city is exactly what Saravor wants.'

The name meant nothing to her.

'Have they got into your head too, Galharrow?' she said hotly. 'Sent you to persuade me to withdraw, show me a taste of power and then tell me it's better to run? You begged me for peace the night the Witnesses slaughtered my men. Well, not this time, Galharrow. You think my resolve will waver in the face of casualties? The Grandspire was primed for one blast, and I know the city doesn't have the phos reserves to strike us again before we retake it.'

'If you attack the city, you're playing into his hands,' I said. 'It's what he fucking wants. You think that he couldn't have killed you here? That he *missed* you? He wants you to attack.' Her pride was overpowering her reason. One day, that epitaph would be carved across her tombstone.

'I will not give up the Range to someone capable of turning their weapons on our own people,' she said hotly. Perhaps the smoke had brought tears to her eyes, perhaps it was the awful knowledge of her own failure, or maybe just the cacophony of screaming coming from the hundred-yard-wide crater. The irony of her statement was not lost on me. 'If you're not with me, get out of my way,' she said.

I tried. I told her everything I knew, I argued every way I could think of. But ultimately, when it comes to argument, facts don't matter. The truth doesn't matter. People will believe what they want to believe because it works in the artificial reality that they have created for themselves. Davandein believed that she was highly competent, and entitled to rule by blood. She could not envisage defeat and Grand Prince Vercanti was fashioned from the same clay. I didn't want to surrender the city to Saravor – leaving him in control of the Engine did not bear thinking about – but she was playing right into his hands. He needed a slaughter, and she was going to give him one.

Spirits know, I tried, but she was stubborn, and there was no time. With every moment that ticked by, disaster threatened. Saravor knew that I was alive, and that I would take any chance to stop him. He would try to eliminate me, and that meant stripping away my resources. His men would hit the office, maybe my house. Maybe Valiya and Amaira.

I threw myself into the saddle.

'I was wondering when you'd show up,' I said. The horse sped along the road, snorting and blowing and I had to let her slow.

The raven alighted clumsily on my fist in an exhausted flurry of singed feathers. It looked in bad shape as it regarded me with a bright black eye.

'What happened to you?' I asked.

'Too close to the Iron Sun when it activated,' the raven

345

said. It sounded embarrassed and in pain. 'Well done for not getting eaten. How did you manage that?'

'Gillings lost their appetite,' I said. 'What do you want?'

'Wanted to see the fire,' the raven said. It plucked at a singed wing feather and tore it free. 'Looks bad.'

'It's bad.'

Couldn't afford to let the horse rest for long. My people were in danger, because of me. I couldn't have them on my conscience. It was already stacked full.

'Fly on ahead,' I said. 'Warn the others. Tell them to go to ground.'

The raven grudgingly agreed and set off, only to return to me a mile farther on, wobbling in its flight. I didn't have to ask why it had come back. It wasn't in its nature to complain, but the Iron Sun's blast had hurt it badly.

The roads were empty, other travellers having wisely found a bed for the night. All three moons were in a tight cluster, red and blue and gold, so bright that the heath was light as day. They caught the light of a sun spitting fire on the other side of the world and sent it back over me.

The city gate was closed, as I'd known it would be. Searchlights had been brought over to the west-facing wall. They should have been on the eastern side, gazing over the Misery. For the first time in my lifetime the barrels of cannon poked over the western wall. The wall here was a formality, only built because cities had walls and when Valengrad had risen eighty years back, the builders had felt it would be incomplete if not fully encircled. It was lower than the eastern wall, fewer towers, but it still had crenellations and judging by the lantern light up there the Bright Order were manning it through the night in case of an attack. Farmers and fishermen playing at war. They wouldn't stand a chance against Davandein's mercenaries, fuelled up on anger, fear, and a need for revenge. Nobody could have listened to those screams and not be moved toward retribution.

I'd take Saravor's patchwork head and see how much laughing he could do with his tongue ripped out.

Above the city, the Iron Sun glowed red with residual heat, hot against the Misery sky. The Talents within would be hard at work replenishing the phos batteries. The citadel's message was one of poorly spelled hope: REJOCE IN THE NEW ORDER, vivid and neon across the world.

I released the horse before taking the tunnel entrance. She would be a worn-out prize for whoever found her. The raven stayed with me, perched on my shoulder as I plodded through the darkness.

'How are you going to stop him?' it croaked at me.

'I'm going to kill him,' I said.

'You think you can kill a sorcerer that powerful? He has Shavada's Eye, and the Witnesses are no slouches. Not to mention the ten thousand men between you and him. And whatever else he is, Saravor's not stupid. He'll be defended – you'll never get to him, it would take an army – and even if you did, you don't know how to beat him.'

'I'm going to kill him,' I said steadily. 'Now shut up, or fuck off.'

'And your friend the major?' the bird croaked in the darkness. 'She's under his power too.'

'I'm hoping that when I kill him, all that goes with him,' I said. 'Him and his fucking devil-children.'

Nenn was a millstone tied around my throat. Maybe killing Saravor would break his hold on her, or maybe it would undo all his past magics as well. When I'd employed his services I'd never imagined that a bond would remain between him and his patients. Perhaps there hadn't been one, until I gave him Shavada's magic. It made me sick: I had given Saravor the power to accomplish all of this.

'Do you think she'll appear?' the raven croaked.

'Nenn? I'm just going to avoid her until it's done,' I said.

'Wasn't talking about her.'

'You want to know if I believe that the woman I love is going to burst forth from the light and be a god for the Bright Order, and wipe out all the badness in the world?'

'Yes,' the raven said, irritatingly close to my ear. 'That.'

'Then no. I don't think that,' I said. 'But if it is her, she'll try to stop Saravor.'

'Good,' the raven croaked. 'The master wouldn't like it if there were more Nameless. Nall is the only one he can even tolerate.'

'Any idea how he's doing keeping the sea-demon sleeping?'

'How would I know?' the bird said. 'I'm just a simulacrum designed for a purpose. I can't hear his thoughts.' It made a coughing sound and went back to niggling at its damaged feathers.

I left the tunnel, tossed a coin to the skeevy-looking youth who loitered in the upstairs room and we ignored everything else about one another. In a way it was comforting to know that even with an army bearing down on the city, with manic zealots up on the wall and a ghostly prophecy about to erupt over their heads, there were still those who would casually endanger their city for money. Some things never changed. When I'd dealt with Saravor, forced the Bright Order to surrender and persuaded Vercanti to appoint a Range Marshal who was less widely despised, I'd need to return here to shut the tunnel down and throw them all in prison.

I moved fast. Tick, tick, tick.

My city had become a foreign place, dark and alien. A troop of soldiers were gathered in a market square, a sergeant drilling them on how to reload their weapons without getting themselves blown up. Holy spirits-damned weapons. The troops looked nervous around their own firearms, and I couldn't blame them.

I walked faster.

I passed the theatre, which despite everything, seemed lit up enough to be running a play. I passed by the communal ovens where teams of bakers shoveled trays of domed bread in with a frantic urgency. I passed Doomsayers shouting their nonsense on every sixth corner, proclaiming that there were mere hours left until the Bright Lady returned. They pointed to the brightness of the moons in the sky, as though an astronomical irregularity was a message meant for us.

I was running now.

Tick, tick, tick.

'No.'

I was too late.

The office door had been smashed in, and there were signs that someone had tried to start a fire. At least it had been closed up, and I'd got Amaira out in time. I drew my sword, felt better for having it in my hand, and then ran to the darkened doorway. The moonlight barely brightened the interior, but I moved quickly, quietly, checking what they'd done. The small armoury that I'd kept in the cellar had been looted, empty racks where pistols, swords and matchlocks should have stood in ordered rows. They'd ripped through my bookshelves, the torn remnants of expensive legal texts scattered across the floor of my office. The locked desk drawers had all been forced. Looking for what? And then I knew. I suddenly, horribly knew what they'd been seeking, and I knew that they would have found it, even though I'd never seen the book myself.

Methodical, meticulous, Valiya had kept a record of each employee. She'd have written down their name, their age, their Blackwing role. What they did for us. Where they lived.

I was out on the street and running before I could draw breath to swear.

We spend our lives worrying about the future, paranoid about the things that may come to pass and upset the delicately balanced structures of our lives. We fear the failure of the harvest, or that our tryst will be discovered, or that our child will be born without eyes or missing a limb. All of that worrying, all the energy we pour into unnerving ourselves, the truth is that it comes to nothing, and it never sees off the real troubles. They erupt, sudden and unexpected, but so obvious, to blindside us and take our worlds, spin them around and leave them different, changed.

I slowed as I reached Valiya's house. I was sweat-slicked, panting, my heart clenched in my chest, and I was too late. It had already happened. A ghostly hand gripped my heart and crushed down with cold, stony fingers. I couldn't breathe.

'No ...'

White-paint letters reading TRAITOR were fresh above the door.

She had locked and barred it, and an axe had overcome that simple impediment, pieces of red-painted wood scattered into the hallway. I didn't want to go in. I sagged against the doorframe instead, for just a moment willing some unknown attacker to emerge behind me and put an end to all this. It was too much. It was all too much, and I didn't want to see what they'd done. But nobody came, and I owed it to them to see.

The house had been ransacked. Chaos, clutter everywhere. Not the ordered rifling of searched drawers either, but a furious, savage flurry of destruction. Axes had hewn holes in the neat little sofas, had smashed delicate landscapes from the walls, shattered the lights, the coffee table, the dresser. A neat, ordered life had been left in ruins.

No sign of Valiya. No sign of Amaira. My breath sat stagnant in my chest, a hard, morbid lungful that I dared not expel for fear that the next inhalation was the one in which I found their bodies. They hadn't fallen in the sitting room, hadn't been cut down in the parlour. Amaira would have hidden. I checked the cupboard beneath the stairs, the privy, beneath the beds, but as I searched I found room after room was empty and my heart began to thump louder and louder in my ears. She wasn't here. They weren't here. Not here.

A noise from the hallway.

I tore into it, sword raised and ready to take my revenge, but it was just an old woman, grey and fearful. She walked with a stick, bent-backed and frightened as she cowered away from me.

Terror widened her eyes, but she didn't try to hobble away. Wouldn't have got far. I must have looked like a devil to her, copper-skinned and yellow-eyed. I lowered my sword, sheathed it. Held out a hand as though she were a skittish animal.

'You've nothing to fear from me,' I rasped. 'The woman who lived here. Did you know her?'

'I did,' the woman said, drawing her shawl tighter around her shoulders. 'And she weren't no traitor.'

'I know,' I said. 'Is she ... did they ...?' I couldn't bring myself to finish the thought.

'They took her. Her and a child, though the child weren't hers,' she said.

Relief hit me like a stampeding bull. I staggered against the wall, choking on the gasps that escaped my shaking chest. My eyes burned and my shoulders locked tight. Oh, spirits of mercy, spirits of fucking mercy sweet and good and fuck you all. They were alive.

The old woman let me get it all out. The elderly know loss and she understood the shudders of exhaustion that now rocked me. Absolute terror will take it out of you. But they weren't safe. They weren't dead, but they weren't free, so now my fears turned to darker places. Would they have

351

hurt them? A waste of time fearing it. They had or they hadn't. But while they were alive, there was hope.

'You're her employer,' the old woman said. 'I saw you come in, from across the street. Valiya said you were a big man.'

She'd spoken about me to a neighbour. Described me. A small, meaningless detail amidst all this chaos but somehow it shined a spotlight on my failure to protect these people that had trusted me.

'What happened?'

'It was those bastard Bright Order men,' she snarled. 'They came and they kicked in her door and set about with the axes. Took the child too. Dusky little thing, only so high. Kicking and biting them she was, or trying. Valiya went quietly. They hadn't roughed her up none. Been praying that they're safe, though I don't know that they can be.' The woman looked past me into the house. 'Truth is, someone comes and grabs you like that, they probably don't mean to treat you kind.'

I looked at the splintered remnants of the door, lying cracked and hewn where they'd fallen. Amaira must have been terrified. They both must.

'She spoke highly of you,' the woman said. Wistful, as though Valiya was already lost and gone. As though being taken was being dead. But if my ordeal in the Misery had proved one thing beyond all others, it was that captured isn't dead. The old woman had grown uncomfortable in the presence of my seething anger. It bled from me like summer heat.

'I didn't do well enough by her, that's for sure,' I said. 'They'll pay for this.'

'Miss Valiya never struck me as the kind to go wanting revenge,' the old woman said. Truth in that. Revenge didn't serve her purpose. She'd only ever cared about getting the job done. Saving others. It was one of the things that I could admit, now, that I had loved about her.

'I know,' I said. 'But first I'm going to find the men who took them. And then I'm going to take it all the same.'

35

Tnota's house hadn't been hit. It was locked up good and tight. No sign of entry, no sign of a struggle. I was calmer now. I'd let the anger fill me, turn me to ice.

I ran on. My feet sent Misery-pain into my shins with every footfall and my chest burned, but I couldn't slow. I was in no condition for this, the weeks in the Misery had taken everything from me, only there was no choice. I ran and I ignored the pain as my old leg wound pulled tight and the barely healed injuries on my chest pulled open and spilled hot blood down my chest.

A man gave out yellow hoods as a Doomsayer explained that at the height of the flare's brightness, the Bright Lady would be born into the world and the princes would bow the knee to her. There was a desperate, ragged look to him, as though he sought to convince himself as much as he did the people he was preaching to. I took a hood, the better not to be seen. Since my arrival the message on the citadel had changed to read DETAIN ALL YELLOW-EYED MEN. Saravor's command, filtered through Thierro. The hood distributor gave me a squinting appraisal, but maybe he decided that his five-and-a-half-foot frame had little chance against my six and a half feet, and he went on with his life without looking back.

'The Bright Lady's enemies approach,' the Doomsayer declared, wild-eyed. 'These last weeks she gestured east toward the old enemy. But today, our friends have seen her offer her hand west toward the new enemy. She reaches out to them, offers the hand of friendship. She walks among us, walks with us! Stand strong with us, good people of Valengrad. Stand strong and see the dawn of her new order.'

Caution would have had me wait, watch the street outside my house, assess the chances of an ambush. There was a strong likelihood that I was running straight into a trap. I was low on gear. I'd have welcomed a brace of pistols, a full harness and a poleaxe if they'd been on offer but I couldn't trust anyone at the citadel, and I had no other means to acquire half an army's worth of equipment, so it was just going to be me, a sword and whatever was left of my nerve, checking if there was anything left here. Caution could go fuck itself: I threw the door open.

The door swung open cleanly – it had not been locked when the Bright Order came – and I could smell phos. A lot of it, the odour of burned energy soaked into the walls. Weapons had been discharged here. Upstairs, Dantry's sickroom smelled of sweat and grime, but he wasn't there. Down the stairs, and down again into the cellar, and the smell grew thicker, almost misty in the air, its residue providing a dim phosphorescence by which I made out the ruin of Maldon's workshop. The walls were painted black with soot and two of the chairs were reduced to charred lumps. A trio of bodies were fused together in the doorway, a misshapen, blackened tangle of indistinct, melted limbs, teeth and fingers. No sign of Maldon, but there was a clear child-shaped silhouette in the soot that coated one wall.

He'd detonated a phos charge of some kind and taken the blast head-on. I wondered if it had given him the release he had been searching for, but if it had killed him, then some remnant of him should still have been there. It wasn't.

I looked across the workbenches. A heavy cloth covered

a gleaming contraption of steel tubes, a crank, and a long, coiled belt. I didn't know what to make of it, so decided not to touch it. As an additional kick to the balls, it seemed that Maldon had requisitioned my parade armour from upstairs and ruined it. He'd welded on extra plates of heavy black iron, and added purposeless hooks and belts in various places. The welding he'd done meant that the plates would be much too thick and heavy for any man to move in, when I'd been hoping it was one bit of kit that would still be available to me.

Fuck. No guns. No phos charges or grenadoes. Not even my archaic armour. Nothing of use.

I was about to leave when I noticed it. A finger had scraped a crude message through the soot coating the wall. *Blue door opposite my old house.*

It seemed an unlikely trap since nobody else knew that Gleck Maldon was still alive, so I beat a path across town, dodging down alleyways whenever I saw anyone that looked like a soldier coming my way. Maldon's former house was close to the Spills, though an arsehole called Stannard had burned it down four years ago.

I found the blue door and struck it twice with the heel of my fist. I slid my hand into my coat and took hold of my knife. Take no chances. Behind the door I heard the click of a weapon being cocked and pressed myself flat against the wall, to the side.

'Who's there?' a voice called. It was comical in a way, a child trying to make his voice deeper.

'It's me, darling,' I said back. Not a very good joke, but it made things pretty clear. A bolt was drawn back, then another, another. Good. I was glad he was keeping bright.

'It's open,' Maldon said, and I pushed through, found he was standing several feet back, a pistol trained on the door. As I stepped in and shut the door, he kept it sighted on me.

'What the fuck happened to you?' he asked. 'Valiya said

356

you were a mess but ... Spirits, Ryhalt. You look more fucked-up than I do.'

'We could argue about that,' I said. Maldon was not in a good way. His left arm was in a sling, and I could see what looked like a pair of flarelock wounds in his chest, patched and stitched by an inexpert hand. His skin was burned and blackened, either raw and red or crisped like bacon fat.

'You look like a monster,' he said, uncocking the pistol and tossing it down on a sideboard.

'You are a monster,' I said. Maldon grunted his acknowledgment.

Dantry emerged from a back room. He still looked gaunt, half-cadaver, but his face broke when he saw me. I went straight to him and threw my arms around him. He was a good man. It might have shattered what was left of my hopes if he'd been dead.

'OK,' he wheezed, and I let him go. I'd crushed all the air from him. He was all skin and bone, no strength to push me away. 'Valiya told me you were alive. I didn't believe it at first. How did you survive?' I shook my head.

'Tell me what happened.'

'Those Bright Order bastards came,' Maldon said. 'Burst in whilst I was in the cellar. They shot me but I managed to detonate a phos canister right on top of them. They didn't think I'd be suicidal enough to pull the control wire out. Should have seen their faces.'

'I saw what's left of them,' I said. 'You got anything to drink?'

Maldon did, of course. It wasn't clear whose house this was, but I got the impression Maldon hadn't much liked the neighbour who'd lived here. Wherever he'd gone, and whoever he'd been, he'd kept a decent enough wine cellar that even Maldon hadn't managed to get through it all in the last few hours.

'It's a shitstorm,' he said. The fire had burned down low,

and we'd spent a pair of hours drinking and trading news while I got my strength back and ate my way through a couple of legs of ham and half a loaf of bread. I told them about the raven's unintentional rescue and the trek through the Misery, though I sanitised it and spared the worst details, which was most of it. The more I ate the clearer my mind seemed to get. I had to pause halfway through to cough and hack out more of the toxic black sludge that seemed to be inhabiting my body now, but I've had worse meals.

'They made Tnota move his shit over to the citadel,' Maldon said. 'Told him he's conscripted out of Blackwing and into the army. They got him training navigators there.'

'So he's safe?'

'Safe as anyone,' Maldon said. 'What did you do to your arm?'

I looked down at the words that I'd carved there and didn't have an answer for him.

'Saravor has to be stopped. If Davandein – *when* Davandein attacks the city, there'll be carnage. Her guns will bring down the gates sure enough, and those mercenaries won't be put off by whatever the Bright Order can muster. They'll go after anyone wearing a yellow hood and gut them, and as they do, Saravor gets the power he needs to feed the Eye. He's going to do it. He's going to become one of them. A Deep King, or maybe something worse.'

'You think he can do that?'

'I think he's been working on it for four years,' I said. 'Ever since he got that shred of power. He saw the potential in the Grandspire, so he took control of Thierro, and through him the Bright Order, while making himself an army of fixed men beneath our feet, ready to take control of the city. Spirits know how many people he's controlling through his fixing. All he needs now is the flare, and for the fighting to start.'

There was a pecking at the dirty window glass and I let the hooded raven in.

'You need to hurry your arse up,' the raven cawed.

'Is that thing Crowfoot?' Dantry asked.

'No,' the bird said, 'just a simulacrum, built to achieve a task. What the fuck are you supposed to be?'

'What task?'

As usual, the raven ignored that question.

'You need to get a fucking move on, Galharrow,' it croaked. 'Whatever you're doing here with this little boy – or whatever he is – can wait. Find Saravor.'

I took a long swig of wine. It probably wasn't a good idea to be on the third bottle already, but we're nothing if not a combination of our worst habits.

'Finding him is going to be hard,' I said. 'Killing him will be harder.'

I rested my forehead on my knuckles and closed my eyes. The impossibility of the task stretched out before me. You don't just walk up to a sorcerer and put your sword through his chest. Or at least, you don't expect that to kill him. Maldon was walking proof of that. But I had limited means at my disposal. If I'd had Ezabeth Tanza at my side, I could have relied on her to send him to the hells, but I was all out of Battle Spinners.

'They have Valiya,' I said eventually. I could barely force the words out of my throat. 'They took her and they took Amaira.'

Neither Maldon nor the raven said anything. No quips, no snide remarks, no mockery. For once they both shut the fuck up.

'They have Nenn too,' I said eventually. 'Saravor has her bound to him and I can't fight her. Not Nenn.'

I was crying. My tears were driven by sorrow, and anger, and the knowledge that there was so little I could do. I couldn't turn back an army.

'Unacceptable!' the raven cawed. Maldon said nothing, his face impossible to read through that blindfold.

'We're down to a goblin-man, a boy, an invalid and a bird,' I said. 'Against a city. Against an army, and a sorcerer who was strong enough to break Crowfoot's wards. He may not have the power of a Nameless yet, but he's only one step away, and I couldn't even protect a woman and child. The game's over.' I sagged back into the chair. 'You were right. We've lost.'

'The visions of the Bright Lady have gone berserk,' the raven said. 'She's appearing all over the city, faster and faster, pointing all over the place. If some ghost in the light hasn't given up, then you damn well shouldn't.'

I shrugged. Ezabeth was powerless to intervene. She was dead.

'You're no good to anyone exhausted,' Maldon said, and it was the first time I'd heard gentleness in his voice since the day I shot his eyes out. 'How long since you slept, Ryhalt? There's a bed in the room over the hall. Go and sleep. I need to go out and finish something.'

The raven opened its beak to squawk something, thought better of it.

The bed had a sour, unwashed look to it, but I could still feel the Misery in my gums, in my nose, feel her bleeding from my eyes and so the relative distastefulness of un-washed bedding was lost on me. I lay down and closed my eyes and thought of Valiya and all she had done for me over the last few years. I thought of how Amaira must have cried, must have screeched and fought when they took hold of her. She was out there now, somewhere, surrounded by enemies. Another child I had failed.

As I lay there, resisting sleep, I thought of Ezabeth, and what she would have said to me. That I'd done my best, that I'd tried my hardest? Even picturing her face hurt, still, after all this time. When I thought of her it was not as the ghost in the light, but of the woman that she had been. The scarred woman behind the veil. Hers was a face that I'd known only fleetingly, but it had stayed with me more clearly than those of men I'd known for years, imperfect and scarred and beautiful and perfect.

She'd have said I couldn't give up. That surrender was not an option. That losing was never going to be the answer. That she'd rather have died trying to save the republic than fled in defeat. I wished I had her courage, and I wished that when I imagined her reaching for me from that impossible distance that I could draw on her strength. Dead and lost, but still she reached out to me, though light and flesh could never touch.

Sleep came, and with it bad dreams of unpleasant things I'd done to people in the past, but dreams are neither prophetic nor something on which to base your decisions. It felt strange to wake up in a dirty peasant house that wasn't my own, and to find that Maldon wasn't there and neither was the raven. I groped around in the kitchen and found some preserved fruit in jars which I ate whilst I sat and wracked my brains for anything that might stop Davandein from attacking, or Saravor from rising to godhood, given that one seemed inevitable and all the pieces were in place for the other.

A siren sounded across the city, calling the men and women to arms. Davandein must have pushed a forced march through the night if her troops were drawing into siege lines now. I listened to that terrible, mechanical wailing, knowing that this was our last reprieve. Davandein was proud, furious and reckless, but she was still a soldier. She'd rest her troops before she began the assault, and the attack would be heralded by an exchange of artillery fire as she sought to bring down the gates, and the city's artillery sought to blast her cannon apart. It was anybody's guess which would succeed, but if push came to shove, she'd send in the prince's Battle Spinners. The flimsy western gates wouldn't stand up to them for long. Saravor had timed his slaughter to perfection.

The day was unnaturally bright, the streets filled with a glassy glare as the sunlight grew in intensity. It was better not to look upward. The Talents in the mill would have to wait until the sun dipped low and the moonlight became easier to spin. It was possible to spin during the day, but hard even with their goggles and looms to spin the right light. Spinning white light was never a good idea, it was almost impossible to control, and trying to was the way that most Talents earned their burns. The moons filtered that light into its separate threads, making it possible to draw the power in relative safety.

The raven pecked to be let in an hour after the siren had been shut off.

'The prince's army is set up just out of cannon range,' it told me. 'They've both fired at each other to test the range, but the Bright Order haven't the means to get any of the big field guns over from the eastern wall so they're relying on culverins, and Davandein's bigger guns don't have the elevation. But there's a lot of sword sharpening going on. She's going to throw everything at the walls before long.'

'Saravor has used the threat of the Grandspire to force the attack,' I muttered. 'She knows that if she lets him have time to power it up again, her whole army will be walking charcoal. She doesn't realise he needs that power for his own plans. The Eye can't draw on the power of dying souls from that far away. He needs them closer – he wouldn't have waited if he didn't have to.'

'The solar flare will give him the phos he needs far faster than normal,' Dantry said. 'He can have it armed tonight. I worked what calculations I could recall from the Taran Codex, and he'll need everything the Grandspire holds to destroy the Eye. He can't afford another blast against

Davandein. He needs thousands to die in the city if he's to draw them into the Eye. She has to do the job for him.'

'But failing that, he has a legion of his fixed men to turn loose on the population.'

I took a slug of wine. Stared at the wall. Took another swig. Opened my cigar tin and lit one up. An average leaf, but anything was hard to enjoy through the taste of the Misery that I had begun to suspect would never leave my mouth. I sat and smoked, drank, stared in silence until the cigar burned down to a nub.

'That's your plan? Get drunk and brood?' the raven cawed eventually.

'I don't have a better plan yet,' I said. 'Maybe one'll come to me.'

'Damn it, Galharrow,' the black bird shrieked. It had all of Crowfoot's old rage in it then, and by the way it flared its black-feathered wings I thought it might fly at me. 'Given the choice I'd have chosen anyone but you. That's what I'm fucking here for, to find your spirits-damned replacement. Fucked if I can find anyone who has the fucking balls and grit that a Blackwing captain needs. The master doesn't make mistakes, but if he could, you'd fucking be it.'

Had the bird been in range I might have throttled it just to shut it up.

'You know why I took his deal? Crowfoot's bargain?' The raven stared at me, eyes like voids. 'Because I was drunk as hell and I didn't give a shit. I didn't care one way or another. He gave me the choice to be bound to him, and to serve, in exchange for two lives that I'll never know anything of. I had nothing left, so I gave him whatever he could scrape from my barrel. I didn't take this job because I'm some noble, selfless servant. I took it because I'm a drunk.'

'Oh, fuck off with your self-pity,' the raven cawed. 'Find your fucking spine. You lost a woman, then you lost another — well my heart bleeds for you. It's the way of the world. A whole lot more are going to lose their women and their men if you don't sort this mess out. Isn't that what Crowfoot ordered? Look after the Range while he stops the Deep Kings sinking the world? Well get the fuck on with it.'

The raven gave three very birdlike caws and then flew off out the window.

I'd like to say its words moved me. But I'd spent weeks walking the endless black sands of the Misery, I'd felt terrible poison flow through my body, and I'd lowered myself into the nightmare. I had pushed through all of that. I'd done more than I'd thought myself capable of. But every man has his breaking point. The baking heat, the pain running through my body, choking on black poison, feeling the Misery work her way through me – I had endured it all, and more. But first Ezabeth, then Nenn, and now Valiya. I was running out of hope. I feared that I would be confronted by Nenn, and she would turn a sword on me, and I hadn't the heart to put one through her. When the Deep Kings had been bearing down on us, Ezabeth had given me hope, but Saravor held every living thing I loved. Even before I'd given him Shavada's dark power he'd been a foe far beyond me. Ezabeth, Nenn and Valiya were the foundation upon which I'd built my strength. Even Amaira had held me up. One by one they'd been taken from me. I wanted to fight. I wanted to stare Saravor in his mismatched eyes and see his confidence turn to bowel-loosening terror. But at the end of it all, I was just a tired, poisoned man without options.

Maldon returned around midday, leading a donkey and cart around to the back of the house. Something heavy enough to make the wagon creak under its weight was stowed in the back.

'That what I think it is?' I asked, leaning against the back doorframe.

'Of course,' he said. 'But I need a supply of phos for it. I used the last of my canisters blowing away those fools at your house. It's just so much iron without it. Do you have any idea how hard it is to get a phos canister when you're not a Spinner?'

'Pretty hard,' I said. 'How'd you get it onto the cart?'

'Paid some locals. You haven't asked where I got the cart.'

'I assumed you stole it.'

'The canisters need to be charged if it's going to work at all,' Maldon said, changing the subject. 'Without those it's worthless.'

'I'm fine here,' I said, pouring the last of the wine into my mouth. I had a bad drunk on me, the kind that makes stupid men lash out with their fists. 'But I do have some terrible news. We've run out of wine.'

Maldon turned on me.

'Enough, Ryhalt!' he snapped. 'It's my job to be miserable and self-pitying. Spirits know, I've fucking earned it. But not today. Now get out there and get me some fucking canisters!'

There was enough drunk in me that I wasn't moved by his outburst. His voice was pre-broken, and his childlike shrieking was, in its way, amusing. Not really amusing. Not really funny. But when you're drunk, you pretend that things are funny so that you can ignore the humiliation.

'Get them yourself,' I said.

Maldon rounded on me.

'You're really going to give up and fucking cry about how shit your life is while the rest of the world burns?' he yelled. 'You think you got poisoned by the Misery, and that's it, time to give up? You lost your women so you're not going to play anymore? Well it doesn't work like that.'

'Who are you to tell me that, when you've tried to take the easy way more than once?' I spat back.

'You want to know what I've lost?' Maldon screeched. 'I can't even *die*. I won't ever touch a woman again not just because I'm a perpetual child, but because I've got no

365

fucking *eyes in my face.* You've spent four years mourning a woman you lost. I'll spend eternity in this rat-sized, mutilated body. Yes, I wanted that to end. But it didn't, and we're stuck together. You cut words into your arm because you thought they mattered. You had grit then, you cowardly, self-obsessed fucking *drunk.* Now get out there and get me ten fucking phos canisters! If I could spin the light myself, I'd fucking do it, wouldn't I? I used to be able to do it like that.'

And as he snapped his fingers in a fury, something utterly unexpected happened. There was a spark, a tiny, thin little judder of lightning between them. Maldon's eyeless face stared at his fingers, his mouth hung open. My mouth hung open.

'Did you just generate phos?' I asked, our argument forgotten.

'I don't know,' Maldon breathed. He sat down hard snapping his fingers, again and again, but nothing happened.

We were interrupted by a fluttering of black wings.

'Tell me things have turned,' I said. 'Tell me Davandein has withdrawn, and Saravor has turned himself over for hanging.'

'It's all shit,' the bird said. 'And there's something new. Galharrow, the citadel has a personal message for you.'

I frowned at the raven, but it had started preening its feathers as though this last were an afterthought. I put on my yellow hood, headed out the front and wandered down the street to get a clear look at the citadel. The bloody neon words were all too clear, alternating between two separate messages:

GALHARROW: THE COURTHOUSE
YOU FOR THE CHILD

36

It would be wrong to describe it as a trap. A trap implies something unexpected, a surprise attack. They weren't trying to lure me in with something desirable. It was a bargain. A deal. A choice.

I stared at those bloody letters as the Misery sky wailed overhead, then that sound was joined by the blast of cannon as the guns on the wall unleashed the first volley. Davandein's attack must have begun. There was no broadside volley, no steady discharge. The guns cracked sporadically, without order. Inexperienced crews.

Only two moons had risen, Rioque was full in scarlet and glistening with promise, Clada was rich and soothing, waxing gibbous in blue. The sun lit the sky in lemon and orange away to the west as she closed with the horizon, the skyline burning with intensity, the brightest sunset I'd ever seen. The moons didn't project their usual light; they blazed with it, the cloudless sky difficult to look at. Even the weather was against me. In the Grandspire, the Talents would be beginning their work, sitting at their looms with scarred fingers, dead-eyed as they spun magic from the light.

That's where Saravor would be. When the battle reached its height, when the bloodshed had driven enough souls into Shavada's Eye, Saravor would go there and turn the power of the Grandspire on the Eye. Then what? When he had what he wanted, would he leave us alone? Claim the city as his own? Or would he flee across the Misery and seek an alliance with the Deep Kings? I supposed, in the end, it wouldn't matter. The city would be torn apart, the people put to a vengeful sword, and most likely I would be dead.

I gazed up at the message. Me for Amaira. Was Valiya already dead? I balled my fists and fought down the shaking. For all my clever schemes and preparations, my intelligence network, my reputation, even my connection to the Nameless ... in the end I was just a man. And Amaira was just a child. Maybe I couldn't stop Saravor. Maybe the warring of the greater powers had always been beyond me, but perhaps I could save one more life before I was done. Was it worth it, trading whatever chance might remain to defeat a dark immortal for an ordinary, annoying child? In this decision, I was alone.

No. Not alone.

Never alone, not even in my dreams.

'I'll stand with you,' she had told me, deep in the Misery. 'I'll be your shield, when you need me to be, but the will to fight has to be yours.'

Maybe it was time to rely on someone else. Trust in something greater than me, which had always been greater than me. I'd held to my sliver of hope in the face of every obstacle. Clutched it hard inside me, regardless of facts and numbers and lies and truths. Because she still reached for me in my dreams. Because the Bright Order had seen her reaching east all the time that I'd been in the Misery, reaching west when I rode out to Davandein. I'd prayed to her in my blackest hour, and all the while, she'd been reaching out to me. Reaching for something. Perhaps she had been nothing more than a hallucination, but if I'd ever believed in anything, it was that Ezabeth would never go down quietly while there was still something to fight for.

Time to put my faith to the test.

I would do what any man does when he loves a child. I

had failed Valengrad, and I saw no way to change that, but Amaira was of no value to them save as a pawn against me. There was really no choice to make.

'Where are you going?' the raven cawed at me, 'don't be a fool. Don't be a fool, Galharrow!' But it stood on a post and watched me walk away without following.

Davandein's guns were firing thick and fast as I picked my way through the streets. Thumps and cracks, dark percussion in the fading light. I doubted the city's light guns could do much to stop Davandein's mercenary artillerymen.

The city was under attack, but you wouldn't have known it from the way people were milling in the streets. Those of fighting age had all been conscripted, a flarelock shoved into their hands, and sent to join the soldiers on the walls, but the old and young were outside, looking up at the sky or chanting prayers to the Bright Lady. They seemed half-oblivious to the impending threat, and only the nervous trembling of a hand or a stammer on the lips betrayed their fear.

'When is she going to appear?' an old man said. 'It can't be long now.'

'The grand prince will be forced to his knees,' a teenage girl declared, reciting the rebel mantra. 'When he sees her appear over the city the new order will begin.'

'I saw her! I saw her!' a woman cried, bursting from her doorway. 'I turned on the phos tubes and she appeared to me from the light!'

I veered around them and kept walking.

Across the city I heard the same thing, time and time again. A man stood on a crate proclaiming that he'd seen the Bright Lady a mere hour ago, that she'd appeared and reached toward him. Her time was at hand, he declared. No one wanted to admit they were afraid, to say that perhaps they should be more preoccupied with the army at their gates, and less with ghosts in the light.

My faith was stronger than theirs.

I watched, nonetheless. I thought, heading to the court-house to trade myself for an orphan child of no great house, no great status, no great skill, that maybe after this I could bear to look Ezabeth in the eye one last time. I'd feared her for so long. Feared how I'd failed her, feared what she'd think of me, what she'd always thought of me. That our brief, candle-flame time together had just been a moment of madness as we stared death in the face.

'Stand with me, Ezabeth,' I said. 'I've never needed you more.'

I knew as I walked toward death that my fears were only fears. That the voice in my head saying I'd never been good enough, that she'd only taken solace in me because she was desperate, was the real lie. It would be good to see Ezabeth one last time before I died. Her real face, scarred and unique. A glimpse of that, I thought, would make it all worthwhile.

A barkeep had dragged a keg of beer out of his alehouse and was giving out free cups as though the coming of the Bright Lady were some kind of carnival event for spectators. I almost took one, but thought better of it. I needed my wits for whatever was to come. They would kill me, I didn't doubt that. But even if the Bright Order were deluded, even if they were dancing to Saravor's tune, most of them were just people. They had no reason to keep Amaira once they had me, and looking back, I'd made far worse deals.

Across the city the sound of small-arms fire joined the largest crunching of the cannon, the sharp whine of flare-locks, the hollow booms of matchlocks, muffled by the intervening buildings.

Soldiers lined the road to the courthouse. Dozens of them, formed in ranks to the left and right, standing to attention with their flarelocks shouldered. Waiting for me like an honour guard. They made no move to take hold of me, or to stop me.

'What's all this?' I asked one of them.

'You're to proceed to the courthouse please, my lord,' he said. He would barely look at me, stared straight ahead, as sweat trickled from beneath his helmet.

'Who ordered you to stand here like idiots when there's fighting to be done?'

'To the courthouse, my lord,' he said.

'I'm no lord,' I said.

The twin rows of men led all the way to the courthouse steps, and to Thierro at the top. He stared down at me, hard-eyed. A new face, the one that had lurked beneath the mask he'd been wearing all this time. He hated me. Hated me with a fierceness that burned like thrice-spun light, reaching up out of his heart until he practically shook with it. He didn't just feel the hate: he *was* the hate. He was dressed in white: white fencing breeches, long white stockings, white shoes with golden buckles. His jacket was white, his shirt gleamed with pearly sequins, and he wore a ruff of finest lace. Sweat had dampened his collar.

'Here you are,' he said. 'Fitting, on this last night, that Crowfoot's lackey be witness to the birth of a new power.' Saravor's words, hissed through Thierro's lips.

'Is that what this comes down to, Saravor?' I said. 'Pride?'

'No,' he said. 'Power. The days of the Nameless dwindle. They will be on their knees when they lose their battle against the Deep Kings, and you will be my message to them.'

He went on into the courthouse.

'Stand with me now, Ezabeth,' I whispered, and followed.

The floor of the high court had been polished to a high sheen, the mosaics bright. There were even more soldiers inside, men and women by the hundred, wearing bright steel breastplates, the coats beneath them dyed a vivid lemon. They wore flarelock canisters, held their weapons to their shoulders, stood to attention. They crowded the tiered galleries overlooking the floor like the viewing boxes at a theatre. Among them I saw many who'd served under Marshal Venzer, Valengrad's finest warriors. They had turned. Of course they had turned, when the shield rose to protect the city from the sky-fires. They'd seen the proof of their faith written huge and glimmering in the night sky. Why wouldn't they believe?

Thierro stood in the centre of the courtroom floor, waiting. I saw Witness Glaun seated like a scarred judge on the marbled dais.

'I've come. Release the child,' I said. My voice rang around in the room, echoed from the marbles.

'Speak when spoken to, knave!' Glaun roared.

'Release the child,' I shouted back.

'Show him,' Thierro said, and snapped his white-gloved fingers. Men emerged holding Amaira and Valiya by the shoulders. My chest lurched. They were both still alive. Valiya was stoic, but her lip and eye were swollen from fist-work. Amaira looked frightened, eyes wide beneath her fringe of dark hair. The worst they'd suffered seemed to be bruises. They didn't struggle. There was no point.

'You have me,' I said. 'Now let them go. They still have time to run before Davandein's warriors get in here and slaughter the lot of you.'

'Silence!' Glaun shrieked. He had a wild look about him. His arms were bare, and there were signs that he'd been slicing at his arms with a blade. Amateur; he hadn't even sliced any words. Fanaticism causes a man to excuse anything in the name of belief. His ends justified his means.

Saravor smiled through Thierro's eyes. A mocking smile. As though I'd missed some hilarious joke.

'You hear that?' Thierro called to the assembly. 'He does not believe! Even with the portents, there are some that cannot – will not – believe. This man before you denies the rise of the new god, has committed murder to try to deny the coming of the new order. You are the chosen few, obliged to watch, and to record for all time, the ascension of a true ruler. When justice is served, destiny shall be realised, here, and now.'

The soldiers cheered. They didn't sense the mockery in his voice. Dupes. I looked to Amaira and she looked at me with terror in her eyes. I gave her a slow nod. She firmed her mouth, gave it back.

'Stand with me,' I whispered.

There was a gasp in the assembled crowd and a spurt of light. I glanced up and sure enough, for a split second I saw it, just as they did. A figure of light. I blinked, the imprint lingering in my vision. A woman wreathed in flame.

'She comes!' someone in the crowd crowed. 'She draws near!'

'She needs him to die, for her justice!'

'She pointed to him!'

But she hadn't been pointing. Her hand had been outstretched.

The soldiers drummed their flarelock butts against the floor, a dry thunder. Thierro waved his hands for silence, and the soldiers around him were blind to Saravor's darkness in his eyes. The flecks of blood in the whites.

'You see, Galharrow? The lady comes to bear witness to the coming of a new age. The Nameless will bend the knee, and your death will send a message to them. You will die here, in the seat of their power, within their hall of justice, and they will know that the new order is coming. That their day is done.'

Thierro was interrupted again by another spark up in the galleries. Another vision of the Bright Lady. Then another. They were coming faster, brief flickers of light.

'High Witness! She draws near. It is time!' Glaun declared.

Amaira was shoved forward; the soldier had a knife to her throat. She shook her head at me. Amaira. Small, bony, disobedient Amaira. An orphan of the war. Nobody of note. Just a girl. A girl who had stuck poems to the bottom of a table, so there would be something beautiful if she died.

'Saravor,' I said. 'You're wrong. This is a game to you. You never understood that true power doesn't stand alone, above men. It stands with and within us. These people deserve more than your lies and trickery. You offered a deal, and I came. But right here, right now, tell your man to get his hands off my daughter, or I swear by every black spirit of the hells that I'll kill every last fucking one of you.'

Thierro cocked an eyebrow at me.

'She's not your daughter,' he said. 'She's some bastard from the oasis kingdoms you picked up in the ruins. Anyone can see that.'

'You can't understand it because you can't see it,' I said. 'That much is clear.' I counted the beats of my heart to keep time. Seven beats, eight. 'You've not ordered him to stand down. Get ready to die.'

Another gasp as the Bright Lady appeared in a momentary flash of raw light. One of the Order soldiers staggered away with smouldering clothes, clutched at a scorched hand.

'The Lady comes!' Glaun cried, 'because the justice done here opens the path! Kill him, High Witness. Kill him and open the path for her!'

'Stand with me, Ezabeth.'

I rolled my shoulders, spat on the floor and drew my sword. I levelled it toward Thierro.

'You think to come at me alone, Galharrow?' Thierro smirked.

'That's always been your problem, Saravor. You're surrounded by men whose hearts you've taken, and you're still alone. I'm not alone. The Bright Lady isn't here for you. She's here for me.'

I advanced on Thierro, point levelled.

'Hear me, Crowfoot,' Saravor said, his voice booming.

'This one is just the beginning. I'll erase all trace of you from our world.'

Light blazed in front of me. The canisters at Thierro's belt flared, detonated outwards as he absorbed a wave of power. It rushed through him, smoking and glimmering from his infused body. The soldiers cheered. And then he unleashed it against me, a blinding white blast of power.

I didn't even flinch.

A wave of heat struck me as the power struck something five feet away and stopped, a beam of writhing phos light creating a screaming disturbance in the air. The power roared, blasts of lightning flaring wildly as the phos arced and cut away from me. And at its heart, she flared into being.

Ezabeth.

The Bright Lady.

My shield.

She stood strong. Magnificent. Five feet nothing, and she was still greater than a giant. A dress of flame billowed around her legs as she grew in intensity, translucent and golden, the blaze of power swelling around her as Saravor poured more of Thierro's spinning into it.

'The Lady!' Witness Glaun cried, and the soldiers cheered. Ezabeth rippled, an illusion, a spirit, ethereal and so distant. She was still too far away. Much too far away for me.

'I cannot protect you forever, Ryhalt,' she said, and her whisper rang like a cannon blast in my mind. 'Run.'

'I'll never run from you,' I said.

Her eyes were awash with pain, the agony of forcing herself into our world. This was it. She was no power-crazed sorcerer seeking ascension. She'd gathered power all along the years for some great purpose. The Bright Order had seen her reaching and thought she quested toward justice, enemies, anything they could have dreamed. But Ezabeth was not a god, she was a woman, and I'd only put it together when I'd asked myself, had I been her, what would I have reached for? This was what she had been building her power to all this time. Not for some mystic rebirth.

She reached for me, her arm rising toward me. Offering me her hand.

'How is he doing that?' Glaun demanded.

'You wanted someone to save you,' I said. 'But there's no god coming to help you, Witness. We have to save ourselves.'

I thrust my hand into the burning light. There was a wall there, a wall between worlds. Ours, corporeal, hard, flesh and bone and iron and sky. Hers, spirit and light, dream and magic. There was no way that a man of flesh could cross into that, and no way that a woman of light could cross back.

But I was not just a man. I was soaked through with the Misery, with Crowfoot's dreadful magic. It infused my body, driven like nails into my marrow. I'd absorbed the tiniest part of that power, and I was no longer just a man. I was no spirit in the light, either. I was something less, and something greater. A bridge between two worlds.

I reached into the barrier, drove against it with all of my strength, my mind, with the black energy that the Misery had imbued me with.

And our fingers touched with a roar like the crashing of thunder, the fall of empires, the breaking of rules long written in the bones of the earth.

Thierro's power winked out, his phos exhausted, and the spirit stood there still, golden and translucent, burning and fierce. Ezabeth's eyes rippled with pain and with power, a ghost in the light become substance. Thierro – and Saravor – staggered back and collapsed. He'd thrown everything he had against me, and Ezabeth had taken it.

'No,' he said, 'She's nothing! You told me she was *nothing*! Just some dead Spinner!' And for the first time, I heard fear in Saravor's hissing. I dropped to my knees. I'd thrown everything I had into reaching for her. Now the heat of Ezabeth's presence, the fire that still surrounded her, seared my skin.

Valiya elbowed the man holding her in the crotch, and as he doubled over she grabbed the hand of the man holding the knife to Amaira's throat. The soldier backhanded her, sending her to the ground. As he lunged for Amaira she ran to me and hurled herself into my arms for whatever meagre protection they could give.

'You have all been deceived,' Ezabeth said. Her voice was hollow and metallic. Not a woman at all. Something greater than us. All around us, hundreds of eyes began to weep blood as Saravor took control of his army of fixed men, while Ezabeth spoke to the soldiers – the Bright Order believers. 'I am not your saviour. I am of the light. I *am* the light.'

'Kill them!' Thierro screeched. 'Fire. Fire!'

'But High Witness, the Bright Lady ...' Witness Glaun looked from one to the other, utterly confused.

Saravor's puppet-men started to come to life, picking up the weapons they'd been pounding on the floor and cocking the rigging levers, a high-pitched whine filling the air as phos canisters connected to firing mechanisms, and five hundred gun barrels swivelled in my direction.

'Run,' I said to the girl at my side.

'No!' Amaira screamed. 'Leave him alone!'

There was no running from this, no dodging that many shots. I tried to give Amaira a smile. It hadn't been a good run, all things considered.

'Take aim!'

'Run!' I said again, trying to push Amaira from me, but she clutched tight to me and I hadn't enough strength to shove her away.

They took aim.

377

I curled around Amaira instead, turning my back on Glaun; a pitiful shield. It was all I could offer her.

'Fire!'

All around us, the thunder of the guns.

37

Perhaps they had all started as believers. Perhaps all they had wanted to see was the Bright Lady born out of the light. They had got their wish, in the end. She was the last thing they saw as they squeezed their firing levers. Perhaps the first man to fire was happy in the split second between pulling the trigger, seeing the light-filled silhouette, and the explosion that tore him apart.

The second man may well have got to experience the same thing. But by the third, or the tenth, or the hundredth, they would have seen nothing, blinded by the blasts as five hundred flarelocks detonated, one after the other.

The roar of the explosions shook the building. The phos detonations crashed against each other in awkward, split-second screams as the light canisters tore apart. The galleries were obliterated, bodies fell like rain. The Bright Order men that had not pulled their triggers were caught in the explosions all around them or else fell to their deaths as the platforms beneath them collapsed, or were crushed by those falling above them. Standing in the middle, surrounded by hundreds of blazing bursts, the wave of heat bore down from all sides, but as the Bright Order died in their hundreds I stood immune. I closed my eyes against the glow, and, when I opened them, I thought that I might have died already.

I paid no heed to the collapsing galleries, or the cries of the burned. Ezabeth blazed before me.

Tears ran down my face. I groped forward on my knees, and we were nearly the same height. I reached out to her, but the walls between worlds were too strong. I had no more strength to reach her.

'Come back to me,' I said, and my voice was raw and broken.

'Ryhalt,' Ezabeth said, and my heart thrashed inside my chest. Her voice had a metallic resonance to it, as though I heard her echoing through a tunnel of steel.

But it was her.

She was here.

'You're here,' I said. But she wasn't. I could see the room beyond her, through her. She had no substance.

'I have little time,' she said, and her voice was achingly sad. 'It has taken me years to build the impetus to reach out to you here. Ryhalt – '

'I'm so sorry,' I said. 'I'm so sorry that I couldn't save you.' I could barely speak. A gantry broke apart and fell to shatter against the courtroom floor.

'Ryhalt,' she said, and the name was an echo of agony through me. 'I made my own choices. I always did. Nobody made them for me. I'm so sorry for your pain, but I don't have much time.'

My pain. She was the one who burned.

'I need you to stay,' I pleaded.

'I am bound to the light,' she said. 'Part of it. Not even the Engine has enough power to undo what I did. But to-night, with the flare and the moons aligned, I have a few moments.'

The spirit of light seemed to shudder, hunched for a mo-ment, but then drew up to her full height.

'I cannot bear it,' I said.

'I can. So must you,' she said.

'I love you,' I said uselessly.

'I love you too.'

My vision was blurred with tears, but even so I saw the smoke-like wisps that had begun to rise from her.

'You have to go, Ryhalt. You have to stop the grey children. I died to save Valengrad. Don't let that be for nothing.'

'How do I stop them?'

The woman of light winced and her ghost-fists tightened into balls, an all-too-human action for a being composed entirely of flickering blue and golden light.

'You're holding it back, aren't you?' I said. 'The fire. You're trying not to show it to me.'

'Listen to me,' Ezabeth said, metallic voice urgent. 'I tried to gather enough power to stop the grey children, but even tonight, in this realm, I'm too weak. I can't stop Saravor, so I've chosen instead to save you. Stand for me, champion. If Saravor manages to use the Eye, he will become as terrible as the Deep Kings. You're the only one I can trust to stop it. You cannot stop the war, Ryhalt. But Saravor is no true immortal. Not yet.' She choked on her own words. The smoking coils rising from her intensified as though she were dry wood exposed to hot embers.

'How can you bear it?' I asked.

The first flames began to rise from her body as one hand caressed my face.

'Because you still care,' she said, and her strange, light-spun face showed both sympathy and sadness as she looked down on me. 'Because I know that no matter how hard it is or how much it costs you – if you have to beat down the gates to the hells themselves – you'll find me and you'll drag me out of here. You're Ryhalt Galharrow. All the hells together won't stop you from reaching me.' Her fingers seared my cheek without even touching me. They were hot, hot as a cannon barrel. I didn't flinch from the heat. I raised my hand and pressed it against the back of her fingers. There was no substance to them, only burning pain which made the magic imbued into my body writhe and twist, rejecting the foreign power. The flames began to lick along her shoulders, her arms. Her face. The pain against my cheek was like a brand, but I couldn't have dragged myself from it. If this was all that remained of her, then I still wanted it. Would endure it.

'If I have to break the sky and shatter the earth,' I said before the statues of Justice and Mercy, 'if I have to tear the mountains from their roots and drown the fucking oceans. If it takes me a hundred years. I will find you. I will bring you back.'

I could no longer see her face. The flames rose over her, stealing her back, but I thought I caught her voice one final time.

'I know.'

And then she was gone.

38

Thierro's body lay twisted and broken on the floor. His chest had been torn open by shards of flying metal. The stench of rotting meat rose from inside him, black, rotting lungs exposed. No amount of cologne would hide it now. He'd been a good man.

'She was real,' Witness Glaun said. He lay slumped against the judges' dais. He was not in a good way.

Valiya was crouched beneath the skirts of the statue of the Spirit of Mercy. None of the debris seemed to have fallen around her. She met my eye, as surprised by her own survival as I was. I doubted that it was simply luck that had protected her amidst the devastation. Pale with shock, she gave me a trembling nod. I returned it, just before a small, spindly-limbed creature managed to throw itself at me. She nearly took me off my feet. Amaira was covered in soot and masonry dust. I looked her over for wounds, found none, and crushed her to me until she had to hit me on the back to let her breathe.

'You came for me,' she said, her eyes full of tears. '*You came for me.*'

I couldn't express what I was feeling, and my face was as wet as hers, so I just held her, softer this time.

'I made you a promise,' I said. 'The seven hells couldn't stop me.' Her arms cinched tighter around my neck. For the first time in a long time, something felt right.

'It was her, wasn't it?' Glaun said. His voice sounded strained. A beam of wood had punched right through him when it fell from the gallery above and he was bleeding a lot worse than I was. Blood on his lips. I set Amaira down, then walked across to him and sat on the steps that led up to the judges' platform.

'It was,' I said.

'Not a trick. Not an illusion,' he said. He must have been in a lot of pain, but there was a serenity to his expression. I took his hand in mine. He had no strength left in his fingers, but they twitched, an acknowledgment of company, at the end.

'No illusion,' I said.

'She was a woman? A real woman?'

'She was Ezabeth Tanza, once,' I said. 'She saved Valengrad and she paid the price for it. But she's not a god. She never was. She was better than that.'

'She was ... glorious,' Glaun managed, before he choked on blood. It bubbled around his mouth. He hadn't got long left, but he'd really, truly believed in the Bright Lady. Might have been the only one among their hierarchy that had. He was guilty of being a fool, but then, we're all fools in one way or another.

'You should have seen her when she was alive,' I said.

'We only saw what we wanted to. I wanted it so badly,' Glaun said. 'All this time we thought her coming was for us.' He choked his way through an unpleasant laugh that probably hurt him more than it was worth. 'But we were wrong. She was coming for you.'

'She always could surprise me.'

He laughed until he died. That's the way of death, sometimes.

Valiya picked her way over to us. Shock and fear had taken the strength from her, but she knelt and closed Glaun's eyes. We shared a look that said too much, and nothing at all. I put a hand on her shoulder and she closed her eyes, content for that moment just to breathe, and stand, and be still.

'What do we do now, Captain-Sir?' Amaira asked.

I regarded her, breathed out slowly. I guess she'd earned an answer.

'Now we kill a Fixer.'

The big guns had all but fallen silent, and instead the constant percussion of matchlock fire warred with the whine of flarelocks. It was no longer restricted to the walls; Davandein's forces had entered the city and engaged in bloody close-quarter fighting from street to street. Shavada's Eye would be feeding on every death, every man or woman that fell sending their spirit's energy flowing toward Saravor, driving him on to victory.

Among the noncombatants, the mood had shifted. They'd not expected the gates to fall so easily. Now they feared for their loved ones.

'My lad's barely old enough to hold his gun upright,' a worried mother said.

'My old girl should have given the fight up years ago,' her neighbour agreed. They had taken down their hoods, the glory and revelation that they had been anticipating seeming suddenly far away. The nebulous promises of the High Witness were now a distant mirage, while the prospect of men with blades had become an all-too-sharp reality. Many still stood out in the streets, but there was a fire blazing by the western wall, a dark red glower over the city caused by a stray shot, or an exploding flarelock maybe. It seemed unlikely anyone was organised enough to put it out. At this rate Davandein would find herself stepping over corpses piled atop a mountain of ash to reclaim the city.

'I was sure she would come,' a father muttered, his children clutched around his legs. 'Where is the Bright Lady?'

Valiya had my arm slung over her shoulder and helped me to walk. My body ached in a dozen different places, the burn across my cheek stung, the old wound in my leg bit deep. Some people tried to help us, but I waved them off and we eventually found horses. We rode the rest of the way to Maldon's hideout.

'How are you going to stop him?' Valiya asked.

'I don't know, yet,' I said. 'If all else fails, I'll take his head.'

'Not much of a plan, Captain-Sir,' Amaira said.

'When we get to Gleck's place, you're going to stay there until this is all over.'

'I hid before,' she said. 'It didn't help anyone any. It didn't even help me.'

'And I thought you looked like shit before,' Maldon said when he opened the door.

'Believe me, it could have been worse,' I said.

'Got them back, then,' he said. He gave Amaira a shallow smile. I think he was fond of her too.

'I hate you,' Amaira said, and he made a face.

I let them clean the burn on my face with cheap whisky. I couldn't feel half the fingers of my right hand, where I'd forced them to bridge the gap between worlds, but I could still curl them, so that was something. I drank the rest of the whisky, of which there wasn't enough. My hands still hadn't lost their Misery shakes and I spilled a lot of it down my chin.

'I have no idea how you can take this much punishment,' Maldon said as he stitched.

'That's rich, coming from you.' I might look like shit, but Maldon looked worse.

A flutter of wings heralded the raven which seemed surprised that I was still alive, though it shouldn't have been. I knew that fucking thing could find me no matter where I was and would know if I died. It was in its nature to know.

'Davandein's troops are in the streets, killing pretty much everything they see,' the bird cawed. 'But they're mercenaries so they're stopping to loot as they go. The Bright Order have fallen back to barricades along Time Street and Second Street. They'll be slow to break, but when they do it's going to be a slaughter.'

'I guess the Bright Order didn't prove an effective force after all,' Valiya said. She'd accepted a talking raven as just another part of the night's strangeness. Compared to Ezabeth's appearance, it must have seemed mundane.

'Useless. Like their weapons,' it cawed. 'They killed a bunch of their own with the misfires alone.' The bird didn't know the half of it. 'The best of Colonel Koska's regulars are fighting a slow retreat but Witness Valentia has gathered a few thousand of her best around the Grandspire. She'll make a last stand there.'

'Saravor is at the Grandspire. That's where he needs to be to open the Eye.'

'Then we go there, and we kill him,' Dantry said. He hobbled into the room on his crutch, in terrible shape. He smelled sour and infected.

'Even if we could get past the troops, Saravor's no ordinary man.'

'You don't have to kill him,' Amaira said. 'He's the head of the dragon, but you only need to clip its wings to bring it down.'

'What do you mean?' I asked.

'The Talents in the Grandspire,' Amaira said. 'The ones Spinning the light. If they can't spin it, then he won't get the power he needs.'

We let that drift in silence between us for a moment.

'You mean ... I should kill the Talents in the Grandspire?'

Amaira met my disapproval squarely, holding her ground. The raven cawed its cheery agreement that she was right. I looked to Maldon, to Dantry. Dantry at least gave a hopeless, disappointed shrug, as if to say he felt bad about it. Valiya said nothing. She was in shock, exhausted, but she continued making an inventory of the weapons at our disposal, laying out the little we had and checking edges and ammunition. She'd been through so much, but still she worked, even if she had next to nothing to work with.

'Even if I had the means – '

'We have the means,' Maldon interrupted.

'Even if we did,' I said, 'it might be too late already. They've been spinning the flare light for hours. He might have enough already.' I looked to Amaira. 'And we have to be better than that.'

'It doesn't have to be the Talents,' she said. 'What about breaking their machines?'

'The Iron Sun,' Dantry said. 'That's where the power's stored. Destroy it before Saravor can use it to tear the power from the Eye.'

'How am I going to do that?'

'I could rig a phos grenadoe. That might work,' Maldon said. 'I used one when they came for me in your cellar. There's a ton of power flowing into the Iron Sun, it wouldn't take much to blast it.'

'You have one?'

'I could modify a canister in a few minutes,' he said with a shrug. 'It's easy enough.'

'Good. I brought you a bunch of them. They're out on the horse. But I'd still have to get past the soldiers.'

Maldon's face lit up and a broad, cruel smile spread over his face. It reminded me far too much of the time that he'd spent as a Darling. He shook his head, and began to laugh.

Time ticked by. It took an hour to get ready.

People died. Time didn't care.

Maldon wound a crank, tightening the armour. The old

388

parade suit had sat in my house, dusty and unused for years. I'd never expected to put it on. It was decorative armour, but the best made in all the states. Maldon's modifications had made it something far, far more. It weighed more than I did, with phos canisters rigged to the lower back. A terrible and impractical idea, really, since they added weight, but he'd done something clever with gears and pistons along the joints that made movement possible. As I flexed my arm, there was a slight hiss, phos assisting the movement.

'I can't walk properly,' I said, testing the range of motion. 'And I can't fight either. There's too much weight.'

'True,' Maldon said, as Dantry helped him with the helmet. It was full-faced, the visor leaving only a tiny slit to see through. They began bolting it down onto the chest plate like an old suit of jousting armour. I hated full-faced helmets. The heat, the muffled sounds within the leather-stuffed interior, the restricted view. I had no peripheral vision, couldn't look left or right without turning my whole torso. 'But the armour isn't there to let you get messy up close,' Maldon said. 'It's to keep you alive. The phos circuits I've added through the steel project a very slight expulsion field. Try not to knock this lever, it will eject the bolts that hold it together and you'll find yourself naked, which probably wouldn't be for the best.' He gabbled away about things that I didn't understand. Magnetism and points of percussion and something to do with the backlash paradox.

'We don't have much time,' the hooded raven said, flapping down to perch, annoyingly, on top of my head. I couldn't turn or shake my head to get rid of it. 'The weapon on top of the Grandspire will be charged within the hour and Davandein's forces have just broken the barricade on Time Street.'

'Are they being held in check?' I asked. The raven didn't even hesitate.

'No.' It had been a slim hope.

I clanked out to the wagon on which Maldon had brought his work. I wasn't going to walk all the way to the Grand-spire in this rig. Valiya offered me two pistols, then looked at Maldon's contraption and put them through her own belt instead.

'Well,' she said. She put a hand against the steel of the breastplate. 'Be strong, Ryhalt. It's down to you now. Try to come back.'

I raised my visor and watched her hurry away into the house.

'I want to come with you,' Amaira said. 'I can help.'

'Stay here with Valiya. Hide somewhere clever. If I don't come back – '

'You'll come back,' she said firmly. 'You have to come back.'

'I will. I promise.'

I closed my visor and turned away. Dantry took the driving seat, Maldon was in the back with me, making last-minute changes, tightening bolts and checking the gears that powered the joints. There wasn't much more to say.

They were right to fear for me, but fear had burned away in Ezabeth's fire. The Misery had not killed me, Thierro had not killed me, and now it was my turn to bring vengeance of the people down on Saravor. He and his grey children were about to learn why you do not, not with the backing of devils, not with the backing of immortals or Kings or the spirits of hatred themselves, fuck with Blackwing.

Saravor had pulled his most dedicated troops back to the main approach to the Grandspire. The streets around it were narrow, and the soldiers had demolished houses to block them and prevent Davandein from approaching save along the Rain Boulevard. They wore cuirasses of polished steel over their golden jackets, cloth-of-gold hoods up over their pot helms. They were arrayed into ranks, hundreds of the bastards, thousands, but they all stood facing outward, poleaxes and matchlocks shouldered. No holy weapons here, no prayers on their lips. They were glass-eyed, devoid of emotion, soundless sentinels. Fixed guardians, all directly under Saravor's control. They were an extension of his being, their stolen lives ready to be thrown away to protect their master, to power his schemes. Witness Valentia prayed before them, apparently oblivious to the lack of chatter, the lack of emotion showing on their ghostly faces. If those were even their faces.

The Grandspire loomed above me. At its peak, an ominous glow brightened the purple sky. What I was about to do was only going to aid him. It was going to be close.

I lumbered down from the cart, my feet striking a heavy, iron clang as my weight fractured the paving stone. I heaved the contraption from the wagon, the phos pistons working, jettisoning tight puffs of smoking light. Maldon's weapon had a weight I could never have lifted alone. The light power hissed as I took a step forward, *clang*, another, *clang*.

'Good luck, Ryhalt,' Dantry said.

'Get out of here.'

'Remember,' Maldon shouted back at me as the cart wheeled away. 'It *is* going to explode!'

Clang, another step toward the troopers. *Clang*. Some of them had seen me now. *Clang*. They were a hundred feet away, spread out in front of the Grandspire in their ordered rows.

The Witness stopped praying, as I drew the attention of her congregation. She turned, saw me, and didn't know what to make of me. I was clad head to toe in black-and-gold steel, and I doubt she'd ever seen anything like the weapon that hung by straps from my left shoulder. But she could probably guess she wouldn't like it. On my back I had a steel hopper full of shot, tens of thousands of matchlock balls. The weight of that alone would have been impossible without Maldon's pistoned armour, and I could still only heave a leg forward once every couple of seconds.

Clang.

'Lower that ... whatever it is,' the Witness shouted. Her voice sounded dim and muffled.

Clang.

This would be the worst part.

'Stand down,' the Witness yelled. And when I paid her no heed: 'On my mark, destroy him.'

I had one hand on the aiming lever. I moved the other to a crank handle. I turned it, and a phos engine kicked in to assist. It was Maldon's masterstroke. The technology, he told me, was similar to that Nall had used to rotate the projectors atop his Engine. The eight barrels, aligned and jutting forward, began to spin and phos crackled in short static bursts as the barrels got up to speed.

They said I'd need an army to get to Saravor.

Maldon had turned me into one.

The motor whined, the phos crackled blue and gold around me, sparks of lightning spearing away in jagged blasts. A dozen gunshots flew past me, another dozen pounded into my armour and glanced away.

I roared and squeezed the firing lever.

39

Gleck Maldon, given enough time, money and assistance, would have revolutionised the face of war. He had been bored, he had been full of spite, and so he had put a weapon of such power into my hands that I knew it should never be allowed again.

A matchlock is a powerful thing. It makes a man a killer at a hundred paces. It cracks with a fearsome sound, requires little skill to use beyond being able to point it in the right direction, but it is limited by the twenty or thirty seconds it takes to get it loaded. Maldon's crank gun had all of the advantages of a matchlock, and none of the disadvantages.

Thousands of rounds per minute.

Fixed men blew apart as the torrent of lead struck them. Hundreds of balls spewed from the rotating barrels, flying wild and indiscriminate. They chewed through the stone steps that led up to the Grandspire, blasting chunks of stone into the air. They chewed through the armoured bodies of men, knocking them backward or cutting them in half. The staccato rhythm of the weapon's thunder thrummed through the air, hiding the screams, hiding the tiny pin-pricks as the desperate tried to aim their matchlocks and return fire. Their shots smacked into me with the force of hurtling boulders, but the phos-bolstered steel held and I was a wolf among mice. *Clang*, I strode forward, easier now as the ammunition depleted, thousands of balls spent and still I turned the crank and the gun thumped out, shot after shot after shot after shot. The weight of the armour eased as I spent pound after pound of lead, the phos pistons warmed and working furiously. *Clang, clang, clang,* I advanced on the Grandspire, firing, firing, an endless torrent of fire and death unleashed from the crank gun's mouth. I didn't have to aim, I just turned the barrels in the right direction and watched through my visor as the world there disintegrated into shattered pieces. I reaped the army of fixed men like a farmer scything corn, and with less difficulty.

Some men took cover behind a barricade of uncut stone. They unloaded shots into me, and one of them smacked hard against the helmet. I staggered, noting that the gun had begun to give out a soft whine. I turned the crank gun onto them and their defences disintegrated, and then so too did they. Matchlocks were being fired on me in desperation, shots ringing from my steel. My left arm locked up within the armour, pistons broken, power suddenly failing. I turned the gun on the sharpshooters who'd put it out of action and obliterated them, the rattling of the gun unceasing, uncaring. My leg stiffened, suddenly more weight on it than there had been before and wild, uncontrolled phos began spilling out in discharging arcs. Heat rose from the gun, hotter than midsummer, and sweat drenched me as the armour overheated too. My time was running out.

Witness Valentia had been my first target. As I clanged past her, up the steps leading to the Grandspire's main door, I saw she wasn't dead, despite losing both of her legs. She lashed out with a blast of light, that struck me square on and I staggered a few steps, only the weight of the armour keeping me upright. I turned the cannon back on her and drilled chunks of stone from the stair, stone dust billowing in cloud.

The whining sound was louder, higher pitched.

I didn't have much time. The plaza was strewn with the

dead and the pieces of the dying, but there were still men out there, men that could fight, and my armour was giving in. I pointed the weapon at them and a handful of shots flew into them, but then the rattle and crack died away, and the barrels spun without their deadly firestorm.

My ten thousand shots were done. Smoke billowed from the gun barrels and poured from the joints of my battered, dented armour. The steel was hot to the touch and I was starting to cook inside it. Sparks spat from all parts of the weapon now, but my enemies seemed to have realised I had no more fire to give from the smoking red barrels, and they grabbed poleaxes and Saravor's last guardians charged me. I yelled as I wrenched Maldon's weapon free of the ammunition feed, heaved it toward them and then clanged into the Grandspire.

The ground floor was aglow with purple light but the mill floor was silent. The Talents were slumped at their looms, chained to them, dead. The poor bastards had been worked until they were no longer needed, then their throats had been cut, carefully and methodically. Saravor had taken the power he needed and then made sure no one else would have access to it.

His dupes were still running toward me, and Maldon's overheating weapon was sitting in their path, screaming a high-pitched whine that I could hear even inside my enclosed helmet. I grabbed the Grandspire's great open door and put my shoulder against it. The pistons screamed, the armour belched smoke and I felt my skin begin to sizzle as the phos machinery, overworked and driven past tolerance, began to buckle – but then the huge stone door grated across the ground and boomed into place. I staggered back into the midst of the looms, as my armour belched smoke and the heat began to sear me. I tore at the straps, ignoring the sounds of men trying to heave against the door from outside. I had a knife and I hacked at the leather straps, burned my fingers even through the leather of my gauntlets as I pried out the rivets locking down the helmet. It was halfway free when a huge thump roared outside, louder than any cannon. Dust rained down from above as the blast shook the Grandspire and pieces of the door cracked and fell inwards in a clattering of rubble ... and then, nothing.

There were no more voices. Nobody appeared at the hole in the door, through which steam and smoke and stray crackles of phos wafted. There were no more sounds from outside, only the hissing and crackling of the armour. The release lever Maldon had warned me of had been shot away, just a stub remaining. I hammered at it until it gave a whine, the bolts blew outward with trails of steam and a pile of hot metal clattered down around me. My skin felt raw, my clothes were scorched, and sweat steamed.

Gasping, I sat on the workshop floor and tried to get my breathing under control. My leg, the old spear wound, throbbed. I pried myself out of the heavy gambeson, sodden and weighted with sweat and dumped it with the steaming armour. I hadn't realised just how many of their matchlock shots had struck me. The armour was riddled with small circular dents. Maldon was a fucking terrifying genius.

This was it. Alone now.

I had a small, turnip-sized phos canister, taken from a flarelock and modified to be a grenadoe, in a pocket. When I tore out the control coil, I'd have seconds before it turned into a blast of light that might just be enough to rupture The Iron Sun. And maybe, if he was close enough, it could take Saravor with it.

Everything in the Grandspire was quiet. Saravor hadn't expected anyone to get past his dead-eyed legion. I coughed painfully in the smoky air, then realised it wasn't the smoke that was choking me. I coughed and spat out more of the black Misery tar until my lungs felt like they'd been scoured with crushed glass, wiped my mouth on the back of a shaking hand. The black slime steamed on the floor, bubbled. No time to worry about it now.

There had been guards in the Grandspire, honest citadel men. They'd been slaughtered, blades in the back and their weapons lay where they had fallen. I took a dead man's sword, an honest weapon with a fully enclosed hilt. He'd taken little care of it, there were specks of rust across the basket. The blade wasn't very sharp.

Sharp enough.

I looked at the stairs. Thousands of stairs. Too many for a man getting old, with a protesting leg, half a dozen wounds and all the worst vices. A well-lit doorway beckoned me instead. Thierro had got the ascending platform working, and there were rows of levers indicating dozens of floors. I threw the last one. Heading for the pinnacle.

I could feel it, as I ascended. A weight, the depth of destiny. The air grew heavier, as a pressure grew the closer I got to the top of the spire. Pressure on the ears, weight in the chest. The weight of spirits. I could feel them as they were drawn in, drifting slowly through the stone, through the air, through my body. Out in the city, people were dying. Guns were fired, spears thrust, daggers rose and fell and the people of Valengrad screamed and died and wondered why, in this last damned hour, the Bright Lady had betrayed them. As the shadows of people's lives drifted past, I had a sense of them. Here, a woman who'd died protecting her children. There, a boy who didn't understand what was happening, they died one and the same, the echoes of their lives like wind against my skin. The disbelief, the sheer unfairness of their untimely deaths howled through them, along with the pain and the sorrow and a refusal to believe it. Each life had its own unique shape and song, flavour and colour, each one was drawn upward to the Eye, and to its master. Songs that ended, never to be sung again.

The platform slowed. An iron rail door opened on a short flight of stairs and I stepped out into the night.

The sky was vivid in purple, and the wind howled around us. The Misery's taint rode thick upon it, its familiar venom and hate on the air. Here, even closer to the Eye, I felt the terrible force of the stolen lives, thickening the air and resisting being dragged toward an even darker fate. Was Thierro here? Had the fixed I'd torn apart already ascended?

The Iron Sun was a globe of black iron, intense violet light shining through the cracks between the plates, enough power to send Davandein's soldiers to hell, if that's what Saravor wanted. But he didn't, and I finally saw him across the rooftop.

Saravor, in the flesh at last. He was just as tall as ever, but broad now, vast and swamped in a heavy robe. He held Shavada's Eye, wriggling and squirming, wet and winding on its maggot-like tail. It was swollen, pulsing with power as it drew in the souls of the damned. A few yards away a figure in a yellow hood stood silently, an observer. Neither of them had noticed me. This was my chance. I drew the phos grenadoe from my shirt. I would have to time it carefully. The throw would have to be good. Too soft and it would only catch The Iron Sun in the edge of the blast, too hard and it might sail away, over the edge of the roof, and detonate harmlessly below.

Fortune had smiled upon me. Saravor's attention was on the chaos in the city streets below, playing out for him like warring colonies of ants. He'd have needed eyes in the back of his head to see me coming.

I pulled the fuse, waited a second, and threw.

Saravor turned, lazily, and flicked one gnarled hand. The grenadoe was cut from the air, snatched from its trajectory, and sailed out into the purple night sky. A moment later it detonated with a bang. A twinkling cloud of sparkling light hung in the air for a few moments, and then it too was gone.

So.

'A valiant attempt,' Saravor said. He smiled, a broad, misshapen expression across his lumpy features. 'But so obvious. That always was your failing, Galharrow. All the subtlety of a broadside.'

'This ends now,' I said. A stupid, futile thing to say. I was already drawing my sword. The blast Saravor had flung had been the same slash of air that Darlings could work and he was forty feet away across the roof. No chance of reaching him before he sent another at me. I drew my sword, set my nerve and my lips curled back across my teeth. I'd take it head-on. Saravor wasn't the only one protected by magic, and the Misery steamed within me at his proximity.

'You want to cut a deal?' Saravor asked. He smiled at me and in it I saw the same old cruelty. He held the Eye out before him, showing me his prize. 'No Bright Lady to save you this time. Your cards are all played. What would you offer me for this, Galharrow? What could you possibly give me to compare with the power I take tonight?'

'The Nameless won't stand for it,' I spat. 'They'll hunt you down and tear you apart.'

Saravor laughed.

'No, they won't. You serve them but you barely understand them. The Deep Kings will kick and scream against someone's trying to *become* like them, but once it's done? A ready-made ally who is willing to learn, to be guided by them? No. They will welcome me.' He rotated the Eye before me.

'What you're doing is inhuman,' I said. I pointed the sword toward him, pitiful threat that it was.

Saravor gave a deep, throaty chuckle, strengthening as if he found that truly hilarious. The yellow-hooded attendant stepped forward and helped him shed the voluminous robe that wrapped him.

'Of course I am,' Saravor crowed at me. 'Inhuman!'

Saravor was not one person. He was several.

One of the grey children stared out from his chest, blank-faced, half-absorbed into the great body. Forearms protruded from his gut, pale and cold as slate, clutching a brittle old book. The Taran Codex. A second of the creatures was melted into his back, its face the back of his neck, arms fused across his ribs. Short brown spines ran in rows down his chest, his back, clumps of tangled hair protruding at random from patches of discoloured skin. An eye blinked beneath his armpit. There was nothing human about him.

'How do you think the Nameless are born but by seizing power?' Saravor sneered at me. 'You think that they were born with it? No. They bent the world to their will. They took their power. Look east, Galharrow. See the Misery your master wrought. You think his power—'

I rushed him midsentence. There was nothing to gain by letting him finish his diatribe on why he, corrupt and twisted and fouler than the canals, ought to be applauded. I had forty feet to cover, and a handful of seconds.

Saravor flicked his hand and a slash of power came at me. It hit me head-on, but it didn't touch me. Sparks flew into the air as the Misery poison that filled me met the Darling magic head-on. Only Saravor was far stronger than a Darling and his blast threw me back, skittering across the floor. I gathered myself, winded, grazed. But still alive. Saravor's many faces looked puzzled.

The Misery coiled inside me, the magic rejecting foreign intrusion. Just as it had when Stracht had weathered the Darling's blast.

'Unexpected,' he said. 'It seems that there is much that I must learn still about this new power.' He smiled.

My body creaked and protested as I rose to my feet. My fucked-up leg screamed harder than the new cuts. Blood trickled hot down my arm, my chest. My skin had more slashes and slices through it than wrinkles now. Breathing came hard, painful in overstretched lungs.

'Fight me. Fight me as the man you used to be, if that's what you ever were.'

Saravor shook his heads.

'You overestimate your own importance. Major, deal with Galharrow. Let him live long enough to see. Long enough for his master to watch my ascension through his eyes.'

The hooded figure stepped forward, and Saravor turned away, looking down on the city again. The woman was dressed in tough riding leathers, gloved hands, riding boots. She drew her sword, a sword that I knew all too well, a sword I'd given her when she first got demoted.

'Ah, no,' I said, as she pushed back her hood. Nenn had the same glassy expression as the men that I'd killed below.

'She was ever my favourite,' Saravor said, as my best friend presented her sword to me. He spoke through the mouth of one of the fused children. 'You know why? Because when I worked on her she didn't pass out. I took a handful of a dead man's innards, I cut hers out and replaced them, and she didn't scream, not once. That's power, Galharrow. And power is all that really matters.'

In a clumsy flapping of wings the raven suddenly crashed down onto the glass platform, frantic and spitting words in a dozen languages. The soul magic in the air was scrambling its brain, but the one word that I understood was all too clear: Hurry!

'Don't do this, Nenn,' I said. 'Look at me. Fucking look at me. Don't do it.'

She attacked through the soul-thick air.

I had sometimes wondered, if it came down to it, which of us would win in a fight. I had the size, the reach, but she'd always had the spirit. I was method, strategy, she was fury and instinct, but there was none of that here, from either of us. She was a drone, mindless and taken, and she struck with single blows, lashing out and withdrawing, none of her skill. None of her deadliness. I parried with heavy sweeps of my blade, but my arms were leaden things and I didn't think I could have struck her down even if I'd had the energy. She was fresh where I was worn to the bone. I staggered back, and then the raven launched itself at her face. She struck hard and swatted the bird from the air, a severed wing spinning away across the glass, and before I could react she drove at me again. First our blades clashed together, and then she caught me in the forearm and laid it open. I lost my sword and she stepped in, quick as a cat, and ran me through.

It was a gut wound. A slow killer like the blow she'd taken herself, once. There was no pain, but I felt the damage inside. Felt what she had done to me. The point had come all the way out through my back. Just like I'd taught her. I went down like a rag doll, feeling nothing below the wound. Blanketing numbness seemed to be spreading upward from it. I'd done a lot of bleeding before, but this was different. This wasn't a little flesh wound. This was my life falling out of me.

I couldn't feel my legs.

Nenn sheathed her sword, drew a knife, laid it against my throat. I had nothing left. My body was failing me. My spine was severed. Nenn, or whatever now occupied Nenn's body, grasped me by the hair and turned my head toward Saravor. To make me watch.

The raven cawed feebly, struggled to rise and collapsed.

In the pulsing light of the iron-bound globe, framed against the purple sky, Saravor drew on the death below. The popping of matchlocks had died away, but the distant screams continued, and I was helpless.

'Nenn,' I whispered. 'Nenn, you have to stop him.' She gripped my hair tighter, made sure I was watching. Made no sound. My vision wasn't good. It was going hazy at the edges and there was a lightness in my head.

There was a groaning in the air, and a sudden coldness as the souls that had gathered around us fled. The Eye shivered, filled with all the dark power it could hold, and Saravor held it aloft.

'It's done,' he said.

'Nenn,' I said again. 'You fought him before. He couldn't make you shoot me. You're not his. Not entirely.'

I felt the edge of the blade prick the skin of my neck. Warning me to shut up.

'You have to try,' I said. Words were coming harder, harder all the time. Hard to remember what was going on now. Something hot and wet on my hands as I pressed them to my gut. 'Fight, Nenn.'

'What can ... I do ...' Nenn gasped. The words escaped like gas from a balloon, expelled in a rush. 'He's stronger ... than me. Than ... anything.'

Saravor carried the Eye reverently, fixed on his prize. The heads of the grey creatures melded into his flesh tried to twist around to see it, ten thousand souls bound into a vessel fashioned from a being of incredible power. He stepped slowly, the high priest of his own religion, moving to stand before the Grandspire's weapon, directly in its path. He raised the Eye before him and one of his grey creatures emerged from the shadows, its face demonic, fingers clawed. It moved to the control panel, where the firing levers could operate the Iron Sun.

'Nenn,' I whispered. 'You have to fight him. If you don't fight, then he wins.'

'I can't,' Nenn gasped. Her knife cut into the flesh of my neck, and her tears dripped down onto my face.

'I know you can,' I said. 'You've always been strong. You've just never seen it. I saw it. Tnota saw it. Betch saw it. He loved you and he wanted you and he'd never met a stronger woman. You've always had the strength, Nenn. Fight him. He's just some fucking monster. You're the woman Betch loved. You're the woman he gave his life for. Don't let some fucking monster take that from him.'

The grey child pulled the first lever down with a clank, and a distant rumbling began below our feet, cogs whirred, gears shifted. The first of the three shields across the firing point withdrew.

'Remember the morning that you watched the dawn rise? On the veranda?'

'I ...' For half a second her grip on my hair diminished.

'He told me – yes. He wanted you to know: yes.'

Her body tensed and now her fingers tightened in my hair.

'He said yes?' Nenn said, and her voice finally sounded her own. Her tears fell fast as rain across my shoulders.

'He loved you,' I said, nearly a snarl. The effort made my head spin. 'We all love you.'

The child pulled the second lever. Iron screeched against iron as the second shield began to rotate, the panels drawing back. I was forced to stare at Saravor's gleeful, awful face. He was bathed in the violet light, exultant. The Iron Sun's beam of power would strike directly against the Eye. I doubted I would survive the detonation. I doubted Valengrad would survive it. I felt the thrumming through the whole Grandspire as the power began to charge for release.

'I loved you too,' Nenn said. 'You're my best fucking friend. Tell Tnota he's a prick.'

She let me go and, crippled as I was, I smacked down against the glass floor.

Nenn raised the dagger high, then swung it down with a scream of utmost pain, worsening as she ripped the blade sideways across her guts. She was still screaming as she forced her hand inside, and dragged out a cluster of entrails. They were stinking and rotten, and she cast them aside, her face bathed brighter and brighter as the Grandspire's weapon primed to unleash its power. I let out a cry of my own as she cast her guts aside, dragged free her sword and with an effort that must have hurt more than all the pain I'd ever known combined: she charged.

'Saravor, you fucking cunt!' she screamed. Lost in his victory, Saravor barely glanced up before she was upon him.

Too late.

She swung, a stroke of pure wrath, the stroke of her life. Somewhere in the hells a dozen bells tolled at once, a clamouring of souls, a salvo of devastation, and Saravor's outstretched arm flew away at the wrist. He had only a moment to realise what had happened. And then the weapon fired.

A brilliant lance of violet fire blazed into the night, a thunder, a roaring scream of colossal power which swallowed Saravor, and for a few moments he bore the brunt of its fury, a rippling shadow caught in the torrent of blazing brightness. His scream was wild as he tried to push against the rush of power, to reach the fallen Eye, still clasped in the hand that had been cut from him. He burned in the light; four seconds, five, then will alone could no longer hold him there and the beam carried him from the roof of the Grandspire and out into the night, propelled through the air. Gone.

The power died, its intensity dissipating to nothing. Slowly, the brightness faded from my eyes.

Silence.

I could see Nenn. She lay facedown, but she was looking at me. I thought that she was dead, but then she blinked, and then she smiled. I smiled back, and she closed her eyes. And then she was dead.

My best friend's spirit left the world. It already felt empty without her.

Alone now. Alone with my death. Saravor had been

stopped, but there must be thousands of dead below. The Range was safe. There was that, at least. I'd done my part. Crowfoot couldn't be disappointed, in the end. He'd keep to his end of the deal, and the two lives I'd traded for my own would go on, wherever they were. For all that the deal had cost me, lying here bleeding out on the roof of the Grandspire. I knew that I'd have done it all again. At least the last moments would be peaceful. Or not.

'You really fucked this up,' the raven croaked.

'Got here in the end,' I said. Speaking was hard.

'Crowfoot will need a new captain,' it said. 'I suppose you could have done worse.'

'We do what we can,' I said, and looked up at the sky.

Quick, small steps. Feet on tiles. My sight had dimmed. Hard to make thoughts come clearly. Lost too much blood. Too close to the veil. Maybe the steps were Death, the Long End, finally come to guide me away. I heard a voice, only it didn't sound like death. Sounded like begging. Sounded like tears. Ridiculously, it sounded like Amaira, and those cold little fingers on my face, trying to roll me over and failing, those felt like Amaira's too. I heard more begging. Then sobbing. Not what a man wants to hear as he slips away into the black.

I tried to smile at her as a cold little hand pressed against the wound, as though it could hold back the damage within. Would rather she hadn't seen this, but I loved her and, selfishly, I was glad she was there.

And then the carrion bird began to whisper to her.

Things got hazy. Vision blurred. Sound got distant. The girl and the raven talked in low voices. Talk of promises. Talk of debts. Talk of a life taking a turn that it shouldn't.

Then there was nothing.

40

I wasn't dead.

That came as a surprise.

Dawn had risen. The solar flare was done, the sky as ordinary as it gets on the Range. Brighter than usual for this time of year maybe, a certain spring freshness carried in from the west. The sky was clear, cloudless, blue in one direction, red and broken in the other. I was still atop the Grandspire, a cold wind blowing in, but someone had wrapped me in a cloak. I looked for Nenn, and saw that someone had carefully covered her, too. I didn't want to breathe for fear it might shatter and spill out what was left of me.

There was no pain. Not in my gut where I knew I was slain, or my arm, my chest, only some stiffness in the old leg wound. I closed my eyes, almost wishing I had slipped away without waking again. Touched my stomach.

Nothing.

No wound, no blood, not even a scar.

It was impossible. My memories had grown hazy toward the end of the night, but I was pretty sure that Nenn had put a sword through me. I checked my back, realizing I could feel my legs again, and there was nothing there either.

I was alone. Saravor's severed hand was gone. Shavada's Eye was gone too. There was a lot of blood on the flagstones. My blood, I supposed.

The city seemed quiet. No guns, no shouts. Davandein's and Vercanti's banners fluttered over the citadel again. It seemed they'd won the day, and got the city under control in the end.

My legs worked when I tried them. Didn't make sense, but not much did. I crossed to Nenn, but I didn't need to pull back the covering to see her face. She'd given me her last smile, and she was with her handsome officer now, or at least, I hoped that she was. I put her sword through my belt, then gathered her up in my arms. I had little strength, but nothing could have made me leave her behind. It was slow going. I couldn't say why I was alive when she wasn't, when she was the more deserving of life, but it was my duty to do right by her now. I carried her through the mess of murdered Talents, across the devastated plaza, its stones torn apart and littered with pieces of Saravor's fixed men. Nobody had come forward to clear that mess up.

The message on the citadel read: STAY IN YOUR HOMES.

I got Nenn's body back to Maldon's refuge, where I laid her out on the table. Maldon and Dantry offered their condolences, but those never help much, and they don't stop you from hurting.

'You did it,' Dantry said, with something that could once have been a smile.

'We managed it,' I said. I placed a hand on Maldon's shoulder. 'You got your redemption, I suppose. Now you can say you saved the city, as well as trying to destroy it.'

'I'm sorry, Ryhalt,' Maldon said. He sounded like he meant it. 'Nenn was one of the good ones.'

'The best,' I said. 'She was the best of us.'

We stood in an awkward silence.

'She should have a state funeral,' Dantry said. 'As a hero of the Range.'

'No,' I sighed. 'We'll give her a pyre out in the yard. She'd have hated a big funeral and they'd only say a load of shit about her that wasn't true. We'll drink and chew blacksap and talk about how she punched those arrogant fuckers in the face when they deserved it.'

'Fucking hell,' Maldon said. 'I'm going to go find some brandy. Dantry, come with me. I can't reach the high shelves.'

'Find Tnota at the citadel,' I said. 'He should be here too.'

They left me alone with the body. I stood by Nenn, feeling that there was something I ought to do, or say, but she was just dead, and there wasn't. She'd have thought me an idiot, so I went and rooted through a store cupboard and found an axe. The yard out the back would do as well as any other patch of dirt.

Amaira was out there, sitting on the picket fence, legs swinging.

'I'm glad you're alive,' she said, only she sounded like she'd already known that I was. Sounded older, too. But then, we were all older, and the battle across the city had probably rushed a lot of kids past their childhoods during the night.

'I have to cut some wood,' I said.

'For Major Nenn,' she said. 'I'll help.'

We split wood for a while, me doing most of the axe work, Amaira stacking the pieces. The pyre had to be big. Big enough for a hero. I stripped off my shirt, broke down the fence and hacked it to kindling.

'Your eyes are still amber,' she said. 'And you're still copper.'

'I guess it won't shift for a while,' I said. If it ever did. I swung the axe again.

'But the other injuries. They're all better.'

'They are.' I stopped, planted the spade in the earth. 'You were there,' I said eventually. 'I heard you.'

Amaira shrugged.

'We all got to be somewhere, Ryhalt.'

'Not Captain-Sir anymore?'

'We all have to grow up sometime. I'm fourteen years old. Can't act like a kid forever.'

I buried the axe in a piece of wood. It was easier to focus on that.

'What deal did you make?' I asked eventually, knowing it was private, that I shouldn't ask.

'A lot like yours, probably,' she said.

'Show me?'

Amaira drew back her sleeve. Across her inner forearm was a stark black-and-white tattoo, like a painting. A hooded, one-winged raven. I stood and looked at it for a while, traced it with my finger. Then I hugged her. I could have said I wished she hadn't, that my life wasn't worth the debt, that she had no idea what she had done. Instead my heart tore just a little further.

'What happened to the Eye?'

'I took it to the heart of the Engine and interred it there,' she said. 'For safekeeping. Until the Nameless come to reclaim it.'

'You got in?'

'The Raven told me the rhyme. The heart is black, the heart is cold ...'

'I know it.' Amaira nodded with a brief, sad smile. It seemed that the raven had told her a lot when she made her bargain. It had fulfilled its task, I supposed. I was angry with Crowfoot, or the raven, which was the same, for taking Amaira. But Crowfoot didn't give a shit if I was angry with him, and in the end the raven had saved my life, so it was better to let it go. I went inside.

'You'll miss her. Nenn, I mean,' Valiya said. The room was dark. She hadn't bothered to turn the lights on when the light had faded, and stood by a window too dirty to see out of. The table was neatly stacked with papers, lists of people. Friends, enemies, suppliers, debtors. She'd been rebuilding, even now. The last, half-written name on the list was my own. It was even darker outside, a single flickering neon sign casting her in electric blue. There was nothing to see out there anyway.

The city had returned to silence and timidity. It slept, whilst we did not.

'Every day I'm alive. And all of the ones when I'm dead,' I said. Valiya looked down into her glass and considered whatever lay in its depths. There was seldom anything good down there. She passed a pen slowly from hand to hand.

'And your Bright Lady, too,' she said. 'Do you think that she's gone for good?'

There was bite in the words.

'For now, at least,' I said.

'Blackwing as we knew it is gone,' Valiya said. 'Blackwing was you, and it was me. Everything we built is ashes and charcoal. Everything we worked for. Everything that we had. Everything we could have had.'

The pressure in the room grew heavier. I took a few steps in but my proximity to her was a hard thing, rough-edged and nothing she'd want to hold on to. A little silence is a dangerous thing, and in quantity it becomes a poison cloud. I could smell her, that sweet jasmine perfume, always too good for its environment. Always a little too refined for this city, for these people. And for me.

'I can't stay,' I said. I looked down at the sparks of darkness beneath the copper of my skin. But there was more to it than that.

She nodded. I'd never needed to tell Valiya anything. She always knew it before I did.

'I understand,' she said. 'I didn't. For a long time. Tnota tried to explain it to me, but I didn't really grasp it. Not fully. The hold she has over you.'

Valiya turned to face me. Calm. She'd cried, but the tears were all spent and only the echoes of their passing remaining in the redness of her eyes, the flush of her cheeks. She pushed her hair back out of her eyes and tied it away. No overhanging fringe to hide behind. It was not a night to keep secrets.

'I owe her,' I said. It was all I could say. We all owed her. More than they would ever know.

'I know,' Valiya said. 'And won't ask you to turn aside from your obligation. I know what she did. I know who she was. And I can't compete with a dead woman. Not with a memory. In these ashes we inhabit, somebody needs to rebuild. Somebody needs to show the Davandeins and the Vercantis how to lead. I will work hard, and I will light a path. I will lead Valengrad from behind the curtain. There's a life there, to be claimed.' She lifted her coat from the chair. Looked up at me, fading like autumn. Rising like spring. 'But I'll not wait for you.'

Her coat flowed over and around her shoulders, a shadow swallowing her. She looked as beautiful as she ever had, and I wished I could have shared it all with her. I was in pain and burned-out, exhausted, and I wanted to tell her every dream I'd denied myself, tell her she deserved so much more than I could give her, and that if I could, I would have broken myself on every rock in my path to deserve her. But there was never time to spare in her world, certainly not for broken men and their regrets, and the drive and efficiency of her life was one of the things that had let me fall in love with her. By leaving me, she'd find and take the life she wanted and deserved. It was cruel to only be able to admit that now.

Besides, there was no point. She knew it all anyway.

'Look after Amaira,' I said.

'No,' Valiya said. She held a sad smile in place on her face, but Amaira's name was the straw that nearly brought her concrete mask down. 'Crowfoot has taken her from me too. She's your responsibility, Ryhalt. Yours to teach, to train. Don't let her down.'

She crossed the room. I should have done something. Begged her to stay, told her that I was sorry. Told her that I needed her.

The door closed, and she was gone.

When night came around we raised Nenn onto her last resting place. I put her sword in her hand, as she would have wanted, and a bottle of Whitelande brandy in the other. I let Tnota start the fire. It wasn't symbolic, I was just tired. Then we drank, and drank some more, and we poured brandy onto the flames and smashed the bottles just as she'd have done.

The sky was vocal tonight, and it serenaded Nenn's soul off to wherever it was going. If it was going anywhere at all.

'What now?' Maldon asked when the fire had burned low, and Dantry and Amaira had gone to bed.

'I made a promise to a lady,' I said. 'A hard one.' I looked down at the ragged words I'd cut into my arm. 'But I think I know how to keep it. It's not going to be easy.'

'Never is,' he said. 'Where do we have to go?'

'You don't have to go anywhere,' I said. 'I'll tell you and Dantry tomorrow.'

'Not the girl?'

'She'd only try to stop me.'

Maldon chuckled and we clinked our glasses together, and drank a final toast to a dead woman who'd been worth more than all the rest of us put together.

I walked through the city in the small hours. The fires were out, and people had defied the citadel's order to remain indoors and were removing the boards from windows or weeping as they embraced the neighbours they'd feared for. They would rebuild, and life would go on, but I felt distant, as though I was no longer one of them. I went to the city wall and leaned against the crenellations, looking east over the Misery. The cracks in the sky glowed a fierce white-bronze, jagged tears through the moonless night and a guard approached me.

'You shouldn't be up here.'

'No,' I said. 'I should be out there.'

I felt her in my bones. Flowing through me, indivisible.

Come back to me, the Misery whispered. *Come back. I'm waiting.*

ABOUT GOLLANCZ

Gollancz is the oldest SF publishing imprint in the world. Since being founded in 1927 Gollancz has continued to publish a focused selection of bestselling and award-winning authors. The front-list includes **Ben Aaronovitch**, **Joe Abercrombie**, **Charlaine Harris**, **Joanne Harris**, **Joe Hill**, **Alastair Reynolds**, **Patrick Rothfuss**, **Nalini Singh** and **Brandon Sanderson**.

As one of the largest Science Fiction and Fantasy imprints in the UK it is no surprise we have one of the most extensive backlists in the world. Find high-quality SF on Gateway written by such authors as **Philip K. Dick**, **Ursula Le Guin**, **Connie Willis**, **Sir Arthur C. Clarke**, **Pat Cadigan**, **Michael Moorcock** and **George R.R. Martin**.

We also have a strand of publishing in translation, which includes French, Polish and Russian authors. Gollancz is home to more award-winning authors than any other imprint, with names including **Aliette de Bodard**, **M. John Harrison**, **Paul McAuley**, **Sarah Pinborough**, **Pierre Pevel**, **Justina Robson** and many more.

The SF Gateway
More than 3,000 classic, rare and previously out-of-print SF novels at your fingertips.
www.sfgateway.com

The Gollancz Blog
Bringing you news from our worlds to yours. Stories, interviews, articles and exclusive extracts just for you!
www.gollancz.co.uk

GOLLANCZ
LONDON